BEND SINISTER:
THE GAY TIMES BOOK OF DISTURBING STORIES

Edited by Peter Burton

Contents

Introduction

There is a long tradition of gay authors writing stories which are at once decidedly sinister *and* decidedly queer. Gothic literature, in which *sinister* is an essential component, was, after all, virtually the invention of gay men, notably Horace Walpole (1717–1797) and William Beckford (1760–1844). There are interesting currents seething away in the former's *The Castle of Otranto* (1764) and in the latter's *Vathek* (1786).

Among the most famous examples of this distinctive genre are *The Turn of the Screw* by Henry James (1845–1916) and *The Picture of Dorian Gray* by Oscar Wilde (1854–1900). Both these writers made more than one venture into this territory. All three of the Benson brothers – Arthur Christopher (1862–1925), Edward Frederic (1867–1940) and Robert Hugh (1871–1914) – wrote stories which could be termed sinister or strange and the most popular of the three, E F Benson, was something of a specialist in what he termed 'spook stories'. E F Benson also wrote several novels with sinister or supernatural themes, among them *The Luck of the Vails, The Image in the Sand, Colin* and *Colin II, The Inheritor* and *Ravens' Brood.*

Perhaps the most famous exponent of the ghost story was M R James (1862–1936) and though neither of the recent biographies has anything to say about James's sexuality, it seems evident that this Provost of Eton must have been at least emotionally homosexual. Perhaps one of the most influential of writers who delighted in disturbing his readers was 'Saki' (H H Munro, 1870–1916) whose shadow falls heavily across the work of such writers as Evelyn Waugh (1903–1966) and Simon Raven (1927–2001).

Other writers worth mentioning include Eric Stanislaus, Count Stenbock (1860–1895) whose 'The true story of a vampire' has been much anthologised, Algernon Blackwood (1869–1951), the unjustly ignored Hugh Walpole (I have long cherished an ambition to see a production of Rodney Ackland's dramatisation of Walpole's supremely disturbing *The Old Ladies* performed by men playing as old queans) and L P Hartley (1895–1972).

Practitioners of the form still happily with us include Francis King, Christopher Fowler, Simon Lovat (for his Ruth Rendell-esque novel *Disorder and Chaos*) and the modern master Clive Barker, who successfully disturbs in fiction and on film.

But what constitutes the sinister? The answer to that question depends upon a set of variables: What does any given author wish to make disturbing? What disturbs any given reader? Is it character and characterisation that causes a chill in the sunlight? Is it locale? Is it situation? Is it subject? Or is it any combination of these? It probably depends on the interaction between author and reader, a relationship that can never be passive.

The seed of *Bend Sinister* was implanted in my mind several years ago, when I was editing *The Mammoth Book of Gay Short Stories*. While commissioning many new stories, I also went back over stories which had had only a brief life because they had originally been published in newspapers or magazines, amongst them *Gay News* and *Gay Times*. I was startled to discover how frequently these *retrieved* stories were of a distinctly sinister nature. Of course, there was one simple and obvious explanation for this surfeit. I had either bought or commissioned many of these stories when working for the already mentioned (as well as other) publications and may possibly be possessed of a particular predilection for this kind of writing. However, I think there is rather more to my perceived opinion that gay authors are especially drawn to the sinister.

Gay authors (before and after what it is easiest to term 'Liberation') have always been aware that they and their like have been regarded as sinister, that homosexuality itself was seen as a fitting subject for disturbing fiction. By writing about aspects of life outside heterosexual parameters, gay writers as outsiders and other were looking with perception and often with deep sympathy at those who were also other. Examples which spring readily to mind include stories and novels by E F Benson, Algernon Blackwood and E M Forster in which survivors from a mythic past contend with and attempt to interact with the modern world and by so doing often enhance the lives of those they touch.

My choice of the title *Bend Sinister* has three diverse sources. Firstly, I remembered being impressed by the title when it was used by the great novelist Vladimir Nabokov. Secondly, I knew 'bend sinister' to be a heraldic term which indicated a bastard line – and enough of the characters in these stories are certainly bastards (if only in the colloquial sense of the word). Finally, and rather more crudely, I was amused by the conjunction of these two words in connection with disturbing tales about men who are popularly assumed to *bend* to achieve sexual gratification.

Bend Sinister contains stories by writers from all across the English-speaking world (though many of them have based themselves far away from their native lands). The authors of the stories range in age from the very early twenties to the mid-eighties and what they find sinister ranges across mutilation, twins, schizophrenia, property dealing, ghosts, obsession, child abuse, addiction and a whole spectrum which disturbs. There should be at least one story in this collection to disturb and, perhaps, cause the kind of dreams none of us wish to experience.

Peter Burton
Brighton 2002

The Changeling Lover
Ian Young

The Changeling Lover
Ian Young

I found my secret lover.
He gave me a silver key.
I made him swear a promise
That he'd remember me.

My lover was a changeling.
He fled without design
And played among the sunny fields
And died before his time.

I felled my lover's tombstone
And dug for him there
And wrenched his body from the earth,
Into rain and air.

And as I took him in my arms,
Who was so blond and clear,
He turned into a clutch of bones
And soil that smelled of fear.

All skull he was and tatters,
With eyes that did not see,
Who uttered, crumbling in my hands,
"JUST YOU REMEMBER ME!"

Famished
Neil Bartlett

in the printed note at the top of the otherwise blank page in my diary. In some countries, apparently, they celebrate the turning point of the year by lighting bonfires in the woods, even by leaping through them in some places; here, sadly, there's nothing like that to mark the occasion. Nevertheless, you do feel that there is, sometimes, a slightly odd atmosphere hanging over the town as the sun begins to set around that time of year, something distinctive, even slightly uneasy. There was certainly something like that in the air as I drove down to the seafront. Expectation. But then you often notice that sort of an atmosphere in a seaside town at the end of a particularly long and hot day. It's something to do with people having come here to get away from their usual lives and being determined not to go home unsatisfied, I think. Perhaps the heat just gets to them sometimes.

Other people, most of the visitors certainly, go down to the beach to be surrounded, but I go there to be alone. For preference, I'll wait until the evening is just beginning to cool, when the only real heat left is that still rising from the shingle, then I can be sure that the crowds will have gone. The beach I use is one too far away from the centre of the town to attract any families, and at the time I choose to arrive there even the young men who congregate there for that very reason have begun to disperse. On this particular evening the sun hadn't started to lose its heat until gone nine, and I was pleased to see, as I parked the car, that the daytime parade was well and truly over. The beach falls away from the promenade in a steep bank of slate-grey pebbles; beyond the pebbles, revealed only at the lowest of tides, is a great expanse of sand, left perfectly levelled and smoothed by the retreating water. It was, to my great satisfaction, an exceptionally low tide that evening, and the sands, for some reason, were quite empty. As I locked the car I looked right up and down the beach, and I couldn't see anyone, not anyone at all.

By long-established custom, this is a beach where men swim and sunbathe naked. For me, this gives my solitary evening visits an extra satisfaction. When I walk naked into the sea, I try to leave all the cares of the day behind me with my clothes. I let myself get taken away from myself. Or at least, that's how I'd put it, if anyone ever asked me.

I have to be careful, these days, when I walk down a steep bank of shingle, but I managed it without too much hobbling. Arriving at the edge of the sand, I undressed straight away, and then just stood still for a moment to let the calm of the evening reach me. Everything was still, not just me; still, empty, suspended. The sky has been cloudless all day, and out on the horizon it was now slowly, imperceptibly shading from a clear blue to a clear, darkening gold. I left my folded clothes on the edge of shingle, and walked out naked into the cooling air. When I reached it, the first few paces of the barely moving sea were as warm as blood; I paused again, and looked back to scan the beach. I am not a man who is ashamed to be seen naked – I have even got used to there being white hairs mixed in amongst the dark, down there – but I was glad that it was so entirely deserted that evening. Entering the water always delights me, and it's a private pleasure. When the water rises against my thighs, I begin to stride more firmly, purposefully, parting it, using all of what's left of my strength; only when it reaches almost to my chest do I lean forward and reach for that first delicious stroke and the full embrace of the sea. Of course, these days, I can't swim as far as I used to, but I always swim as far out as I can, and certainly far enough out to be quite alone, far enough for all the world of the beach and of the town and of my daily routine to fade away entirely to silence. When the sea is as mirror-calm as it was that evening, the only sound out there is the sound of your own regular breathing, the slight repeated swish and ripple as your hands cleave the water. Once, out there, a dolphin rose right beside me, with a sudden sigh and gurgle as its back broke the surface. It scared me half to death.

That evening there were no dolphins. One solitary gull dipped down, and the touch of its beak briefly rippled the mirror. The quiet was absolute. I swam until my shoulders began to gently ache, and then trod water for a moment to gather myself.

There, suddenly, six feet under, was the cold of the offshore current, tugging at my feet, reminding me that the calm surface was deceptive. Enjoying the twist and stretch of my back as I did it, I turned and kicked back for the shore. Swimming, especially swimming naked, I feel as self-possessed as anyone of my age ever does. In the water, I suppose, I am still a reasonably young man.

The sand was cooler when I walked back across it, but there was still just enough warmth radiating from the shingle for me to want to sit and let the air reach all the parts of my skin the towel hadn't quite got to. Out to sea, the sky was beginning to shade from opal to carnelian; the air thickened, and the gold of the sun itself began to deepen as it sank towards the sea, and blaze. When I looked down at the backs of my hands, even my white skin was gilded.

High above, a silver sickle moon was just beginning to appear.

I'm not sure how long I had been sitting there, just watching the colours slowly changing, and thinking, and trying not to think, but it certainly took me by surprise when I became aware of the noise of footsteps on the shingle behind me. Not long, I suppose; I hadn't had time to get cold, and I still hadn't got dressed. I didn't look round, at first; but then when I realised that there were two pairs of feet, and that they were getting close, and in fact seemed to be sliding and crunching down the bank of shingle directly behind me, I thought that perhaps I should. I remember that as I turned, I was reaching out towards my folded clothes with my right hand, as if I had some instinct to cover myself. Even at my age, you never quite get out of the habit of expecting trouble. I turned, and looked up, and there standing over me, standing almost shoulder to shoulder, were two of the most beautiful young men I have ever seen.

Being alarmed was just an instinctive reaction. There were two of them, after all, and before I'd heard the sound of their feet right behind me I'd been sure I'd got the beach to myself. They seemed to have come from nowhere, and now there they were, two of them, looming up right over me, and you could see how young and strong they were straight away, how well built they were, their arms. Oddly, even though they were standing only about six feet away from me, they weren't looking at me, but over me, straight out at the expanse of empty sand and the setting sun. They were both shirtless. The one standing slightly closer to me raised his right hand to shield his eyes; they were a startlingly pale shade of purest blue. The same blue as the sky had been only moments earlier. Opal.

I couldn't help but stare. The low, level light of the sun was colouring the skin of their bare chests and arms just as it was mine, gilding it... and then the one with his hand lifted to shield his eyes spoke. He said, not really to me in particular, and quite quietly, almost under his breath, just the one word, "Perfect."

Of course, he meant the sunset. And he was right, it was. But as I crouched at their feet, looking up at him, and at his friend standing there shoulder to shoulder beside him, and at the way that the sunset was turning the two of them, with their two calm, handsome faces gazing out to sea, into a pair of perfect, matching statues, it was all I could do to stop myself blurting out the words which were on the tip of my tongue, which were yes, yes, you are...

"Yes, yes, you are, both of you."

It would have been a foolish thing to say, but not an untrue one. Because they were perfect, both of them.

Of course, to very beautiful people their own beauty is a fact, a commonplace, a constant condition, but to the rest of us it is always a surprise, an astonishment. They appear among us, completely unaware that to us they seem to have come from a different world entirely. That's what these two were like. Now I know you might say that physical perfection like theirs is all over the place, these days. After all, you can buy it in any newsagents, you see it every twenty minutes on the television. And there do seem to be more and more of them looking like that in this town every summer – shirts off, holding hands in public, matching pairs often as not. Still, they stopped me in my tracks, these two, when I looked up and saw them standing over me like that.

Quite turned my stomach over. Knocked me out. Took me back. Or whatever the saying is. Bodies so perfect you can't quite believe it.

And I haven't told you the most striking thing about them. I couldn't work out what it was as first, but then I realised. They weren't just a matching pair, these two, they were identical. I know it's the fashion these days, matching haircuts, the same carefully shaped muscles, the matched, wary expressions, you see them all the time – but these two were actually identical; they were that oddest, uncanniest of all pairings, twins. Everything was an exact repeat; the pattern of raised veins on the backs of their beautiful hands; the white-blond hair; the line the waistbands of their trousers made across their flat stomachs; the slight frown each of them had from narrowing his eyes to gaze at the setting sun. As I said, or rather, didn't say, perfect.

I never like it when I catch myself staring at the young. It's hardly proper, at sixty-five. But I don't think I showed anything of what I was thinking, and all I said, by way of a reply, was just, "Yes, yes, it is. Lovely."

The one nearest me – it's ridiculous, but there's no other way for me to put it, I can't say 'the taller one' or 'the one with the longer hair', because they really were identical in every respect – the one nearest me asked me if I thought the weather would last, and I said yes, yes, I thought it would. I hope you're right, the other one said then, quietly – and I noticed that they both had the same faint trace of an accent, something half-American. It went with the look, somehow; shirtless, cleanshaven, blond.

I asked them if they were just visiting for the day, and they told me that no, they were down for the summer. At that point I remember suddenly thinking that perhaps it must sound like I was trying to make conversation, that perhaps I should leave them alone to just enjoy their sunset in peace and quiet, after all I didn't want them to think for a moment that I was trying to...

"What about you?", said the one closest to me.

"Oh, I live here," I said.

When I said that, the second one said something that rather surprised me. Or rather, the way he said it surprised me – very suddenly, and looking straight at me, whereas before he had been gazing steadily out at the sea and the sun. He asked me if I lived on my own. Now, as you know, that's often a very important question in conversations with strangers, and I felt very... well, surprised.

"Yes," I said, "that's right. On my own. What about you two?"

I suppose it was the boldness of his question that made me risk such a forward one in reply. Of course, I would never have asked it if I hadn't already been sure that they were – well I mean, obviously I was safe, obviously there was only one reason why young men would be out walking on that particular stretch of beach at sunset, there was no reason to be shy. There was a pause, and before he answered me they turned and looked at one another, both of them turning at exactly the same time.

When their eyes met, the gentlest of half-smiles lit their faces, and oh, suddenly, I recognised that look. Or, rather, I thought I recognised it. I remember all that, that feeling of sharing a tremendous secret – but then I wondered if maybe with twins, with twin brothers, maybe it's like that anyway? He reached out his hand, and the other one took it in his. The half-smile on their lips grew, slightly – it was more an intensification of feeling than an actual change of expression – and I saw the grip of their linked hands shift, momentarily, the interlacing of their fingers subtly strengthen.

I looked back up at their faces, from one to the other, and the half-grins grew, and they seemed to have forgotten about me for a moment, and then suddenly, as one, the two pairs of palest-blue eyes turned full on me, and the answer to my question was quite clear, it was absolutely clear from the way he said, in that curiously level, quiet, half-American voice, "Oh us, we're together. Yes sir; together."

I pride myself in not being easily surprised, and certainly not shocked, but, well, it must have shown in my face. They deliberately left me hanging in silence for a moment, still smiling, before the other one said, "It's OK, most people are pretty surprised. We get used to it."

"I'm sorry," I said, "I didn't mean to..."

"It's OK, really."

He looked out above my head again, as if to prove that nothing had been said to disturb the calm of the evening. I turned to follow his gaze, and saw that the sun was just dipping to touch the horizon, laying a path of gold across the sea towards us.

All three of us watched in silence as it started to sink from view, reddening through every shade of fire and flame as the sea took it. I don't know if it was the liberating effect of my swim, or the sheer beauty of the sunset, or its strange stillness, or the unexplained frankness of these two extraordinary young strangers, but I suddenly felt completely free to talk. I felt safe. Normally, great beauty overawes me, but for some reason, for just a few minutes, as that particular evening cast its spell, a feeling of something like intimacy loosened my tongue. I surprised myself – I still do, sometimes.

"How long," I said, "How long have you been together?"

The fingers shifted their grip again, slightly.

"Nearly nineteen years."

I'm sure that normally, whichever one of them whose turn it was to deliver their punchline said that – because I had the curious feeling that this was perhaps all rehearsed, was at least familiar, that they had told this story to other men besides me – the response was incredulous, or at least confused. But the way I remember it, they seemed to me, standing there, gilded by the setting sun, already so fantastical, so perfect, that this final outlandish detail seemed no more than fitting. Of course, of course they were only nineteen, even with bodies like that; of course the two of them had been a pair all their lives. Of course their being lovers was only the natural extension of their exquisite, unlikely and complete union. It was midsummer's eve, after all.

"That's wonderful," I said – what else could I say? – turning away to look back at the sea, and doubtless to hide the look on my face. I'm sure I was trying to smile, but I could feel how easily the smile could break, how close it was to breaking.

Jealousy is always shaming, even in front of complete strangers. The sun completed its sinking; the show was over, and the silence of the beach intensified. I was just reaching out again to my pile of clothes, thinking to get dressed and quietly leave the beach to the lovers, when behind me one of them spoke.

"Well, nice to meet you, but I guess we'd best be going. This is our first night in town."

"Where are you staying?" I said, pulling on the first sock that I'd picked up, keeping it polite.

'"Nowhere, yet."

"Well, good luck – the hotels get very full at the weekends, you know." (Why is it that socks are always so hard to get back on, on the beach?)

"Oh, I'm sure we'll find somewhere. Or someone."

Something about the way it was said made me stop tugging at my reluctant sock and look back up at them. Had I heard right? The sky was starting to darken behind them, and I'm sure I'm not imagining or misremembering this bit, but when both of them looked at me again, in unison, which they now did, and in a way that made the statement seem more like a question, their eyes, if I'm not mistaken, seemed, somehow and just for a moment, to glitter. And it was very clear that they were waiting, waiting for me to respond. And for just one mad, stomach-churning moment, when they looked at me like that, I thought that this really was an invitation.

So little actually gets said, doesn't it, in these conversations, but you imagine so much, don't you, and so quickly? I imagined them in my car; which one of them would sit in the front, or would they stay together, on the back seat, I wondered? I imagined unlocking my front door with them standing on the pavement behind me. I imagined the three of us walking up my stairs. I imagined all sorts of things, believe me. I knew that all I had to do was smile before I replied, and if they were asking me what I thought they were asking me, admission would meet admission, need would meet need, and something unspoken would become quite definite. But what was it that was being asked of me, exactly? What was it they wanted? There was something about there being two of them, and about the fact that I kept on imagining them behind me, imagining not being able to see what they were thinking – and they were so strong, and they were such a pair – when they make their move, I thought, they'll move as one, as a pair; swift, sudden, strong. What could they possibly want with me anyway, I thought? What possible geometry could they have in mind? Why on earth would two such beauties approach me, a man of my age, when they had a whole summer town full of young men to prey on? I hesitated, and hesitated, and in that hesitation, as I looked from handsome face to handsome face, despite all my fears, I heard a thought spoken out loud inside my head. I didn't actually say it, but I definitely heard it, and in my voice, and I mean not my voice of forty years ago, but very definitely my own voice, sixty-five, quite clearly, saying, come on, it's not as if they're going to eat you.

And then I said no. I don't mean I said "No," out loud, but I thought it, no. No. Not me. And what I finally said, said out loud, after much too long a pause, was, "Oh, I'm sure. I'm sure you will."

The one who'd done most of the talking kept looking me right in the eye, and smiled, and I'm sure it was a different smile this time, something colder, and harder, and much less handsome, and then he said, "You know something, I think you might well be right."

Then he turned to his friend – to his brother, I should say, because I'm sure they really they were brothers, it can't have been just an act – and said, curtly, as if he was speaking to his dog, "Come on then, I'm famished."

And that was it; as suddenly as they'd appeared, they went. Have you ever seen a terrier drop a rat as soon as it has snapped its neck, drop it with a sudden and complete lack of interest and move on to the next one? That's how they were with me. They walked right past me, down the shingle bank and onto the sand. As they walked away into the deepening dark they never once altered their direction or paused to look back at me. I said nothing, never even thought of shouting after them – I knew they wouldn't stop, knew that whatever it was they were looking for, they hadn't found it.

Ahead of them, at the far end of the beach, I could see that the lights of the pier and the seafront were all on now, sending out their multicoloured dot-and-dash messages of desire. The sickle moon was clear and bright against the dark blue velvet of the sky, and I can remember thinking that for an encounter this strange, it should have been full, it should be a full moon tonight. The two of them should break into a loping run as they head for the town across the sands, their gait should shift and suddenly reveal them as a pair of wolves, of dog foxes; one of them should even pause, lift his head and sniff the night air. After all, I thought, it was an odd word to use, 'famished'. With those arms and chests, they looked less famished than any young men I'd ever seen – and it wasn't just the flattering light, every inch of those smooth, matching, sculpted skins was indeed perfect. But then young men talk like that on summer nights, don't they ? They're never hungry, only famished. Starving.

Ravenous.

I watched them go until I could see them no longer; it took some ten or fifteen minutes for the gathering darkness to first smudge them, then erase them. At the moment they disappeared, I suddenly realised that I was still naked, and shivering, actually shaking. I groped for my folded clothes, dressed hurriedly, and drove back home as fast as I could.

I can see them still, walking side by side and absolutely unhurried across that great expanse of bare, smooth sand, sand that the fading of the light is now turning that unearthliest of colours, a dark, sombre violet. Above the pier, the moon is hanging as bright as a promise. High above the awakening town, Orion strides out across the midsummer night, his sword heavy at his belt, his faithful hound at his heels, nose lifted, scenting, eager for the first quarry, the first blood.

I really should be in bed. The rain is slashing at the window now, my shoulders are stiff and I know that when I open my eyes it will be dark, and it will be cold, and that I'm sixty-five, sixty-five. That strange meeting on the beach seems less of a memory now, more of a fantasy or hallucination. I'm always least reliable when dealing with beauty; I always remember men as being more handsome than they really were.

I remember their skin. Their hands. I remember their eyes.

I wonder if they'll come back this year. And if they do, and if I meet them again – as the sun is setting, say – I wonder if I'll say something different this time. I wonder if this time I'll say yes. I wonder if I'll invite them back here to this room.

After all, as I said, it's not as if they could eat me.

Ten Letters From Toby
Sebastian Beaumont

Ten Letters From Toby
Sebastian Beaumont

March 3rd

Dear Neil,

I am writing to you because I think I might be in trouble.

You know how in 50s and 60s sci-fi movies when you turn off black-and-white televisions the picture gets smaller and smaller until there is just a dot in the middle of the screen? Well, I think I'm like that dot. I used to be a full picture, but now I'm getting smaller and smaller. And one day I'm going to disappear altogether.

It hasn't been unpleasant – diminishing – because all my usual preoccupations have become meaningless. I no longer worry about getting into trouble with the DSS. I simply don't care. Even the fact that I haven't gone down to sign on for a while doesn't worry me (I find I can't leave the flat at the moment). I was supposed to go to an interview with my 'Client Adviser' last week, but I couldn't be bothered. In the past it's made me feel such a failure when I'm faced with a real live person who's asking me awkward questions about what I'm doing with my life. But that's okay at the moment. I didn't go to the interview, so it doesn't seem real to me. Right now I feel fine. Well, not fine exactly, but not unhappy. Not stressed out. Hey, you always told me I shouldn't be so stressed out. Well, now I'm not.

The junkie next door but one sold me some *serious* sleeping pills the other day, and they're just kicking in, so I must go to bed.

love Toby

March 4th

Dear Neil,

I want to tell you something. Last year my sister had a cleaner called Justin. He was pretty good at his job, but he was just her cleaner. I'd never even met him. I just knew that my sister had a cleaner. Then, one day, this bloke walked up to me in that club at the top of Leith Walk and said, "Are you Alison's brother? You look just like her." It turned out that he was a drag-queen DJ called Belinda Blowjob and he was paying off his student loan by putting on a fortnightly club night and by doing cleaning jobs during the day. He'd recently got an MA in printmaking from Glasgow.

So?

So, this world is full of strange people. Or people you look at in one way and see as dead ordinary, and then if you see them in another way they're extraordinary. I mean, this guy was walking round my sister's house dusting her ornaments while back home he had a folio of *amazing* artwork (I saw it later) and he'd be polishing her mirrors while trying to decide what kind of cabaret slot to do that night, and whether to wear sequins or lime-green rubber.

Oh, yes, I'd better get to the reason why I'm writing this letter – the reason why I wrote that letter to you yesterday in which I didn't come to the point...

Last night I was reading a novel in bed – *The Blood Countess*, based on fact, about this 16th-century Transylvanian Countess who murdered 650 virgins because she believed their unsullied blood would give her eternal youth (talk about violence being the *real* pornography, the author is *sick* and so am I for reading past page 60). Countess Bathory. It didn't work, of course – the eternal youth bit. Well, I knew it wouldn't because those things don't happen in real life. But just for a moment, while I was reading the book, it seemed as though the whole thing was true – that you really *could* live forever if you drank the blood of virgins. Crazy really. I mean, it was only a novel. But then, the murdering Countess really did exist, and what made it so creepy was that in the context of the fiction I could believe that she was still alive somewhere, *right now*, like in the next room or something, still living and devouring virgins.

Anyway, that's not the point either. The thing was that when I finished the book and stretched out my hand to turn the light off, I realised that it wasn't my hand. Oh, it was attached to my body, and it looked like my hand, but I realised that the shape of my hand had been taken over by a shadow that was slightly smaller in all respects to my real hand and was somehow occupying the entire inside of my fingers, palm and forearm, so that although it was covered up by my skin, *underneath* the skin there was something else that wasn't a part of me. It was dead scary. I kept on waving my arm about, trying to catch this weird shadow out, but it always moved as fast as I did so that it never showed.

But I knew it was there.

What is even scarier is that my fingers hardly work, because the shadow's kind of deadened them. Luckily it's my left hand so I can still write this.

I've just read back what I've written. Do you think I'm going mad? It's occurred to me that I might be having a nervous breakdown, but because I don't have a job or a family, or a lover since you left, there's no one to give me an opinion on that. Maybe that's why I'm writing to you – maybe *you* can tell me. But you never wanted to talk to me again, and I know you meant it.

Never mind, you can decide for your own amusement.

Anyway, I haven't finished what I wanted to say about Justin the drag queen.

The night I met him he was chatty and friendly and put me on the guest list of the club that he hosts (in the end he wore the lime-green rubber). It's at that place across the cobbled courtyard down by the Grassmarket that often has live music. Not a brilliant venue for a club night of Justin's kind, but it was pretty busy all the same. His cabaret slot was crap, but I think it was supposed to be, and everyone loved it. He wore this huge sixties beehive wig and camped around and I thought, "*That's my sister's cleaner!*" And the weird thing, like the *really* weird thing is that I've got to know him quite well since then, and he's actually dead ordinary, and I thought: first he's nobody, just my sister's cleaner – and everybody knows that cleaners are ordinary people – and then he's Belinda Blowjob being totally weird to a shrieking audience; and then, of course, he's just another ex-student trying to pay off his student loan, someone who wants a job and a home and a lover. Just like me – just like you. *Dead ordinary.*

I never told you this but when I was a kid I used to be able to make myself invisible. I would get on a bus and concentrate really hard on being invisible, and the conductor would come along and ask the person next to me for their fare, and then the person after me, but he wouldn't stop and ask me for mine. It gave me a thrill to know that by the power of thought alone I'd managed to make him unable to see me, and it made me believe that the world is a stranger place than we can fully understand.

It was my great secret, that I could make myself disappear at will. I didn't tell anyone at school. I only did it every now and then on the bus, but it made me feel really different, in a good way. It made me feel that I wasn't ordinary and dull, like everybody else. It made me tingle with pleasure when I thought about it. It made me feel important and sort of *powerful*.

The only problem is that I finally worked out what actually happened on those buses. Years later I sat in front of the mirror and concentrated and concentrated on becoming invisible, hoping that I would fade away before my very eyes. But, do you know what? I just looked crazy. My face went puce and my upper lip jutted right out and my eyes started to bulge, and I thought, "I was never invisible. That bus conductor left me alone because he thought I was a nutter".

I had to laugh about it, though it was sort of sad, too, and it made me think that all the extraordinary things in life are probably dead ordinary underneath if only you learn to look at them in the right way.

Must go, love Toby

March 12th
Dear Neil,
I realised yesterday that if I'm ordinary, and everything I've ever done is ordinary – no matter how crazy it seems on the surface – then I can't be mad, because ordinary people don't go mad.

That was a relief. I was so pleased I even went and signed on. I'm in a bit of trouble about missing my Client Adviser interview, but I'm going to talk to someone about it, so I hope I can sort things out.

love Toby

March 13th
Dear Neil,
By playing around with semantics I managed to persuade myself I'm sane – a fact that I now realise more than half proves the opposite.

I've been reading a book by Patricia Duncker – *Hallucinating*

Foucault. There's this bit in it where she says: *'But there is another kind of loneliness which is terrible to endure... And that is the loneliness of seeing a different world from that of the people around you.'* Well, that describes me perfectly. I mean, that shadow in my hand, for example. It's crept way up beyond my elbow now – nearly to my shoulder, in fact. *That's* a different way of seeing things, isn't it, to be aware that there's a secret shadow inside you that's taking you over? And knowing that you see things differently *does* make you feel lonely, in a strange way. But what I've experienced is no less valid just because I'm the only one who's experienced it. I mean, this shadow is either there or it isn't. My perception is either true or it isn't. I tried explaining this to the woman who lives downstairs from me – she's the most ordinary woman you could wish to meet – and she looked at me as though I was mad. And I thought, "I'm not a nutter, I'm ordinary like you. You just *think* I'm a nutter". And it made me feel that I was different, but only because *she* thought I was different and not because *I* thought I was different.

Incidentally, this *thing* seems to be leeching me in some kind of parasitic way, because I keep feeling exhausted and somehow, well... bloodless.

love Toby

March 23rd
Dear Neil,

My legs have been overtaken by The Shadow. I keep on jerking my body from side to side in the hope of moving my legs fast enough to catch the shadow out. One of these days I'll manage to move so fast that it can't keep up with my body and then it'll be out in the open and I'll be able to grab it and kill it, or something. If I've got the strength left, that is, what with this inexorable blood loss.

I went to the doctor about it – it took pretty well all my emotional strength a) to make the appointment, b) to go to it, and c) to explain the situation.

He clearly thought I was mad. He told me not to worry and that it would go away of its own accord. He said it was probably stress-related and told me to take some vitamins and iron – he did at least admit that I'd become unnaturally pale. He also gave me some tranquillizers that

I have now flushed down the toilet (a big mistake – I could have sold them to that junkie next door but one).

love Toby

April 4th
Dear Neil,
I crapped in the bed last night. I was so shocked when I woke up. I still can't believe I did it. But the shadow's up over my waist now and my legs have completely stopped working and it seems my gut control has stopped too. I had to pull myself out of bed using my one good arm. It took me half the day to get dressed and get the sheets washed (god, they stank).

Toby

April 12th
Dear Neil,
I've seen my adversary! It's 4.00am and I've just woken up and realised that the shadow still thought I was asleep, so I leapt up, and I was right! In the bed there is a shadow, minus head and shoulders, and it's exactly the same shape as me! I knew it. *I knew it!* It'd taken over nearly my whole body so I know that if it ever gets back into me, I'll be a goner. I've crept out of the bedroom (I have full use of my bodily functions now that it's not inside me), and come out here to write this letter to you, and I'm so pleased. I'm so pleased it's true that my internal shadow is real, because seeing it like that has proved that I'm definitely *not* dead ordinary like I'd always feared I was.

I'm still weak, though. I looked at myself in the mirror and you'd hardly recognise me now, I've got so gaunt and wasted.

I'll go back into the bedroom and face up to that parasitic *thing* when I've posted this. Wish me luck.

May 15th
Dear Neil,
Sorry about the delay in writing you this letter. Jesus, I've had a

tough month. As you've probably guessed I *did* go back to face my shadow, and I came out of it badly. I leapt onto the bed and grabbed hold of it – but there was nothing there! That's when I knew it had got back into me and I was in *real* trouble. I don't remember much about what happened after that because I was kind of choking from inside and everything was going dark, but I must have made a lot of noise because the next thing I knew I was being strapped to a stretcher and loaded up into the back of an ambulance. I thought they were going to take me to hospital, but they brought me here, so I guess I must be mad after all.

love Toby

May 19th

Dear Neil,

Hey, it's not too bad here. They don't think I'm dangerous, so I'm allowed to walk in the grounds on my own. The rhododendrons are out – purple and white and deep, deep red. This place used to be an almost-but-not-quite stately home, so it's got that Victorian landscaping, with a small lake that's almost entirely choked with weeds and lilies. From the common room I look out across the Firth to the shores of Fife and the mountains beyond, which is what I'm doing right now as I write this. There are all sorts of people here, and some of them seem to me to be the absolute epitome of ordinariness. They'll come over and chat to me over tea and I'll think "Why are you here?" They're always asking me why *I'm* in here, and I can't bring myself to say, so I don't think I have a right to ask them back.

I talked to the psychiatrist who's been assigned to me and I told him all about my shadow and he was really interested and came up with all kinds of stuff about how it was just a manifestation of my sense of failure. He said I'm not a nutter at all, and that lots of ordinary people have nervous breakdowns. It happens all the time. I just need to get home and get motivated and get a sense of 'self'. Apparently.

By the way, I'm sorted out for a while after I get home. I'll be getting sickness benefit for at least three months, so I don't have to feel pressurised into looking for work. It seems it's useful going nuts every now and then.

As far as my blood goes, I still feel exhausted all the time, and they're doing tests on me to find out what's the matter, because they can't work it out, and I still look so white and gaunt that it makes me seem even weirder than the people in here who are *genuinely* mad. It's a mystery, apparently. I have extraordinary blood!

June 3rd
Dear Neil,
Well, I'm home again.

So, it seems I went mad – in an ordinary sort of way. I was trying to figure that out and it suddenly hit me that everyone is both ordinary and extraordinary at the same time. Wasn't that what I was saying to you about Justin the drag-queen cleaner? I was saying it, but I wasn't *thinking* it; I wasn't *feeling* it. Well, I may not be a drag queen or a cleaner but I guess I've got my odd side and my ordinary side just like anyone else. I reckon that a person appears to be either sane or mad depending on your first experience of them. Take that woman downstairs, for example, the one I told you about before, the ultra-dull one. She still thinks I'm completely barmy. You should have seen her face when I met her on the stairs this morning (she's the one who called the police and ambulance on the dreaded night that I confronted my shadow). She didn't say a word when I greeted her and thanked her for her help. She sort of pursed her lips, rolled her eyes, made kind of warding-off gestures with her hands and quickly stepped inside her flat and closed the door on me. "Well," I thought, "just look at you!"

I'm sitting here, drinking tea and putting my feet up. I've still got a long way to go before I get my strength back. They haven't found out what's up with my blood yet. But at least I'm sane.

24th June
Dear Neil Deakin,
You don't really know me, though we were introduced once, and I saw you a few times on the stairs. I'm the woman who lived downstairs from Toby McLean. I've been keeping an eye on him, because, to be frank, I've always been worried about him. Ever since you stopped coming round, that is.

Poor Toby died sometime last week. I hadn't seen him for nearly a fortnight, so I went up and let myself into his flat – I knew he kept a spare key in the spider-plant pot in the stairwell window, I've seen him hiding it there more than once. The last time I saw him he looked very unwell. In fact, he virtually assaulted me in the doorway of my flat, shouting something about me getting an ambulance when he had his breakdown. I thought, "I'd better keep an eye on him". He didn't seem at all well.

I found him in the sitting-room. He can't have eaten anything at all after coming home, because he was so thin. He looked underweight when he shouted at me in my doorway, but I wouldn't have believed it was possible for someone to lose so much weight so quickly. He was barely a skeleton, and so pale.

I don't suppose you really want to know the gory details, but Toby had some paper by his side, and a pen, and your address, so I reckon he must have still been in touch with you. I suppose the police will have been round to talk to you, but I thought I'd write anyway. I always thought you were good for Toby. And maybe you'll miss him. It's nice to think it won't only be me.

Killing Time
David Patrick Beavers

Killing Time
David Patrick Beavers

The water gushed around and over his boots as he clomped along down the hill. Normally, the navy nylon jacket with its polar fleece lining kept him warm and reasonably dry, but this sudden cloudburst was like being beneath a waterfall. Saturated to the skin in just a few minutes. The umbrella was all but useless. At least his satchel was still new enough to repel the sheets of rain slapping against it, but who knew just how long that would last.

Matthew plodded ahead down the hill toward the bus stop on the corner of Fuller Avenue. A sheltered stop with large, plexi-glass walls that were supposed to hold movie advertisements between the double panes. Instead, the plastic sheets were scarred with graffiti and splattered with all sorts of foul, viscous fluids. When the stop-hut was newly built, having replaced the old, rotting wood and cast-iron bench, it had recessed lighting, but the city long ago halted the replacement of the fluorescent bulbs that people stole. The only light at this hour of the morning came from the mercury vapor street lamps. Usually, the light bleeding into the stop from these sources sufficed, but it was not bright enough to read by.

He squinted through a curtain of his dripping bangs. Off one curb. Stomp-splash over asphalt. Up onto the other curb. Home free, he thought as he ducked beneath the shelter of the hut. His sudden appearance startled a woman who'd been sitting, yet half dozing, on the bench.

"Sorry," he said as he put down his umbrella.

"I'm glad to see you," she said.

She was Linda. A somewhat full-figured woman who worked as a temporary para-legal for one of the law firms in one of the high-rises near where Matthew worked. She, like Matthew, loathed taking the bus, but as his car's engine was being rebuilt and her car had disappeared along with her soon-to-be-ex husband, they were both forced into public transportation by need and economy. They chatted a lot during these early morning hours while waiting for the bus.

"You got here before this miserable cloud burst," he said.

"Barely."

Matthew set his satchel down on the bench, then abruptly combed the excess water from his hair. "At least the wind's not blowing too much."

"You need a mirror?" she asked as she opened her purse. "I've a compact."

"Naw. Thanks, though. It was still wet from the shower, anyhow."

"It's bad enough being out here on good mornings, but this…" She sighed and leaned a bit forward to peer down the hill.

Matthew craned around for a look as well. They could usually see the bus – the 217 – way down the hill at the stoplight. It was almost a quarter of a mile away from them, but visually it was a straight shot. Linda leaned back and checked her watch.

"It'll be late," Matthew said.

"I know."

Matthew moved his satchel over a bit toward Linda, then sat down at the very edge of the bench. How he'd rather be back up the hill, in his apartment, in his warm, toasty bed. He scanned the windows of the apartment buildings across the street. All the obsidian black panes spoke volumes of people still happily slumbering while he and his bench-mate sat in the dark surrounded by wetness. As he absently stared ahead, he noticed the rain suddenly cease to fall. He looked up at the sky. Black clouds now shone a silvery gray, but they were still as thick as cotton batting. The wind picked up slightly, soughing through boughs of pine and fronds of palms that grew all around. Linda drew her coat tightly about her.

"Kind of pretty, don't you think?" Matthew said.

"No, I don't." Linda scanned the sky. "Gives me the creeps."

The silvery gray suddenly burned a brilliant pink and fiery gold, illuminating the world around them. Linda began to count as they both stared at the sky. Just as she got to ten, the thundering double boom of a megaton cannon ripped through the silence. Linda inadvertently jerked back from the noise.

"Blanket lightning," Matthew said softly.

"Well, God or ol' Ma Nature needs to roll that sucker back up and stuff it way in the back of the closet."

"Better this than thunder bolts," Matthew said.

"Shhh..."

"What?"

Linda motioned for him to remain silent. After a moment, she looked at him. "No dogs."

Matthew listened. The neighborhood apartments were home to hundreds of pet pooches. Usually any loud noise set them off howling their disdain to one another over the blocks of stucco and glass. It did seem odd that not even one dog pitched his baying pipes to sound the alarm. Linda rose and stepped to the curb to peer down the hill. She remained there for a minute or so, as if she could somehow simply will the bus to appear and pull up beside her. Matthew glanced at his watch.

"Do you see anything?" he asked.

"Not even a car," she said softly. She turned and sat back down. "Come to think of it, I haven't seen a car go up or down the hill since I've been here. Haven't seen the eastbound bus, either, and it usually gets to the stop opposite the street a few minutes before our bus comes."

"Well, it's only Tuesday," he offered. "The club animals aren't usually out on Monday nights. And they're usually the only ones racing around the streets at this time of the morning, still hopped up from the night before."

"Did we miss having to set our clocks back or something?"

"Daylight Saving Time ended last month."

Linda fished in her purse for a cigarette. Matthew offered her his lighter. She inhaled deeply, then let a long stream of smoke blow out. "You want one?" she asked.

Matthew did want one. He was trying to quit. "No thanks," he said.

"Every time I light one, the bus sure enough comes."

"Well, it broke down twice last week. Takes time to get a back-up bus."

Matthew got up and looked down the hill. Nothing. He stood there and watched the stoplight change from green to red then back to green. Just as he turned to sit down, there was another silent, minor flash of pink overhead. He glanced up and could see the clouds were turning black once more. A few seconds later, an explosive double boom wrenched the air, then the clouds opened up again. It was as if a gigantic, cosmic tap had been turned on full force, the sheets of rain slamming on the roof of the hut like a breaking tidal wave. Water swelled up from the street, over the curb, flooding the sidewalk beneath their feet. Matthew and Linda scrambled up onto the bench, just standing there dumbly, staring at the roiling, rushing run-off below them. The din within the hut was deafening. The whole structure vibrated steadily.

"Now this just sucks!" she snapped.

"It'll pass! It's just another cloudburst!"

"That's what everyone told Noah!" she said as she pitched her cigarette into the rushing stream.

"Well, there sure as shit isn't time to build an ark!"

"Listen!" she said sharply.

Matthew listened. Even with the din all around them, he could hear a distinct slap-slap-slapping of splashing water. Soggy feet running along drenched pavement. Running. Fast. Another one trying to make it to shelter. Matthew quickly shouldered his satchel and scooted closer to Linda. Another brilliant flash of golden pink and violet light lit up the sky, followed immediately by the most deafening blasts of thunder. Linda grabbed onto Matthew as the sound swept around them. The lights on their side of the street went out without so much as a flicker of warning. Matthew glanced at the plexi-glass wall just as a man slammed into it with such force that the entire hut swayed. Linda shrieked. Matthew's heart skipped wildly. He watched as the man bounced away from the wall and fell onto his back. Matthew dropped his satchel onto the bench, then jumped down into the ankle deep run-off cascading down the sidewalk. Linda grabbed him by the collar.

"What're you doing?!"

"He's hurt."

Matthew pulled away and went to the man.

The cloudburst diminished in a matter of seconds.

The dazed man was already trying to rise. His overcoat was saturated, his suit slacks were ruined. As Matthew helped him up, he noticed the man clutched his dress shoes to his chest. He had been running barefoot.

"You have to help me," the man said hoarsely.

"Come on," Matthew said softly. "The rain's letting up."

The man let Matthew assist him to his feet, then clung tenaciously to him. Matthew eased him along into the modest shelter of the hut. Linda crouched on the bench, shifting her purse and Matthew's satchel out of the way.

"You have to help me," the man pleaded.

"Are you okay?" Linda asked. "Did you hurt yourself?"

"Hurt?" The man was confused by the word. He stared at Linda, then turned back to Matthew. "Help me?"

A trickle of blood dripping from his nostrils spread like runny watercolor over his wet chin. "It's just a bloody nose," Matthew said. "Doesn't look like it's swelling."

Linda handed Matthew a wad of tissue. Matthew blotted the blood from the man's face.

"Can you tell me your name?"

"Name?"

"Your name, hon," Linda added as she awkwardly kneeled beside him. "Can you remember that?"

The man stared vacantly at the shoes he held. Matthew eased a small piece of balled-up tissue into the man's left nostril to stop the flow of blood.

"Keep the tissue up there for a second or so," Matthew said.

"Oh..." the man said absently. "Okay..."

"Can you remember your name, hon?" Linda asked again.

The man pulled back from Matthew, suddenly aware of the foreign object now lodged in his nostril. He clumsily brushed it out. "What're you doing?"

"You've got a bloody nose," Matthew said.

The man snatched the tissue from Matthew's hand and daubed at the wound himself. "I'm fine!" he snapped.

Matthew and Linda both pulled back. "Okay! We're just trying to help!" said Matthew as he moved around the bench closer to Linda.

Linda said nothing. She wouldn't look at the man. Matthew sighed silently.

The rain once again stopped as suddenly as it started.

"Joseph," the man said. "I'm Joseph."

Linda picked up her purse and stepped out towards the curb.

"Is it coming?" Matthew asked.

"Is what coming?" asked the man.

"The bus!" Linda snapped. "The stupid, friggin' bus!"

Matthew shouldered his satchel and moved out to the curb. "I'm about ready to go back home and call in sick."

"I don't have any more sick days this year," Linda said with a resigned sigh. "Crap. This is just crap."

"It won't come," Joseph whispered.

Linda spun around abruptly and lit into him. "I don't know what your fucking problem is, what you fucking think you know or don't know, and I don't wanna know, so just shut the fuck up!"

Matthew placed a hesitant, hopefully calming hand upon her shoulder. Linda yanked away. He turned back to Joseph. In the shadows, the man looked to be somewhere in his thirties. He was taller than Matthew, but thin. The soggy overcoat swallowed him up. He still clung to his shoes. Well-polished wingtips, either black or dark brown. The man simply stared vacantly at some point of oblivion around his bare feet. He turned his attention back to Linda, who was now furiously smoking another cigarette, her eyes focused solely on the downward slope of the street.

"Maybe," he said. "Maybe we should just walk down to Sunset and catch the 304."

Linda remained with her back to him, but she did glance at her watch. "Murphy's Law," she said.

"Meaning?"

She turned to him. "If we walk down to Sunset, you know that damned 217 will finally come flying up the hill here." She turned back around to stare down the hill.

Matthew sat down, next to Joseph. He wasn't sure what to say. On any other day, the man might be just like any other man just waiting for the bus. The shoes he clutched looked expensive. Even the ruined overcoat had that air of overpriced design to it.

"Your nose has stopped bleeding," Matthew said.

He seemed to have heard Matthew, for he nodded ever so slightly.

"Where're your socks?" he asked.

The man raised a hand, hesitated, then felt around for a pocket. "Socks?" he said. "Socks."

He focused his attention on one free hand fishing through a tangle of twisted, drenched fabric. A startled, yet pained yelp escaped his lips. He stopped moving, but just for an instant, as if a thought were suddenly forming in his mind. He pulled out his hand and fixated on his ring finger. A bead of blood swelled up on the side, next to the nail. Gravity tugged at the drop. It trickled down the finger and across his palm, then effortlessly dripped onto the pavement.

"Useless..." Joseph muttered to himself.

"Come on," Linda said quietly. "Let's get the 304."

Matthew heard her, but could not stop staring at Joseph's bleeding finger. He felt her tug at his sleeve. He slowly drew himself up onto his feet.

"It comes in ten minutes," she said. "We can make it."

"What about him?"

"You wanna babysit a whacko? Fine. I'm going."

Linda stole away quietly. Matthew hesitated for a moment then picked up his umbrella and followed her across the street and down the steep incline of Fuller Avenue, their footsteps dully thudding on the sidewalk.

"Too many freaks in this town," Linda said.

"You think he's high or something?"

"I think he needs to be medicated," she snapped. "Damn fool's brain's scrambled."

Matthew sighed. "Rain's stopped at least."

Linda bristled and suddenly stopped short. Matthew heard it, too. The rapid slap-slap-slap of bare feet on pavement. They both looked back. Joseph was barreling barefoot down the hill towards them at breakneck speed, his overcoat billowing out like a sail behind him, a shoe in each hand. He launched a wingtip at them. Linda and Matthew ran. The leather projectile clocked Linda in the shoulder, the force sending her stumbling, then falling onto the pavement. Matthew bent down to yank her up. The second shoe grazed his head, then bounced down the hill. Just as he got Linda to her feet, Joseph slammed into Matthew, tackling him hard. Matthew's umbrella went skidding off into the street. His satchel slipped in front of him, cushioning his collapse onto the concrete.

"Run!" he screamed.

Linda scrambled ahead. Joseph's knees bore down on his back, pinning him to the sidewalk.

"Help me," Joseph whispered hoarsely.

Matthew let out a growling shriek and bucked furiously. Joseph spread over him like an oil slick, adroitly wrapping the strap of the satchel around Matthew's neck. The constriction of his windpipe was severe. Matthew stopped fighting. Joseph's hand suddenly appeared before his face. He held a syringe.

"It has to work." Joseph's words were emphatic.

Out of the corner of his eye, Matthew saw Joseph clench the syringe between his teeth. His free hand yanked Matthew's jacket up. Cold concrete met bare skin. Matthew sucked a dry gasp down then freed his right arm and swung his elbow hard into some part of Joseph. His assailant grunted sharply but held fast, reining his choke-hold. In an instant, the syringe was back in Joseph's hand. He abruptly stabbed the needle into Matthew's stomach and held it there.

Matthew could barely feel the sting. Though a slight sensation, even the tiniest shift of his body or of Joseph's atop him made the intrusive needle feel more pronounced.

Seconds felt like minutes. Joseph withdrew the needle, then clumsily pocketed the syringe. He rose up, sinking his weight onto his knee, smack in the middle of Matthew's spine. He leapt over Matthew and ran down the hill.

Matthew fought to untangle the strap wound around his neck. Pulling himself to his feet, he saw Joseph had recovered one shoe and was bounding over to the other. Matthew spotted his umbrella in the gutter as his right hand felt his stomach, his fingers rubbed hard at the injection site. He lunged for his umbrella, caught it up by the handle, and tore down the hill in pursuit of Joseph. The madman let out a loud, joyful whoop and sprinted like an Olympian on fire down the remaining blocks toward the intersection at Sunset.

Adrenaline pumped through Matthew as ran. He tried to yell, to shriek at the top of his lungs, but not a sound came out of him. A sudden, sharp pain shot through his head. He winced, staggered a few steps, then caught hold of the top of a short retaining wall. He steadied himself and drew in a few deep breaths.

Dawn was breaking through the thick clouds. Black night bled indigo. He pushed off again, walking fast down the sidewalk, his left hand keeping purchase on the wall.

He felt lightheaded as he neared the corner. There was no covered bus stop here. Just a bench. The mini-mall across the street was dark. The streetlights were not as bright. He strained to keep his focus on the surrounding area. There was no sign of life, even around the shrubbery flanking the buildings.

Where was Linda? The police? There were always cops on Sunset at this hour. Chasing the night trade away. He squinted to see the blocks east, then west, but the dull ache in his head blurred his vision.

The burning, stabbing pain that cut through his thigh nearly brought him to his knees. He stumbled back against the rear of the bench.

Where was the madman?

Where was Linda?

What had Joseph done to him?

Another current of blinding pain ripped through his head. His body convulsed as if a machete had hacked through him. A seizure, he thought. He looked up into the indigo sky. A fucking seizure? Indigo faded to black.

Matthew lay there unconscious on the sidewalk. A trickle of blood leeched out from beneath his temple where the concrete had scraped skin away. He could not hear the soft, steady footsteps approaching him. He could not feel the tug of the thumb that peeled his eyelid back, nor the gentle fingertips that felt his neck for a pulse.

"He's out cold."

Rougher hands fished a wallet from his back pocket, tearing out the few thin bills, then dug keys from the front. Coins spewed out, caught up by the tangle of jangling metal.

Linda snatched the wallet from Joseph, withdrew Matthew's Driver License and whispered the address it listed, then she placed the license back in the wallet and the wallet back into the pocket.

"You hit me with your shoe, you jackass," she said.

"The hazards of our trade. Can't be an accurate madman all the time."

"How much insulin did you inject in him?" she asked.

Joseph shrugged as he thumbed through the jumble of keys. "Almost eighty units or so."

"Well, get your ass gone. And be quiet when you go through his place." She dug in her purse and pulled out a cell phone.

"What'd he say about his neighbors?"

"He told me yesterday that the upstairs people were gone on vacation. The old man next door's almost deaf, but the couple across the hall start their day as regular as clockwork at seven-thirty."

"Doesn't look like he'd have a pot to piss in."

"His pot's platinum."

"Ingots, you said."

"Two. And two in gold and four in silver. Left to him by his lover."

"Heavy metal inheritance."

Linda shrugged. "He said was going to have them appraised this week along with some bits of jewelry."

"He said in passing conversation."

"People say lots when killing time," she said. "He was going to take them to be appraised this week. Get going."

Joseph pocketed the keys, slipped on his shoes, then left. Linda waited until he was out of sight, then dialed the Emergency operator. Theatrical tears flowed forth.

"Hello? I need an ambulance and the police. There's been a mugging."

Outback
Kevin Booth

Outback
Kevin Booth

I was finally initiated into sex at nineteen – when I met Dale. It was in the Mildura grape-picking district of Australia. I was working through the summer to save for my big OE, or overseas experience. It was a hard job: twelve hours a day, sun-up to sundown, six days a week in forty-degree heat. But it was outdoors, the change I needed from the last nine months of swotting and essay-writing at University down in Melbourne. That harsh outback sun at least lent me a rich bronze tan and bleached my hair to a shining white gold – like the boys I was later to discover in those mass-produced, Californian porn videos. It was also a chance to tone the muscles I had developed at the pool over the last few years into a harder, more rugged body.

I had come out here alone. My regular friends had all gone for jobs in the city. Yet, the idea of doing something alone – totally alone and unknown – had appealed in a mysterious sort of way. I had started off on the pear and peach harvests further up the Murray river, then as the work dwindled, I heard about the grape-picking in this area and hitch-hiked down.

There were about twenty or thirty of us, mostly students, shacked up in huts on the property – and I mean shacked. Each hut was four walls and a tin roof. In general, the only window had no glass, just a piece of sacking to keep out wind and rain during the occasional summer storms. Furniture was two, one-up, one-down bunks. It wasn't important. The sheds really only served as a place to sleep and store your gear.

I didn't make friends easily with the other workers. After dinner, in the evenings, when the rest of the crew sat around smoking joints and telling sex jokes, I generally lay in my bunk reading, or took myself off for a walk around the vineyard. There wasn't much to see: just more of the red earth and rows of vines we worked among all day. The nearest pub was fifteen kilometres away and only a few of us had cars, so we were a pretty closed world for at least six days of the week.

I found a retreat. Not much of one, but it was somewhere to go, to be away from the dreary world of harvest-working. At the end of the property, there was an old, abandoned water-tower. When it had split its seams a few years back, the owners had had a new one put in. You climbed up the ladder of rusty, iron rungs embedded in the concrete and you reached the roof – probably the highest point for a few kilometres in all directions, except for the new tower close to the homestead. This lookout gave me the shabby illusion that I had somehow escaped from everything down below in the world of the grape-pickers. Moulded into the roof was an open hatchway, and then more iron rungs which led down into the belly of the tower. I didn't go down into the tower – I had a sensible fear of snakes and spiders which I was sure must infest the dark, empty cistern. I preferred to lie on the roof and stare up at the stars, imagining myself on a trip that went far beyond the Mildura grape district, to Asia, or Africa, or Europe. I tried to imagine the same voluminous cloud of stars shining down on Venice, Bangkok, or Marrakech.

Dale arrived about a week after I did. Coming back from picking at sunset, all of us piled onto the tractor, we passed him on the track. Jake, the foreman, realised he was a new one – he wouldn't be walking that track for any other reason – and stopped the tractor to give him a lift. He tossed his pack aboard easily and hopped onto the clanking trailer with the rest of us. He was strong and muscular, with the hardened, outback squint of a country worker and a carved, lean face over which crawled a dusty shadow of blond beard. His shoulder-length hair tied back in a pony-tail, and the gold ring in his left ear made him look more like a pirate than anything else, except he was caked from head to foot – like everyone else – with the red dust of the country.

He introduced himself briefly and didn't say much more for the rest of the journey back to the huts.

The next day at dawn, when he appeared with the rest of us at the trailer, he was wearing a pair of faded-red jogging shorts, an old tee-shirt and trainers. Clanking behind the tractor out to the picking site, my eyes were pulled more than once to the healthy bulge quietly visible underneath that red nylon, but luckily he didn't notice. His tee-shirt would come off in the first hour and he would stay that way throughout the long day. His body was hardened and tanned from seasons under the outback sun and he moved with the mercury fluidity of an untamed animal.

He was also a loner. When we got back to the huts at dusk and the rest of the group would flop down, prepare dinner, roll a joint and relax, Dale took himself off to the bathroom – a euphemistic expression for a shed partitioned in two with a row of grimy taps over a rusty trough – to wash and shave. Then he would go back to his hut and change into long trousers and a clean shirt as if preparing to head out for a night on the town. The strange thing was he never went anywhere. He just sat outside his cabin playing with a huge bowie knife that he always wore at his belt. He kept himself to himself and no one really forced the issue. A sort of lone-wolf energy emanated from him which made you wary and not quite sure about approaching.

I noticed him for obvious reasons. Although, in those years, I seemed to be perpetually captivated by some hunk at Uni who I would admire from far off for months, Dale was different to anything I had experienced up till then. What I saw in him sounded a new chord in me – a lot scarier. The inherent violence humming through him and his hard, blond, outback looks combined into an enthralling sexuality. The man was pure sex. Within a few days of his arrival I was completely obsessed, finding any opportunity to get within careful gazing distance. I say careful, because I never let him see I was watching. Any time he looked towards me, I felt my world crumble in and I would mentally drop to my knees, holding out supplicating arms in adoration. I was incapable of meeting his eyes. He didn't seem to notice. He didn't seem to notice or take interest in anything. That was my impression of him, at first.

Then one day, after he had been there about a week, I came down the row to where the others were pouring out tea and coffee and lighting up for our 'smoko' to find him resting with his back against a picking basket, staring at me as I approached. I went red immediately, and could not look at him. I felt like a girl all of a sudden. I grabbed a mug of tea and sat a little way off. Yet, he continued to stare at me, as if I was some weird specimen in a zoo. I didn't have the guts to challenge him and concentrated on my tea. I didn't like this change, because his look wasn't friendly, but impersonal and slightly antagonistic. I had been dreaming for a week of him looking at me just once, letting me get close, but now I found this cool observation really upsetting. I finished my tea quickly and went back to work early.

Nothing else happened then. We finished the day. At lunchtime, at afternoon smoko, and on the ride back to the huts, he was once more his usual self, oblivious to me and the rest of the world. So, naturally, I couldn't take my eyes off him.

That evening, as I was washing my dinner things in our luxury kitchen-bathroom suite, I felt someone watching me. I turned, and there he was again, eye-balling me with the same challenging, aggressive stare of the morning. He took his time, looking me over, and then with the slow confidence of a fighting dog, he sauntered up.

"You from Melbourne?"

I nodded. I found his closeness off-putting, and I knew that he realized it.

"Thought so. Your accent. I'm from Adelaide. Well, just outside. A place called Morgan. Heard of it?" I shook my head. "You haven't missed much. Only the flies go there. You a Uni student?"

"Yeah. I'm studying Lit., English and American."

"You all look the same, you Uni students. There's a certain look. I can pick it a mile off."

I didn't think this was true, but I let him have his way. He seemed to know what he was talking about. Besides, the look in his eyes left me feeling that 'Uni student' was more of a euphemism for some other category of sub-human existing in the back of his mind. I didn't like the inference.

"See you round, then, Prof."

And he meandered off again in his casually aggressive way.

I heard movement. I was lying face-up on the roof of the tower, dreaming of love or death in Venice. Someone was climbing up the rusty ladder. I froze. Images of madmen hurling innocent victims from great heights paralysed my limbs. A head popped over the side of the tower.

"G'day. So this is where you hide yourself away in the evenings."

He hauled himself onto the roof and sat looking out at the rows of vineyards which stretched in all directions. We sat there for a good couple of minutes without speaking. I couldn't think of anything to say and he obviously didn't want to. He noticed the hatchway.

"What's down there?"

"I... I don't know. I've never been down."

He looked at me as if he thought my lack of adventurousness was a crime against the great Australian national character.

"Well, let's have a look."

"There could be snakes... or red-backs..."

"Are you scared of snakes?"

"No. I just don't want to... I prefer it up here."

He did not appear to hear me because he was already swinging himself down into the darkness. I looked down after him. I honestly didn't want to go down. I heard him reach the bottom, then I saw his lighter flame illuminating the space in a warm glow.

"Are you coming down or what?"

I began to climb down. Each rusty rung tingled with the potential prick of some venomous creature. I felt like I was descending the first level of Dante's Inferno. Below, we were in a cracked, concrete cylinder, reasonably empty apart from a certain amount of rubbish on the floor. Rubbish which could be the hiding place for innumerable snakes and spiders. His lighter went out. I freaked.

"Light it again!"

"Just a minute."

When his lighter clicked safety into the cave once again, he was holding a candle stub in his other hand. He grinned at me.

"*'Be prepared'*," his tone mocking the Boy Scouts' motto.

He lit the candle and propped it in the centre of the floor. He looked around the space. So did I. That took about three seconds; there wasn't much to look at.

"This is cosy, n't it?"

I agreed. Where we would go from here in terms of conversation, I had no idea.

He licked his lips and a surprisingly pink and innocent tongue popped out of his violent, handsome face.

"You ever been to Adelaide?" I said I had not.

"I used to go there a lot. A few of us would go down in the ute. Great place. Too big for me, but the birds are to die for. Pirie Street, have you been there?"

I said I had not been to Adelaide.

"Hard to cruise though, the birds."

He sat down on a packing case which someone, God knows who, had hauled in there. I couldn't work out how they would have got it through the hatchway. He took out tobacco and began to roll a cigarette. Every time he looked at me, his eyes glinted black and gold in the candle flame. I sat down against the wall, first checking carefully to see it was free of poisonous insects.

"There was this place outside Adelaide we used to go for laughs. The faggots went there to get fucked up the arse. Lot of faggots, specially at night. They all look alike, the faggots do. There's a certain look. You can spot them a mile off. They look like... a bit like how you look."

Our eyes locked in the pause. I tried to form a denial, then he laughed maliciously. I almost shit myself. I had been sprung.

"We just used to drive around and scare the shit out of them. Didn't do anything, really. Just give 'em a scare, just for laughs. Get 'em in the spotlight, yell at 'em, pop off a couple of rounds."

He paused and lit his cigarette, taking his good time. As he began again, he looked at me sideways, rather slyly, as if calculating his next move.

"Once I went up there on my own. I'd had a few and I had the rifle in the back of the ute. I thought I'd get some target practice on the queers' bums." A long drag on his cigarette and another look to see how I take the expression 'queer's bums'. "So I'm standing next to the ute finishing off a beer when this bloke comes cruising up, really casual, like he didn't know what he was doing there. 'Got a light?' he asks me. I give him a light. Next thing: 'What do you like?' straight out, as if we've been bum buddies from the year dot. I decide to string him along 'What do you like?' I ask really campy, like I'm one of them too. All the time I'm thinking about the rifle just behind me in the back. Then straight out he says: 'I like sucking dick'. I almost zapped him one, right there. I would have. But then I got this idea. See how far I can string him, I thought. Then I'll zap him after. 'Mine'll cost you,' I say. Wouldn't have said it, but I didn't think he'd go for it. Truth is, I was down to my last fifty cents."

He shot me a look, slightly annoyed, slightly ashamed, daring me to challenge him. Suddenly, he seemed unsure of his dominance of the situation.

"Besides, I knew I could always zap him after. Well, the faggot straight away pulls out his wallet and hands me a twenty. I couldn't believe it. Then he gets down, unzips me and goes to work. Gave me the best fucking blow-job of my fucking life. Can you believe that? A fucking faggot! I hate faggots... I hate them... But I tell you, he gave me the fucking blow-job of my fucking dreams. Made some fucking money after that, I tell you. I was the most popular boy on the block with the fucking queers. Not the kind of thing you tell your mates though." I wondered why he was telling me. He started laughing.

"Faggots! All they wanna do is suck dick. Suck dick or get fucked up the arse. They'll even pay you for it!"

He looked at me still laughing, but his eyes were wary as if he had just made a momentous confession. Which he had. No one had ever talked to me about gay sex as frankly as he was. Then he stopped laughing and just looked at me arrogantly, summing me up through narrowed eyes, as if daring me to call him a faggot. Although, by confessing, he was making an assumption, which I saw reflected in his eyes, as he studied me with his curious mix of contempt and intimacy. Through his hardened squint, now not so hard, but softened by the night and the candlelight, he was not making any admissions of faggotry. But in his candid, scornful way, he was definitely calling me one. His next question confirmed it:

"Don't have twenty bucks, do you?"

He stared at me shrewdly, waiting for some response. I swallowed and forced a stilted half-laugh but did not know what to say. After a moment, he erupted in condescending laughter and went on.

"One guy asked me what he could do for twenty bucks. For twenty bucks, you can suck me off. That's what I said." Another lightning glance, summing up. "So he asks me what he could do for fifty. I told him, for fifty bucks you can suck me off two-and-a-half times, cock-sucker. So then the joker gets smart and comes out and asks me what he could do for a hundred. I said, 'What do you want, a fucking season ticket?' He split pretty quick."

I laughed in obedience at his joke, but even in my own ears it sounded thin, fake, and full of terror. He stared at me like some half-crazy, hungry wolf, waiting for the moment to strike.

"What do *you* like?" he trilled effeminately as he had done in his story, then laughed again. I looked at the ground, wondering how I could get out of this cell and back to the encampment without things getting violent.

His attraction flowed out at me like a venomous drug, clogging my reactions. I was now petrified, but part of me was willing to stay, let things develop as they were heading. The sensible thing would be to get up, make some excuse and split back to the huts. This guy was dangerously crazy, and had a serious problem with gays, but my terror lay firmly on top of me like an aggressive lover, holding me down.

Dale had his right knee drawn up in his position on the box, his back leaning against the wall of the cylinder and his left hand resting casually on his crotch. He looked me straight in the eyes and his left hand began ever so imperceptibly to move up and down. I looked at his crotch. I knew what the game was going to be. I could not avoid it now.

"I always seem to be able to pick the queers. It's a special skill I've got. They've got a kind of a look in the eyes, and there's always something kind of girlie about them."

I mentally checked my own looks, my own stance, my walk and anything else I might do that could give me away to a potential gay-basher. I did not think I was particularly effeminate, but maybe he was right. Maybe he was able to see a special glint in my eye, which no one else saw. But then, didn't they say it takes one to know one? Not that I was about to challenge him at that moment, in that space. I mentally bit my lip and let him have his way.

Dale got up and stubbed his cigarette out on the ground. I stood up, preparing to go too, wanting to get out of there, fast. But he just walked to the ladder and leaned against it, facing me, blocking my exit, watching me with starving wolf menace. He put his hand on his chest and kind of caressed himself, letting his fingers slide down into his belt-line. Then, deciding something, he pulled his shirt over his head in a rough, animal movement and let me observe how the golden hair on his chest caught the light from the candle.

"That's what I saw in you, the first time I saw you. But then I thought, no, give a feller a chance. And I waited. But you can't take your fucking eyes off me. I thought, nah, he just wants to be your friend. Some friend! Can't look you in the eyes, can't take his eyes off you, and goes all kind of girlie every two minutes. Something's up, I thought."

He paused and gave me the chance to defend myself. I said nothing. I noticed the bowie knife hanging from his belt. I had not seen it before, because of his shirt.

"Hot tonight, don't you reckon?" he whispered. His voice still carried a trace of his mocking effeminacy. His fingers danced over his chest, ruffling the hairs, following the course of his curling hairs, down towards his waistline. "Don't you wanna cool me down?"

I did not know what he meant. Or I did not want to know what he meant, but I knew what he meant. Looking into those cool, ice-blue eyes, my heart began to thump hideously loudly against my ribcage. Faggot. If you move now, if you show him you are a faggot, you are dead. But he was waiting. He gave a kind of shuddery, menacing stretch, arching his back and tensing his muscles. Then daring me silently to touch him, he waited. Raising one hand, – Don't do it – I screamed silently at myself, I touched his chest – almost touched. I let my hands brush through the hairs, the electric contact and the warmth from his torso was unreal, nothing I had experienced before. I wondered why I had never before noticed the energy a person's body could emit. Years of sporadic physical contact in my terror-filled school sports classes had never produced such a brutal emotion. I began caressing those hairs gently, timidly, with knuckles and fingertips.

I would have gone on, but he did not want that. He took hold of my wrists and placed them at his belt – with incredible, slow deliberateness, and with real arrogance. I brushed the cloth of his jeans softly with my knuckles, feeling his heat, but not daring to let him feel my presence. He still waited. I reached for his belt, unbuckled it, fingers fumbling with the unknown catch, I felt – I knew – I was a faggot. He made no move to help me – naturally, *he* wasn't a faggot – and continued staring at me, a rather evil smile painted on his lips. His total immobility confirmed his absolute dominance of himself and the situation. I got the belt undone. I reached for the top button of his jeans and undid it, exposing a tuft of lower belly hair. I began to undo the other buttons one by one, which were quite stiff so that as my fingers worked on the buttons, they pressed into his jeans and I was able to feel the lump of his sex. I got the last button undone and pushed his jeans down over his thighs, hardened and toned from all the bending and lifting in the fields. Now he was wearing tight-fitting, white, cotton briefs. The contours of his sex formed a mesmerizing bulk through the cloth. I raised my eyes. He still hadn't moved, just continued looking at me with that funny smile on his face. Finally he spoke:

"What are you waiting for, Prof? Go down."

He placed his hands on my shoulders and pushed me down quite roughly onto my knees.

I could smell the sweat of his groin, close up to my face. He hooked his fingers below the waistband of his briefs and pulled them down, letting his fat fleshy trunk flop out in front of my face. He took hold of the base and waggled the thick head before my eyes.

"Come on. I know you want it." The faint sneer in his voice was aggressive and antagonistic.

The fact was, in that moment I did not. It was heavy and thick with a wide, flat head. He waved it to and fro, like a venomous cobra slowly hypnotizing me. There was a drop of something – urine? pre-cum? – on the pink head which was gradually easing itself out of its fleshy cowl. It was undoubtedly the ugliest thing I had seen in my life. I could not believe he wanted me to stick this thing in my mouth. I could not believe that this worm-like piece of flesh was what I had spent most of my adolescent years fantasising about. He obviously sensed my reluctance, and his impatience became apparent. He pushed his hips at me.

"Come on, open your mouth."

I opened my mouth and he stuck it in. I closed my mouth around it and he began to slide it back and forth in my mouth. It was hot and stank of sweat. I started to suck on it like candy. He jerked.

"Not with your teeth! Not your fucking teeth, idiot!"

I covered my teeth with my lips the way children do when they imitate toothless grannies. He seemed more satisfied and began to move his hips with more confidence. At one moment he placed his hands on my head and jammed my face down onto him. It made me choke. I almost vomited.

"Get it together."

His scorn was blatant, but a hint of another emotion crept in: need. At this moment, during this act, he needed me. He needed me to continue and not stop. I felt for the first time a connection, something that we might be able to develop together. He paused in his movements a little as he waited for me to recover. The next time he rammed it in, I was ready. He began to ram against the back of my throat for several hard strokes and then he would cool off and let me swallow back the bile that was always on the point of exploding into my mouth. I was not enjoying it at all. It was hard work. But I thought I should keep going and try harder if at least one of us was going to get anything out of the experience.

He began to thrust in and out in fast, shallow strokes. I responded by clamping my lips loosely around him in an 'O' shape, letting him do the rest. I watched the patch of hair on his lower belly as it charged towards me with every thrust. It was no longer golden, but brown with moisture. His balls were slapping against my chin. I felt him speeding up. He was not wasting any time. He banged into my throat violently at every thrust. I gagged at every stab of his thick pole, but he stopped taking notice of me. I managed to look up at one point and I saw him, with eyes closed, immersed in the sensations provided through his penis. I tried not to gag any more. I did not want to make him angry, with or without his knife. And I knew he was not going to allow me any other option. I could feel my own dick hard inside my underpants, pre-cum oozing through onto my tracksuit bottoms. I wanted to touch myself, let my dick out and give myself release, but I was afraid of what he might say. He was right. I was a faggot. This was what I was meant for – giving a real man head.

His rhythm accelerated. His breathing changed gear. His hands gripped my head with extra force. Suddenly he stiffened and rammed himself deep into my throat, choking me. My nose was buried in his pubes, drinking in his thick, masculine smell. He held himself there as I fought down my vomit for several seconds, holding onto his buttocks, then he was cumming in jerks and spasms in my mouth and down my throat – warm, viscous, salty, bitter, sweet – until my mouth was full and I did not know whether to swallow, but I had no choice and I swallowed. As he pulled out, his dick spat a wad of cum onto my face, hitting my cheek and dripping down my neck. Pushing me violently back, he turned away. He squeezed a last few drops out of his penis onto his fingers and wiped them on the wall. I fell forward onto all fours and spat a mouthful of his cum onto the floor.

"Cocksucker, I thought you liked that," was his comment.

Panting heavily, he hitched up his trousers and buckled his belt. He grabbed his tee-shirt and slipped it over his head as he turned to the ladder. He did not even spare me a glance.

"See you later, you queerboy." he muttered. "I'll come and see you the next time I can't afford a hooker." Then he turned fully towards me. "Remember, you tell a single motherfucker about this… and you're dead."

He disappeared upwards into the night.

I stayed in the tank then for a while, watching the candle flame slump lower. The taste of his cum was strong in my mouth. A snail-trail of his cum on the wall reflected back the candlelight softly. I could not organise my feelings in my head. I felt horror. I felt fear. If I went back to the encampment now, would I find a hoard of gay-bashers with him at their head ready to lynch me from the forklift? I also felt disgust. Disgust at his sweat and semen coating the inside of my mouth, but also disgust at myself and my body and my own penis, which was hard and had been for the entire experience. I felt like a faggot. But I loved it. I slipped down my tracksuit pants and took hold of my meat. I began to pull myself off. I spat on my hand for lubrication, rubbing myself with his taste, with his sperm. I dropped back down onto my knees, feeling him standing over me again, feeling his hard pole sliding in and out of my mouth. His desperation, his need. I felt how I had served him like a slave, using my mouth to give him pleasure. For the moments our fellatio lasted, I had felt complete, a fitting receptacle for his use. My meat strained outwards at the thought and I moved my tongue around my mouth, relishing the taste of him in me. I felt my own sperm tingling in my balls the instant before it began to rise. As my milk erupted out of me I felt him push into me, jamming his manhood down my open throat and cumming into me with redoubled force as I splashed my own cum onto the concrete wall of the tower.

I had managed to cum right on top of his stain on the wall. Our jism dripped down together, sparkling in the candlelight. I sagged against the cool concrete beside it. Then I leaned forward, stuck out my tongue and licked some off the wall, swallowing our juices together.

I felt dirty, but I felt free. For the first time in my life I had submitted to those feelings that had threatened to dominate me for years, and the freedom of degrading myself before another man gave me an overwhelming pleasure.

I did not want to return to the camp that night, but after cumming, I felt like getting away from that tower as fast as possible. Logically, I knew he was not going to tell anyone anything, because basically he was as guilty as I was. But when I arrived at the camp, I took the back way and slunk into my cabin like a shadow. I fell asleep quickly, despite the emotions billowing in my heart and the thoughts battering my brain.

The next morning, it could have all been a dream. I did not see him on the trailer. He must have got up late. At morning 'smoko', he was nowhere to be seen. It was only after we had returned to work, for the hard slog before lunch, when I was hoisting a basket into the middle of the row, to be picked up by the trailer, that I saw a flash of red cross the space between the vines, a hundred metres down the row. With the excuse of getting water, I ambled down to the track, and there I saw him, pack on back, faded red jogging shorts above tanned thighs, slowly heading out with his lone wolf pace, towards the highway at the end of the block. I suppose, I know, I felt a deep relief, but also a gut-wrenching pang, knowing we would never have more relationship than what we had had in the cracked water tower, certain we would never see each other again. Maybe it was not the most ideal sexual experience I would ever have, but it had been the first. I felt grateful to Dale for having initiated me into that profound, mysterious rite of sex and also for having somehow, unknowingly opened a tiny shutter for me to glimpse the wavering path of my future destiny.

The Notorious Dr August
Christopher Bram

The Notorious Dr August
Christopher Bram

There was rain the next day, not a downpour but a light cool drizzle. It settled the dust and slowed the ferment of poor Tom. I was now on familiar terms with Kemp, though I'd known him longer dead than alive.

We passed through a hamlet whose doors and windows remained closed against us. A dozen dogs of all breeds and sizes trotted after the wagon, begging for a taste of what smelled like bacon.

Isaac held his silence all morning. He sat hunched against the light rain, closed like a fist around something in his heart. My own heart was not nearly so keen as my stomach. Suddenly, out of nowhere, Isaac angrily asked, "Who am I? Who in God's name am I? I was a fool to want respect from that soldier trash. Not the respect owed the Kemps. I am not Kemp's Isaac anymore. That world is over. That world is finished. I am in God's hands now. The body of Thomas Kemp is in my hands, but I am in God's."

I thought it was his hunger talking, the inebriation of an empty belly. His mention of God didn't disturb me. People in that age were always dragging God into the conversation. I was from a family of freethinkers myself, and we weren't quite atheists but believed in a Supreme Being as vague, unworldly, and beautiful as... well, music.

"Providence," said Isaac. "It is all Providence" – and I only pictured a city in Rhode Island with a perennially disappointing box office. "The house of Kemp is of nothing now, and I am left to Providence. God will do with me as He will. If He wants me to be happy in Goshen, so be it. If He wants to drop me into the flames of perdition, that is His right."

Freedom was not very appealing if it left you a slave of God, I thought, but kept the thought to myself.

Words continued to tumble out of him, furious, hard-bitten accusations, directed not at me but like an argument with himself. The fires of hell led to home fires, fires of the hearth, and he spoke of the

Kemps, his master and mistress, and his sister, Lucy. Stupid Lucy, ignorant Lucy, a foolish woman who thought that the Kemps were Providence itself, that the Kemps would provide. She once told him, "Don't go talking like that, Ike, or you makes our white people thinks you wants to be free" – he used his darky voice to imitate her. But the Kemps, too, were children of God, and God the Father saved only a handful of His children from the fires of hell. Isaac hoped Master Tom might be in heaven, but that was for God to decide, not the Kemps.

I didn't know what to make of this crazy, aimless hell talk. Isaac seemed so much older and wiser than me when he was silent. But underneath his manly mask was confusion, uncertainty, and fear. Religion provided words for his emotion. Strange to say, it never occurred to me that Isaac might have gone mad. Years of slavery followed by such sudden, violent freedom could unhinge any man's mind. But when you're young, the entire world seems half insane already.

I did not dare offer him solace, not even a pat on the shoulder. I didn't know what to say except "Food. We need to find food. You'll feel better when you get something to eat."

He raised, his eyes to heaven and scornfully shook his head. But then, as if noticing his own hollow pit, he sighed, and said, "Yes. You're right. Food for the body. Then food for the soul."

For all his religion, Isaac never opened his throat in song during our journey. We had no musty hymns or exotic Negro spirituals on our long ride east, neither 'Asleep in Jesus' nor 'Roll Over, Jordan'. There was no music in Isaac, and what tunes we had were all provided by my pagan flute.

The sky began to clear toward sunset, and we saw a grand house in the sunshine up ahead. A stately brick box stood by the road, rain-washed and flittering behind a miraculously intact white rail fence. It looked like a mirage at first, a pocket of plenty in that impoverished land. Yet there was no livestock in the yard, no human beings by the barn or slave shacks. The place appeared deserted. We rode through the gate, hoping there was a garden out back where we could scrounge forgotten vegetables.

I went up to the front porch and knocked on a heavy oak door. Nobody answered. I looked through a window, the glass so old that it swelled and crimped like running water. The low sun poured through elegant rooms inside.

An ancient colored woman hobbled across the yard, her head tied up in a rag turban.

"You there! Auntie!" Isaac shouted. She hurried off, afraid to even look at us, skating her rag-bound feet over the clay.

I tried the door. It was unlocked. I opened it slowly. "Hello?" I called in. There was silence inside. Even the clock in the front hall was still, the hands stopped at two-forty-five, or maybe nine-ten: I remember only that the ornate clockface wore a sly, subtle smile.

"Don't go in," said Isaac. "You want your head blown off?"

But I'd already entered, and Isaac soon followed, stopping at the threshold to wipe his feet. "Rich folk," he whispered. "Old-time gentility."

Shafts of dusty amber light stretched through rooms full of fancy furniture from another era. There were no dustcovers on the chairs and sofas. Who lived here, and where had they gone? I couldn't guess. No portraits hung on the walls, only a single pale square of the fireplace that suggested they'd taken their image with them. But they'd left behind a piano. A great oblong box squatted in the back parlor, an old Broadwood imported from England. I went over and opened the keyboard. The keys were black and brown, like an ear of Indian corn. I tried a few notes. The treble end was hard and metallic, like broken chimes, but the lower octaves sounded fine.

While Isaac went into the other rooms, I sat on the stool and fingered the keys, hesitatingly, as if it had been years since I'd seen a piano and couldn't remember how it worked. I was pleased to touch an old forgotten self again.

A tune came to me, one I didn't recognize. I let a pattern of notes trickle from my fingers. It began, in fact, as simply a set of finger movements, something physical rather than audible, a spider dance performed, by my right hand. I played, the phrase slowly, then again, more quickly. The phrase led to a new phrase, and another. I improvised an answer with my left hand. Something like this...

C-sharp minor, an agitated, unhappy key. That may have been only the out-of-tune piano, but it began to pour from my fingers, race out of my hands, a cascade of notes like the presto agitato of the 'Moonlight' Sonata, which surprised me, since I'd been unable to master those pounding rapids on my own. Like this passage here. A similar steam engine of bass but with new phrases racing alongside, angry shouts and heartbroken laments. It grew under my hands like a fire, into a blaze of sound, a holocaust of chords and arpeggios, a furious, weirdly exuberant, sorrow.

On that hollow, jangling carillon of a piano, I played better than I had ever played before. But the music did not originate in me. It came from somewhere else, leapfrogging my brain and going straight into my hands.

There it was, the lush composition dictated to me by the spirit world, only I didn't know it at the time.

When it stopped coming to me, when I ran out of notes, I let it softly die. And I sat there, staring at the black-and-brown keyboard, gripping my suddenly ice-cold hands between my legs.

"Does it have a name?" said a voice.

I nearly jumped from my skin. But it was only Isaac – I'd forgotten I was not alone – drawn back to the parlor by the roaring piano. He looked impressed. It may have been gibberish to him, pure cacophony, but I'd been flying like a locomotive, which would have amazed anyone whose ideal of speed was a buggy ride.

"I don't know," I said. "I don't know what it's from. It just came to me."

I remained shaken, alarmed. I wondered if the piano was haunted and had somehow used me to play itself. Or had the muse come from the corpse in the wagon outside? It had sounded demon enough, though I doubted that the ghost of Thomas Kemp would speak in the style of Beethoven.

"Nobody here," said Isaac. "Everyone's run off. Except that old woman out back."

"There's no dead people upstairs?"

He treated the question as perfectly natural. "The rooms are empty," he said. "But there's pickled tomatoes and preserved peaches in the pantry. And a feather bed upstairs. A master's feather bed," he announced and added, with a stern note of defiance, "I'm sleeping in a master's bed tonight."

We did not light a fire or candles that evening for fear of attracting a passing patrol or more deserters. We gorged ourselves on the tomatoes and sweet jarred fruit by moonlight. Food eased my anxious mind only so much. I remained nervous. There were no clues where the owners had gone, why they had left their house in apparent haste. I unhitched Antigone and brought her indoors, afraid she might run off or the old woman out back would steal her. The tall horse balked at the front steps and the door, but finally lowered her head and entered, stepping like a lady to the manner born. Putting her with the piano and sofas, an armful of hay on the carpet, was a nice sacrilege, equal to a slave in a master's bed.

I did not want to sleep alone in that handsome haunted house. "Is there room for me?" I asked Isaac. The sharing of beds was commonplace in my century. "Or I'll sleep on the floor."

He shrugged. "Sleep where you like. It's a big bed."

I followed him upstairs to a moonlit room and a canopied bed like a mound of snow under a marquee. We undressed to our shirts and got in. Climbing clothed into that downy heap would have been as unthinkable as taking a bath in trousers. I was so tired, so empty that I didn't stop to think that I was sharing a bed with a Negro. Everything seemed to pour into me – linen, feathers, and Isaac. I sank into a deep sleep.

I dreamed that I stood in a forest, a burning forest with flames like music. Each fire had its own key, major or minor, a roar of sound like an idea of sound. Men screamed silently in the musical blaze. I caught glimpses of them in the flames, Kemp and Crawford and the sick captain. I was dreaming of Isaac's hell, only I stood unharmed in the midst of their punishment. The flames did not burn but merely warmed me.

I woke to find myself pressed against a man's warm back and backside, with my hand in a very intimate place. I knew it was Isaac but continued to hold him, the smooth, hard root of the man. It was good to touch something so familiar, like touching the piano downstairs. We ride our souls in sleep like horses, and sometimes the horse knows best where to go.

He softly moaned and stretched, and suddenly became still. He was awake; I was terrified that he'd be angry.

"This is magic," I claimed. "I know magic tricks and spells." My half-awake sleep self hoped that he'd be too innocent to know what I was doing. I lightly rubbed his lamp, as if to make a genie appear.

He let my hand continue a moment. "That ain't magic!" he snarled. And he swung around, grabbed my wrists and pinned me, so violently that I expected him to slap and punch my face. But he had my shirt up under my arms, his knees between my legs and his tongue in my mouth. I had never been kissed. Uncle Jack didn't believe in kissing. It felt wondrous, like eating magnetic air.

My mind stood apart from my body, amazed by Isaac. The bite of his beard and press of bare hips were a revelation, a show of warmth and passion never hinted at by his stony daylight self. My body was delighted with the attention, my hands fascinated with his back, the skin like rough silk, the great weight of him. He wrapped his arms around me for the naked lightning of souls, first mine, then his, with a loud duet for flute and trumpet.

We lay there, heart to galloping heart, our breaths in each other's face, our hearts stripped of their foreskins. His open eyes were so close to mine that I seemed to look into the infinite spaces behind the stars. Then his head jerked back and he stared at me, sharply, as if seeing me for the first time, understanding that he had been intimate with a man – a white man.

He blinked, he frowned. "That's how we do it," he muttered. He rolled off, turned his back to me, drew himself into a ball, and promptly fell back asleep.

I remained awake, breathless, amazed. It had been nothing like my sessions with Uncle Jack, which were all in my privates. This time my entire body, head to toe, heart and soul, had become a private part. I cautiously scooted against Isaac's back, put my arms around him and fell asleep, too.

When I awoke the next morning, Isaac was already up and lacing his shoes. "We better get going," he said in his usual stony manner, as if nothing had happened in the night.

But I already knew. His silence was in yet another key, a different indifference. I was immediately ashamed of last night, frightened by what he must think of me. My shame contained not only fear but a strange new fondness for Isaac, a tenderness that made me crave his respect.

Downstairs in the parlor Antigone towered over the squat, dead piano. She looked more profoundly wrong by day than she had I moonlight. I led her back outside. Isaac and I breakfasted on jarred fruit, with as few words as possible, and loaded a box of jars into the wagon. He didn't mention last night, so I didn't dare mention it either. Soon we were on the road again, the sinister mansion rumbling behind us and disappearing in the misty trees.

The morning was cool and damp, uncomfortable for us but a kindness to the corpse. If only we could've preserved Tom like fruit in a jar.

Finally Isaac said, "I had a dream last night. A sinful, childish dream."

"I know," I confessed. "I had the same dream myself."

He refused to look at me. "It's bad enough to do it as a boy," he said angrily. "But now I am a man. A free man. I must put away childish things."

"Forgive me," I said. "It won't happen again."

"It better not," he declared. "Or I'll leave you on the road. Out here in the middle of nowhere." He blamed me, and like a criminal or a man in love, I took full responsibility.

"It will never happen again," I insisted. "I promise."

Because I knew he was right. It was a boy's vice, and we were no longer boys, not after all that we had been through.

"Fine," he said. "Good. We need never speak of it again."

And I was relieved, overjoyed that we put it behind us so quickly. I could not tell him about Uncle Jack, of course. And I couldn't ask about the black boys with whom he had done his childish thing. I gladly passed over the latter. Picturing pickaninnies in each other's arms would have been too humiliating, making me feel that I was no better than a slave myself, a shameless beast, and no longer white.

The Weeds
Perry Brass

The Weeds
Perry Brass

It was nearing the very end of his second week in Provincetown –
almost October really – and Joe Richman and his partner were staying
in the last cabin at the end of Uncle Pete's Wharf on the West End of
town. Uncle Pete's had been there since the 1920s. It was a series of
ramshackle little cabins, and the last one, the one they took for two
weeks, was surrounded on three sides with gorgeous views of the whole
harbor of Provincetown. When the sun rose on the harbor, the small
cabin was cloaked in gold and red. It was a beautiful place to stay, but
by the second week Joe was already feeling that strange, empty feeling
he had always had in Provincetown; that feeling of a being a bit player
on a stage set, wandering around after the play had been declared over;
or that feeling of being a guest at a party to which he had never really
been invited. The town at the picturesque tip of Cape Cod was
charming but shallow, and as the Indian summer shivered into autumn,
and the water in the bend of the harbor on the bay side got bone-
chilling, that strange feeling started to close in on him even more.

It was time to leave. Definitely.

But Joe's lover, Pen (short for Pendexter) McPherson, a sweet,
chubbyish, buttoned-down lawyer and occasional amateur jazz pianist
– by nature closed in enough – was not about to be bothered by any
competing closed-in feelings, especially in Provincetown on his
vacation. Pen loved P'town and treasured his times there. Joe felt like
a idiot complaining about the place. Most of the time Pen stayed in the
cabin and read, or practiced the piano at Sally's, a small bar further up
Commercial Street, where he had become a regular and where they
invited him to tickle the keyboard with his variations of 'cocktail
classics' when he was in town. Pen was an invited guest and smiled
smugly when Joe made his crack about being an uninvited one. "I was
the one who invited you, Joe," he said, and Joe smiled, too. It was silly
to try to make his feelings known to Pen, who had a different feeling
for the Cape than Joe did.

For Joe there was something ghostly about P'town. Especially after the season, when the regulars who hid out from the summer tourists came back into Commercial Street – dozens of mentally handicapped types spawned from intermarriages among the Portuguese natives. And hoards of loud, geeky high-school kids suddenly appearing from down Cape. But even stranger were the old Provincetown gays, who had been there for a decade – at the absolute minimum – who worked behind the scenes as waiters or busboys. They started to go back to the beach dunes after the summer professional cruisers had returned to New York or Boston. It was the old boys who gave Joe the creepiest feeling. They were boys, too, with their wrinkled boy faces – the same faces Joe remembered from vacations back in the 70s and 80s, and he saw their hungry, vacant faces back in the dunes now. They were faces that never even looked at you. They had seen so many tourists, had cleaned so many tables -- and they were still there. They talked among themselves, dishing, gossiping in hoarse, shrill, empty voices that Joe heard as evening fell on the dunes or on Commercial Street in front of the Town Hall, where they parked their bicycles and he would walk solitarily among them and they would pretend not to see him, because some of them knew him, too.

"You're not going to get into trouble again?" Pen asked with that same smug smile that made Joe feel more sorry for Pen than angry. Pen kept life at an arm's distance from himself; something lawyers and other professionals were trained to do. Life was clients or patients or, in other words, other people. Pen was in bed with a book. It was still early in the evening after dinner, a quick one they had put together in the cabin, and Joe was making himself ready to go out.

"No," Joe said patiently. Of course he knew he would. It was silly not to when he was bored and slightly bothered as he was then. He finished combing his thinning hair in the cracked mirror next to the sink. It was part of the charm of Uncle Pete's that each cabin had its shaving mirror in a different place, none precisely in what could have been the bathroom. In 'Gull's Nest', the last cabin, the shower-with-toilet had no sink, so the galley sink next to the door had to do for vanity as well as dishes.

"I'm serious," Pen said, putting down his book. He was reading *Emma* again. He always took a large box full of books with him to the Cape, and then bought even more while he was there. "I don't want another scene like we had last week, okay?"

"I don't want that, either." Joe smiled. What had happened was awful, but it had made him feel younger, desired, really. He told Pen good-bye. "I won't be that late," he said, and then he walked out onto the deck of Pete's to watch the sky over the harbor. A crescent moon, cold and crystal-white, was being raked by purple-black clouds across its thin face. A shiver ran over Joe's body, and he hunched his shoulders and pulled his light cotton windbreaker closer to him.

He walked around to the left of the pier and saw the light on in Ralph's house. Ralph had a house directly next to Uncle Pete's Wharf. What a strange coincidence it had been – Ralph, edging fifty and still very handsome; they had met on Commercial Street early one evening, and it turned out they were 'neighbors'. And Ralph said "come by for a drink" but did not mention his 'roommate', a waiter, insanely jealous, as it turned out, who came in while they were innocently having a Coke by Ralph's fireplace and asked a few questions of Joe ("Where are you stayin'? How long you gonna be here?") and then huffed out.

"He's not angry, is he – I mean about me being here?"

"No, he's just not very good with strangers."

"And how are you?"

"Much better," Ralph said, and turned his clear, beautiful blue eyes on Joe, whose heart started to speed up. A moment later they were in each other's arms, but Joe did not feel comfortable about it – that look from Tim, whose lower lip seemed never to leave a pout, that look did not help.

"I think I'd better go," Joe said.

"Don't leave because of Tim," Ralph whispered. "We have an agreement. He knows that I'm" – he paused and then hit the right word: "sexual... I find you very attractive."

"I find you the same way, but maybe we'd better not do this here."

'"He's at work now. He won't be back for a long time."

Joe believed him and they had their clothes off and the fire was going. Joe could hear the waves from the harbor lapping outside and he was enchanted with Ralph's muscular, hairy body and the soft sweet way he talked, almost in a kid language, the language of Provincetown. When Joe kissed him, Ralph said, "Oh, boy..." He seemed shy and sweet and closed his eyes, pulling Joe next to him, while their sex became hotter, more urgent, until Joe felt all of his feelings – the need to be loved, that awful need to be loved that Pen did not fully satisfy –

flooding out of him, and he realized that he had told Ralph that he loved him, and most awfully enough, he did. Soon, they were cleaning cum off each other in the shower, when Tim came back and the fury began.

Joe's heart stopped as he watched Tim attack Ralph, kicking him and beating him, while Joe managed to get his clothes back on. "You fucking slut! Get out of my house and never come back!" Tim screamed at Joe.

"Tim, this is... don't hit him, too!" Ralph shouted.

"I should kill him! You *never* do this, Ralph. Why with this one? What did he do – suck you off? Do things I won't do?" He turned to Joe just before Joe got back out the door. "Listen, jerk, you ever hear about Aids? I don't want you bringin' Aids to our house. We been clean for years – both negative – so keep your goddamn Aids outta here!"

Joe managed to get out onto the street, but the ugly little drama did not stop – Tim followed him, and grabbed him, tearing Joe's shirt. Joe hurried down onto Uncle Pete's Wharf, and with three or four people out looking at the rising moon, Tim berated him, threatening to kill him if he ever so much as looked at his lover again. Finally, Joe was able to get back to his cabin, just as Pen came to the door.

"What's going on here?" Pen asked calmly, a fresh cigarette in his hand.

"Are you his boyfriend?"

Pen smiled. "Sure, what of it?"

"I think you should keep better control o' him. He don't have the right to bust up other people's homes!"

"What did he do, break in?"

"No, I caught him with my lover."

"Takes two to tango, my friend. I'm a lawyer. Would you like for me to call the police now, or later?"

"You can call any cop you want," Tim snarled. "But if I ever so much as catch him on our wharf again, I'll kill him."

Pen smiled again. "And if I ever catch you on our wharf again, maybe I'll do the same. Why don't you grow up, friend? And why don't you keep your own boyfriend on a leash?"

"Fuck you..." Tim turned his back and walked away; and that was the last memory of Tim Joe had, but not the last memory of Ralph. The memory of Ralph was burned into him – and as much as he wondered how such a beautiful, soft-spoken, sweet creature could have such a monster for a lover – he could not help thinking about him, knowing that he was only one pier away from him, but now impossible to see. Joe thought of every way to get to him, but something always held him back, either his own fear of Tim, who was obviously psychotic, although in Provincetown, notorious for long, drunken winters, that diagnosis seemed past the point; or his fear of hurting Pen. Pen looked forward so to these vacations in P'town, getting away from all his office troubles back in New York, hanging out with a group of cronies on Commercial Street he had known for years. They were his Provincetown friends and he would never see them any place else except there; but they all planned their vacations on the Cape together, and how could Joe ruin that, make it so that Pen might not want to come back again to a place that he loved?

So there was the orange-colored light on in Ralph's house, with its own shorter wharf right next to Pete's. The light itself, all golden in the night breeze, tore at Joe's heart. They would be leaving the very next day and something told him that probably he would never see Ralph again. That was the thing that hurt so much: that he might not ever see Ralph alive again. The sheer pain of it cut at him, just ripped into him. Joe had so many friends back in the city that he would never see again, men taken by Aids, and now there would be this man, that he had fallen so passionately for after just a short amount of time – what could it all mean? It was impossible to analyse, but wasn't losing someone to Aids as terrible as losing someone to fear?

He walked back up the pier and then onto the West End of Commercial Street. His heart drummed inside him while he opened the short picket gate to the walk in front of Ralph's house. What would he do if Tim suddenly appeared? But he knew there was no turning back, and the golden light from the back windows of the house, the light he saw from the tip of Pete's Wharf was soon on him. He peered through the window, without any caution now, openly, and there he saw Ralph who looked up at him. Ralph tiptoed to the door.

"You'd better get out of here," Ralph whispered. 'Tim's in the other room."

"I've got to speak to you. Can you leave for a moment – just tell him you want to go to the store or something? I want an hour with you – can I have that?"

"Okay. I'll try."

"I love you," Joe suddenly blurted out.

"I know," Ralph whispered. "I'll meet you up the street in about ten minutes."

The ten minutes seemed to last an hour, as raven-winged clouds drifted back and forth over the starved moon, at times even blocking out every bit of silver light from it. Finally Ralph in a black silk bomber jacket and white, drawstring pants showed up.

"Let's get out of here as quickly as possible," he said. "My car's around the corner on School Street."

Without another word, they hurried over to Ralph's car, got in it, and Ralph began driving. "I told him that I was going over to the East Side. You know the gallery openings are tonight. Tim hates galleries, but since I paint, he allows me to go to them."

"*Allows* you?" Joe felt as if his heart were in pain, as if the strange chemistry between Ralph and Tim had produced an acid that had spilled over onto a third person. Himself.

"Yeah," Ralph said, turning the car down to the road to Herring Cove Beach. "I don't like it. I don't – let me tell you. Tim has a lot of good qualities. He literally built the house we live in – he can do anything with his hands. But I feel trapped like a bird in it."

"Do you think it's just Provincetown that does it?" Joe looked out the window at the dark moors waving with sea grass and the bay, black as silk, beyond it. "There's something, I don't know, suffocating about being here."

"I don't know, either," Ralph said and he suddenly reached for Joe's left hand and kissed it. "I wish you did love me. I wish all of this was really real and you weren't going to leave tomorrow."

He parked the car in the lot closest to the dunes. There were several other cars there already, and they got out and began walking along the beach. Ralph had a blanket with him and about half a mile down they spread it between two dunes and then took their clothes off and made love with the stiff breeze rippling over them. It was the most intense, complete love Joe had made since he was a teenager, when his first urgently hungry pangs for sex had been fed – and it was frightening in its intensity and completeness. It wasn't just getting off and cumming, but it seemed to come from his very soul, his very marrow. His brain opened up and accepted Ralph. They were two men in their forties – Joe at the beginning and Ralph at the end of it – and they were both involved with somebody else, but there was nothing there at that moment for either of them except one another. Perhaps that was the beauty of Provincetown itself – right there at the very end of that sandy spit of land on Cape Cod, that you could be so alone there and then find somebody else there also. Joe knew it; and when it was over he found himself crying. Tears were actually coming out of him.

"We'd better go back," Ralph said. "If I'm out any longer, Tim'll come after me. He'll end up going to the openings just to see if I'm there. He's done that before."

Joe looked out at the sky and the water. There was the wind off the water and he felt very cold now, that he was no longer connected so intimately to Ralph's warm body. He put his clothes back on and felt weighted and tired.

"He must hate himself," Joe said. "How can he live in this gay place and hate himself so much and hate other people like himself?"

"I don't know. I asked myself that years and years ago. What's your boyfriend like? I guess he's not that possessive."

"No," Joe said. "He's not."

Ralph got up. "Let's go," he said. He began to pick up the blanket, and Joe had to get off it. Together they shook it out, and Joe felt that he needed shaking out as well – that heavy, depressed feeling would not leave him. He could not bear the thought of getting back into the car with Ralph, and then saying good-bye to him and then having it all finished.

"I want to stay for a while," he confessed. "I'll walk back."

"Do you think you should? I mean, it can be dangerous here – " then suddenly Ralph smiled. There were other men cruising on the beach, that was for sure. He looked at Joe, then kissed him very softly, holding Joe's face in his hands. "So you really want to walk back?"

Joe nodded.

"Good-bye, Joe," Ralph said, and then started off, until he disappeared around a bend of dunes.

Joe was sure that he if walked somewhat further east, in the direction away from the beach's paved parking lot, he could cross a dry, safe flatland onto the narrow road back into town. The wind was not in his face, and he pushed on in the dark across the rocky beach. There were a few other men out but they did not approach him. Some of them were in pairs. They were obviously lovers or boyfriends, or men who had just met and were discovering the electricity of strangers on the beach at night. But no single man approached Joe as he went on by himself.

There was a narrow lighthouse at the very head of the cove, and he could see it and followed its blade-thin ray sweeping into the blackness out beyond him. Finally, almost at the place where he knew he could turn in and be safe from the beach, he looked down at his feet and saw a glistening mass of amphibious, green weeds lying in the spongy sand at the waterline.

The weeds looked melted in layers into each other, pitch-black below and pea-green above, with bubbles of light, oily and soft, like little pearls of warm liquid, pulsing through them.

There were places where they exuded a horrifying, sticky jelly, and some of that stuck to his soaked sneakers. He began to skid on it and he could not stop himself. He toppled over and fell flat on his face. The oozy, sticky weeds sucked at his brow, elbows, and fingertips. He had to get up. Cautiously, he arched himself slowly, gripping his sneaker toes into the muck, while the black, cold waters of the bay drilled towards him. His arms and legs were now wrapped with the weeds and they coated his clothes with their gummy strength, at once passive and turbulent, holding him down. The water pushed over his face, sopping into his nose, making him realize now – completely – that he was not asleep: this was no dream, anymore than his involvement with Ralph had been. This was not simply another strange but negligible complication of his vacation in P'town, a vacation that had led to other strange complications.

He tried hard to pull himself out. Then he realized that the weeds were no longer empty. They were filled with bodies. He could see them, individually, distinctly; but he understood that they had no more substance to them than the glistening jelly released by the weeds. He tried to scream, but the jelly washed at his lips, and he knew that the bodies were now passing by him, floating in this luminous, glowing substance that had become diluted by the cold, inky waters of the bay.

There they were, dozens of men – boys – he had known. They had all died; they were the dear, dead friends that he had loved. Boys he had lived with in New York years ago and had read about in the *New York Times* and men he had picked up and loved who were dead now, too. But he could not join them, not in this horrifying jelly. He arched himself up further and with every last bit of strength he had, or would ever have, he pulled himself up from the glistening mass at the water's edge.

Then he looked up. There were men watching him. He recognized some of them: the men with the old boy-faces from the 70s and the 80s, the slowly ageing gay waiters and busboys of Provincetown he saw furtively in the dunes in the fall. They were just watching him, passively. No one was helping him; no one. Then he even saw it. A ripple of light – maybe from the naked moon itself – passed through them, and some one was being carefully guided to him. Thank God, he thought. Ralph has found me. Only he knows I'm here. He felt prostrate from exhaustion on every level – what a strange vacation he'd had while Pen read books and played the piano. The light, the movement, came closer to him and he reached out towards Ralph who now had his hands around Joe's throat and was dragging him this way up to the dunes so that the weight from Joe's body filled with the slime of the weeds and the grip around his neck caused all the air to leave him as he looked up and saw Tim's angry face.

"I told you I'd kill you if you ever came back on my wharf."

The other old boys, who had been there for so long and would be on Cape Cod the next year and the next, who always wore the most wonderful boyish clothes from the little shops on Commercial Street, scooped out sand from the dunes until a deep pit was formed and then they threw Joe's body down into it. They put their arms around Tim and told him not to worry. It was all right – protecting the dunes around Provincetown was necessary for everyone. Then one of them went back to Pen and told him quietly that somebody who had been seen staying at Uncle Pete's Wharf had also been seen swimming out as far as he could that night in the bay; and that if Pen did not see his friend again, they'd be happy to look for him in the morning.

Justice Armstrong-Jones
Scott Brown

Justice Armstrong-Jones
Scott Brown

"Mr Scott," David looked down at the sheet of paper in his hand and then back up across the courtroom. He knew everybody hung on his every word. Frank Scott's life hung on his words. The reporters sat with pencils poised, they were waiting for those words. He could see the news later: 'Justice Armstrong-Jones told Scott...' The responsibility was huge. David loved it.

Frank Scott stood, hands behind his back, hair tied back in a ponytail, his face baby soft and beautiful, his eyes, so blue, so strikingly blue, his expression quizzical, his head cocked to one side, looking, staring, straight at and probably through David on the bench. David had this guy's life in his hands, the jury had found him guilty and now it was up to him. This was the moment he had waited for, this is what he had worked towards. He had presided over the first televised court case in England and now it was the grand finale.

Frank Scott had stiffened at the sound of his name from the judge's mouth. David had slipped his half-moon spectacles on, and now leaned forward on his elbows. Frank Scott was a beautiful man. David would have gone with him, which was a worry. His gaze met the defendant's and held it. David saw the danger in the eyes, wondered if he would have seen it before today. He wondered if it would have been too late by the time he saw it. Scott continued to stare at David and David in turn stared back at him. The whirr of the video cameras recording was the only sound for a moment as the whole world went silent, David wondered how many millions of people were watching him.

"Mr Scott," David repeated. There was a pressure release from the whole courtroom as the words were spoken. Frank Scott stared at David, unmoved, unfazed. David would have seen it in the eyes, this kid was evil. "A jury of your peers have found you guilty," David swallowed, the sound was magnified by the microphone.

Frank Scott stood unmoved. "Guilty of a crime it is unimaginable to even begin to comprehend having taken place in the real world."

One of the jurors started to cry. It wasn't the first time. The evidence had been graphic. Scott's handiwork had been paraded around the court and around the world. He was a nasty man and the tears were not for him. "Mr Scott you are, without doubt...," David paused as he thought of what he was going to say. Of course he knew exactly what he was saying, it was just right at this moment the world was watching. This was his moment, his pause was for dramatic effect, it worked, everyone literally leaned forward and waited. David almost smiled "... evil," he said quietly, confidently. The reporters scribbled on their pads, this was power.

"You gained people's trust, you became part of their life, and you then took their life." David removed his glasses. "The right to give and take life is retained by one being, and that is God Almighty. You, Mr Scott, are not God; you, Mr Scott, are a person who has taken the rights of the free world and tried to corrupt them; you, Mr Scott, are what I would see the devil as if he should ever visit this earth. Without care, consideration or conscience you took the lives of innocent people."

Frank Scott smiled at David as he spoke, David broke the stare and looked down at the piece of paper in his hand, the paper shook. It was the first time he was aware that he was nervous.

He slid his glasses back on and pulled the paper up onto the bench. He was nearing the end. "As I have said, you are evil. People like you have waived the right to live as a free member of society. You, Mr Scott, will not re-enter society again; you have been found guilty of the murder of seventeen men, Mr Scott, for each murder fifteen years is the sentence." A huge hubbub erupted around the courtroom, David would usually have used his hammer but he enjoyed the respite, he had created the furore and he would let it fade of its own accord. And it did. David sipped from his glass of water. Frank Scott looked at him, unmoved. David was sure he hadn't worked out that he would never leave prison. "Your sentence, Mr Scott, while being eccentric, will nowhere near compensate for the pain and loss you have caused a large number of people. This world will be a better, safer place with you off the streets. You are a danger to a section of our community, the gay community and that community can now feel safe once more."

David looked at the journalists and the TV men, they were hanging on his words, the jury smiled, the galleries were happy: at last a judge who took the law and stretched it so that the criminals paid. He would be the centre of debates for weeks to come. David Armstrong-Jones, too harsh or a breath of fresh air? He had achieved what he had set out to: "Mr Scott, you are a very young man, twenty-one, and while it saddens me to put you away for the rest of your natural life, it saddens me more that one so young could be so possessed. I am sorry you have to spend so long in prison, I only wish that I could pass the death sentence because that, Mr Scott, is what you deserve." David had just opened the biggest can of worms and he was going to get into so much trouble, the live television carrying the message out to the world, the reporters grabbing a great story: 'Judge demands reintroduction of death penalty'.

David didn't care, this was his ultimate moment of glory, for he had milked the trial for nine weeks now. "Instead of the death penalty, as I have said you will serve fifteen years for each of the murders you committed, the sentences to run consecutively, you will be sentenced to serve two hundred and fifty-five years in prison." There was another burst of noise from around the court and again David let it die of its on accord. "I recommend the term is served without parole, you, Mr Scott, will live the rest of your natural life behind bars, and you will die behind bars, I would suggest you never walk free on this earth again."

The gasps at David's opinionated remarks shook others into conversation. Frank Scott stared straight on throughout. David looked into the defendant's eyes and Frank Scott raised his eyebrows. "Order, order." David banged down his hammer three times and abruptly the noise ceased. David didn't know what all the fuss was about. He could say what he liked in his summing up, it was his courtroom and the trial he was presiding over was his trial. He had earned the right, so what if he overstepped the mark, what the hell, it was controversy, that's what they wanted and that's what they'd had. Shut up and praise him.

"Take him down," David banged his hammer in a final act of closure, the court was again awash with noise.

Frank Scott was over the front of the dock as the prison guards moved in to take him down. He sprinted across the courtroom floor and propelled himself forward and up off the witness stand and onto the bench where David sat looking on, frozen in time, shocked at what was going on. But he knew someone would save him. What so shocked him was that Frank Scott had left everyone in his wake and was now pulling off David's wig and tugging at his red robes. The screams and shouts around the courtroom were coming from everyone, a huge surge of people was up and moving, reporters scribbling, camera rolling, it was all on television, they couldn't write this stuff, David now knew he was part of history, it was all he could think of. God he would be front page news tomorrow.

"I didn't do it," Frank Scott screamed as he shook David's robes. "I didn't do it, I said I didn't do it, why don't you believe me." The robes were held with one hand as a right hook scraped David's chin. Scott's foot kicked a guard square in the face. More policemen rushed in. He was losing the battle, and then was pulled off the bench. He had been close though, close enough for David to know that his blue eyes were beautiful, the eyes of a god, the exact eyes he would have gone for. David would have gone with him and he would probably now be dead like all the others.

"I didn't do it," Scott shouted one last time as seven policemen smashed him to the floor, his arms up his back. David heard the pop as his shoulder was knocked out of its socket, the cuffs go on regardless. Frank Scott was pushed down the stairs and into oblivion. David was pleased that the British justice system was getting tougher and that he was part of that toughening system.

"Are you okay?"

"Judge?"

"Sir, how are you?"

People were fussing, but David simply smiled.

"Fine. I'm fine."

He put his wig back on and straightened his robes. Everybody was looking, cameras were pointing. David realised his chin was bleeding. He was a hero. He banged the hammer twice and silence fell as he shouted for order. He was in a hurry now, briskly thanking and releasing the jury, promising them they had made the right decision. The usher then stood and walked forward, David had given him the nod, formal proceeding were not over yet.

"All rise." His voice echoed around the large courtroom.

Everyone stood. David then rose and walked down the few steps and through the door, out of the way, straight into chambers without looking at or talking to anyone. He closed the door and poured a whisky. Sitting back in his large chair, he smiled. He had probably just made headlines in all the papers across Britain, maybe even some in the US. So long as there wasn't a major earthquake or some other disaster tonight, he was certain that all of Britain would know who David Armstrong-Jones was by breakfast tomorrow.

He had delivered the sentence at eleven minutes past four, but because of the scuffle and the time it took to get everything back in order it was a quarter to five before he was able sit back and savour his whisky. His hands shook as they held the cut-crystal tumbler, though the whisky it contained was calming his nerves. He pondered on what he had just said and done, and he knew he meant all of it. Frank Scott was a nasty, vicious killer. He'd picked up, dated and murdered seventeen gay men. He'd said he hated gays, yet he had fucked everyone of his victims before killing by a knife through the heart as he rode them and they were coming. He hated gays and he wanted to cleanse the world of them. David shook his head. Poor weird child. David was justified in what he had done.

The psychological profile had said the killer would be in his forties. Frank Scott was twenty-one – a bit out there. No DNA. The case was flawed. But Frank Scott had done it – however beautiful his eyes, however furious his protests, David knew it was all shit. The boy was guilty. He deserved to hang.

David had another whisky with the two counsels as they slowly reviewed the case, Jennifer Good insisting there had been a huge miscarriage of justice, while Geoffrey Black argued that at one stage the boy had more-or-less confessed. David pointed out that the best place for the kid was behind bars, at least the gay community was now safe. They went around in circles just arguing the toss. It wasn't relevant, it was just that Jennifer absolutely hated losing.

At the start of the case David had been worried about where things would go, during the case he recognised the power he held, not to mention the iconic status bestowed on him by the gay community as an out gay judge who was being tough on the serial killer of men like himself. Now, at the end of the case, he saw himself as a protector. He had cleansed the streets for other gay men, the fear of and warnings about a predator in Soho could be consigned to the past. He had made the place safe again. It had all been his doing. He was a celebrity. He had already seen the news and the response to his remark about the death penalty. It was surprisingly good. He looked at his watch, it was after seven, and he was hungry, hungry for food and hungry to taste the success he had just won. He shouldn't, he couldn't, but he must. He wrestled his conscience for all of two minutes and decided to take himself to dinner in a restaurant, a dinner on his own. He didn't want to talk about things, he just wanted to reflect. His life would be different as soon as tomorrow's papers came out. Tonight, he was simply David, simply free.

He took himself in his convertible BMW to Soho, the birthplace of his iconic status, and sat for dinner on his own at the front of his favourite French place – where the food was glorious, the price reasonable and from where he was able to watch lots of young men in tight clothes walking past the window. He was happy. He could eat in peace and happily watch the parade of enticing male flesh. Maybe later he would slide off into Soho's core and into a bar. Maybe he would pull, maybe he wouldn't, it didn't matter though, after tomorrow everyone would know who he was. The whole community would want to thank him. He was the saviour. He was the one who reignited promiscuity. They would all want to fuck him then, and they could. They could form a line and fuck him in thanks. He had no problems with that whatsoever.

He finished his main course and motioned for the dessert menu. Although he was on a diet, today was a bit special and he could always allow himself a strawberry cheesecake. It didn't matter, he'd swim an extra ten lengths tomorrow.

The bar wasn't as busy as it had been when he'd been there in the past. Still, tonight was Tuesday, he'd always been there on Saturday before, naturally it would be busier then. Still there was enough talent on show tonight, enough for him anyway. He sat at the bar, his glass of whisky in his hand, the hand that no longer shook, a hand that had delivered the justice he so dearly believed in. The cheesecake had been good, the whisky was fine, expensive but fine. He was completely content, completely relaxed. He made eye contact with a man at the back of the bar. It was a reflex. David didn't even like the look of him that much. He looked Italian. He didn't like Italians, not sexually anyway. Still, if he had to he would. The man wasn't ugly, he just wasn't his type. From tomorrow he would have his pick, but today was today and he'd have to rely on someone wanting his slightly overweight body and his greying shaved head. David knew he was a great person but he also knew all gay men shopped with their eyes and he knew he wasn't the great eye candy they all look for. He was more of an apple than an éclair, after all, and though we all know apples are good for us we all really fancy that éclair, David was an apple, always had been, always would be. Maybe from tomorrow he would be toffee apple. He could only hope.

"Another whisky, please." He slid the empty tumbler over to the stunning barman whom he hadn't even bothered to look at. There was no point: one, the guy was beautiful but plainly thick, two, he would never hop into bed with him, so there really was no point. He served drinks and took money. That suited David. He also knew he would never get the boy into bed because he probably never watched the news or read a paper. He would never know who David was. Shame.

"Can I get that for you?"

David looked around at the guy slipping into the seat beside him, a middle-aged guy. David never went for men of around his own age, but there was something... maybe his Arab looks, maybe his accent. David felt a tingle dance along his spine. This man smelt really sweet.

"No." David turned to the barman as he placed the whisky in front of him.

"No?" the man's voice questioned.

"No, but let *me* buy *you* a drink." David turned and smiled at the man, who smiled back at him.

"Whisky too, please." David turned to the barman who was already pouring the drink.

It had been a long while since he'd even thought about going with a man nearer his age. Well, a man in his forties. David was fifty, or forty-two, depending on who you asked. Today he was forty-two, so was the Arab. Jem, he said to call him. Jem short for something much longer that David would never be able to pronounce. So Jem it was. Jem was in the rag trade, he designed clothes. He wore good clothes too. His tall, slim, strong figure was the perfect clothes-horse for what he sold. David looked at Jem's wrinkle-free face, his thin fine lips and his cropped brown hair. He didn't look forty-two: neither did David, but in his case that wasn't a good thing, his lie was becoming telling.

David let Jem buy the next round and he then bought the one after, whisky flowing, Jem gently touching his knee. David not objecting, thinking maybe, maybe he'd been stupid chasing all those young kids, maybe he should never have paid for a rent boy, maybe he should have spent his time looking for guys like Jem, men nearer his age. Okay, the youngsters have energy and sex appeal, they can bounce around for an age and sex can last forever, but when it's over, what do they do? They talk, David knew nothing about Westlife, nothing about *Pop Stars*, or *Pop Idol*. He was a judge, he didn't get time to watch much TV. Christ, the kids are good to start with but you really do want to kick them out after a while.

Jem, though, was an older man. He looked good, his green-blue eyes changing colour before David's own eyes. In one light they were green, in another they were blue, either way they were sensual and knowing, Arab eyes full of knowledge. David was struck, he had fallen, on the very night before he could have a passport to sleep with whoever he liked and he had gone and fallen in love for the first time in his life. He could see it all, he could introduce Jem as his lover, in the past it had been awkward, the boys were twenty, twenty-two and he was a forty-five/fifty-year-old judge. He couldn't take these boys to meet MPs, although they had probably already been there. It wasn't right, but with Jem it felt right already. By the sixth whisky Jem was stroking David's ear, his hand rested on his thigh and David had his hand resting on top of Jem's.

"So come on, we've spoken all night about me and my work. What about you and what do *you* do?" Jem's fingers stroked David's head, and for the first time in his life David felt like he was being cared for in a way he had never been cared for in his life. Here was someone wanting him for once. This was what a relationship should feel like, wanting on both sides. Jem wanted *him*, David had never really been wanted by the others – the kids who wanted paying for sex, or the ones who just demanded to be kept in DKNY gear. Jem knew nothing about him, he just wanted him for who he was on face value. He felt the courage to lean forward and plant a kiss square on Jem's lips. Jem responded and the kiss lasted a few seconds, David's eyes closed, feeling the softness of Jem's sweet Arab lips. He opened his eyes and Jem's cool green stare was holding his, his eyes warm and loving. Maybe this was for life. Maybe David had just met the elusive Mr Right. "I'm a judge." He was confident, he didn't elaborate. He was just a judge, a man who made the justice system work. He didn't tell Jem that he was also a gay crusader.

"Wow, how exciting that must be."

This was the first time a potential partner had ever taken a real interest in him. David nodded, it was.

"Here's me making dresses while all the time you're Mr Lord Judge Justice la de dah." Jem smiled mockingly and he appreciated the joke.

"Well, the girls always need clothes."

Jem squeezed David's legs in retaliation to his bitchiness. "And I always thought that judges were decrepit old things."

"And I'm not?" David questioned.

"No, my dear, you are very very far from being old and decrepit."

Jem smiled and kissed him again. David was in heaven. "Shall we go to mine for coffee, its just around the corner."

David nodded.

"Why not, I'll have to get the car in the morning anyway."

Jem held his hand out and pulled David up from the stool.

"Who said you were staying the night? I said coffee." Jem raised his eyebrows.

"We all know that in the gay world coffee means sex, it's just another word for it, it should go in the dictionary under other meanings." David winked and pulled on his jacket. Jem slipped a hand into his and they walked out of the bar. David had never been so happy.

"Tell me about your day today then, did you send anyone to prison?" Jem asked as he led David across the road.

David smiled. He could tell him the story, and the truth, but he didn't see the point, he could tell Jem knew all about it. He wasn't the kind of guy to miss such a case or the attendant publicity. He was just playing dumb to prevent David's ego growing. He obviously wanted to hear the story from him. Fair enough.

"I've been working on this small case, you might have heard of it…" David began. As the streets grew less populated, Jem slipped his arm around his waist. David hugged him back and kissed his cheek. What a great day.

"Shall we have sex then?" Jem turned and looked David in the eye as he locked the door behind them, his finger flicked a switch on the wall, lights burst into life and the little flat warmed up immediately.

"I thought you said coffee," David questioned, taking hold of Jem's waist and gently kissing the tip of his nose.

"I thought you said coffee meant sex," Jem said, raising his eyebrows in camp response.

"Why don't we have coffee and sex?" David reasoned.

"That's why you're a judge, so fair yet firm." Jem broke the hold and led David into the living room, the space was fashionable yet comfortable. It was evident that a designer lived here, the place had so many contemporary things. It was in stark comparison to David's traditional, comfortable home full of his antiques and good furniture.

"Nice place," David mused as Jem walked into the kitchen and flicked on the fluorescent tubes and the glare of the stainless steel blotted out the street outside.

"Tea or coffee?" Jem called from the kitchen as he filled the kettle and flicked it on.

"Oh, dear boy," David protested, "Coffee is one thing and means sex, tea is a whole different ball game which means love and marriage, never offer a man tea unless you really mean it." David picked up a large spiked piece of glass with a thousand colours in it and jumped when he saw Jem's head poking around the kitchen door.

"That cost seven thousand pounds, so be careful. As I said tea or coffee?" he smiled the cutest smile as he said it.

"Coffee," David stated in his most authoritative manner. "I'll have tea in the morning." They held each other's gaze as the kettle bubbled into life. Jem smiled and was gone. David made himself comfortable on the sofa.

The huge four-poster bed was fantastic, the white linen sheets perfect and fresh, the double bath they had shared was amazing, Jem certainly had all the creature comforts that made life bearable. They had dried each other, Jem taking care of him like no other, then he had laid him down on the bed, his soft voice so gentle on David's ear, then his breath so hot as it traced the length of his naked body, his tongue sending impulses of electricity through his relaxed body.

He took David in his mouth and slowly, teasingly worked away. David was constantly close to climax but he was never taken to that precise point. Jem was an expert, he was reading David like a book, taking him to a certain place – but never beyond. His attention was back on David's mouth and the strong kiss was immensely arousing. David felt he was in love and the more time he spent here the more he was falling. He could feel all of Jem's hot body pressing against his and that made him even wilder.

Jem laid back and let him try to please him in the way he had been pleased. David was good and Jem squirmed about all over the place. David smiled. He could give head like no one else. Jem's salty taste was going in his mouth. He knew it was nearly over. Poor Jem was at that place. David stopped. "Fuck me," he whispered, his breath travelling along Jem's stomach up his throat and into his face.

He nodded hungrily. "Okay, I'll get a condom and some cream." He made to move but David caught him.

"Don't bother."

"Okay." Jem looked worried but excited at the same time, fucking was in his mind, it always is when the dick takes control. David opened his mouth with pleasure as he forced himself down on Jem. "Ow," Jem started to protest but soon slid into David without much more fuss.

"Ssshhhh," David put his fingers to his lips as he started to slowly ride up and down on Jem's dick, Jem's breathing heavy, he had been really close when they had started so it wouldn't take long now, as long as Jem enjoyed it he would be happy, time, size, ability, it didn't matter if you were happy, if he could satisfy his partner then he was happy. David just enjoyed the mechanics of fucking. Fucking was good, it must be the happiest way to go if you died fucking.

"Oh, shit." He drove upwards into David who leaned back to allow Jem to finish off with full flowing drives into him, then he felt it, the come. Jem pushed in with his hips as David sat forward. "Ow." Jem's face contorted with a confused mixture of pleasure and pain, David was smiling as Jem finished coming and gasped for air, his eyes opened and he looked down, he couldn't speak, he couldn't breathe.

David smiled, both of their eyes looking at the glass spike that had pierced Jem's chest and now pulsated with the beat of his heart, the beating getting slower, Jem's eyes confused as to why.

David slipped off Jem and dressed. He had a lot to do before dawn to make sure he covered his tracks, he always had a lot to do before dawn in order to cover his tracks. It worked too, he had come this far. He smiled as he buttoned his shirt. How famous he was going to be in the morning, especially now that he had a new murderer to crusade against, copy-cat killings, it was all part of the long-term plan. God, they were going to love him.

Justice Armstrong-Jones. Everyone was going to know him, and that alone sent a shiver down his spine. It was all coming together.

In the Interests of Science
Peter Burton

In the Interests of Science
Peter Burton

As the letter was post-marked from Bath I knew it would be from James Howard. Since we first started to correspond, a little over half-a-dozen years ago, I have received a letter or postcard from him every three or four days. He writes about the most trifling things. The correspondence seems much more like a conversation, a dialogue, with points raised and discussed in some detail from one letter or postcard to another. I suspect that as Howard doesn't possess a telephone – he has an almost spinsterish dislike of any kind of domestic appliance, a loathing of the more technical advances of more recent years – correspondence is a substitute for conversation.

Howard's constant barrage of letters and cards can be rather tedious; especially as I feel obliged to write some kind of reply almost upon receipt. I know that a silence of more than two or three days is likely to bring forth a whole series of rather cross postcards which demand explanations as to my lack of prompt reply. Usually Howard appends some irritated postscript in which he complains about the decline in good manners, the steady erosion of civilised behaviour. He relates this decline in manners to the accelerated speed of our contemporary society. The point is taken; for a while future letters receive my immediate attention.

Although we have corresponded so regularly over these last few years, I have yet to meet Howard. I now feel it is unlikely that we shall ever meet – the contents of his latest letter intimate this. The letter – written in Howard's usual terse style – came as something of a surprise to me:

Dear Bob (he wrote)
You may have heard that I am to be married in three weeks. The woman is pleasant enough – a comfortable widow of middle years. She has two young sons. I shall be leaving Bath – not without regrets, as I have known many happy years here – and moving in with my wife at her home in Bristol.

As Estelle knows nothing about my homosexuality, it is obvious that my collection of books and periodicals on the subject must go. It wouldn't do for her to suspect anything – most especially as I shall be adopting the two lads. I am sending my collection of (shall we say) dubious literature to you under separate cover and would appreciate your arranging the sale of the same through one of your bookdealing chums. A cheque would be appreciated in due course. I cannot impress upon you enough the need for absolute discretion in all future correspondence.

All best wishes – Howard

Something about the letter disturbed me. I am not sure that I can exactly pin-point the details which made me feel slightly uncomfortable – I suspect it was the generally furtive air about the whole letter. Somehow I could envisage the unsuspecting widow; picture the two sons. What age *were* these two boys anyway, I wondered. 'Young' is such a misleading word – and for someone of Howard's age, which I have always presumed to be around sixty, twenty could seem 'young'. To me the expression 'young sons' rather suggested two boys about eleven or twelve, but then I am twenty years younger than Howard. Certainly, if the boys are pre-teen they will have nothing to fear from Howard – and maybe, anyway, his rather eccentric tastes will preclude these adoptive sons from his desires.

I suppose I should explain, fill in the few details I know about Howard. Details will give reason to my feeling of disquiet.

I have published several books and a considerable body of journalism yet, though I make a living from my writing, I am not well known. I would not expect to see any of my books prominently displayed in a major bookshop, nor placed anywhere on the bestselling lists. But I am happy; that is the most important thing. And it was through my writing that I first encountered Howard.

A little over six years ago, I published my first book: *Cricket and the British Consciousness*. The book hadn't sold sensationally, but it had sold enough copies to make a paperbacked reprint worthwhile. I was rather proud of my effort. James Howard is a cricket fanatic. He had read the paperback edition of my book. His first letter to me was thus addressed care of my publisher. That first letter was friendly enough – a brief acknowledgement of the merits of my book with comments (pedantic comments) on several minor inaccuracies in the text. I duly replied, promising to correct the errors should there ever be a second edition of the paperback. As with most 'fan mail,' I expected my reply to be the end of the correspondence.

By return of post, I received another letter from James Howard. In this letter he raised points about England's poor showing in the recent Australian Test season. This time I didn't reply immediately. A week passed. I then received a postcard from Howard in which he asked if I'd received his previous letter. I thought this rather odd. How was he to know that I wasn't away, or that I was extremely busy and unable to catch up with my mail? I began to form a mental picture of James Howard.

Bath I have always remembered as a beautiful old spa, filled with good bookshops, pleasant pubs, and several excellent restaurants. But it has always seemed basically a city of middle-class and old or elderly people; maybe even a place of retirement. William Beckford, I remember, spent his last years there, after the sale of Fonthill Abbey.

Beckford's biographer, the compelling but snobbish diarist James Lees-Milne, had spent his old age in the supremely beautiful Lansdowne Crescent. Howard, I suspected, must be a retired gentleman – perhaps ex-army or from the colonial service. My supposition wasn't too wide of the mark. I was subsequently to discover that he had been attached to Military Intelligence, where his outspokenness and *outré* behaviour characterised him as something of a loose cannon.

My thoughts of the army or the colonial service produced a somewhat clichéd mental impression of a rather squat, red-faced man, probably with a thick but neatly clipped moustache. I imagined him dressed in thick tweed suits, heavy walking shoes and, perhaps, carrying a stout stick for use on hikes around the surrounding Somerset countryside. Cricket, I knew, was his game. I could also imagine him as a golfing enthusiast, maybe keen on fishing. I certainly didn't imagine him as one with any interest in literature. Nor in sex. At least, I tended to picture him fumbling drunkenly with local prostitutes in Aden or Bangkok or Cairo. In these last two suppositions I couldn't have been more wrong.

Two letters a week from Howard became a regularity. At first these letters discussed the current cricket matches; politics – remarkably, he proved to be rather a socialist; current events about which we were both only as informed as our newspapers. In one letter Howard enquired about future writing projects. I was then preparing my second book, a novel about public school life and set just before the last war. This letter received the most astonishing reply; astonishing, at least, because it cut right across several of my preconceptions about James Howard. I will quote only a brief passage from it – *'I expect you will be writing about the exotic hothouse atmosphere which prevailed – probably still does prevail – in those places,'* he wrote. *'Assignations in Chapel, love-notes furtively passed in class, long summer days with happy afternoons spent behind the cricket pavilion with one's particular friend. Oh, I remember it all so well!'*

This wasn't at all the kind of thing I expected from the James Howard I had created in my mind's eye. My reply was discreet, though I suggested that the finished work would undoubtedly please Howard and bring back happy remembrances of things past.

It was after this letter that the correspondence became much more personal, more intimate. Cricket, politics and world affairs were relegated to the more obscure reaches of our letters. Now our letters were taken up with discussion of the public school novel; from *Tom Brown's Schooldays* to the most recent examples of that absorbing blend of fiction and fantasy. From the public school novel we moved on to the exhilarating adventure yarn for boys, once so popular but now superseded by trashy thrillers and lurid volumes of sexual exploits. Howard even brought into this conversation by correspondence novels of war and novels of science fiction. Throughout these books we were especially interested in observing the streak of homosexuality. It was in the discussion of some of the science fiction and war stories that I began to perceive – dimly at first – the nature of Howard's particular fascination; his particular *bent*.

Injury and affliction seemed to absorb Howard. He discussed it at length – and I noticed that there was always more of a fascination with some volume in which one of the characters had to go, as it were, under the surgeon's knife. This interest was most apparent when Howard was writing about war novels – I remember a detailed discussion about a novel by Martin Boyd. Howard had been positively entranced by a sequence in which the hero meets again a beautiful boy – half of whose face had been shot away in a First World War shell attack. Blindness was another recurring theme in Howard's letters. I distinctly remember a letter in which he wrote at length about blindness in fiction – citing one of Samuel R Delany's science fiction stories as a classic example. And I remember a letter in which Howard talked about one of Burroughs' novels – *The Wild Boys*, I think – commenting that some of the boys were *'provided with interesting disabilities'*.

It was apparent that Howard was fascinated by boys; with an exaggerated sense of literary values he claimed Michael Davidson's *The World, The Flesh and Myself* as one of the major works of autobiography in the twentieth century. This fascination with boys I could understand; it was an absorption I shared. But this interest in violence and the fruits of violence convinced me that Howard's interest was in more than just boys.

The clincher came in a letter in which Howard wrote about a youth he had met on a train journey between Bath and Bristol; was he, I wonder, on his way to meet his 'comfortable widow'?

The boy, it appeared, had been Howard's only companion in the carriage. Somehow they had begun a conversation – haltingly, I imagine, as I cannot picture Howard as the type of man who would easily make conversation with strangers. It was neither the conversation nor the boy's looks which had seemed to interest Howard. Towards the end of the letter, he had written: *'He had been in an accident at his place of work. He had lost the middle and index fingers from his left hand. I confess, I felt an almost overwhelming desire to take that incomplete hand in mine, raise it to my lips and kiss those pathetic stumps. I resisted. I suppose I shall not see the boy again.'*

Howard, I decided, was fascinated by boys. But he was most strongly drawn towards *mutilated* boys.

The barrage of letters and cards which seemed to proclaim this obsession disquieted me. Mutilation, injury, amputation – it seemed markedly unhealthy. I was soon to find out how extreme was his interest in this peculiar field.

Not so long ago, while dining with two close friends, I happened to mention my strange correspondent and his equally bemusing obsession. One of the friends – a journalist for a tabloid newspaper – asked the name of my peculiar friend. I told him. He then asked where James Howard came from; I told him. I asked if he knew him.

"No," my friend replied, "but I do know of him. In fact, some years ago I wrote a story about him for my paper. I'm sure it must be the same fellow. There couldn't be two like him down in Bath."

The port was passed again; we lit cigars.

"What was your story?" asked our host.

"Gruesome," explained the journalist. "Kinky and gruesome. You see, this James Howard amputated his left leg. He hacked it off, just below the knee, with a meat cleaver. And he very nearly died from loss of blood."

"But why?" I asked.

"As I remember it, Mr James Howard said that he'd hacked off his arm in the interests of science!"

Howard's package of books and periodicals arrived. Through the good offices of a friend in the second-hand book trade, I had managed to sell the various volumes. Payment was not large but, I presumed, it would satisfy Howard. I typed out a letter congratulating him on his forthcoming marriage, asked one or two questions about the widow and her sons, enclosed the cheque and posted the letter.

This morning I received my last letter from James Howard.

Dear Bob (he writes)

Thank you for your good wishes and the cheque. The amount seemed rather small; are you sure that you filled the cheque out correctly?

You ask about the woman I am to marry – though I cannot think why you should be interested. I have already told you that she is a widow, of middle years, comfortably situated. Her husband was killed in a motoring accident six years ago – when the boys were eight and ten respectively. Though his wife was not in the car, the two boys were. They were both blinded and received dreadful injuries. It is my intention to become a friend and helpmate to the boys – and, of course, to their mother.

I have been considering our correspondence in the light of my marriage and have decided that it might be a good thing if we ceased to write.

I will destroy all your letters and would appreciate your doing the same with mine.

I shall remember you with affection.

etc. etc.

I shuddered as I finished reading the letter. Then I thought back over all I had learned about James Howard. Somehow it all seemed horribly sinister. Maybe I am just over-reacting.

But enclosed with the letter was a small coloured snapshot. Scrawled across the back, in Howard's bold and familiar handwriting were the words: *Jamie and Derek, my adopted sons*.

The photograph showed two boys of about fourteen and sixteen. Their blind eyes, beneath mops of fair hair, seemed to gaze towards the camera. Their faces showed hope and expectancy and a wonderful innocence. But I felt my heart lurch, as I realised that in the horrible accident which had killed their father both boys had lost limbs.

The Pink Tower
Richard Cawley

The Pink Tower
Richard Cawley

Alex smiled, behind closed eyes, as the colour gradually began to change, to lighten through his eyelids. At the same time he felt a barely perceptible new warmth spread over his face. It was time now, he knew from experience, to open his eyes. Yes, it had worked again. There was the great apricot disc in the sky, suspended, just above the horizon. Well, as yet, the horizon was still very indistinct, but he knew it was there.

In front of him, from the edge of the pink rocks, where he sat reflected in the still deep pool, the sea stretched away, perfectly flat and gleaming, to the vague division where it met the pale six o'clock sky.

This particular morning was even better than usual. The faintly pine-scented breeze, which had no effect on the mirror pool, slightly ruffled his hair; his nondescript mid-brown hair, how he wished it was blond, even dark brown would be better, anything but...

A mere metre or so below him, the pool was perfectly flat. Sheltered by its low surrounding wall of rocks, it always was. The sea however wasn't always perfectly smooth, but today it was. He liked it like that. He felt, he almost believed, that if he actually believed hard enough, he could step off those jagged pink rocks and walk along the pale dazzling pathway which stretched across it straight to the shining orange disc of light.

Even as he was thinking those brief thoughts, the sun had risen noticeably, centimetres, he held out his hand sideways to measure, the width of at least two maybe three fingers! Yes, it was the quite best yet. It looked, he thought, just like the cover of one of the 'books of thought', which had so fascinated him in the window of a religious book shop, on a rare trip to South London.

Orange graduated stripes of light, radiated up and out, piercing a long low band of wispy clouds, with gaudy stains of pink, peach and apricot. In a photo, on a book cover, or a poster, it would have looked ludicrous, vulgar, sentimental; the kind of thing his parents would take great pleasure in ridiculing. His oh-so-tolerant, liberal, educated parents.

Yes, today was definitely the best to date. The best in almost three weeks. His morning routine had been exactly the same since the third day. The third day of this, their first holiday on Corsica. He would wake just as the first faint light began to distinguish the triangle of white nylon net at his feet from the darker thicker fabric of his small nylon tent. It was that first light, coupled with his painful erection which would wake him.

It never took long to deal with the second factor. He would unzip his sleeping bag as quietly as he could, conscious that his parents always slept with the caravan door open. He would then close his eyes and conjure up visions of the dark-haired older boy on the beach. The one who played endless ball games in the sea, in front of the spot where he always sat with his parents. His parents with their endless books. This year to his intense embarrassment, it was Harry Potter. Harry Potter! They were constantly making little Harry Potter jokes and references to each other.

Afterwards, he would pull on his shorts. They would be just next to his lilo, with the bottle of water, the torch, the insect repellent and the toilet roll. He had asked for a toilet roll of his own, just in case he needed to 'go in the night'. He wondered if his parents suspected? He never got up to 'go in the night' at home!

He had discovered the jagged rocks with the deep fascinating pool, a magic pool surely, on the third day of the holiday. For the first two days he hadn't spoken. He wasn't sulking, as his parents insisted he was, on purpose. It was just that he was so depressed. Ever since he could remember, they had spent their summer holidays on the same camp site, by a river in the south of France. He found it hard enough anyway to make friends, to mix with other kids; well, at fifteen, he realised, he wasn't really a kid any more; but at least there, he had had a few friends. Not the big crowd, not the sporty ones who loved canoes, jumping off high rocks and making a lot of noise. There was just Brendan, the other English boy, with red hair, and the Dutch twins, all odd kids, like him, but they got on, played their own games, talked their own talk, lived their own funny little holiday lives.

But here, it was all so different. All the kids on the beach seemed to have known each other for ever. And besides they were all so beautiful, the girls, with their long hair, not that he cared, and the boys, all French, and all so sporty, so athletic he would never even dare...

Then on the third morning, he had wandered off alone, at dawn, to explore the silent, sleeping camp site. He had taken a different fork in the dirt path, not the one which led to the beach, from their neat little encampment under the pines. He was fascinated, as he dawdled along the dusty track, to see the different states in which people had left their temporary domains, before retiring for the night. There were a few caravans, but mostly tents. Some encampments were pin neat, with everything put away for the night. The folding tables wiped clean of every crumb of baguette and every last drop of spilt rosé. Others, however, looked as if a small tornado had paid a recent visit, with tangled piles of folding chairs, burst inflatable beach toys and tables littered with empty bottles, dirty glasses, overflowing ashtrays and hard puddles of soot-streaked candle wax, studded with suicidal night insects.

His parents belonged to the first category of campers. The 'don't forget to put the matches in a plastic bag in case there's a heavy dew.' category. The 'Why not take the rubbish now, darling, while I make us a nice mug of camomile. It'll only attract the ants' category. Why did they have to be so bloody 'responsible'? They had already started muttering about circuses, and animals losing their dignity, as soon as the posters had appeared tied around several trees, the day before. He longed to see the circus. He knew there wouldn't be any tigers or other endangered species. Probably a goat and an old dog. He still wanted to go. They would take some persuading, though. He'd seen one before, a small family-run French circus. A boy, well a young man, obviously the eldest son of the family, had performed all the acrobatic acts in the show. He wore nothing but spangled tights and a head band. Alex had fantasised about him for months afterwards.

After walking for about five minutes, he had suddenly come upon the 'magic place', the pink, jagged rocks. There were no longer any tents. The ground was too rough and there was no shelter. He clambered down from the now-narrow path. One particular rock, a smooth one, made a perfect seat. No one around. Total silence. Except for a faint lapping sound as the sea barely nudged the little cliff.

Just inside the rocky barrier which held back the flat mirror sea, was a large rock pool, big enough to swim in. Well, maybe five or six strokes from end to end, he calculated. He stared into the pool. It was incredibly dark. It seemed very deep.

Then he sat perfectly still on his smooth throne of pink rock and stared straight ahead, into the perfectly quiet stillness, the soft pale grey emptiness. He felt suddenly strangely calm. Totally relaxed for once. At home.

After sitting quite still for some time, he turned his head slightly, ever so slowly, to the left. He was very conscious of the movement. He knew it was an important moment in his life, momentous! There was the island. It seemed much closer than it did from the beach. Was it because the early morning light was so different, or was it really closer?

The beach, where they had spent most of the last two days, curved deeply to make a perfect semicircle. On the left, looking out to sea, the pale yellow sand turned gradually into a low rocky peninsula, covered in part by low undergrowth. Then, separated by what appeared to be just a small stretch of water, the long low island rose gradually out of the sea.

The island stretched about a third of the way across the bay, or so it appeared, from their habitual spot in the centre of the beach, directly in front of the café. The other, right-hand extremity of the perfect little semi-circular bay ended in a shorter headland, again covered in low scrubby pines, myrtles and a plant with strange little hard red fruits which his father had pronounced to be 'arbutus'. Alex was shown a photo in the guide-book as proof. His father always needed to know what everything was called.

Where the dry scrubby undergrowth ended, the pink rocks began. His special morning place, his pink rocky throne and the still magic pool. If he were to dare... just to dare, to lower himself into that dark liquid mirror, would it welcome him? Would it close slowly, gently, over his head, take him to its own still depths, its silent magic world, away from the pain, the teasing? He tried not to think those thoughts, however tempting, however pleasant it was, to lose himself in them, to escape from reality.

Jan had been the only therapist he had ever listened to, had trusted, out of a long succession who had tried to 'help' him as a 'disruptive child'. Jan had tried to explain that the less he allowed himself to wallow in these 'dark thoughts', the easier it would be to cope, to cope with the 'normal' world. Jan had never reminded him to sit up straight or criticised him for slouching. Yes, Jan had been definitely OK.

Swimming was the only sport which vaguely interested him, and then not because it was a sport, it was just that he loved the feeling of the water sliding over his body, supporting him, almost holding him back, but then allowing him to slide, wriggle free, constantly moving forward. He loved the solitary sensation, even in a crowded swimming pool. Wearing his goggles, he spent most of the time, well over half, he calculated, with his head under the water. Just him and the water, away from the hard, noisy, brutal world.

He had swum a little on the first two days of the holiday, but not with any enthusiasm. He had been so depressed. It had merely been a means to an end, a way to keep cool in the blistering sun. But then on the third day, everything changed. The pink rocks, the silent pool, they must be magic, otherwise how could he possibly, suddenly, feel so different? He began to notice things; notice how pale the sand was; "And how clean!" his parents had added, evidently pleased that he had at last spoken. The sea, he suddenly became almost deliriously aware, was no less than perfect! It was warm, but not too warm; and clear, totally clear and transparent.

He swam, in sheer delight from the centre of the beach, to its left-hand extremity, where sand gave way to rocks, and then back to where his parents sat reading. He stood up, the water no more than waist height, and paused for a couple of minutes, then swam, this time a little faster, to the other end of the beach, and back. He looked at his watch. Just over twenty minutes. Easy! Half a mile or however many metres that was? Exactly the same time it took to swim thirty-three lengths of his local swimming pool.

"Half a mile!" his father would always comment. "Good start to the day! If nothing else goes right today, at least we have the satisfaction that we've swum half a mile," he would add smugly. Didn't he notice that he repeated the same thing almost every morning? Still, it was the only activity which he and his father ever really shared, on a regularly basis. They had persuaded him to take it up because of his 'bad posture', but Alex had found he liked it.

He did love his father, both his parents, but for some reason he found it almost impossible to show it. They would never understand. They could never understand, be part of his world, the world inside his head. And he could, would, never be able to join their world, not properly, that is, no matter how hard he tried, pretended, when he was trying to be 'normal'. He could never join their world of endlessly watching television, while professing to hate every second. Their world of ostentatiously recycling bottles and constantly despairing about the Sunday crowds in IKEA. A world where adults constantly, and publicly deplored 'what was going on in the world' where they agonised loudly, over the plight of flood victims, abused children, hunted foxes... and then did nothing; watched television, recycled bottles and trailed miserably around IKEA on Sunday.

Half a mile! He would swim another half mile later, after lunch. It would be good for his body, his despised skinny body. Perhaps if he kept it up for the whole holiday, building up to two, even three miles a day, his body would become more like the dark-haired boy's. The boy who constantly played ball games in the sea. The boy of his dawn fantasies. He was there now, this time with a frisbee, directly in front of Alex, as he lay on his stomach, on his dolphin towel, facing the island.

It wasn't until that third day however that he really noticed the tower. It stood in almost exactly the centre of the island: he held his hand up in front of his face, to measure: on the highest point. It was a square tower, or so it seemed, from where he lay, but was slightly uneven, as if some of the top had crumbled and fallen away. Two of its four walls were visible from the beach. The left-hand wall, being farthest from the sun, was dark, in shadow, until the sun moved round in the late afternoon. The adjacent wall, the sunlit wall, glowed pink, the same pink as the rock of the island on which it was built, presumably to protect?

There were no visible openings in the shaded wall, but high in the pink wall, the one nearer the sun, was one solitary dark window. The door? Perhaps it was round the other side, facing the horizon, out of view. Or perhaps it was directly under the dark narrow window, hidden by what appeared to be a clump of trees.

The other thing which had so changed his mood on that important third day, was the 'family' which settled next to them on the beach. There was only one child, a boy of perhaps seven or eight, Alex guessed, plus two men. The men appeared to be quite a bit younger than his parents? Difficult to tell though, because they were both so slim with fit, toned-looking bodies. Unlike his father, who despite his daily half-mile swim, was decidedly overweight.

What thrilled Alex most however, was the fact that the two men would occasionally touch each other affectionately, as they lay close, next to each other on one large towel. Once he even saw them kiss, briefly; yes they actually kissed each other on the lips; a proper kiss! Of course he had read all kinds of stuff in books, magazines, newspapers, even seen things on television, about gay men, their life-style. And he would often speculate, fantasise, about people he knew, who he though could be, might be, like him. But he had never actually come into contact with, actually, physically seen two men who were definitely, without shadow of a doubt, homosexual.

Even better, the child seemed perfectly happy with the situation, aparently oblivious to the fact that his situation was different to that of most other children. How he envied that little boy. Maybe if he had had two daddies, he would feel more normal?

He had never openly discussed his gayness with his parents. He was sure they would be more than happy to, they were so 'liberal' and 'open-minded'. In fact they would probably be thrilled. At least then they would have a handle, a label, to explain why he was so different, instead of them just being lumbered with a 'difficult' child, a 'disruptive' child, a slouching child who was a bit 'weird'.

His reverie was broken.

"I think we'll do something a bit different tomorrow!" His father suddenly announced. "A bit of a spin. Start to discover a bit of the island. We'll get up really early and drive into Porto Vecchio for breakfast, then on to Bonefaccio. It's less than an hour away. I've looked it up. It looks really picturesque in the guide book. The old town's built on a cliff. Should get some good photos if the weather's like this..."

"Suits me, darling," his mother added, "Not having to cook breakfast for once. Anyway, I think a bit of a break from this sun wouldn't be a bad idea. I adore it, of course, this blissful doing nothing, but I don't want to end up like a leathery old crocodile, and at our age..."

She was always going on about their age! It amazed Alex. Parents were old, just old, what could it possibly matter. Anyway they were married, had each other, what could it possibly matter what they looked like now? And as for the 'blissful doing nothing' his mother claimed to adore ... she never stopped, not for a second, from the moment she woke up until bedtime. She was always either cooking or shopping or tidying. Even on the beach, she had to be doing something. She couldn't just lie there and look at the sea, the island, the tower. She probably hadn't even noticed the tower. No, even on the beach, she had to be reading a book, or agonising over a crossword, or talking, even if it was just saying how wonderful it was to do nothing. She had to comment on everything, share it with everyone else. Why couldn't she just enjoy something? Experience it for its own sake, on her own, quietly. She always had to comment on everything, as if looking for approval. Make sure she was enjoying the right things, the same things as every one else. Being normal.

"Yes, a bit of a spin. That would be lovely. Might find some interesting local produce. Apparently the cheeses are really special, and the charcuterie, you know the pigs, roam free, half wild, in the forests... I mean the little supermarket at the gate's fine. In its way it's really good, for a camp site. I'm not really sure I fancy the meat though. I mean that boy... Not that I've anything against piercings... Alex darling, what about you? would you like to go to Bonifaccio. You all right, my boy?" She tilted his chin back slightly with her fingers.

On the one hand this action irritated him, her slightly patronising tone, talking to him as if he were recovering from a long illness. But at the same time he was pleased to be consulted, not to be taken for granted.

"You seem much better today? Happier? You do like it here don't you? I know you miss your little friends, Brendan, and the twins, but I'm sure you'll make lots of new friends here. There are lots of children... well, young people, your age? Daddy and I have already talked. We love it. The weather is just so much better, seems more reliable here. I've forgotten how many hours of sunshine they have each year... We're sure we'll want to come back, again, next year... You do like it her, don't you darling?"

"Yes, Yes. I'm going for another swim," he muttered.

"Don't tire yourself out. It's terribly hot this sun. We're quite a lot further south you know. Takes it out of you. And don't forget you've got all those pine kernels to crack for me before dinner... "

He had found them the day before; small, funny-looking little sooty things. He had been examining the ground. He often did when he was depressed. Even when he wasn't depressed he loved peering at small low-down things. When he was in the country anyway. Not so much in London. He loved observing the things which no one else ever noticed, while they were busy raving about 'the view', 'the sunset', 'the landscape.' That's why he had so loved the 'Borrowers' books, about a race of minute people, who utilised all those tiny things he loved. He also like the fact that there was no magic in the 'Borrowers' They just used their initiative and 'borrowed' all the tiny things that had been lost or discarded by humans.

'Harry Potter' of course was fine, and like all the other kids at school, he hadn't been able to put them down, but 'the Borrowers'... He remembered every detail, every little thing that happened in the 'Borrowers' books...

He had managed to crack one open. He had placed it on a flattish stone; he had found a stone with an indentation, to stop the little nut rolling away; then bashed it with another stone. The first hit had no effect. The second strike worked, but it crushed the creamy little oval, seed inside.

"What's that, darling? Is it a pine kernel?" His mother, obsessed with food, suddenly became very interested in what he was doing. "I didn't realise that's what they looked like. I'd never thought! Oh how wonderful. Let's collect as many as we can. I'll make fresh pesto. They've got lots of fresh basil in the shop at the gate, well, unless it's all gone. They do seem to have it regularly though..." She began to scrabble about in the dirt, sifting through the dry yellow pine needles, like a mad thing. Completely over-excited, as if she had discovered gold! "Come on. Let's all look . We'll need loads for pesto!"

And so he sat, at the white plastic and aluminium folding table, in front of the awning, cracking open the sooty, hard little nuts with a garlic press into a bowl. It was incredibly slow, hard work, but there was no hurry. His mother had decided to make fresh pasta, and was now getting terribly hot, rolling out the dough on the table inside the caravan, with the aid of an empty wine bottle.

She really was a bit of an embarrassment, Alex mused, as he worked, his mother, with her food obsession. "I read cookery books like other people read novels!" she would boast. Why it was something to boast about, he couldn't possibly imagine. It wasn't even an original expression. He knew she must have read it somewhere. He used to wish his mother would give him the kind of food that he heard the other kids at school talking about. He wished they might occasionally have burgers or take-aways, or even Bolognese sauce, instead of bloody pesto. But no, even after a hard day at work, she would wear herself out, grinding spices for a Thai green curry, or shivering outside the back door grilling organic vegetables on the BBQ.

It wasn't until he had spent that disastrous weekend with Brendan and his mother in Dover that he began to realise that perhaps it wasn't such a bad thing after all to have a mother who was obsessed with food.

Brendan's mother had given them microwaved Chinese take-away, left over from the night before, on white toast for breakfast! And they had been allowed to choose which chilled ready-made meal they would like for Sunday lunch, when they had visited Tesco's the night before.

They had eaten all their meals on their knees in front of the television. There was a tiny formica-topped table in the little kitchen, but there was no proper table anywhere in the flat, not a table that you could sit down and eat at.

The whole weekend had been a failure anyway. Brendan had been quite a different person from the boy he use to 'hang out' with in the south of France. In Dover, in the scruffy little ground-floor flat he lived in with his mother, a French teacher in a local school, he spent the whole time, when they weren't in the supermarket or eating in front of the television, glued to his computer.

For once, Alex actually felt quite content, relaxed, cracking the sooty little nuts, and watching the little Chinese bowl grow gradually fuller. He looked at his mother through the open caravan window. She was brushing back her hair from a sweating forehead with the back of her left hand, whilst taking a good swig of white milky liquid from a small glass in the other. It was Pastis. They always drank what the locals did when abroad. "Although," Alex had heard his mother repeat so many times, and often to the same people, "it never tastes quite the same at home, back in England."

It was like the set of boules they had excitedly bought one year, in an end-of-summer sale in a giant French hypermarket. Alex could have told them that they would never get them out of the box once they got home.

She caught him watching her. "You all right boy? How you getting on? Nearly enough? I mean are you really all right. Not too fed up? I mean about France?"

"No. It's cool. Nearly finished." He was surprised at the sound of his own voice. It sounded oddly normal? Almost adult!

"Oh darling I'm so pleased. Daddy and I really love it here, don't we, Peter?"

"Mmm. Yes, kitten," his father, who was totally absorbed in his guide book, replied absent mindedly, putting down his glass of Pastis and blindly feeling for an olive from the saucer in front of him. Alex pushed the saucer towards the groping fingers. He shuddered. He couldn't bear it when his father called her that. Kitten! Nothing could be less kitten-like than his mother, with her heavy shoulder-length blonde hair, streaked here and there with grey, and her big red hands which were at that moment cutting the roll of pasta into long ribbons.

"Thanks, son." He took an olive and looked up, giving Alex a concerned but affectionate little smile. "Listen to this, it's really fascinating." Alex suspected it wouldn't be even slightly interesting, let alone fascinating. It didn't matter though, his mind was already totally occupied. It had suddenly come to him in a blinding flash. He had read all about destiny and coincidences in a book of his mother's. She loved reading all that stuff. Yes, the tower, the pink tower, it was so obvious now. It was there just for him! That's why his parents had brought him to Corsica. To this particular place. They wouldn't realise of course, but yes, that was it. He must just get to the island, somehow, to the tower... and then, then, he knew, with total one hundred per cent certainty he would meet... yes of course, it was fate, 'the one', he would meet 'the one'.

He would be perfect. Better than the boy in the sea with the ball. He would make everything all right, make it... well, just make everything all right. 'The one'. He would be 'the one', he just knew it. All he had to do was get to the tower? But suddenly his daydream was interrupted by what his father was reading from the guide book. It actually was fascinating he suddenly realised, really fascinating!

"'... And indeed, the type of red granite which so impressively dominates the landscape of the Estérel hills to the west of Cannes on the Côte d'Azur can be seen on some stretches of the Corsican coast.'"

Red granite! Red, pink! Yes of course. It wasn't just his romantic imagination. The rocks, the island, the tower built from the same stone, probably quarried from the island, were all pink. Geologists, guide books might call it red, but it was pink. His tower was pink. And this, his father reading about it from a guide book, at exactly the same moment... It was an omen. He had read all about it in his mother's book, to look out for coincidences. This was more than a coincidence, it was a definite sign!

They had arrived in Porto Vecchio before nine.

"It really wasn't as far as it seemed coming the other way, you know, when we arrived, was it, darling?" his father had announced, rather too loudly, as they sat down in the smart little café.

"I'm not sure I actually want a croissant. I mean they are terribly rich, aren't they? It might be fun to have one of those squares of pizza in the window. I bet they're good. The tomato sauce must be homemade? What about you, boy? What d'you fancy?" his mother had continued. "Peter darling, we mustn't forget to get some money out of the wall. There was one at the Post Office. We just passed it. You have got the cards, haven't you?"

It had taken them a long time to find somewhere to park in Bonefaccio, even though it was only just after ten-thirty as they settled down on the terrace of small cafe/bar, high up in the old town, overlooking the extraordinarily brilliant blue sea.

"My God, just look at that yacht!" gasped his mother.

"I know it's terribly early, but it is eleven-thirty in England..."

"What? Oh! Well, actually darling, it's only nine-thirty. We're an hour forward, not back. but I know you're going to have a beer anyway!"

"Well, we are on holiday. What d'you fancy, old girl." Alex disliked 'old girl' almost as much as 'kitten.'

"Well, d'you know I think I'm going to have a kir. We did get up very early, and if you're having a beer... What about you, darling?" she turned to Alex. "Orangina? Coke? Go on, you can have a Coke if you want one. You haven't had one so far this holiday..."

"No thanks. I'll have a mineral water; a still one. Please," he replied curtly and automatically straightened himself up in the yellow plastic chair. He didn't really want a still mineral water at all. It was just that he hated being talked to like that, like a silly little kid. He thought that by ordering a still mineral water, they might begin to take him seriously, to realise he was an adult, well, sort of.

"Well, she's no better than she thinks she is!" his mother proclaimed as the drinks arrived. It was one of her pet expressions, a 'borrowed' one. She was craning round, back over her shoulder looking down at the yacht again.

Alex followed her gaze. A woman was leaning down over the railing at the front of the huge white boat, to reach what appeared to be a newspaper, from a man in smart knee-length white shorts and a blue and white striped top. With her other hand she was preventing an enormous white straw hat from falling off her head. She straightened up, turned and disappeared with the newspaper into a dark doorway.

"I suppose she might be going to a wedding!" his mother sneered, and then suddenly flashed him and his father one of her 'special' looks. That particular look was something else which irritated Alex. It was a look he knew so well and meant 'Keep your voices down, those people at the next table are speaking English!' Why was she obsessed in foreign countries about not letting other English people know that they were?

The group of people, who seemed to hurl themselves at the next table, on the terrace, were not just speaking English, but shouting it, and with strong American accents. This time another well-practised look from his mother. This one involved eyes briefly raised to heaven, and meant simply 'Oh, my god' and for once Alex agreed with her. He tried not to look, but had to turn, as a voice whined.

"I need money, for the football machine. Which is my water? I don't know which is mine now!"

The table was covered in half-empty small plastic bottles of mineral water, there must have been six or seven.

"Dunno honey. This is mine. My lipstick. Howmuchyaneed hon?" drawled a woman with wiry dark brown hair who was dressed in tight pale blue shorts, with a blue and white striped singlet and white socks and tennis shoes. She was chewing gum and both her bra straps showed conspicuously. She was also sweating profusely. "Here doll," she gave some money to a pouting teenage girl, who turned, without thanks, and joined a large group of children who were arguing noisily around a football game.

"Wish we didn't have to walk all the way down again. I mean, hell, it's cute an all up here, but once you've seen one of these old towns..." she turned, as if expecting an answer from a big balding man, who Alex suspected, was her husband. He ignored her and turned to another, smaller man, who was wearing spectacles, and Alex thought, reasonably acceptable clothes. The big man was dressed in a banana yellow jogging suit, the same colour as the plastic chairs, Alex noted with faint amusement

"Yer want something to drink?"

"Yeah. Coffee," the smaller man replied without looking up.

"Girls?" He was ignored.

The owner of the café, who was standing by the table, looking down in disbelief at the forest of bottles, was becoming visibly agitated.

"Two coffees," the big man bellowed. "*Café au lait! Due,*" he yelled. The owner turned on his heels and stormed back into the bar. His neck, Alex noted, had become quite red.

"Couldn't we get a cab back down?" the woman in white shorts whined. She had removed the sock and shoe from one foot and was closely examining each painted toenail in turn.

"Just to think, I have to phone all the way to England, just to speak to that boat!" A new voice. Slow and deliberate. A voice intending to be heard. Slightly supercilious. The kind of voice which expected to impress.

Alex carefully observed the second woman properly for the first time. He instantly disliked her, even more than the rest. She was standing leaning over the wall, alternately looking down at the boat, and then at the other three adults, to see what effect her words were having. She was expensively dressed in a loose beige linen top and ankle-length skirt. She wore lots of gold bangles and a pair of large sunglasses, on her head to hold her immaculately arranged straw-coloured jaw-length hair in place. She dialled a number and put her mobile phone to her ear, carefully sliding it under her hair.

"Yes, good morning. Are the Lindemans on board?" A pause during which she looked around again, to gauge the effect her words were having. They were having little if any effect, as far as Alex could judge.

"Oh hi..."

"Yes, we got in last night. Our little boat... I'm looking down at yours now. We're up in the old town."

"Oh, only this morning! You're off this afternoon. Round the island!"

"Oh no, we'll be gone long before then. Just a couple of days..."

"Well, yes, we'd love to..."

"Right now. Why not? We could come straight down..."

"Oh no. That's real kind, but no. There'd be too many of us. Just

David and I. The others will stay up here, with all the kids. Anyway with you not being used to kids an all, they'd be... they won't mind. Anyways we just got up here. There's lots to see. Old churches and stuff." She looked sideways at the dark-haired woman. Her conversation seemed to be having no effect. The other shoe and sock had been removed and she was now totally absorbed in cleaning her horse-like teeth with a metal pin which she had removed from her wiry hair.

Much as Alex detested this brash little group of people, he was annoyed when his mother suddenly gave one of the little sideways nods which he knew was her coded message for 'let's get out of here quick!' He was intrigued by the little scenario and wanted to know the outcome. Whether the ugly couple in ugly clothes really minded being dumped? Whether they would begin to bitch about the woman with the phone when she swished down with her husband to pay a house call on the obviously influential Lindemans on their flashy yacht? Whether they minded being left with the gaggle of rude unruly children? How many were theirs? He would never know. His parents were already in the bar, discreetly paying for their drinks.

"Hey, this is good! Is this what you picked up in the café in Porto Vecchio?" Alex was flicking through a small glossy booklet on Porto Vecchio and its surrounding attractions, published by the local tourist organisation. Look, it's got a map of our beach, of all the local beaches. And it's got the island..." He wished he hadn't said anything. He had never mentioned the island, or the tower to his parents.

"Yes, it's really quite excellent isn't it? It's got all the local hotels. With prices and everything. You know, if we ever fancied coming back here for a week, say at Easter. Too far to bring the caravan for a week. There are probably some good cheap flights at that time of year."

"The flowers must be stunning," his mother chipped in, "and I bet they have chanterelles on the market, I've never tasted fresh ones. Well, not bought them and cooked them myself. You all right, boy?" She swivelled round in he seat and gave him a rather relieved-looking smile. "You certainly ate enough at lunch! In fact, I've never seen you eat so much."

He tried to give her a 'normal' smile, then as soon as she turned around again, he began to measure with his fingers. Yes, he was right, to swim from his morning place, by the rock pool, it couldn't be more than a mile. Less perhaps, and he'd already swum a mile yesterday! Not all in one go. In two halves, with a couple of tiny breaks. But in a week or so...

"It's so bloody hot now. What d'you say we stop in Porto Vech. On the way back for a nice cold drink. I only had a couple of glasses of wine with lunch. Might get a *Guardian* too..."

The circus had been a bit of a let-down; particularly as his parents had actually suggested it; asked him if he wanted to go! He supposed they were trying to humour him, for being so 'good' and not 'difficult'.

Much to his disappointment, the only acrobatic bits in the show were performed by two young women with surprisingly beefy thighs, considering how much exercise they got each day. There was an older man, who acted as ringmaster, did a few tricks with a dog and walked a tired-looking llama around the ring a couple of times. Two small kids, a boy and a girl, seemed to do most of the work in most of the acts, and there was also a young man in his early twenties. Much to Alex's disappointment, however, he wore a baggy clown's outfit for the whole show, so the tensed muscles he anticipated, and had hoped to file away in his secret fantasy scrapbook, never appeared. He couldn't really even tell if the young man was good-looking, behind his plastic nose – his mother commented that it looked exactly like "one of those miniature cheeses with the thick red waxy skin" – and his thick clown's makeup.

The biggest disappointment however was the non-appearance of the little boy with his two daddies. Alex had been sure they would bring him.

There was one real bright spot during the evening, however. It was when, half way through dinner he had gone to the toilet for a pee. The circus didn't start until nine, and as it was in the small dry field at 'the gate', where the tiny supermarket and restaurant were, his father had suggested they dine out "*Moules frites* eh? Give your mother a break?"

Alex was already in a very good mood. His parents had, for the first time let him drink undiluted wine. They usually allowed him one glass, thinned heavily with water 'Just like French children'. His pizza had been brilliant, and the tall fair-haired boy who was making them at the little counter in front of the blazing outdoor oven, was good looking enough to keep his mind away from his parents repetitive conversations. "I can never roll my pizza bases out as thin as that. Do you think it's the flour?"

There had been only one cubical; unisex. It was one of the hole-in-the-floor kind, with two little flat oval foot pedestals protruding from the stained white porcelain, and intended to keep the user several centimetres above the business in hand! He hated using them anyway, but particularly when he was wearing sandals, so he stood with his back to the door and aimed as best he could for the hole in the middle.

Afterwards he had been so pleased with himself for having managed not to splash his feet, that he suddenly realised that he was examining himself closely in the large mirror above the wash basin. He normally totally avoided mirrors, would walk past them quickly. Sometimes he would even try and clean his teeth with his eyes shut. He hadn't really looked at himself properly in a mirror for at least a year.

Was he imagining it or were his shoulders actually filling out his tee shirt more than usual, instead of just looking like a wire coat hanger had been left inside? He pulled up one sleeve, bent his arm and tensed it. Yes, he could actually see a little muscle, a bicep, a faint one admittedly, but it definitely made a rounded shape on the top of his arm instead of it just being thin and stick-like. Well, he was swimming a mile and a half every day now, without stopping once! The swim would take him over an hour. Perhaps the exercise really was beginning to have an effect?

He leaned forward peering into the glass and ran his fingers through his hair. It had grown quite long. Surely it was lighter? Had the sun bleached it? His mother's hair was blonde after all. It certainly looked quite a bit paler against his tanned face. Was he really that brown? Well, they had been in the sun for almost three weeks now. He smiled at the tanned face in the mirror. Tomorrow. He was ready. Yes, tomorrow, if it felt right when he got to the magic place.

It was still dark when he woke. He looked at his watch, the fluorescent hands. Just after five-thirty. He didn't put it on as usual. Everything felt different. For one thing his penis was completely flaccid. It was a sign. The first time since he could remember.

He sat up and listened, frozen, to check that no one was awake in the caravan. He mustn't be disturbed. He could say he was going to the toilet, but they would wonder why he was gone so long. Anyway, just a voice, a single word would spoil it. Break the spell. If this really was the day. The day he was to meet 'the one'. The day when all the pain would be over. He knew he mustn't speak to a soul. He must be pure, unsullied, ready. Not even a word.

He pulled on his shorts and tee shirt, felt for his sandals. He had managed somehow to escape from his sleeping bag without unzipping it. There was still the the zip on his tent to deal with, but it performed in perfect silence for him as usual. The sun-tan oil, which he had secretly rubbed into it, seemed to work excellently. He smiled to himself. All was running smoothly. He stood up carefully and stretched his arms way above his head in the dark. Although outside the tent, he noticed, there was already a faint light spreading through the sky. He could just make out the shape of the pine trees towering above him. He thought carefully for a second, then carefully backed out of his sandals. They would make too much noise. In bare feet, he would be able to feel if he were about to tread on a brittle twig. Break it. Make a noise.

The dusty path felt surprisingly cool on his bare feet, even though the air was quite warm. Sometimes he trod on little stones. They hurt, but he didn't care, soon nothing would matter anymore. He knew for certain, but for a second, he stopped still on the familiar path. He really did know, for certain, it was fate, the omens, that if he could get to the island, he would be there, 'the one', but then? What then? He had never allowed his fantasy to continue beyond the moment of meeting. He was saving it for the real thing. Of course there would be sex involved, but then? A boat perhaps? He shook his head. If he let himself think about it like that, it wouldn't happen, it would break the spell! He walked on quite quickly.

He stood staring out into the pale colourless morning. The island was still just a dark shape. It appeared to be so far away, but he knew it wasn't. A little under a mile. He had checked and double checked, measured with his fingers. He had even allowed himself to ask his father's opinion. "Yes, son, a mile I reckon, probably a bit less."

He pulled his tee shirt up over his head, then folded it neatly. He normally never folded anything, but it felt important, part of the ritual, religious almost. He laid it on the rock next to his feet. The rock which normally formed one of the 'arms' of his special morning throne. Next he stepped out of his shorts and added them to the little pile, then stretched his arms above his head. He felt a faint breeze slightly ruffle his pubic hairs. It felt strange. It was the first time, he realised, that he had been totally naked out of doors. It felt wonderful, right. Anyway, it would make the swimming easier. The breeze which was tickling his genitals – his penis was beginning to stir – was having no effect on the sea. Again it was mirror flat. Good, it made the swimming so much easier, even the slightest little swell, splashing in his face, as he came out of the water between each stroke for air, was distracting. It was important that his mind was perfectly clear, focused on his goal. He must 'hold' the spell.

He suddenly remembered something. He bent down and fumbled in the pocket of his shorts for his goggles. He had carefully put them there the night before. He put them on, checked the fit, then pushed them up onto his forehead. It was time. He picked his way gingerly over the sharp rocks at the other side of the pool. He didn't want to cut himself. He wasn't afraid of the pain, the blood, he just didn't want any distraction, and besides he mustn't be marked. For the first time since he could remember – he'd checked thoroughly in the little mirror in the caravan – he didn't have a single spot, or even an insect bite! He mustn't cut himself, he must be perfect, totally unmarked, for 'the one'.

He sat on the edge of a flattish rock, just a few centimetres above the water's edge. Conveniently, there was another perfectly placed rock just beneath his feet, it was going to be much easier to launch himself off than he imagined. From the beach it was easy, but this was the first time from rocks...

He pulled down his goggles, checked them one last time, took a deep breath, then fell forward, gently, silently into the waiting sea. Only once, about fifteen minutes after he had set off, did his confidence waver. He stopped, pulled up his goggles and trod water, suddenly aware of his smallness, just a tiny speck in this huge sea. He looked back at the shore, how strange it looked from where he was. He couldn't of course see the pool now, just the rocks, a pale band above the sea before the dark pines began. He turned back again. Ahead, the island! It seemed suddenly much closer. His confidence flooded back into his body. He wasn't even slightly tired. His practice had worked. He could swim for ever! The sky was rapidly growing lighter; it would soon be dawn; but the island was still, as yet, just a dark silhouette. Suddenly he noticed the shape of a small bird flying across his vision. It was high in the sky, above the island. Its tiny dark shape disappeared behind the dark mass of the tower. Alex waited for it to reappear in the sky on the other side of the tower. It didn't! It must have landed on the tower, maybe on the ledge of that single narrow window. The final omen!

As he reached the island, it seemed much higher than it looked from the opposite shore, from the safety of that perfect semicircular sandy beach. It loomed above him now. He had started to be worried that it might be difficult to get ashore. Of course he shouldn't have done. Right in his line of vision, he saw a small beach, a small steep pebbly beach. Of course it was meant. All part of the pattern.

He dragged himself up out of the water, then slipped back a bit as the pebbles grated and shifted under his weight. He made another effort, then stopped, panting slumped on all fours, head hanging down, forehead touching the wet round little stones. A small solitary figure, slumped panting on a dark pebble beach.

Then suddenly, the magic actually began to happen, as he felt a strengthening new warmth; the first rays across his shoulders. He stood up, stretched, puffed out his chest, threw back his head. Had there been anyone there to see the miracle, the transformation, they would have not seen a tired thin adolescent boy, but a tall young god, a mythical creature, newly spawned by the sea, his slender perfectly proportioned athlete's body flashing gold in the first low blaze of sunlight. A gilded statue from an ancient Greek temple. Idealised youth, a perfect example of healthy young manhood.

He ripped back his goggles and flung them onto the ground. He wouldn't need them now, he knew. He brushed his hair back from his brow with one hand. Had there been a mirror, he would have seen it pale and shining, the colour of ripe corn, in the growing light. He gazed up at the pink stone of the tower, smiled and started on the last, the final part of his quest. His heart was almost bursting with happiness, beating fast, loudly with excitement. He could hear it clearly, like the crashing of waves, it grew louder as he scrambled up the rocky hillside. He kept his head down, to be sure of his footing. He mustn't slip now. He used his hands to pull himself up with the low hard bushes. He stopped halfway to look up for the time. He didn't notice, or feel, the cuts on his hands and legs. His heart leapt! The door! Exactly as he had expected, behind the clump of trees. Not much further to go. Minutes...

*

It was made of wood, pale dry-looking wood, bleached by the sun. Bigger than he expected. It looked very firmly shut, but there was no aparent lock, no keyhole. Perhaps it was bolted from the other side? No, it couldn't be. It was meant. This was the moment. The noise of waves seemed louder.

There was a rusted metal handle on the right-hand side of the door. It looked as if someone had bashed it with a hammer, a rock, it was almost flat against the door. He just managed to squeeze his right hand through it, knuckles wedged tight against the dry wood. He wedged his hand in a little further. The door seemed heavy, solid, he would need a good grip. He put his other hand flat against the wood, braced himself and pushed. The door didn't move at first, but then it suddenly gave way with a lurch. It didn't swing open to the left as he had expected. The hinges had long since rotted away or been stolen, removed. The door fell forward. Alex, hand wedged behind the rusty handle, fell with it, down the high jagged cliff, mouth wide open, but no scream came.

On the white yacht, the Lindemans sat opposite each, hidden behind their newspapers, separated by the debris of their low-fat, high-fibre breakfast.

She was reading the *Daily Mail*. She preferred it to *The Trib.*, the only American newspaper on sale in the newsagents in Bonefaccio. She adjusted her rimless half-glasses and peered at the date on the top of the front page.

"My God, Sheldon, doesn't time fly, it's over three weeks since we were back here. Remember those hideous people from back home came to visit!

"Why in hell I was stupid enough to give them my mobile number? It was the day we set off on our trip round the island..." She paused, nodded in a self-satisfied way and continued. "If you ask me, she should have waited a bit longer for the nose job, until she could have afforded a better one!"

"Shut up, honey, listen, this is terrible, listen." He was reading the local newspaper. He did this every morning, with a dictionary next to him for the difficult words. After all he had all the time in the world now he was retired. "Listen, hon. It's awful, real sad. I think I got it right." He looked up a word in the fat dictionary. "'*The naked bodies of two young men were found at the bottom of a cliff on an island near Porto*

Vecchio'," he read aloud. Then, after poring over the paper for another couple of minutes, "It seems they were exploring some old ruined chateau thing? One boy was only fifteen, it says. English apparently, staying with his parents on a campsite. Shit, they must be devastated. The body of the other guy, they reckon he was eighteen or nineteen, hasn't been identified yet. Shit..."

"And what, I'd like to know, were two teenage boys doing, alone presumably, on an island, with no clothes on, nude! What was going on, that's what I'd like to know?" Mrs Lindeman peered over the top of her rimless half-glasses and over the top of the *Daily Mail* with a knowing look.

"Shut up! For Christ's sake, just shut the hell up for once, woman!"

She was surprised to see her husband's eyes welling with tears.

Fog Over Amsterdam
Jack Dickson

Fog Over Amsterdam
Jack Dickson

That's how it started. How it might end, I'm not quite sure. I can still feel the warmth of his body, curled against mine. Still smell a stranger's blood on my skin. And the number he called in some Netherlands crack lab remains stored in my mobile phone.

Delays of up to eight hours were announced on all flights from Casablanca's Mohammed V airport into Schipol. I was on my way home from Cairo, taking the long way round. At half-seven, the 5.45am languished on the runway, its passengers loaded back off again. The sun was rising in the distance. A harassed-looking blonde rep from KLM was asking for volunteers to give up their seats to 'people with families' and travel the following day. Anyone taking up this offer would be given money, taxi fares and a night in a five-star hotel, with all meals.

I have no great love of 'people with families'. Nor did the thought of identikit so-called luxury in a concrete monstrosity with room service tempt me much. But even if I reached Schipol today, I'd miss my connection. So I nodded to the blonde rep, who relieved me of my boarding pass and baggage ticket then eyed me efficiently. "I shall ensure your luggage is loaded off the flight, sir. Please wait here". Then she was off in a whirl of blue KLM insignia and clacking kitten heels.

Ironically, the flight re-boarded an hour later. My erstwhile travelling companions shuffled back towards Gate 17B. I wondered which already-screaming ankle-biter had the privilege of sitting in my seat. And I wondered who else had been fool enough to fall for that 'eight-hour delay' line.

I'd clocked him earlier, of course. The way you do. Short – an inch or so shorter than me. Slender. A shock of ebony curls. Eyes you could dive into and never come up for air. Dressed in black trousers and matching jacket, and wearing a tight white polo-neck, he could have been my age. He could have been younger, I suppose. Not older, although Arabs keep that dark, dark hair well into their sixties. When

I'd first spotted him, 4am in front of the check-in desk, he held a nylon record bag and the attention of an older, darker-skinned man, to whom he was chatting amiably. Now, he sat smoking, tipping his ash into the base of a large Kentia palm. The record bag was nowhere in sight. Nor was the older, darker-skinned man.

As the departure lounge cleared, we made eye contact across the emptying space. He yawned and smiled. I smiled back then returned to my vigil for the blond KLM rep. Obviously, only two of us – for reasons of our own – had been tempted by a night in Casablanca.

A full four hours after her initial approach, Ms KLM reappeared. "Mister Dickson? Mr 'Arris?"

His name surprised me. Maybe I'd picked it up wrong: he didn't look of mixed parentage. We both stood up.

She smiled her airline smile: "Follow me. Everything has been arranged," and marched off, kitten heels clacking.

I looked at him. He looked at me. He yawned a 'what have we let ourselves in for?' yawn. I grinned and we followed.

Everything had been arranged. It was merely that, like life in general, time beats to a different drum in Morocco. She escorted us back through Immigration Control. I scrutinised the *Casablanca Police* stamp on my passport, thinking this would all make an interesting after-dinner story. In her tiny office on the main concourse, she issued new tickets, fended phone calls and faxes while talking on her mobile in French. From time to time, she and Mr Harris babbled in Arabic, punctuated by his yawns.

The sight of her silver-grey mobile nudged my conscience: I should really phone home, let them know what was going on. As ever, my wife had her phone switched off. I left a message. "Stuck in Casa overnight, sweetie. Give me a ring back when you get this."

As I disconnected, Mr Harris was frowning at his own, somewhat antique model. He raised it to his ear, shook it, raised it again then peered at it.

"No signal?" Finnish technology never lets you down: I'd made calls via mine from inside pyramids.

He rolled those dark, liquid eyes. "Charge is low." His English was good, and American-accented. Which for some reason surprised me. I held out the Nokia. "Be my guest."

He took it with a smile and punched in a series of digits.

"Mister Dickson?" Kitten Heels' razor voice took my attention. I looked away to concentrate on what she was saying, while Mr Harris rattled on in Dutch, in the background.

"I give you the taxi money. You and Mister 'Arris will be travelling together today and tomorrow morning, yes?"

I nodded. Slender brown fingers sat the Nokia back in front of me. I always look for wedding bands. But on Mr Harris's left hand the only decoration was a chunky silver pinkie ring.

"Now..." Ms KLM opened a drawer in her desk and produced a cash box. Opening the cash box, she withdrew a stack of Moroccan Dirhams, secured by a somewhat perished rubber band, "... two thousand each. For inconvenience."

It sounded a fortune, but I knew it wasn't. Mr Harris looked at me. We exchanged smiles.

She counted out our Dirhams and I felt like a schoolboy with his allocation of pocket money.

"Lunch, dinner and breakfast at the Casablanca Holiday Inn, Mister Dickson – five-star hotel." She moved to her fax machine, which had been spewing vigorously since our arrival.

I watched her tear off a section of paper. Mr Harris was flicking through his Dirhams, black eyes shining. Maybe it was a lot, if you lived in Casablanca. I wondered, for the first time, if he did.

"Please show this at reception..." She handed us each an A4-sized sheet, "... now I shall book your taxi and we shall be all set." She leant back in her chair and smiled. Phones were still ringing. Someone else was talking over my shoulder, enquiring about flights to New York. As far as Kitten Heels was concerned, one problem – that is, us – had been disposed of. Then Harris spoke to her in Arabic.

The smile faded. She rattled something back.

He stood up and moved towards the door. My hand settled on the sleeve of his black jacket and for the first time I touched him. "What's up?"

He looked at me. "Don't you want your bag?"

You travel as much as I do, you learn to ignore your luggage. My battered Adidas sports bag had, accordingly, slipped my mind completely. As I rose to join him, he shook his head. "Give me your... baggage ticket... I shall find both."

It seemed a kind gesture. I fumbled for the information in the pocket of my jacket and held it out. "It's big, black... it has Adidas in white on the..."

"I shall find it. You wait here for the taxi." He moved seamlessly from the room, leaving me with Kitten Heels and the guy who wanted a flight to New York.

Midday came and went. Mohammed V began to look more like a North African port of transit. Moving out onto the concourse to smoke, all human life paraded past: women in burkas dragging kids, women in miniskirts with laptops, men in everything from joggy bottoms to pristine white sheiks. But no Mr Harris.

A new travelling companion made his presence felt – impatience. I debated just leaving then and there: if Casablanca baggage-handlers wanted to keep my luggage till the next day, it saved me the trouble of carting it into the city and back. But I couldn't leave. I had the taxi money. I couldn't just... abandon Harris. So I set off to look for him.

While the rest of the world is tightening its security arrangements, Mohammed V airport is moving in the opposite direction. Passport and stilted explanation at the ready, I paused at the Khalashnikov'd guard who lounged at the exit to Baggage Reclaim. He smiled and waved me through: my white face, I suppose.

Scanning the area, my eyes paused at the service counter, around which a gaggle of passengers were verbally harassing the overworked clerk in a variety of languages. Still no Mr Harris. Then I spotted him. He was standing alone and smoking, eyes focused on the one moving luggage carousel. Perched on top, a jade green Samsonite made its languid progress in and out of view.

I wandered over. He addressed me before I could open my mouth: "They say our luggage may be lost..." His eyes never left the carousel. "... or out on the runway, somewhere. They do not know where it is. They're not even sure it came off the flight."

I tried a shrug. "KLM have lost it, it's their responsibility to compensate us..." I remembered the light in his eyes at those thousands of Dirhams, "... screw some more money out of Blondie back there and..."

He turned. "I need that bag." For a moment, a different light shone in those dark, bottomless eyes. Then it was gone. He smiled, and I noticed the tar stains on his otherwise immaculate teeth. "You're right – let KLM pay us more." He yawned, and unexpectedly rested an elbow on my shoulder. "Man, I need to catch up on my sleep!"

We got an extra 500 Dirhams each – about four pounds sterling. Mr Harris seemed pleased. Seeing us together, our taxi-driver presumed he was my 'guide' and, accordingly, directed all comments to him. Harris, on the other hand, had taken to addressing me as 'Jaques', although where he caught a glimpse of my passport I have no idea. Although I sat in the back, he made a point of talking in English. I had heard him converse in at least four other languages so far, but English was the one tongue our driver didn't seem to speak.

"He's asking me if you're a good tipper." His dark head swivelled round. "If you have a lot of money, and if you are worth..." He groped momentarily for the phrase. "... ripping off?"

I laughed, catching our driver's mercenary eyes in the mirror. "And what are you telling him?"

"I told him you are paying for me to stay with you at a five-star hotel..." He grinned, "... and that any money to be made from you is mine."

I continued to laugh, enjoying our bond at the expense of the preconceptions of others. I paid the driver from the bundle of Dirhams the KLM rep had given us. And this sense of playing with expectations continued in the Holiday Inn's reception.

The interior was mock-Moroccan. The staff were local, to a man, the guests either western or Japanese. They looked at Mr Harris like he'd be more at ease serving in the restaurant. But he charmed them – the way he'd charmed Ms KLM, and the taxi-driver, and everyone else I'd seen him with since we'd met, just a few hours earlier. In his black jacket and white polo neck, he seemed every inch the urbane cosmopolitan traveller.

A beautiful blond couple in Martinique joined our lift at the fifth floor. They addressed each other in low, cool voices and got out at the ninth. Harris yawned. "Dutch. You can always tell. The Dutch look like they never sweat."

As did he. I smiled. "You know the Netherlands well?" I'd yet to discover if his cancelled flight earlier that day was business or pleasure.

"I work in Amsterdam – should have started back..." He consulted what could have been a Rolex but was probably a fake, "... four hours ago. But I arranged for a colleague to cover for me."

So the phone-call had been not to a wife or a lover. But a place of work. Casablanca. Amsterdam. Even then my mind knew there was a link. Superficially, the two cities were light-years apart. On a deeper level, the connection was obvious.

The lift pinged. The doors slid seamlessly apart and we got out.

Beyond the token paid to indigenous styling, the interior of the Casablanca Holiday Inn is identical to a hundred other Holiday Inns in a hundred different cities. Bland. Faceless. Shabbily identikit and not even particularly luxurious. With its sad-looking doorman and *faux*-marble foyer, it was another of those hermetically sealed bubbles favoured by travellers who wished to pick at a foreign land, as one would do a Greek starter, rather than throw oneself into the entrée.

But shabby or not, it was impressing someone.

Mr Harris ran the pads of his nicotine-stained fingers along the faded flock wallpaper as I searched for our rooms. His eyes were child-wide and he'd managed to stop yawning. I watched him, hiding a smile at his obvious fascination. A drugs dealer who'd never seen the inside of a five-star hotel? The clothes spoke of a role fairly high up the distribution system. The awe said he was some poor mule, lugging unprocessed kif to the next link in the chain.

I found our rooms. He was still taking in the lampshades and carpets, neither of which looked liked they'd seen a cleaning hand in quite a while.

I gave him his pass-card. "Listen – you want to freshen up and we can maybe catch lunch?"

He yawned again and ran a hand through oil-black curls. "All I want to do right now is catch up on my sleep." My disappointment must have been obvious. Because he smiled, "Dinner?"

My cock twitched like a teenager's. "Seven?"

He nodded, eyes moving from his pass-card to the slot in the door to his room.

I grinned and took it from him, wondering what or who had kept him up so late the previous night. As I unlocked his door for him, his mobile rang noisily somewhere about his person. He rolled his eyes and waited till it stopped.

Fifteen minutes later I had washed, pissed and set off to find toothpaste in Casablanca, on a Sunday.

For the next five hours he flitted in and out of my mind. I found toothpaste, and for some reason bought two tubes, along with two toothbrushes, two individual disposable razors and a rusting, overpriced can of Gillette shaving foam. I found cheap cotton underwear and a knockoff Umbro polo shirt, then wandered around the Place des Nations Unies, smiling at the children with their balloons and the ancient Berber men selling tea.

I shaved. I showered. I sprawled on the king-sized bed, flipping between Al Jazira and CNN and thinking about Mr Harris less than six feet away, through the wall. Seven pm on the dot, I was outside his room, clutching duplicate toothbrush, toothpaste and razor and rapping on the flimsy surface. Beyond the door, his mobile was ringing again.

Dressed only in black underpants, he eventually appeared, still rubbing sleep from those pool-like eyes. "Five minutes?" Before I could reply, he staggered back into the gloom, beckoning me.

Watching that slender, coffee-coloured body merge with the dark, I knew he could take as long as he wanted. But he was surprisingly efficient. With the curtains still closed, I only enjoyed the briefest of glimpses of him as he dressed. His lack of self-consciousness surprised me. The unexpected intimacy with someone I'd known less than eight hours struck me as unusual. He switched on the bedside lamp and grabbed the fake Rolex. In the light's dim glow, the small handgun beside his pillow wasn't so unexpected. The fact that he slipped it into his pocket, seconds later, was.

In the restaurant, dinner was everything I have come to expect from five-star chains. The only dish they couldn't ruin was the *harira*. We ate our spicy lentil soup and he told me about himself.

He'd been born and raised in Casablanca. His family still lived here. Ten years earlier he'd moved to the Netherlands to work, and had been home for the weekend, to see his mother. It was every cliché in the book. "It is cheaper from me to come visit my family, than for them to visit me. And I can help them out..." He fumbled for the word, "... financially."

I nodded, smiling at the dutiful son and trying to work out how old that made him. "You get home often?"

"Twice a month." The black jacket had been removed and the tight white polo neck clung to his slender body like lycra. "It is very..." He searched for the word, "... handy to have KLM. Everyone at Schipol knows my face."

I smiled, watching long muscles stretch and flex beneath the white as he reached for more bread.

The main course arrived. I poked at, then ignored it. Harris wired into what could have been beef but was probably camel. "You are not English I think, Jaques?" He looked at me, a mouth full of food.

His French pronunciation of my name made me feel like someone else. "No, not English."

He munched on, nodding. "Irish?"

I smiled, catching the waiter's eye and pointing to our empty glasses. "Scottish – Glasgow."

"Ah... *Braveheart*!"

I was still laughing when the waiter appeared with two more *Flags*. Beyond, the restaurant was starting to fill up. A party of what had to be German Saga tourists trickled in. A few guys on their own. A woman dressed like Isadora Duncan. The mixture was eclectic, very Casa.

"'Arris!" The shout was gruff and came from behind.

I glanced round. A tall well-built man in a leather jacket was striding across the room towards us.

Mr Harris stood up. They embraced warmly, and immediately began to talk in fast, Moroccan Arabic. At the first pause in the words, I made a motion for the guy to join us. He eyed me curiously, looked at Harris then nodded curtly when my dining companion introduced me in English. Not privy to his name, I sipped my *Flag* as their conversation dipped in volume and they moved away. The stranger produced an envelope from the inside pocket of his jacket. Harris took it, slipped it into the inside pocket of his own. Then, as abruptly as he'd appeared, the well-built Arab embraced Harris a second time, before striding off towards the lift.

"Sorry about that..." Harris rejoined me at the table.

"No problem." I pushed my plate away. It was immediately seized and removed by a hovering waiter. "Your friend should have stayed – I'm sure KLM would stretch to dinner for three."

"That was my brother." His mouth laughed. "And he had plans." Those pool-like eyes remained fixed on the closing doors of the lift, and I found myself further intrigued.

By nine we'd finished and moved into the bar, to spend the rest of KLM's expenses money. Or rather, I did, since payment for the over-priced *Flags* seemed to be my prerogative. We talked about Cairo and my love of North Africa. He told me Egypt was a powder keg, and Mubarek would join Nasser any year now. We decided, in the light of events in the US, he was probably right. The conversation meandered onto nepotistic lines. Harris talked about his family, and his plan to get his brother Salem a job in Amsterdam.

"Casa's great..." He leant back in a plushly upholstered chair, apparently more at ease now in his five-star surroundings, "... if you've got money."

In the background, a white-jacketed, dark-skinned pianist played show songs on a baby grand in need of tuning. I almost expected Rick to appear from somewhere, or to see Ilsa draped over a stool at the quiet bar.

"Money can buy you anything here..." He tugged a Duty Free Marlboro from a soft packet and stuck it between full lips.

My hand fled for my lighter.

"... but no money?" He continued to talk as I lit his cigarette. "No hope." He smiled at me, over the flame.

I thought of him and his family. Of the missing luggage. Of the mysterious work in Amsterdam and the more intriguing envelope from well-built Salem. And the gun. Was it the atmosphere? The smell of mint tea? My imagination? Maybe he worked in an Amsterdam bulb-packing plant and was merely paranoid about muggings. "Think you can get your brother a job?"

He exhaled and nodded. "Anyone can do the work. It's not..." He searched once more, "... rocket-science."

I grinned at the idiom. "What is it you do, in Amsterdam?" My curiosity wouldn't leave it alone.

The briefest of frowns creased the corners of his eyes. "I am in... how do you say it? Farm... farma..."

"Pharmaceuticals?" I supplied, in a low voice.

His face lit up. He laughed. "Yes – pharmaceuticals!"

The merest shiver trembled through my groin. This after-dinner story was going to be better than I'd expected: my night with a Moroccan drugs' mule.

He leant back further in his chair and smoked. I mirrored the movement. Because I was going to spend the night with him. Of that there was no doubt in my mind.

Eleven pm came and went. We talked about Scotland. His linguistic skills. The fact that the mini-bar in both our rooms was locked. Our hands brushed several times. As did our knees. He'd taken to resting one foot against my ankle, under the table. And moving it occasionally to rub against my calf. All the signals were blaring. Just before midnight, he looked at his wrist. "Would you like to meet my mother?"

It wasn't the most unexpected question I'd ever been asked. But it had to be up there in the top five. I laughed. "What, now?"

He stood up. "I promised I'd drop by – she'll be home by now." He struggled into his jacket. "If you'd rather get some sleep it's..."

"No, no..." I joined him on my feet, tossing a hundred Dirham note onto our table, by way of a tip. If the way into his pants was through his mother, that's how it would be.

The twenty-minute bus journey cost about ten pence. Harris seemed to know both the driver and a fair number of our fellow passengers. My white face stood out, a smear of cream on coffee. A number of mobile phones rang. Twice, they were Harris's. Night was falling as the streets became wider, the buildings more modern. And more ramshackle.

Mrs Harris – for want of anything better to call her – was tiny and smiling. She embraced us both as sons and addressed me in excellent French. The reason for our visit became apparent. Harris handed her the bulk of his KLM expenses-money. I felt like an impostor as she sat fragrant dishes in front of us, and enquired if we were hungry.

Thanks to the Holiday Inn's cuisine, I was. We ate. Several small children clustered around Harris, who ruffled their hair and crushed small denomination notes into their grubby hands. On the far side of the room, an elderly man sat glued to a Moroccan soap opera in which light-skinned women broke the hearts of swarthy men in dark husky voices.

The *thé de menthe* flowed like water. Tiny glasses of some clear and vicious grain spirit appeared. The taste of the mint was flavouring everything. I have no idea what we talked about. Various family members and neighbours appeared to meet the Scottish guest. I was kissed and hugged, my hand seized in a myriad grips. In his pristine white polo neck, Harris caught my eye several times. I tried to read the glances but my vision was starting to swim. At some point, I saw him pass the envelope to the elderly man in front of the television. I would have wondered why his brother hadn't delivered it himself, if my brain had been in a state to wonder.

More hugging. More kissing. Mrs Harris called me *mon fils* and wished me *bon voyage*. Next thing I knew the wind was in my hair and we were back on the dark streets. An arm looped itself around my waist. Somehow, my own found his.

With the sound of children's voices fading, I pushed Harris against a wall and held him there with my body. He seemed very small and warm, his mouth minty. His cock was hard against my hip. Or it could have been the gun. I wanted him then and there. With the smell of rotting vegetables and the Atlantic wind beating at my back. He pulled his mouth from mine and kissed my neck: "We have rooms. We should use them." The words were a breathy whisper on my skin.

So when the first taxi appeared, back on what passed for a main road, I hailed it and kept my hand in his crotch on the journey to the Holiday Inn.

Naked, he took my breath away. His cock was uncut and thick. He wouldn't let me use a condom. "I want to feel your seed inside me," he murmured, as I gripped the back of his smooth neck and pushed myself into his taut, dark hole. At some point during the second fuck, my hand moved back to his cock and he came while I was in him. Rearing up and back, I met my own eyes in the mirror above his bed. His moans filled my ears. His dark body writhed beneath mine.

Later, we dozed, our legs tangled in a sticky soup of spunk and sweat. I was just about to drop off when his mobile rang. "Leave it." I kissed his hair and reached for him.

With a surprising strength he wriggled free and bounded across the room. I lit a cigarette and sighed. The Arabic was fast and breathless. And I somehow knew what was coming.

He turned, lifting the Rolex from where he'd sat it two hours previously. "The taxi will call back at 4am…" He smiled. "You should really get some sleep."

The message was clear. My cock still tacky and sore from him, I returned the smile and dressed. He accompanied me to the door, kissed me one last time. "See you in three hours, Jaques."

Fifteen minutes later, back in my own room, I heard the door to his open. Then close.

I don't know where he went or who he met. But I know what he did. An hour later, soft knocking at my door woke me from a post-coital sleep. He stumbled into my room, a black rucksack over his shoulder. I thought he was drunk. When he threw up in the bathroom and I saw the blood on his white polo, my mind flew to the gun. I held his head as semi-digested globs of what could have been beef but was probably camel sloshed around the toilet bowl. I tried to remember how to treat bullet-wounds. He peeled off the polo neck and began to wash it in cold water. His dark skin was greasy with sweat but undamaged.

His hands shook. The sink slowly filled with reddening water. I gripped his bare beautiful shoulders as he rinsed and rinsed again.

Finally, I made him sit on the toilet with his head between his knees while I draped the sopping polo neck over the shower rail and cleaned up the mess.

Neither of us said anything. As I slept with my arms around him, sirens screamed somewhere beyond the Holiday Inn's hermetically sealed windows.

At 3.58am, we stood in the Holiday Inn's foyer, waiting for our taxi. Harris was yawning again. But at least he'd stopped shaking, and the white polo-neck was dry.

At 5am check-in, there was a message for me, from Ms KLM: our bags had been located and would be waiting for us at Amsterdam. I wandered over to where I'd left Harris, and found him deep in conversation. The middle-aged guy with the steel-rimmed glasses laid a hand on the shoulder of the black jacket and leaned in closer. I smiled, caught Harris's eye then joined the end of the queue, wondering if he'd check his rucksack through.

When he joined me for a coffee, sometime later, I saw he was still carrying it. I told him the good news about our luggage. He seemed happy. We talked of general things, seated either side of the small table. It was one of those morning-after conversations where most of the magic has burned off, like fog over Amsterdam. To tell the truth, I was happy we hadn't been given adjacent seats on the flight. And it had nothing to do with the sex or the blood. Or the gun.

On the plane, I watched the middle-aged man with the steel-rimmed glasses buy Harris drinks. Three hours later, we touched down at Schipol.

Back in Europe, security was tighter than ever. As Ms KLM had promised, his record bag and my black Adidas hold-all were waiting in the Baggage Reclaim attendant's office. Beside the luggage carousel, I spoke to him for the last time.

"Good luck, eh?"

"And to you too, Jaques." He grinned, yawned and threw the record bag's strap over one shoulder. We shook hands like the night ships we were and I headed off to the Gents. Just in case.

In a locked cubicle, I unzipped my rucksack. The gun was shoved down in between a tube of toothpaste and yesterday's underwear. I removed it, slipped it into my pocket and unlocked the door. After washing my hands and the small firearm, I wrapped the gun in paper towels and pushed it into the wastepaper bin. I didn't blame Harris.

I'd probably have done the same myself. Then I made a short call on my Nokia.

I have no idea what he had in that record bag. Or the rucksack he'd acquired after he'd shot whoever he'd shot, earlier that morning. If anything. But since September 11th, no one likes to take any chances. By the time I reached 'Customs', Schipol airport police were already acting on 'information received', as it is invariably described. Harris's luggage was open on a counter. A pair of officials were going through it. Another two, both armed, stood either side of him. Some people stared. Others, like me, walked quietly through, glad it was someone else. I could hear his quietly protesting Dutch. He sounded calm enough, if a little bemused.

In a concourse Benetton, I slipped the package I'd collected in Cairo to my usual contact. From there it would pass to one of our cells, somewhere on mainland Europe. From there, it's in the hands of God.

"la ilaaha il – lal – laah"

But every time I stop over at Mohammed V, I still think about Mr Harris.

Making the Miami A-List
Neal Drinnan

Making the Miami A-List
Neal Drinnan

It always gets me how guys in America have those names. It's like everyone is named after a movie star, a state, a geographical feature or some hippy-shit affirmation from the seventies. How is it every time you meet someone in a bar you know their name'll be Kiefer Loas, Garland Wells or Courage Hurtz. Never just Peter or David like in Australia.

In California they'll tell you Peter is really bad numerologically – 'it doesn't kick ass in anumerological way'. So I guess if you come from an uninspired American home-town and you have one of those regular names, you change it. Then you'll be someone new? When you arrive in California or Miami. Well, new for about fifteen minutes.

South Beach Miami, 1990 something. Bella's sick in our room, there are no medical clinics open anywhere and the woman at the hospital laughed in our face. "Sure, Honey, you can see a doctor but it's gonna cost you three hundred dollars to walk through that door and another hundred for the pleasure of seein' the man, so jus' how sick are you, girl?"

Me, I never bothered to recover from my jet lag, it was a malaise too but a more surreal one than the flu. I was awake all night, asleep half the day. The August sun melted me – daily – into a pool of my own stinking Crisco. "Why'd we have to stay so close to Bar Hombre, Bella? You know I'll be round there just as soon as that bowl o' butter sizzles into that wild wild west." She coughed. "Your cocaine beckons, fresh from the farm, Sugar."

She peers out the window as if she can see Columbia in the distance, then she sneers as a limo crawls past our hotel blaring Kenny G. I know that smile, we often share it. She used it when she shamelessly released her tits from her Astro Boy halter-neck at the Disney Parade, she used it when she left ketchup-drenched napkins, spilled Diet Coke, cigarette butts and disgusting cheeseburger waste in the monorail that ran from The Epcott Centre to Disneyworld. That smile and those eyes say 'America is trash but we love it, don't we

Boyo'. Bel has already shot five rolls of film in Disneyworld. She wants to do an exhibition of fat people eating junk food called 'Enough Already'.

When she gets better she's going to start on Trailer Parks – she wants me to find her some. Now she makes sad *Camille* eyes at me. "Go. I know there are some Cuban boys just dying to meet you," she throws her head back dramatically, she fancies she's Tallulah Bankhead. "I'll be fine. You go on ahead." Cough, cough. She's my kind of martyr.

The truth is she's the one who was doing the Cuban boys before I even arrived. She had the neighbourhood sussed right out. She knew what the queer boys were up to, way before me. "They're all going to some hu-u-uge party in Fort Lauderdale where Ru Paul or some shit is playing – loads of drugs, you name it – but don't go up, word is tix are sold out and you're lookin' down the barrel of $200 for a scalper ticket. As soon as the party's over they all head straight down to South Beach – we're talking sex on the streets. I'm told the boys are walkin' barely talkin' lolly pops and half the bulge they carry in their trousers is their C-O-K-E stash. It's gonna be no place for chicks."

Bella was right. I had left her for these party zombies. I had been taking candy from strangers, stepping into shadowy men's cars for snorts of coke; what would Mumma say? Teeny little baby snorts fresh in from across the border – "Leedle beet goes long way, Hombre".

That's when I met Skipper. I didn't ask "why Skipper?" He was blonde, 26 and Californian. His Mom and Dad had made millions out of *in vitro* fertilisation programs and designer babies. I guess he was an early model. He had strayed, played and ultimately stayed in Miami after some spectacular summer of love several years ago. God knows what the truth was with Skip. He "fuckin digs surfing man" yet there's no surf for miles. He was "going places", yet he shared a low-life hotel room at the Kabana Manana with a junkie-bouncer called Zolar. Skip carried a little more weight than he should have but was still doin' Twinkie like he was twenty.

When I was coked, he was cool, or so I must have thought. Coke kept the tragedy of it all at bay. His transient life seemed the way-to-go and that edgy, neurotic bouncer who pretended like he owned him seemed like an integral part of the side-show. Miami is a long way to go for pure stuff, but hey, who needs beautiful natural surroundings when the coke's so wild it can make John Goodman look like Keaneu

Reeves. The more coke Skipper got into him the more kid-like he became. "You like my big cock, sure you do. You wanna fuck my tight ass? You can't wait can you pussy-boy." He'd ask me his questions, or someone's questions, heard on a thousand porn videos. Then he'd answer on my behalf. My own coke rushes rendered me less than charitable, but more, or less, his porn equal. Somehow I held back from saying "you wanna suck some Aussie cock or eat out some downunder boy-pussy?"

Skipper had the fidgets big time. "Give him special K to slow him down. Give him more coke if you don't want him gettin' bored," groaned Zolar from behind a body-building magazine in the corner of the room. Zolar had promised he was going to work in ten minutes – a half-fucking-hour ago. "He kinda digs watching, he gets me really pissed but he's cool," whispered Skip.

Skipper's got his ass in my face, hoping I'll do some eating but I'm not hungry right now so he gives up. He's going through the pocket of his jeans and pulls out a xeroxed invite to some sex party. "Gotta be cute to go to this," he says with pride, his blue eyes looking even more dark and ringed now. I try to stick my finger up his ass, it's kind of open and it looks like it could use something, but he reiterates what he'd said before – "only cock up there goddamn it. You can eat it or fuck it but that's all."

He's pouting like a kid and I can't help annoying him because he's been after my money the whole time – more money than he's worth – but I'm having fun.

He gurgles something, "A-list fuckin' queens, you know what I'm saying."

"What are you saying Skipper, what are you saying, cutie?"

"Don't you even have A-list queens in Orrrstralia."

"Sure we do."

"Well, that's who'll be there."

"Different ones, I expect."

"Well, a different A-list."

"What did I jus' say, fuckin' A-list queens'll be there."

"Yes, but not the same A-list that we have in Australia."

He looked blankly at me, "You're a dumb fuck, I gotta tell ya. Are we goin' to this sex part-ay or are we gonna look at that ugly bouncer, 'til I'm sick to my stomach?"

The bouncer threw a sock at Skipper, who smelt it. "That is sooo gross," he whined in his best Valley boy.

The invitation had a picture of a flamingo with its head buried in a bucket of cocaine and some grainy porn shots of someone being fucked from behind. It didn't look like an A-list invite to me, but what the heck. I'd had me enough of Skipper's ass anyway.

"You got money for a cab?"

"Sure," I say pulling my pants up.

"I'm ready for part-ay action," said Skipper, still covered with lube but pulling his clothes straight over the top. "Sticky me," he said with an ass wiggle.

Skipper had no money. I'd worked that out over the past couple of days. The bouncer paid for the room and I knew if I was to be honoured with the company of this tarnished dream-boy, I'd have to fund all our excursions.

"I shoulda put some of that moisture crap on my face," he said in a lucid moment of self-realisation. "You're fine," I said, moistening my finger with saliva and reaching over to rub a smear of dry cum from the section of belly that peeked out from beneath the crumpled Versace T-shirt he'd found on the beach right outside Versace's house.

"Maybe he'll be there," I said.

"Who?" he snapped with a sudden venom that made me hope that bucket o' coke was still happening when we got to the party.

"Versace, of course."

"Huhh, in your dreams Aussie boy – I know dudes who've tricked with him."

"I don't wanna fuck him," I said.

"Are you outa your mind! He is a god, he could fuck me any time, even without a condom."

I thought back over the several hours of trashy sex we'd already done and there had been no insistence on me wearing a condom during that. Now he was making it look like a rare privilege bestowed only on *nouveau* Miami aristocrats. Suddenly I felt emotional, like crying. "I'm too sensitive for this game," I thought as the chemicals turned on me for a moment. My poor Californian *in vitro* heir had already squandered his fortunes and was now pretending he possessed them to squander once more. The poignancy was almost too much to bear.

I look at the T-shirt – the pink stain near the V came from a strawberry shake I'd bought him earlier. "He's a messy pup," I'm thinking, "inside and out."

"Here's the joint," he yells, looking at the screwed-up piece of paper, trying to check the address. He spits some gum into the invitation, screws it up and drops it on the floor of the cab. "Thank you driver," he adds real sweetly, while I try to make sure I'm handing over a twenty-dollar bill, not a fifty.

"I don't think this is Madonna, Versace or Calvin Klein's house somehow. Do you?" I spare him the humiliation of bringing up the A-list thing again.

The house is a bleak little bungalow with S&M garden gnomes and there's a trailer park at the end of the street which I must tell Bella about. Storm clouds are swirling all about and from inside we can hear a few low pornographic rumbles and some sort of creaking sound.

The door is open so we wander in.

There are three men watching a porno on a brown Draylon three-seater. Two of them toy joylessly with flaccid, depleted-looking cocks while the other expressionless dude slaps his semi-engorged monster of a thing from one thigh to another. Slap-slap it goes, and Skipper watches it for a minute then turns to me. "Slap-slap," he says. He looks at the guy and drawls "Yes Sir, I'll have me some of that donkey dick," then he wanders into the next room. I contemplate the other boys on the couch. One looks Puerto Rican, but he doesn't look like he's dying to meet me. I wonder where the bucket o' coke is, but leave vulgar questions like that for my companion to ask. After fifteen minutes of watching a film about two fourteen-year-olds fucking near a motel swimming pool and listening to the slap-slap of Mr Personality's cock, I went in search of Skipper.

Each room down the hall harboured some sort of lurid action; the first contained the obligatory middle-aged queen strung up in a leather and chain harness, his ass a creamy yawning cauliflower of Crisco and fist. The chains were swinging and creaking, in time to his monotonous moans. I smiled at him in a way that conveyed an acknowledgment of his hunger but a failure, at that moment, to share his appetite. There was a black-plastic-sheeted room with dim lights, eager writhing torsos and the fragrant hint of urine and poppers lingering in the ether. The last room had a bed, a weight station and a Versace T-shirt hanging from the door knob.

My boy was busy, working as hard as he could. His face was crimson, his Joey Stefano bubble-butt stretched to the max. "Meth," he whispered to me with a hint of helplessness – or defeat – in his voice.

"Crystal Meth." I looked behind him and saw two guys struggling to stay inside him – it was awkward but they were managing. I felt my own cock stir but short of taking crystal myself, not much was going to happen. I was feeling very clear-headed. I reached gently to touch the cocks as they squirmed and duelled for dominance in Skipper's insatiable ass. "You're one greedy assed, drug-fucked doll-baby, aintcha?" grunted one of his intruders.

"Unghghg," was all Skip could muster.

My fingers touched the balls, the greasy, hairless bases of the battling shafts. I felt along them into my friend's ass and, discreetly, I moved behind him to whisper something to the eager sires. "Would you like to put a rubber on while you fuck my friend?"

I may as well have called the fire department. "Who brought the fuckin' Orssie? Hey Dude, we're partying in here – you don't like it, you don't gotta stay." So I didn't. I wandered out to the brown couch and tuned into *The Simpsons* because the other guys had vanished and the porn vid had finished, leaving white static dots on black velvet oblivion.

In the bedroom Skipper's ass and perception stretched as far as they could. I imagined him flying. Arms stretched over the Florida Keys, the freeways, shopping malls and gas stations. He flew over the deserts, canyons and oil refineries back to the safety of his home. But he couldn't land when he wanted to. He felt something hot and wet running down his legs – hot cum, excess lube, wet shit. Who could say. Tears welled and burned his eyes because he could not land anywhere any more. He'd left all that safety behind.

Suddenly the tears turn to hot-hot-wow, his drugs are working again. These guys are seriously partying – taking him apart – worshipping him – Skip, Skip, Skipper. Every hue of every color in the great American dream washes over him. He's a movie star, an astronaut, the goddamn President of the United Fucking States. Music thunders from the stereo – *I love Am-er-ica* – and he opens that sultry meat oven of his ass as wide as he can to catch all the exciting possibilities. Skip smiles as the frayed web of his mind acts like a dream-catcher. "Work hard sweet blonde boy, you'll be what you want – an interior designer – a rock star – the dude who announces airplanes at Miami airport." He thinks these things as color and heat pump through him like magical crystals and the song blows his fucking mind.

I find him his T-shirt. We can't go back to his hotel because the bouncer is doing something gross, illegal and secret. We can't go to mine because Bella is sick or maybe that Cuban boy is around protecting her from the crack dealers who painted the room next door with their own shit. Or maybe I just don't want him there.

"I'm hungry," he whines. "I wanna stay at The Delano."

I want to stay at The Delano too, though I'm not sure I want to stay there with Skipper. He looks pretty wasted and smells a mite whiffy. He wants hosing down. "What the Hell," I think as I get us a room and we wander across the marble floors to the lifts. We walk past Amazon women who seems to walk on glass stilettos and are accompanied by two Great Danes on diamond-studded leashes. Skipper looks like a very trashy bit of street hustle now. He looks as though he's been in a car wreck or beaten up but he's so out of it he doesn't care. "Get in the bath," I say when we arrive at the room.

"I want food."

"You want room service?"

"No, I want something from the diner." Skipper only likes food from the gleaming silver diner so I will have to go and get it. He's lying in the bath smoking a crushed cigarette.

"I wanna strawberry mailed, Cajun fries and a breakfast burger – you got that?" He waves his hand dismissively and laughs at how he's lording it over dumb-fuck me.

"I got it," I say, but I'm getting over "it" too. He's not the catch he imagines himself to be.

In fact, at this point, I am definitely the prettier boy.

I think about this as I walk the five blocks to the diner and wait half an hour for his food. I take it back to the hotel. He's nodded off in the bath, with the remains of the cigarette packet floating on the top of the soapy-oily water. I leave the food there, go down to the lobby and pay for the room. I have a chill at the thought of him drowning, then another at the thought of him trashing the room or spending five drug-fucked hours on the phone to LA. I have spent hundreds of dollars in twenty-four hours; he's a bottomless pit, unlike my credit card.

In the lobby of my real hotel, Bella sips a cocktail. She's 'all better' having found a Cuban doctor who 'works outside of the American health care system'. We both smile at the oxymoron. "You smell of sex and fast food," she says as she kisses me. Suddenly one of the crack dealers comes head first down the stairs into the lobby. The Texan bar girl says, "Lordy, Lordy, here we go again." We sit at the bar while a gunman drags the bloody figure out and bundles him into a waiting car. I look to Bella. "I thought they would have been kicked out after the shit-painting episode." Renée-Beth, the bar girl, gives me one of her 'I'm telling you this in confidence' expressions. "I think there was a lot of money involved there, hon." She moves closer, her voice a whisper. "The other guys, the ones from New York, raped two girls last night – and no one's saying a word." I look to Bella in confusion, she makes like she's zipping her mouth up. I'm perplexed and Bella says, "they settled out of court". She looks at Renée-Beth who is her "best friend" now and they are nodding their heads in unison. "If I lived here, Renée-Beth, I'd get me one of those darling little pearl-handled guns like that prostitute had who we saw last night."

"I know, I love those ones too – you know they fit in the smallest pocketbook." She looks at Bella's ample bust. "You know you could even keep it in your brassière." She reaches over and touches the cup of Bel's bra. I look at Bel and raise my eyebrows.

One of Bella's Cuban boys appears outside and leans against the balcony with his skateboard. Bella pretends not to see him. I realise I haven't slept for days. "I'm going by-byes, girls."

"What happened to that 'Gilligan' or whatever his name was?"

"Oh, we broke up."

"How'd he take it?"

"Up the ass, Bel, always up the ass."

She screws her nose up and crosses her legs. She looks at Renée-Beth. "Boys are yucky sometimes." Renée-Beth nods in agreement. The Cuban boy loiters on the steps, skateboard under his arm. "Bella's still sick, Carlos baby, maybe you come again tomorrow," says Bel, dismissing him in her momsy voice. She turns to Renée-Beth, "Maybe we can go to that Miss Thing bar tonight?"

"Sure we can, Hon," says Renée-Beth, stacking the beer glasses noisily.

I take some sleeping pills and listen to the whoopin' and hollerin' as another evening's action intensifies amid lengthening shadows on Collins St. Each night there is new drama, fresh atrocities of both violence and aesthetics. Bella never gets herself in as much trouble as I do, and Skip, well he, at least, got to stay at The Delano. I drift off. I can hear 'I Love Am-eri-ca' booming from a car somewhere. I'm already dreaming of tonight at Hombre, of that friend of the bouncer.

He was out-of-it the other night. Skip had shaken his head. "He likes to be real fucked-up before he takes anyone home." I giggle to myself – the pot calling the kettle black.

A talk show blares from the shit-smeared room on one side, a Latino girl is fighting with her boyfriend on the other and I smell Skip on me. It's a mixed aroma, a *bouquet-garni*, mixture of unwashed laundry, fast food from the diner, lube and something still not erased from his childhood. Something creamy and Californian, an essential ingredient in the bi-national casserole and something folks love to eat. He's simmering away in that big old hotel, fixing to serve up that same dish, piping hot, tomorrow. *"Bon appetit,"* I murmur to a dusky Bahama sky that resembles cling wrap and I surrender to my sleepy pals.

A Lodge in the Wilderness
Stephen Gray

A Lodge in the Wilderness
Stephen Gray

He had obviously targeted me in the crowd collecting for the big event. My first thought was wallet and cash, but when I checked my pockets all I had was the room-key dangling from its wooden crocodile, which I had not yet left at reception. After a swim and shower, I was sweating again. I glanced sideways at him for he was talking over my shoulder. He did not observe European-type space, because he was touching my flank, and he was sweating, too, his face shining. In a word, he was the Zulu buck type, a swain.

He was asking where I'd come to Natal from (Johannesburg), how, by car? (yes, by car) – oh, such a long way, did I have someone with me? I was travelling with my photographer; it was his car actually, strictly business.

Said photographer appeared with his usual wreath of equipment over his safari gear. "Did you see that giraffe, right up to the fence?" he asked. I nodded. He clacked his room-key, so I gave him mine to deposit as well. We were doing a publicity pack, I explained, for this whole organisation.

The last luxury bus braked in the dust and they staggered out of their air-conditioning: mostly French, these ones, but many other groups. They were complaining about more possible chunks of buffalo and warthog and would they have to wash their salad all over again for themselves? Tourist phobias, I thought, as the buffet spread perfectly satisfactorily before us, around the arena, with dozens of obliging assistants under tall white hats in the shadow besides, to cut up their fare for them. It was my night for being chosen. One Parisian lady told me exactly what had been lost from her room the previous night: her passport, her air ticket, her travellers' cheques, her jewellery, her clothes, the photo of her husband. All she had left was her daughter clinging to her, equally shipwrecked, in the heart of darkest Zululand. They were brought two punches by the lad who had befriended me, one with cane spirit and one without. They had to taste and exchange them. But what had they seen in compensation? They had seen – a lion.

He was not on the staff here. His brother was, there behind the prawn stir-fry, shaking his ladle at us. But we had the identical reaction: we were shamed that our country had so let the Parisian down. Only one lion. Later, the photographer received an even fuller itemisation, while the girl curled up in his lap close to the fire. Her African experience.

I was trying not to appear too keen, but Kenneth (he told me his name was Kenneth Nkosi) persisted. He had finished school now, there was not a position to be had in Mhali, beyond poaching or illicit trade. As I had heard it all before, the immensity of deprivation and the despair of backward, clueless places, my heart was hardened. He was one of how many offspring? – fifteen. Well, at least he was well dressed in fashionable short-sleeved shirt and slacks and trainers, that summer's range from Mr Price. He did not have the stretch marks of much undernourishment, nor the hollow-eyed look of Aids.

I seated him at my table in the alcove, opposite me. His handwriting was as neat as his English was cautious. He passed across his address. Not that I would ever visit the hut where he lived on maize and beans. Already I could see myself stacking an extra plate, with his brother's collaboration, and this lad's face falling into it.

For the rest it was Amstels and, coming out of the bush past the floodlit pool and the rocky hill, the velvety sky pinging with fireflies, the bonfire whooshing up with aromatic flames – the Zulu warrior troupe, that is, the local Standard Eights in strips of hide and cow's tails, stomping and snorting to the big drum, with their girls in peltries ululating and clapping. Of course they belonged to the Traditional Dance Union (minimum fee R400), and they would receive at least half of that as a donation towards buying themselves soccer uniforms. Plus whatever the now cheering and whistling crowd of tourists pelted them with they could keep. I left it to the photographer: go for the rows of rotating bare breasts.

Kenneth's chatting up of me had rather run its course, but he was not going to move on to score elsewhere. All right then, we were friends for life, as one becomes when settling into a long night ahead. We went into repeat: yes, he had passed his matric, which is a very considerable achievement in those parts. We had got to his favourite, favourite subject, when another brother of his joined us – the big one, rather hostile-looking. He wedged himself between Kenneth and me, sullenly, I thought, and demanded a beer like ours. Where Kenneth was yielding and rather dainty, this head of the brood was the one who had done the battling on their behalf. Kenneth looked awkward, but was giving nothing away.

When it came to help yourself time, I offered to stand them both whatever they liked at the trestle-tables, stretching right from the bar to the bird-hide. Larger brother declined. Kenneth I got away from him; while we were in the queue I whispered to him, just stay with me tonight, get all your brothers to leave us. He was pumping me about chances for piece work. He could approach no one else there, as after their shouting experience drink was taking over. Who was going to pack up any sweet Kenneth and fly him back to whichever wealthy country they came from?

Large brother was still sulking at the table and, although he was probably just socially awkward, he had a way of holding himself I did not like, as if his shoulders had frozen in a shrug. But still, to be good-humoured, I tapped my beer can against his. My particular drinks steward silently appeared, showing no alarm that I should be entertaining his kind. He surely should rustle up another round for us all.

I nodded, and that is the point in this story where Kenneth, opposite me, opened his mouth to pile in his first forkful. I was about to follow suit when the elder Kkosi, his one shoulder six inches above the other, asked me how much.

I could see Kenneth looking straight at me, then at his fork. He speared a cube of pawpaw. I said what did he mean how much? They were welcome to join me to make a pleasant company, and as I was on a freebie I probably wouldn't have to pay anyway. Yes, to make publicity, an attractive sell.

Publicity for fliers and brochures and in-flight magazines and web-sites, all that, to draw even more busloads of luxury tourists to this poor armpit of the continent, to the only place they could decently stop over. The photographer interrupted. Certainly, the sizzling ox turning on the spit, basted by grinning assistants, with the Milky Way in the background, was tempting.

The elder brother repeated the query; how much was I prepared to pay?

I asked him how much for what. I had stumbled into my few blurts of the vernacular to pick up the pace.

I was not going to hint openly that Kenneth might out of sheer convenience like to stay with me overnight, so as to get an early start if he was to guide me round the historic sites – Rider Haggard mountains, the cultural village, the weaving cooperative and the inevitable game sanctuary, not to mention rowing about the lake, doubtless with the stranded Frenchwoman whom I saw was dancing barefoot now; she must have lost her shoes as well. I was not going to reveal if I'd pay for any personal pleasures.

He said for Kenneth. Kenneth gazed at me full face.

I looked down at my plate for something as plain as a pea. Then I said to his ward and guardian: "If Kenneth has nothing better to do and takes me round tomorrow, I will give him a very generous tip. That's the deal. I need local colour, you see, to fascinate these people." I gestured across the patio and the lawns lit with fairy lights to indicate for which invading horde I needed to devise the hype.

"Five hundred," said the brother, whose name I had not even gathered; each time he raised his conspiratorial mumble, so the tape was too loud. That table alongside was all the way from Buenos Aires: they were going to clear the decks and demonstrate the tango.

"You must be mad," I said. "Five hundred is much too much."

Five hundred rands was half of what each and every one of those suckers was paying for the night and, what with our foreign exchange crisis, it was nothing at all to them. For me, five hundred plus petrol is not much more than I'll earn on this entire job.

Large brother said we could go to the ATM at the shopping centre nearby, right now, and be back in ten minutes. No one would know. I could just see myself, followed by the three Nkosi brothers, stepping over muddy puddles in the moonlight, tapping the numbers into the machine in its safe enclave, receiving the payout and then handing them the notes. They would count them over and over again, then shake hands with me in manly agreement. And Kenneth, over whom the deal had been done, would stay behind as they walked away. How many other brothers do you have who will surround me at the outlet and empty my account? And leave me beaten to a pulp? I say never. *Never* has become a good Zulu word, as in never the poverty relief programme relieves poverty, as in never the days of the Zulu impi on the march will come again. You're all just tourist attractions now.

I added, if I wished to cash any money I would use reception. I did not need an escort.

"He can cook for you," the spokesman proposed.

"Like his brother," I replied, who was smiling towards us, stirring for the hundredth time whatever assortment he had in his wok. "This one wants to grow up and be a teacher – teach geography, all about the world. It seems he has the talent to do it? if he can get further education or whatever."

"He can sew," said the brother.

To my amazement they were studying me for some sign that I understood their proposition. Which was: cooking? sewing?

"Sewing," I said. I could just see Kenneth making big stitches in my seams on the balcony of my flat, when I had a tailor on the corner who did the job for R15.

"You do not have a wife," said large brother.

If I had, I would have said I did have someone to cook and sew for me. I almost replied, I do not need a wife – or a son.

"What else could Kenneth do for me – be my bodyguard, I suppose? Johannesburg is not a safe place these days. That's why I always like to come back to Zululand." It's so primitive, I almost added, but I would have meant less streetwise.

"For five hundred he do cooking, sewing…"

"Garden," Kenneth interposed.

"Garden – digging, he do planting, he do watering, he do raising…"

"Yes, but I live on the second floor."

"He do – washing, he do drying, he do ironing, he do packing in cupboard, he do windows, he do polish brass, anything. Five hundred rands is not much."

"Then he is my servant," I said.

"He do anything you ask."

"And what claims would you family have on him?"

"No family, no family. You are his only family."

I have understood, at last. There are no jobs here, many mouths to feed.

The staff wheels in a trolley with a huge cone of pudding melting in blue flames, eliciting the expected rush of parties. The younger ones have started their rave the other side, but they come flocking.

"I don't want a slave," I say. "Look Mr Nkosi, look Kenneth – this is the twenty-first century. No one wears chains anymore. I don't want to buy anybody, own anybody." I have spoken firmly enough for Mr Nkosi, so addressed, to be clear. He blinks, wipes his scarred face and departs for the toilet. He has been here before, tried this con on others, for he knows the trajectory. The crowd parts before him as if seeing a real Zulu is too much for them.

Kenneth slumps crestfallen meanwhile.

"Look, Kenneth," I take the opportunity, "you approached me, not the other way round. I only want you for one night, do you understand? It's just a thing between you and me. Keep him and your other brother and your whole family and whoever else's involved in your ramp out of it. Just us." I rub my fingers together, and then look at them rubbing. I am embarrassed at myself.

He is deeply embarrassed, too. We have sunk to such basics of crudity in this noble land of honourable affairs. Humbly he will wait as I fetch the key. I will bid a loud good night to the photographer, who now certainly has his plans as well. Kenneth will stalk unseen down past the greenhouses and wait in hiding behind the shrubbery until the light comes on at my glass door, while I go the public route under the walkways, especially now that we're caught in a shower that sweeps across the scene, causing major scurrying and retreat of foodstuffs. Dancing guests are so drenched they might as well jump into the blue pool. I will open my door in a regular way, put the lock on closed, leave my key on the television past the bowl of fruit. He will have his own towels to bathe and dry himself and I will have opened the wine to let it breathe. Otherwise, I'll settle for my same old drinks steward, but he was so clumsily nervous.

I understand everything now. He has set up the whole scenario. He comes over yet again to see that we are up to speed on the booze, and he winks – not at Kenneth, which would give away the entire conspiracy, but at me. He knows my taste, after all, wants me to be exceptionally content with his hotel.

I glance at Kenneth, so confident when he first sidled up to me. Now he is cringing, has a beaten quality which I would rather not witness.

My turn for the toilet. I take a walk about, just to cool off, breathe deeply and nod at the staff at various points, as if we have all become big friends by now. They know I will not be gone out of their lives at dawn like the rest, the decorated people whom they can neither understand nor care about. Just pick at, with the endless politeness of the poor. I stop at reception for any messages from my office and make the necessary transaction. I return and the photographer is carrying the sleeping French child to the mother's stripped room.

At the table Kenneth is playing with his glass. They are going to persist. I ask his brother to get us three plates of ice-cream. The moment his back is turned, I count five one-hundred-rand notes out in front of Kenneth. I expect him to grab them for himself.

When the brother returns, he has a tablespoon of melt each. Kenneth has not put the notes away. He passes them crisply to his henchman and they are gone under the table into his jeans. The three of us nod at one another to indicate he have done a good deal, as agreed upon. I take it that the deal commences as of now.

Then the proprietor approaches across the merry damage, apologetically slapping me on the back: "It isn't always like this, last night you saw how quiet it was, usually we're more organised. As long as everybody's having a good time." He is one of those boss types. When he notices them the two Zulus jump to attention before him, not sure if they are going to get a slap on the back like me or their faces punched in, in deference to me they actually get their hands shaken, and much relieved Zulu jocularity – establishing kin with the kitchen, ah the old High School and ah over that side of the cotton fields, far far, until he concludes: "You see to it this type from Johannesburg writes nice things about all of Mhali. I don't want any controversy now." And as a salvo: "On the house, on the house!"

Indeed, the times have changed. A few years ago, they would not have been allowed on the property. A few years before that, this was their King Shaka's rhino-hunting ground and so we are the trespassers.

I call Kenneth to my side and his brother, whatever his name is, is sufficiently discreet to pull away. In fact, with all the sensitivity in the world, he goes to the drinks steward, who takes one note from him. They then break it together at the bar. The steward takes him to the cigarette-machine. By this time the plan of subterfuge is completely outlined. Kenneth has his route.

But the brother seats himself again, while I am ready to leave. I have no matches, so he empties his pocket of a rag or two, a spanking new Swiss army knife, the head of some car-part, at last a grimy folder of matches. We do nods and grunts.

I take my promenade, let myself into my room and lock the door, plonk the key on the television. I turn the basket of fruit so that the bunch of grapes faces to the fore. I pop the cork and arrange the two glasses. I am adjusting the lighting when the phone goes. The photographer, he wishes to apologise for deserting me all evening, but he has top shots. What time tomorrow for the mountain? Guess what: they are no trouble, can the marooned woman and young come too? I almost ask why.

How can I tell him that something even more unlikely has happened to me: that I have actually, in this day and age, purchased, cash down, a living, breathing shall we say – dependent – of whom I am the holder, who must answer to my every beck and call; who, after he has given me my money's worth, may fully expect his freedom, and to be put through training college as well most likely? But I do not say any of that: I merely agree that 7.30 will do, before it gets too hot.

I put down the phone and am adjusting the second facecloth when there is a tapping noise on the glass door. But I cannot be sure, because the thunderstorm has turned around.

I go to the curtains; distinct tapping once more. I pull them apart. I reach for the handle, working on a simple Esco key, which seems a bit unsophisticated. But I turn it nevertheless, as I am about to have my dream of rural Zululand come true.

And there is not the stumpy old drinks steward, who will do at a pinch, because he has many more mouths to feed than himself. Even now he is running the leftovers home in his mind to his kraal, assessing the bones of the ox for marrow and the nubs of the carrots and the disposable bits of candle and the gross, fattening rinds of imported cheeses.

Nor in the backlighting of the storm, alas, is the lad called Kenneth, who of course was called nothing of the kind, and who in studying earth science was only expressing his desire to get away, to anywhere except where his destiny had placed him, and which he would never escape, and who, despite his intelligence and his ambitions and his rural talents to develop and his superb physical beauty, was hungry first, hungry as in starving to death. He had to eat to survive.

And with the television forecasting sunny skies over Kwazulu-Natal, plus a few thunderstorms to be expected in the evening, as was only normal at that time of year, there was the no-name elder brother awaiting me, as if he had a chip on his shoulder, all bitter and twisted; as if he hated the way his Kenneth was so pretty and softly spoken that white men went for him – like a kind of bait, the kind of bait you could always rely on to wind in your fish from the river, and land it out of the muddy red swirl? and club it to death.

Only he was not fishing now, but hunting big game. In his hand he had his knife open. Knife as in knife, just the silver blade, its tip concealed under his third finger with the stock up his cuff.

I should have recognised that it was him before I unlocked. I could tell from his silhouette in a flash which one it was, and that he was not the one I had expected. But now the door was wide open and there he was, as I should have foreseen, expecting to confront me.

"I'm sorry," I said rather lamely, "with all the noise and everything, I didn't quite catch your name."

He looked rather sheepish. "Enoch," he said.

"Come in then, Enoch," I said. I opened the door wider for him to enter. I left it open, but closed the curtains.

He was as surprised as I was, and turning I could see him close the knife and surreptitiously work it into the pocket of his windbreaker. I indicated the armchair, which he fell into – then he jumped up because his jeans were making the satin wet and I indicated never mind. I sat on the bed opposite him.

"So, Enoch," I said, "that's a nice missionary name. What's your proper name, Enoch?"

"Enoch," he repeated, "it's my real name."

"All right," I said. As he was not a great talker, I led by gesture. I poured him a glass of wine and handed it to him. Before I could pour my own, he had the glass clasped in both hands and half empty.

I made a guess. "Are you having trouble with your vehicle?"

Yes, it was an old Toyota pick-up and they were expensive to fix. Ay, he cursed and raised his eyes and, more to the point, patted the bit of spare part in his pocket.

"All right," I said, "so I've given you quite enough for that. What do I get in return? Zulu people are always very level people, I always thought."

I shoved over the grapes and he broke off a handful and spat the pips into his palm. I went to the coffee table and brought him a saucer, into which he deposited them.

I faced him again. "You have extorted money from me, and yet you intended to kill me just now. Why do you think that, Enoch? It's *me* who should kill *you*, if you take my money, not so, and give me nothing for myself? How can things come right that way?"

Enoch would not raise his eyes to mine. All that Sunday school training. I topped up his glass. The storm proceeded. The curtain ballooned out like a skirt, then dropped down.

Then he asked the big question that had been troubling him all night, and which the drinks steward had in his wisdom seen, and Kenneth or whoever he was had not seen at all. But Enoch took some leading up to it. "Why you give Kenneth...?" he started.

"I haven't given him anything you haven't taken," I said. "*Would give* you mean. I'd give him a place to stay and food and the new necessary clothes, so that he could advance, go to college, all that, make something of himself, for himself. He's very presentable and bright, and what the heck is there for him here?"

"You mean... like adopt?" he said slowly.

"Not adopt, just take on, you know..."

He was perplexed. "But in Zulu land we don't like that, never."

He made an unflattering sign, folding his palm about his thumb.

I was about to put that idea right out of his head when the phone rang. It was the front desk. The security guard had reported my outside door was seen to be unlocked. Please would I check immediately, that was the bad side fronting the squatter camp.

I checked, but before I locked it and closed the curtains fully, I noticed the tango-artists in the foliage with some female indigenes. They would not behave like that at home.

"Enoch or whatever," I said, feeling quite drained as I sat, "I think maybe give me my money back, less the cigarette packet of course, and we'll just – forget any of this happened. You can see, I must work tomorrow. Write lots of nice things about you to bring lots and lots of those tourists here and make jobs for you, and for playing soccer and you driving around, making your business, everybody happy. That's the policy now, I didn't make it, you see. Happy, like happy for everybody."

"Yes," he sighed, deeply tired too.

"Come, let's call it quits," I said. I put my hand across on his knee, buddy-like. He'd been double-crossed before, and was being double-crossed again. But he was not untouched.

He reached for the notes in his pocket and peeled off the four into my hand. The rest? – the remains of a hundred had gone to Kenneth, and Kenneth was not even his name, nor even Enoch's brother. And the stir-fry artist was brother to neither of them, though they all came from the same clan. In Johannesburg we didn't call them clans; they were gangs.

The bigger question of all of course was why Kenneth and *not him*? But I told Enoch that, if he had his own vehicle, he should be married by now. For Enoch the new South Africa had arrived too late. He knew that, but we could not say it aloud.

What he did say to me, in effect, was did I have any idea what a wife, any wife in Zululand, *cost* these days? He had done the requisite fighting for one (the scar on his forehead), dug dirt in the white man's gold mines for one (the shape of his hands), had driven trucks for one (the tilt of his shoulders). But without a wife, he was technically still a boy.

He wanted to smoke; it was a non-smoking room.

We had arrived truly at the end of a man's social order, if the day had come when boys had to be taken for wives. The people were now coming to an end. End as in Judgment Day and all the Wrath of God.

He stood and wobbled and asked if he could use the toilet, after all those beers on the house and now the wine. I pointed. He took his windbreaker off first, as if he would not make it there fully dressed. By the way it fell on the carpet, I could see the knife was sticking up in the pocket. He had forgotten about it, intentionally I hoped.

I made sure the curtains were firmly closed and put on the bedside lamp. There was the copy I had churned out, with my glasses on top. So I read through the clichéd blandishments I'd managed so far. There was a lot more room for romantic tosh though, all the buzzwords: 'darkest', 'aflame', 'Big Five', 'community effort'. How about a 'lodge in the wilderness'? I could hear the tomtoms throb in my pulse.

Eventually I guess Enoch had played with the flush mechanism, the comb and the free soap in its black wrapper and pressed the plunger on the body lotion dispenser and sniffed the shampoo and bath crystals sufficiently to emerge as he wished to be. Apart from his Calvin Kleins, he looked just like your wildest savage.

Dream House
John Haylock

Dream House
John Haylock

Malcolm Cox was in late middle age and on the point of final retirement. He had spent his life in South East Asia: first in the Colonial Service in Malaysia and when that country became independent in 1957 he was seconded to the Foreign Office on a contract basis and acted as an adviser to the British embassies in Indonesia and Thailand. When his contract expired he managed to get a job in the Family Planning Section of the United Nations office in Bangkok. His friends joked about this appointment. Malcolm had never given a thought to the planning of a family. He was a bachelor and like many unmarried men over forty he preferred his own sex to the opposite one.

Malcolm had never had an affair. His life had consisted of a series of brief liaisons that had rarely lasted more than a few months. While a Colonial Service officer or a Foreign Office adviser he had had to be circumspect, only indulging in surreptitious encounters; at times concupiscence had caused him to court danger, but luck had been with him and he had escaped disaster. Now in Bangkok he was freer than he had ever been. None of his colleagues at the United Nations branch cared what he was or what he did. Love, alas, did not come his way. Who could, love him? He was sixty-five, bald, with a red face mottled by years in the sun, and tarnished and uneven teeth. His charm and intelligence, however, offset his unprepossessing appearance.

During his years abroad he had regularly gone on leave to England, but less and less did he feel at home there; he had little in common with his old friends, most of whom were uninterested in South East Asia and looked bored when he expatiated on polities in Thailand or unrest in Indonesia. On the death of his widowed mother, he sold her house in Crowborough, whose society he had always found stifling, and bought a flat in Kensington, equipping it with the family furniture – he was an only child. On leave in London, he felt a stranger and after a few weeks he was more than ready to return to South East Asia. When final retirement arrived and he said goodbye to Bangkok for good and took up residence in his Kensington flat, he soon began to pine for Thailand. He would sell his flat and build a house, his dream house, there. But where? With no companion?

One balmy spring evening he took himself to a Thai restaurant in Kensington, and there he experienced a *coup de foudre*. Suriya, one of the waiters, was most appealing and exceedingly handsome. Malcolm pleased him by speaking in Thai, though after a few snatches of conversation they were able to have while the young waiter was busy serving other diners they reverted to English, in which language Suriya was fluent. Malcolm's Thai was rudimentary.

"When are you free?" Malcolm asked Suriya as he was paying the bill.

"In the afternoon," the Thai replied without hesitation.

"I live near. Here's my card. What about tomorrow?"

"OK. Four o'clock."

Malcolm gave Suriya a generous tip and on the threshold of the restaurant he put both palms together and looked the young man deeply in the eyes. Suriya returned the *wai*.

That night Malcolm contemplated Suriya and his appearance. He guessed that he came from the north of Thailand, from Chiang Mai or Chiang Bai as his complexion was pale, but not of Chinese extraction as his dark-brown eyes were unhooded. Would he be willing, Malcolm wondered. The fact that he had quickly agreed to visit him was encouraging.

Precisely at four Suriya turned up at Malcolm's flat. Dressed in a polo-neck pullover and jeans, he looked more attractive than he had in his waiter's uniform of ill-fitting white jacket and black trousers. Broad-shouldered, he was of medium height, a little shorter than Malcolm; his manner was assured; he had none of that deference and diffidence often found among South-East Asians. He sat on the sofa when Malcolm, saying "Do sit down", waved an arm towards it. Malcolm sat in an armchair.

"What about tea?" he asked his guest.

"That would be nice."

Malcolm rose and went into the kitchen and put on the kettle and got out cups and saucers, milk and sugar.

"May I help you?"

Malcolm, reaching up to a shelf for the tea caddy, found Suriya by his side. The kitchen was small. They looked at each other. Malcolm leant forward to kiss Suriya, but the young man moved his head and only allowed Malcolm's lips to brush his cheek.

"Shall we go into the bedroom? We don't really want tea, do we?" Malcolm turned off the gas.

"Up to you."

Suriya wasn't very co-operative in bed but nevertheless Malcolm remained enchanted; it was the young man's presence that counted; his lacklustre performance didn't matter. When at the front door, Malcolm brought out his wallet, Suriya said, "I'm not like that."

On his second visit Suriya told Malcolm that he came from Chiang Mai province; it pleased Malcolm that his guess had been right. Suriya's third visit took place on a Sunday, his day off. After they had had a shower and put on their clothes, they sat in the sitting-room. Suriya accepted a glass of whisky.

"I'm not gay," he said to Malcolm, "but I like you."

"And I like you very much."

After two glasses of whisky, the young Thai confessed to having married an English girl in Chiang Mai, but they were living apart. "I hate her," he said. She was now with her parents in Sudbury.

"Why did you marry her?"

"She wanted to. She attract me. It was crazy but I did."

"And now what?"

"We have big row. She tell Home Office I married her to get residence in England. The Home Office they say I must go back to Thailand. I appeal. I think it will not succeed."

"Which do you want, to stay here, or to go back to Thailand?"

"I wanted to stay here, but now I think better I go back."

"What about your wife?"

"I can cancel the marriage. In Thailand no problem."

Malcolm thought for a moment and then said, "I like the northwest of Thailand. I want to go and live there, to build a house there, my dream house..."

"Dream house?"

"The house I've always wanted to have, a place to end my days in. I dislike this flat and living in London." Rashly, Malcolm added, "Will you help me?"

"Help you?"

"Build my dream house."

"I cannot build."

"You can speak Thai; you know Chiang Mai."

"I have no money, no money at all. The restaurant they pay very little. I work without permit."

"Don't worry about money. I'll look after the money side of the bargain."

Malcolm put his furniture in store and his flat on the market. He and Suriya flew to Thailand, together – first class; Malcolm wanted to impress.

In Bangkok, where they stayed in a five-star hotel for a week before going up to Chiang Mai, Malcolm visited his old friend Anthony Hunter, a denizen of Thailand for over thirty years, Anthony had run a travel agency which he had recently sold and was basking in the proceeds. His house, which he had had built to his own design, was comfortable and groaning with Thai *objets d'art*, many of which were valuable. Malcolm was so besotted with Suriya that he fretted when the young man went out on his own as he was wont to do, but not before pleadings and protests had taken place. It was on one of Suriya's evenings out that Malcolm went to see Anthony, who lived among the wealthy in a district which took nearly an hour to reach from the centre of traffic-jammed Bangkok.

"You're out of your mind," Anthony said when he had heard Malcolm's plan to build his 'dream house' with Suriya.

"I'm in love," explained Malcolm.

"Love!" Anthony put into his exclamation the utmost contempt. "At your age 'love' is silly, boring and risky."

"Silly, possibly, but boring?"

"Boring to others, the lovesick only have one subject of conversation."

"Risky?" queried Malcolm.

"Yes, because the house has to be in the name of a Thai, unless you're an accepted resident like me."

"I know that. The house will be in Suriya's name, but I shall lease it from him. I can trust him."

"How long have you known him?"

"Seven weeks."

Anthony finished his whisky. "Yuth!" he yelled, and almost immediately his servant padded barefoot into the sitting-room. He held up his glass. Yuth took it silently and then accepted Malcolm's.

"I don't know what I'd do without Yuth and his wife," Anthony said.

"Suriya is straight."

"Good God!"

"He's not gay. He will do it with me. Our chemistry works."

"Oh?"

"I don't mind if he fucks girls – he married an English one, but that's another story; he'll always come back to me."

"How do you know?"

"He's promised."

"Good God, Malcolm, I didn't realise you were gullible, and you've lived, out here. You're like an innocent from England."

"I know what you're thinking. You're wrong. It'll work out. You'll see."

In Chiang Mai, Malcolm rented a furnished flat in a condominium and he and Suriya began their search for a suitable site for the Dream House. They looked at a number of plots within the city and then in housing estates on the outskirts, but none pleased them. Malcolm bought a Japanese pick-up and Suriya learnt to drive. He was happy with Suriya; he put up with his absences, which were frequent, accepting the fact that Suriya's family lived in a village ten miles from the city. Malcolm was not invited to meet his widowed mother, whose two unmarried daughters lived with her.

About twenty miles from Chiang Mai, near the town of Lamphun and therefore still on the fertile plain watered by the River Ping and its tributaries, Suriya discovered a new housing development which had only just started. Malcolm was delighted with a plot of land, which was for sale and had been planted with two rows of *lamyai* (a kind of lychee) trees and cultivated for vegetables. It was about three acres in area, near an irrigation canal, a row of casuarinas marked the west boundary; banana trees grew here and there.

"We'll remove those," said Malcolm, referring to the bananas. "They're so untidy."

The purchase of the land was a protracted business. During the proceedings, which were conducted by a Thai lawyer and Suriya, Malcolm flew to England to arrange for his furniture to be shipped to Thailand and to see a doctor; he'd had chest pains for some weeks; Suriya had been kept in ignorance of them.

Meanwhile, Suriya, with the help of an English resident of Chiang

Mai, who was knowledgeable about architecture and builders, had plans drawn up, and they were ready for Malcolm's return.

In London a specialist had told Malcolm that he had a spot on his right lung which was almost certainly the beginning of cancer. Malcolm did not tell Suriya.

The Dream House with all the frustrations and delays of building slowly came into existence and work was started on a Thai-style house on stilts in the grounds for the driver and another for the gardener. Suriya had successfully persuaded Malcolm that it was necessary to have a car as well as a pick-up and a Honda Civic was bought. The young man also cajoled Malcolm into agreeing to build in the corner of the estate a bungalow for himself. "But," Malcolm objected, "you will have your room in the main house."

"Sometimes I will want to have my mother to stay," he explained.

"I see."

Connected to the main house by a covered teak passage (all the floors were of teak) was the guest wing consisting of a bedroom, bathroom and as sitting-room. This was completed first and Malcolm and his friend lived in it while the main house was being built.

A doctor in Chiang Mai confirmed the diagnosis of the London specialist and Malcolm had to start a painful course of chemotherapy injections. He told Suriya his dire news.

"What I do if you die?" he asked, distressed yet practical.

"The house will be yours. It's yours now. It's in your name. On paper, I'm your tenant."

Malcolm's illness spurred him to get the house completed as soon as possible. When the high steep roof had been erected the house stood out in the flat land around it like a temple. Inside the main part, the arrangement was simple: the whole of the ground floor except for the kitchen and other offices consisted of a large living-room. There were two sets of sofas and armchairs, occasional tables, cabinets and desks, two grandfather clocks (one modern, ordered by Suriya locally), and near the kitchen a long dining-table that could seat twelve. Most of the furniture had been in Malcolm's mother's Crowborough house. A number of oriental rugs here and there adorned the floor. The huge room faced west. French windows gave onto a veranda on which were rattan chairs and tables.

A staircase of baronial proportions led up to the first floor, where there were two bedrooms and a wide balcony. Each bedroom had a door into the one bathroom. Malcolm had insisted on having only one bathroom in spite of Suriya's pleas for two. Malcolm had his reasons.

The injections that Malcolm had to endure were agonising; they weakened him and tired him; he slept badly. He exhausted himself urging the builders to expedite the completion of the Dream House.

"We are improving the district, giving Thailand a piece of architecture that will become a national treasure one day," he told Suriya.

"You think so?" said the young Thai sceptically.

"Yes, and you must keep it up when I'm gone."

A swimming pool was dug and boulders were brought from a garden centre in Bangkok for a rockery, which hid a hut for the filter machinery. An expansive lawn was planned. When Suriya, after consultation with the gardener, had recommended second-grade turf, which the gardener could supply, Malcolm had insisted on having the top-grade kind, which had to come from Bangkok.

The whole project augmented by impulsive decisions (like having a swimming pool, a lily pond with carp) had exceeded the original estimate of £100, 000 by £75,000 and was not yet finished. Malcolm had to sell more shares on the London market than he had budgeted for.

He was impatient to have a house-warming party as soon as possible. Flowers in bloom (mainly marigolds and petunias) were planted in the beds, and lilies in the pond, in the middle of which was a statue of an ephebe, which Malcolm had found in an antique shop in Chiang Mai, and round which the carp swam; the driver was fitted out with a dark-blue uniform; the cook and the two maids from the nearby village were instructed by a restaurateur from Chiang Mai how to prepare a buffet. Invitations were sent to friends in Chiang Mai and Bangkok. Anthony was asked to stay in the guest wing for a few days. Suriya asked Malcolm if he could invite an Australian and his Thai wife to the party.

"Are they friends of yours?" Malcolm asked suspiciously.

"I met them in Chiang Mai. I told them about the house. They were very interested."

"Oh well, all right."

Although Malcolm was in considerable pain he managed to be jovial during the party, a lunch-time affair held at the beginning of December when the sun is less fierce. It went off well, starting at noon and going on till four. Guests, both Thai and foreign, drank copiously, ate voraciously, sported themselves in the pool and vociferously explored the house and grounds. Malcolm barely spoke to the Australian and his Thai wife. Both of them, though, on their departure, told him they greatly admired his home and this pleased him. His Dream House was a reality.

After the guests had gone and the host and Anthony were sitting on the veranda enjoying the fading light and the magnificent glow in the sky, Malcolm said, "It was a success, wasn't it?"

"Indeed," replied Anthony.

"They liked the house, didn't they?"

"They were ecstatic about it."

Malcolm beamed.

"I wonder why Suriya brought that Australian and his Thai wife," he said. "Did you speak to them?"

"No, but I noticed they seemed to inspect the place very thoroughly."

"They praised the house highly to me as they were leaving. I told Suriya to tell the maids to go home when they've cleared up. I don't know what we're going to do about supper."

"I've eaten much too much, Malcolm, to have anything more."

"I'll get Suriya to make us an omelette. He's good at omelettes."

"I saw him drive off in the Honda just now, when you were upstairs."

"Oh?" said Malcolm, visibly disappointed. "He often goes to Chiang Mai in the evening and sometimes doesn't come back until the early hours. After all, he's young." Malcolm rose from his rattan chair and looked out at the casuarinas, now black marks against the night sky. "He's been an inestimable help over the house," he pondered, aloud, "I couldn't have done it without him. He's worth every penny of the allowance I give him." He emitted a sob, cleared his throat, and added, "Let's have a drink."

Anthony was shocked when breakfast was brought to him by a maid, who dropped to her knees at the beginning of the teak corridor and wobbled the tray along to a table, which had been laid outside the guest quarters. "How abominably feudalistic of Malcolm to allow such outdated deference," he muttered to himself.

Malcolm didn't appear until the middle of the morning. "Has Suriya come back?" he asked Anthony, who was on the veranda reading.

"I don't think so. The Honda isn't outside."

"He may have gone to his cottage for the night so as not to disturb me. You didn't see upstairs yesterday. Come up, I'll show you."

While mounting the grand, but uncarpeted staircase, Malcolm remarked, "A carpet has been ordered, I was hoping it'd be ready for the party, but of course it wasn't. Here's my bedroom."

They entered a spacious room which contained not only a double bed and other bedroom necessities, but also a desk, a filing cabinet, a safe and several bookcases. Like the sitting room the aspect was to the west. They went out on to a balcony and admired the garden, the pool, the *lamyai* trees, the casuarinas and the land beyond.

"Suriya's bedroom is next door." Malcolm indicated the adjacent room that also gave on to the balcony.

On the way back through Malcolm's bedroom, Malcolm opened a door that led into a bathroom, which was perfectly equipped with bath, two hand basins and a separate shower compartment. Anthony was surprised to see an upholstered lounge chair placed against the wall next the shower. "What's that doing there?" he asked.

"I sit in it when Suriya's having a bath, but recently he's taken to having a shower and he draws the curtain."

During their descent, Anthony looked out of the landing window and saw the Honda approaching with a truck behind it. "Look, here comes Suriya."

"It's the carpet, I bet," said Malcolm. "One day late. Suriya must have gone out to guide the truck here."

That is exactly what Suriya told Malcolm he had done. His face was blank, his eyes were dead when he spoke to Malcolm. Anthony guessed he was lying and that he had met the truck by chance on his return from a night out in Chiang Mai. Suriya busied himself directing the laying of the red stair carpet. When it was done the staircase looked most imposing.

"Splendid," said Anthony. "Positively palatial. A carpet for princes to descend."

Malcolm was pleased.

Soon after the party and Anthony's visit, Malcolm's pains became so excruciating that he had to ask Suriya to take him to hospital. He was dead in a few days. Suriya informed none of Malcolm's friends of the death. He had Malcolm's remains cremated and arranged for them to be sent to Malcolm's next of kin, a cousin and heir to his estate in England.

In his Thai will Malcolm left Suriya the Dream House and the balance in his Chiang Mai bank, which came to less than five hundred pounds. The allowance ceased. Suriya couldn't afford to keep up the property. He sold the Honda, paid off the staff except for one gardener, moved into the cottage and contacted the Australian and his Thai wife who had attended the house-warming party.

The Australian, tall with a wrinkled, sun-tanned, leathery face, had a businesslike and persuasive manner and beat down Suriya's asking price of £200,000 to £150,000, paying £100,000 down with the promise of stumping up the rest later. Having a Thai wife simplified the purchase since the house could be in her name. Suriya agreed to the Australian's offer. A £100,000 was a great fortune to him and he was anxious to get rid of the place. The Australian said that he and his wife were planning to have a sort of factory in the grounds, but he didn't elaborate on the matter.

A year later, Anthony, who had been furious with Suriya for not telling him immediately of Malcolm's death and only writing him a letter after the cremation, went up to Chiang Mai and out of curiosity visited the Dream House. He was coolly received by the Australian, whose dumpy, brown little Thai wife was absent or didn't appear. He did not seem to remember having met Anthony at the house-warming party. With reluctance, the new owner consented to Anthony's request to see the garden and accompanied him on to the lawn, which was well kept, the rockery too. The pool seemed in good shape and the *lamyai* trees and the vegetable plot were flourishing. When Anthony went towards the guest wing, the Australian said, "We haven't bothered with that. It's empty. Come and have a beer." Anthony sensed that he didn't want him to see inside that part of the establishment.

They had a beer together in the sitting-room, which, Malcolm's furniture having presumably been sold by Suriya, only contained a sofa and two armchairs covered with a light-green plastic material and a glass-topped occasional table. They sat in this oasis in the vast room. The Australian had no news of Suriya. When Anthony rose to leave, the Australian leapt to his feet, clearly relieved that his uninvited guest was going.

Four years passed before Anthony revisited Chiang Mal; again he drove out to the Dream House. He was staggered by what he saw. The gates had gone, the front door too, the tessellated floor of the porch loosened by weeds, in the middle of the lily pond, green with chick weed, still stood the ephebe, now headless.

Inside, the place had been stripped; it was a shell; only the concrete and brick walls showed the building was once a house. On the now banisterless cement stairs were vestiges of the red carpet. The bedrooms were bare and open to the sky, the floorboards gone, the bath also, the hand basins and the fittings, but the armchair, its cover in shreds, its springs and stuffing protruding, was still there. The teak balcony balustrade had disappeared.

The garden was unkempt, wild, a jungle. The trees had grown, a raintree had become enormous; the lawn was covered with a straggly creeper and self-sown bushes, the trunks of the casuarinas were wrapped in wiry thorns. The pool, half smothered by branches, still held water, but it was black, foetid and like the pond green with weed. A tree screened the site of the rockery, the boulders had gone. Amidst the chaos here and there bougainvillaea blossomed, and a young flamboyant was in bud.

The *lamyai* trees had expanded into huge spheres of dark green, but were not past yielding a crop of fruit.

In the vegetable garden was a man tending a patch of garlic. Anthony, who spoke fluent Thai, approached him. The man, whose brown face was deeply wrinkled, wore a straw hat, a grubby T-shirt and threadbare jeans. He looked alarmed when Anthony strode up to him and he gave evasive answers to questions about the house; but after some coaxing and the sight of Anthony's wallet he opened up. It seemed that all of a sudden the Australian and his wife were gone. They left in the night, leaving behind most of their clothes and all the things in the house. The old gardener intimated that their flight had something to do with drugs and the police were about to pounce. He said he had been Malcolm's gardener and was kept on by the Australian after Suriya had left. He got no pay now and thought he had the right to cultivate vegetables and harvest the *lamyai* trees.

When asked who had ransacked the house, the gardener said he didn't know. Anthony tapped his wallet and learned that the local villagers had done it. The temptation was too great to resist. Teak is valuable and the contents of the house were not worthless. Finally, Anthony inquired if there were any news of Suriya. The old man had no knowledge of his whereabouts.

Anthony pulled from his wallet a five-hundred baht bank-note and gave it to the gardener, who put his palms together making a *wai* and thanked him over and over again.

As he was driving away along the approach road that weeds had reduced to a path, Anthony thought of the bathroom armchair and its sad, dilapidated state. He recalled Malcolm's expression of delight when he had said referring to the guests' reaction to the house, "They were ecstatic about it." Anthony had not told Malcolm that he had heard an elderly English peer mumble to his companion, "A sheer folly, my dear."

Mirror Man

Steve Hope

Mirror Man
Steve Hope

The pub was already quite full when the stranger arrived, as he had hoped: he was less likely to be noticed and remembered. He ordered a mineral water as usual, since it could be drunk quickly, he would keep his wits about him, and, in any case, as always, he had his car. Parked far enough away not to be associated with visiting this particular pub, of course.

"That's one pound exactly, darling," sang the young barman. Like the stranger's, his eyebrows were plucked, but he hadn't been content with symmetrical neatness. They were as sharply pointed as a swallow's wing. His fluttering hands were so weighed down with jeweled rings it was surprising that he could lift them. The stranger was nauseated. Might as well be a fucking woman, he thought. Don't know why some of them don't chop it off and have done with it.

As he handed over his money, the barman asked: "You new in the area, love? Don't think we've seen you before." His eyes sparkled. Did the little creep fancy him? He must discourage interaction. Be forgettable. Not stand in the way of the barman's fixing his attention on lots of other guys in the bar, as he surely would; there were lots of nice-looking ones in tonight. Queers would think so anyway, he supposed.

"Just on business," he grunted, and looked down pointedly at his drink. The barman took the hint. He said no more and went over to another man just arrived at the bar.

It was half-past nine, and the pub was filling up in earnest. The stranger was gratified at how many men had shaven skulls, earrings, jeans, and short leather jackets just like his. His camouflage was near perfect tonight. He remained at the bar looking at the huge mirror behind the bottle shelves with the absent gaze of a barfly. The tables and settles behind him were full of men, mostly young, mostly fashionably dressed, all laughing and talking loudly and absorbed in each other's company. Pickings might turn out to be meagre here. In a corner, two boys kissed passionately next to a couple of old men who ignored them and argued about whether to go to Ibiza for Christmas. Wish I could do them here and now, thought the stranger. Then the ideal candidate came into the pub.

He saw him in the bar mirror first, of course, framed neatly in a gap between two bottles of liqueur. He was alone. As with so many others in the pub that night, his style was much like the stranger's. His head was shaved, his eyebrows were plucked, and he wore leather and denim. Where the stranger was dark and stocky, however, the newcomer was fair and slight. This last was an obvious advantage if he put up much resistance. The fair man stepped up to the bar and retrieved a wallet with several credit cards in it from his inside pocket. He proffered one across the bar, asking for a pint of lager and cash back. On his wrist was the rich gleam of gold. He suddenly smiled invitingly at the stranger, who knew his victim was marked.

"You new here?" asked the fair one, echoing the barman's question. This time the stranger's response was much more encouraging.

"That's right. Well spotted," he beamed.

"We all tend to have the same look about us," said the other man, still smiling brilliantly.

"This is your first time here, too?" asked the stranger, just managing to conceal his glee. Here was someone showing signs of affluence who was also unkown here.

"Well, my first in this pub. I live locally but don't go out much, to be honest. You live around here as well?"

"No," said the stranger. "I'm a stranger to the town as well as the pub. Just on business here."

"What do you do?"

"Freelance accounting."

"Does it pay well?"

"Can do."

"My boyfriend and I both travel a lot through our jobs," said the fair man. "I sell fitted kitchens and he's in conservatories and double-glazing." The stranger felt a little discouraged. The man's referring so pointedly to a boyfriend might be a bad sign. It could prefigure an invitation to a threesome; or it could equally well mean that he only intended to be friendly and had no intention of going anywhere with him. But the stranger was soon reassured. "We both make pretty good money," continued the other man, "but the trouble is we end up passing each other like ships in the night. Today's a good case in point. He's staying somewhere up North and I'm all alone at home. Next week it could be the other way round. Good job we don't mind each other finding a bit of fun when we're apart. Passes the time and gives us some good stories to tell." His smile grew even wider.

"Maybe we can find a bit of fun together," said the stranger cautiously.

"That's just what I was thinking," said the fair man. "What sort of thing are you into?"

"Just about anything if I'm with a really tasty guy." Of course, he hated coming out with stuff like that, but he knew exactly what queers said and he had to say it if he were going to get anywhere. Exactly where he might get to wasn't yet clear; very often he didn't even have to lay a finger on a man to get everything he wanted. Just the hint of a beating was enough, and sometimes not even that. Queers were so spineless. One afternoon he went home with a crisply suited businessman who innocently told him that they would have the run of the house, since his wife and children were away for the weekend. The stranger left five minutes after arriving, a gold watch and over a thousand pounds in cash to the good, simply by threatening to come back later and tell the man's wife how he spent his free afternoons. He'd only used his flick-knife once, on a chap who started using his fists when he'd demanded money from him instead of giving him a blow-job. He cursed the unconscious and bleeding form in the dark; he only had a tenner on him after all. Occasionally he roughed blokes up when he already had the goods, just for the sake of it, especially after having sex with them. He hadn't done the sex bit very often, of course. It was just to see why anybody would be into that sort of sick-making stuff, and he never could. Anybody who seriously got off on it was asking for a beating.

The fair thin man told him he had a nice chest and package, and the stranger smiled, genuinely gratified. That was one thing you could say for queers: they knew a real man when they saw one. What should he do with this one? Roll him in an unlit and secluded spot or go all the way home with him? He was alone for the night and seemed pretty well off. That could mean rich and easy pickings at the house.

"Don't know about you," the fair man was saying, "but I'm pretty horny already. I bet you have that effect on lots of guys."

"That's what they tell me," said the stranger softly.

"I bet they do. So, unless you'd like to have another drink, I'm game to take you home right now."

"That's fine by me."

"Shall we go to my place? Or maybe your hotel's really close by? You decide."

"We'll go to your place," said the stranger. "My hotel room's not very comfortable and I reckon they're a bit iffy about taking people back." The fair man nodded at this and finished off his lager.

It was only ten o'clock, and the streets they walked through were still quiet. After a few minutes the fair man stopped, looked furtively about, planted a lingering wet kiss on his mouth, and then stepped away again, smiling mischievously. The stranger's cock swelled, and he smiled in return. He would get this bastard. After several minutes' walking, the fair man suddenly turned into a pedestrian underpass which reeked of urine. All the lights were out, and the ground was strewn with broken glass. The fair man stopped again, and turned to face the stranger. His shaven skull was silhouetted by the faint glow of street lights at the far end of the underpass, and his face was invisible.

"Right, you fucking queer," he said. "Get your money out."

"I'm not queer," said the stranger. "*You* are. You get *your* money out, if you know what's good for you." The fair man thrust a hand into a jacket pocket and pulled it out again. There was a click, and a blade shone in the gloom.

"Stop pissing me about," he said. "Hand your money over or you'll get this stuck in you. Not the cock you thought you were going to get. Dirty queer." The stranger drew a smooth metal object from his pocket, and a second blade sprang out.

"I know exactly what I'm going to get," said the stranger, "And what you'll get if you don't give me all your money right now. And that poofy gold bracelet you've got on while you're at it. Got a bloody nerve calling somebody else queer. Fucking bender."

"You're all mouth. Queers haven't got the nerve to use a knife. I have. I'll do you in a second. Now give me your fucking money."

"In your dreams, poofter," said the stranger, "and that's what *you* are, not me. I'll show you bloody nerve. Only queers kiss the way you did."

"Only queers smile and chat up like you did, and open their mouths the way you did when I kissed you." They fell silent, and stood motionless, their knives held out before them in the evil-smelling dark.

Monkey Business
Alan James

Monkey Business
Alan James

After the first few days, a fortnight seemed much too long; Tony had only come anyway because it was such a cheap package, the single supplement wasn't too steep, and the travel agent had recommended it.

"Oh, I've been there loads; you'll find plenty to do. The old town, Chinatown they call it, is very bustling, and the people are very friendly." The agent had, if anything, been a bit over-friendly himself when he'd said that, looking quite knowing, or smarmy, perhaps, or maybe familiar was more the word; but possibly, of course, it went with the job.

Certainly, the beach hotel was okay, the service was good and the food was acceptably lavish; but one flicky-roof Chinese temple looks very much like another. "I'm templed out," Tony heard an American woman say in the lobby, and he knew how she felt. Still, he dutifully took the free shuttle bus into town every morning – it was too hot for the beach, anyway, and Tony burned, instead of tanned – and trudged round with his *Insight* guidebook.

The old town centre was bustling, so much so that it was difficult to decide quite where to stop for a drink or a snack: one major street seemed devoted to back-packers, with thumping reggae pubs blaring out very loud wailing; and other, more Chinese, streets were filled with rather frightening food arcades where you had to know exactly what you wanted, and nobody had any patience for you. There was only trash to buy, but Tony bought some anyway, for the girls in the office.

But after a while, things started looking up, as Tony began to discover a number of fairly swish businessman's hotels scattered around town, which did very good and cheap buffet lunches. Tony was very fond of his food, and decided to make the most of it, add to his ample waistline, forget for the duration the diet he was half-heartedly following at home, and have a sort of one-man gourmet tour; so, it became Thai one day, Indonesian the next, Chinese, Indian, Italian even. Eventually, he fell into the habit of lingering pretty much the whole two or three hours of the set lunch-time, taking a book, his free newspaper from the hotel, and cheap local cigarettes; he found the unfamiliar local cakes and desserts especially good. Sometimes, an hour or so later, after dozing for a while in one of the comfortable chairs in the hotel lobby, soothed by the sound of tinkling fountains and the cadences of *shmaltzy* music from a grand piano, Tony would find the hotel coffee shop, and have tea, with very un-local, but extremely delicious, generously-cut wedges of pecan pie, or Black Forest gateau; so the holiday settled down into one agreeable, gastronomic blur.

One lunch-time at the start of the second week, as Tony rifled through his bag on the seat beside him, he found that he had forgotten to bring the Nevil Shute which he had bought from the hotel bookshop, and only had his guidebook to accompany him through the Special Cantonese Dim-Sum Buffet at the Shangri-La. He was aware that he had missed a few 'attractions', and started to check down the list of numbered sites on the double page showing the town map. The only thing for which he could muster up any enthusiasm was the Botanic Gardens; Tony had quite a collection of exotic house plants – now temporarily under the care of his sister – in his flat, and thought he would like to see what the local flora looked like in its natural habitat. By the time he had finished lunch, which had been extremely delicious – such a lot of new flavours – it was around three-thirty. Tony knew where the local bus station was, just around the corner from the Shangri-La, but it had always looked like a confusing, noisy, seedy place, and he couldn't resist taking one of the taxis from the Shang porch.

The ride was interesting; inland, through lush suburbia, the spiky foliage and tall palms visible over white-painted walls exciting, as a foretaste of what he might soon be wandering amongst, in the Gardens themselves. The road which led to the Botanic Gardens eventually skirted a belt of jungle-like rainforest at the base of a step incline, at the top of which was supposed to be a small hill station, dating from colonial times: the whole roadside area was dotted with Indian temples, set in clearings, surmounted by high, tapering masses of writhing statuary, painted in the most garish of colours; where, amongst the deities and bare-breasted dancing-girls, Tony could also make out naively-depicted birds and animals – peacocks and elephants, certainly, and, he thought, monkeys. At ground level, real goats wandered about the temple precincts, tethered by long chains to coconut palms, and chickens scuttered in dust-baths by the side of the grass verge; behind the temples, up in the foothills, were smaller buildings, shrines perhaps, reached by long, steep-looking flights of steps.

The Botanic Gardens were, frankly, disappointing: considering the tropical climate, Tony had imagined something more like the interiors of the great glass-houses at Kew, beautifully landscaped around pools scattered with giant water-lily leaves; but here, the main focus seemed to be on a circular jogging-track, laid with multi-coloured concrete pavers. There was a rather dried-up stream, its bed littered with discarded plastic bags, crossed by brightly-painted metal bridges, each one apparently a much-simplified copy of a famous bridge somewhere else in the world; and the most interesting of the plants – orchids, anthurium, strelitzias – were growing in large, walk-through cages of sagging chicken-wire, all locked up. Even the labelling on the ordinary-looking trees was a bit peculiar; everything seemed to be a legume, and Tony knew enough about food to know that *legume* just meant vegetable in French. Also, there were no monkeys, not that Tony had any particular interest in monkeys, but the guidebook said that they could be seen and fed at the Botanic Gardens.

The guidebook, however, like most of its kind, was a little out of date. At one time, the café at the entrance to the Gardens had sold bags of peanuts to the tourists, who had fed the colonies of hill-monkeys, which in huge numbers had noisily descended daily for hours of easy feasting; but then people had started bringing in bags of rotting fruit, and simply tossing them onto the lawns where the monkeys gathered, so that the entire place had become a ripe-smelling dumping-ground, littered with torn plastic. The monkeys had also started ravaging the Gardens, more for wickedness, it seemed, than any other motive, and it was then that the gardeners had started to move their plants into the ugly metal cages.

Eventually the authorities had started surreptitiously culling, and rifle-shots could be heard echoing round the foothills, which had led to a minor scandal via the newspapers; so peanut-selling at the Botanic Gardens had been banned, and the vendors had moved to a spot a few hundred yards away along the road, where the wooded hills swept right down to the walkway, and soon that place had become a rubbish dump, too.

Tony was very hot, and sweating, after his tramp around the Gardens: he sat at the café just outside the gates, and ordered a coconut; he had enjoyed the young, smooth, green coconuts at the hotel. The top was shied off, and Tony drank the clear, refreshing liquid through a straw, afterwards scooping out the milky, jelly-like flesh with a spoon. He asked the stallholder where the monkeys were, and the man pointed down the road, back towards the town; Tony could see the end of a line of cars, parked by the roadside under the overhanging trees, and a coach or two drawn up on the grass verge opposite, so he decided to stroll down and have a look.

As Tony drew nearer, he could see people, both adults and children, throwing things into the bushes, and then he realised that there were monkeys scampering about all over the place, some in the middle of the road, some climbing onto the cars, many shinning up and down creepers, or hanging from the branches of the trees. When he reached the line of parked cars, Tony could see what a mess the place was in; the whole of the jungly bank was littered with plastic bags spilling out rotten fruit, and there was a strong, fetid smell. The monkeys didn't even seem to be bothered about the fruit, but were much more intent on the bread which most people had brought.

It was certainly an interesting spectacle, and it was wonderful to see the creatures swarming about at large. The most intriguing were the mothers, carrying their tiny young beneath them; Tony was fascinated by their miniature, black hand-like paws. Every so often, one or other of the males, with his pointed little red pencil of a penis exposed, would jump on a female and copulate for a few moments. Other groups would come crashing down through the trees, or along the cables which, strung from poles, followed the walkway, and a fight would ensue: entwined balls of fur, spitting and shrieking, would roll into the roadway, right into the path of the fast-moving traffic, which swerved and hooted around them; more than one of the creatures had a damaged tail, or was missing a limb, and one particularly aggressive male was dragging a deformed and flattened back paw along behind him.

As Tony stood watching, a small baker's van – really just a blue-painted wooden box on the back of a motor-bike – pulled in; the driver threw a large plastic sack onto the piles of fruit, and phut-phutted off again, as stale, mouldy bread and cakes tumbled about. This caused an enormous scramble, and the locals and other sightseers standing around laughed to see the fighting and biting. Tony could see the monkey with the flattened paw tearing into the plastic sack with his teeth, turning round to screech and snap at any who came near him, before loping off, batting some sort of loaf in front of him along the road.

There were smaller monkeys, though, which seemed to be more timid, and looked around them with eyes more watery than fiery, and these didn't join in the fray. An old man with a handcart was selling bags of food for a few cents, so Tony bought something in a pack, six flattish buns in a clear cellophane wrapper. He opened the packet, took out one of the buns, and broke a piece off to taste it; inside, it was a bright yellow, embedded with red and green nuggets of something or other, and was very dry and stale, and very sweet; Tony had noticed how highly-coloured so many of the local baked goods were. He broke the bun into pieces, which he threw towards the monkeys nearest to him, those which hadn't joined in the general mêlée; they came very near, taking the pieces quietly, and eating them in front of him, then looking up for more, so that Tony could study their humanoid paws, and the markings on their fur.

He fed them two or three more broken-up buns, before a troupe of larger males bounded over and muscled in. Tony threw the remaining buns into the group, and put the wrapper into his rucksack, as there didn't seem to be a waste-paper basket around, and he didn't want to be guilty of adding to the mess of litter around him; looking into his bag, he saw a bundle of white napkin, and remembered that he had stashed away, for later, a few dim-sum that he hadn't quite been able to manage at lunch; thinking that they would by now be heavy and greasy, he threw those to the monkeys, too, trying to aim for the more timid amongst them, but they were always pushed aside by the others.

Tony thought it would be best to return to the Botanic Gardens for a bus or, hopefully, a taxi, and started to retrace his steps. When he was about half-way there, he noticed a small clearing amongst the trees and bushes to his left, which he hadn't seen on his way down; glancing in, he saw a track through the undergrowth, leading up into the wooded hillside. It looked cool, green and inviting, so he took a few paces in.

The foliage on either side was beautiful, and frightening, all at the same time: above a general carpeting of plants with huge, heart-shaped leaves, like giant arums, there rose great grey-green spreading fans of tall pointed blades; vastly high, slim tree-trunks reached to an open-work green canopy, which was pierced by long, diagonal rays of bluish

light, falling across thick hanging creepers, and arching stems of
bamboo and rattan. Tony wandered in a little further: from a patch
of lilac flowers, a large butterfly fluttered up and hovered for a
moment in front of his face; it was perfectly black and velvety, with
its smaller, lower wings elongated into elegant tails. Tony was
entranced; this was more like it... the exciting reality, and the
atmosphere, of the piece of wild forest, more than made up for the
bland municipality of the Gardens.

Tony started to wander up the track; the gradient was easy, but he
was sweating with the humidity, and his backpack, though small,
began to pull at his shoulders. A large bronze lizard, its skin glinting as
though varnished, scampered across the track in front of him, and he
began to feel very adventurous; he paused at a junction to peer down
a path running off to his left, from which direction he seemed, in the
stillness, to hear the attractive sound of running water.

It was almost too much effort for Tony to remove his backpack to
search in it for something to wipe his forehead, as he didn't have a
handkerchief, and the sweat was now running down into his eyes, and
stinging; he tried using the front of his T-shirt, but it felt heavy and
clammy. His feet were red and swollen, for he always forgot to rub
them with sunscreen lotion, and they were criss-crossed with white
marks when he took of his sandals; the idea of a paddle in a hillside
stream was very appealing, so after a moment's hesitation, Tony
decided to trust in his ears, turn to the left, and follow the narrow,
winding track. Overhanging greenery had made of it a sun-dappled
tunnel, which lead eventually to a bowl-shaped, rock-filled clearing in
the jungle; the water which Tony had heard was gushing from the
hillside over a group of fallen boulders, forming a pool which filled the
shallow depression in the centre of the space, then tumbling off,
gurgling as it went, over more rocks, down the densely-wooded slope
which fell towards the road.

There were two men in the clearing; one sat on the rocks by the
edge of the pool, with his back to Tony as he emerged from the path,
and the other, in swimming-trunks, was squatting directly beneath the
fall as it cleared the boulders, the water falling onto his head, and
spreading out around him in a protective, glassy bubble. The scene was
inviting; the film-set jungle, the creepers falling through shafts of
light, the sparkling water; but, seeing the man bathing, Tony was shy,
and felt that he must be intruding in a private place. Still, he stood and

watched, enjoying the daring thought of stripping off his own clothes, and freely stepping into a hillside pool.

The bather stood, and, taking a piece of soap from a rock, began to lather his torso; the white foam ran down his body, and drifted into the pool, streaking the moving water as it slid away. Tony abandoned all thoughts of a bathe, sadly comparing his own white, flabby body with the dark, broad-shouldered, slim-waisted figure in front of him. The man rinsed himself under the fall, and looked up; he raised his eyebrows and grinned, evidently surprised to see the white man standing there, and called out something to the man sitting at the water's edge, who turned round, also smiling when he saw Tony standing a little way behind him.

"Hey, John!" Tony turned round.

"No, you, hey, John!" The two men were laughing at him. The bather had come away from the waterfall, and Tony could now see that he wasn't, in fact, wearing swimming-trunks, but thin cotton briefs, which had become transparent with the water; as he watched, the man took them off, wrung them out, and threw them onto a rock, then, picking up a towel, began vigorously to rub his dark, shoulder-length hair. Tony didn't swim, and he didn't go to a gym, despite telling himself that he should, when looking at the photographs of smiling men with perfect physiques on the covers of *Men's Fitness*, as he collected his copy of the *Radio Times* each week from Safeway's; it was a long time since he had seen the naked body of another man, and he watched, fascinated.

The bather said something to the man seated on the rocks, and they both looked at Tony and laughed again: Tony thought that perhaps after all it was rather odd, him just standing there watching a naked stranger drying himself; maybe even offensive, although the two men seemed happy enough. Nevertheless he was just thinking he really ought to go, when the seated man called to him again, "Hey, Johnny, come!"

Tony walked the few more yards to the end of the path, and entered the clearing: the man who had called to him was sitting in a patch of shade, and patted the rock at his side, where Tony, hot and sweating, was glad to join him; taking a Marlborough from a packet, he offered it to Tony, who took it, and they sat there side by side, smoking.

The bather seemed in no hurry to dry and cover himself. From his closer viewpoint, Tony could see that the man was tattooed, around his biceps and across the upper part of his chest, with some lines of sloping, Arabic, possibly, script; the darker markings against the dark skin had not been so noticeable before. The man's body could hardly have formed a greater contrast with Tony's: in front of him was a lean, firm figure, with the smooth torso slightly lighter than the limbs; the dark patch of hair around the man's thick, circumcised penis, and the black, wiry hairs on his calves, still held drops of water, which glinted in the sunlight.

Tony was well aware of his own appearance: thinning ginger hair, big face scarlet and dripping from the heat, belly dropping over the waistband of his shorts, T-shirt lank and piebald with damp; the man sitting with him, a paler man than the bather, Chinese perhaps, threw away his dog-end and said, "You come to bathe?" But any thoughts of removing his clothes had long since left Tony's head.

"No. I came for a walk. To look for the monkeys." This was apparently very amusing; the Chinese man laughed, and the bather grinned and repeated "Monkee, monkee"; he was still very slowly drying himself, and talking to his friend, who translated for Tony, "He thinks maybe, if not you come for bathe, you come for looking?"

"Looking?"

"Looking at him." The men laughed some more.

"Oh, I didn't know about this place. Honestly, I just came for a walk."

"So you don't like to look at him?" The bather was drying his hair again; Tony noticed that his armpits were almost as smooth as his chest, and that he wore a metal amulet on a chain around his neck.

"No. I mean, it's not that I don't like to."

"He is very handsome man."

"Yes, I suppose so."

"Very handsome. Me, I not so handsome like him." He translated for the bather, who laughed.

"Well, of course you're... I mean, your looks are different, that's all." Tony was beginning to feel caught up in a web of private jokes. The bather was talking to his friend again.

"He say, maybe you like to bathe with me?"

"Well..."

"Or maybe you don't like."

"No, of course – you mean here?"

"Can go another place, smaller place. Uphill one."

Uphill didn't sound the most attractive direction to Tony. "You mean, climbing?"

"Not so far. Little way only."

"Well, I'm not sure." Still naked, the bather picked up a rubber band, and drew his hair back into a ponytail; as he did so, his features took on a more simian aspect. Coming over, he squatted in front of his friend, from whose shirt pocket he took the packet of Marlborough, giving one cigarette to Tony, and putting another into his own mouth. From the same pocket he took a lighter; then, having lit both their cigarettes, he dropped packet and lighter back into the other man's pocket, finally tweaking his friend's nipple, through his shirt. Turning to Tony, he stretched out his hand, and made circular movements with his fingers through the gingery hairs just above Tony's plump, mottled knee. It was an extraordinary sensation. Tony was aware of how unprepossessing he looked, especially in the heat, and regretted the shape he had allowed his body to become; but certainly, the others showed no signs of repulsion.

The bather was speaking to the Chinese man, who translated, "He say, all white men have red hair."

"Well, not all. Not that many, actually."

"But that is what we say. *Ang mor*, red hair. Sometime we say, *Ang mor gow*, red hair monkey. So, red hair monkey come to look for local monkey." This he translated for the bather; it was obviously very amusing, as they both laughed quite a lot; the bather grinned at Tony, showing small, pointed teeth, and added something else.

"He say, how about this one?" The Chinese man rubbed his flies.

"This one?"

"Is also red?"

"Red?"

"The hair, is also red here?"

"Oh. Yes, actually it is. Quite red."

"He can see?"

"Oh." Tony was glad he had a cigarette to play with. But the bather stood up, laughing; he threw away his butt and stood smiling down at Tony, hand on hips. He really was standing very close; Tony could see no more drops of water on the dark skin. He noticed one or two long black hairs on a mole near the man's navel, which was quite prominent, as if clumsily tied; he wondered if, since the bather had touched him, he was allowed to touch the bather, but in any case he wouldn't have dared. Turning to his clothes, the man pulled on a pair of old jeans, and a faded Hard Rock Bangkok T-shirt; he rolled his damp briefs up with his towel, put them into a plastic bag, came back to Tony, smiled, and said "Good-bye," before saying a few more words to his friend, and walking away along the path.

Standing, the Chinese man said "Okay, come" and, after skirting the pool, started to climb up a rough track behind the waterfall; it didn't look too steep, so Tony thought he might as well follow, for a little while at any rate. Before long they came to a large boulder, which the Chinaman clambered over, followed by Tony, who had a little more difficulty; behind was a small pool, fed by a trickle of water, and surrounded by rocks.

"Here can bathe." The man took off his T-shirt, and looked at Tony. "Okay?" Tony looked back at him. The humidity in the breezeless forest was weighing down upon him, and with the extra exertion of the climb, the sweat was again pouring down his forehead; to sit in the cool water would be very pleasant. The Chinese man was fairly short, and not slender, as the other bather had been: his pale belly was well-rounded, the waist undefined, and the full breasts beginning to sag, with a pierced jade disc, like a flattened green Polo, hanging between them, on a gold chain; Tony didn't feel at such a lumpy disadvantage with this man, and could comfortably have undressed in front of him... even sat with him, for a while, in the small pool but somehow, he thought he would go back to the hotel. The Chinese man didn't seem to mind; he took off his shorts, and sat in his briefs cross-legged in the pool like a little plump Buddha, smiling at Tony, and calling after him as he scrambled back over the boulders, "Tomorrow you come?"

Speeding back to his hotel along the coast road. Tony had an empty feeling inside; it had certainly been his best day so far, but why had he been so timid in the forest? How exotic it would have been to have bathed in the pools there... the only time, too, that he had had anything other than 'hotel' contact with anybody local.

The following day, Tony had lunch at the Sheraton. They were running a Japanese buffet, which was quite interesting, but also quite dainty, so Tony found it a challenge to select enough of what he liked which was substantial enough, and he didn't like to go up too often; but in fact, he didn't intend to linger as long as usual. A taxi took him back to the Botanic Gardens, dropping him in front of the open gates, on which he turned his back, walking instead down the road to the gap in the undergrowth which gave onto the hillside track. His backpack was heavier than usual, as he had stuffed into it one of his hotel towels (plus, from lunch, double-wrapped in a couple of Sheraton napkins, some rather un-Japanese-looking, but tempting, chocolate cookies, which he hadn't given himself time to sit and eat, but thought instead might come in handy for later).

Tony was wearing his swimming-trunks under his shorts, just in case, as he certainly couldn't have wanted anyone to see him in his underwear; but he hadn't tried them on before packing them, and they were too tight, making him feel hot and nylony, and leaving deep red ruts where they had chafed the tops of his legs, as he had noticed in the Gents' at the Sheraton, so really he could have done with taking them off. Today, he wanted to feel adventurous and free, and to be just as local and jungly as the men he had met at the pool, and sit with them, and bathe, and offer them his cigarettes.

The rainforest greenery was just as lovely; the sunlight shone through the leafy canopy high above in dusty-golden shafts, and the arching bamboos and great sword-like leaves thrusting up beneath them made suitably romantic tropical silhouettes against a bluish haze. Looking up, Tony noticed a magnificent stag's-horn fern bursting from the forked trunk of one great, spreading tree, and mauve-pink blossoms – which may have been wild orchids? – sprouting from another, but he didn't spend quite as long gazing round today; instead, he headed up the track, turning left at the junction to follow the path to the waterfall. His backpack already felt unreasonable heavy; the sweat was beginning to sting his eyes again, and he realised that he had forgotten to bring a cotton handkerchief to wipe his face.

There was no one by the pool, either seated on the rocks or in the water; Tony felt a pang of disappointment, but looking at his watch he thought that he might be an hour or so earlier than the day before, and of course nobody had made any precise appointments, so he could hardly expect someone to be around at the very moment that he himself appeared. In any case, there was plenty more of the hillside to explore, but first he needed a sit-down, so he sat where the Chinaman had been sitting the day before, on the large, smooth rock at the water's edge.

He could hardly be bothered to take off his backpack, but he wanted to smoke, so he did; it was quite damp at the back, and he could feel his T-shirt sticking to his shoulder-blades. He sat and smoked a cigarette, wishing that he had thought to bring a bottle of water; still no one came, so he smoked another. But sitting and smoking hadn't stopped Tony sweating; the humidity, under the forest canopy, was again intense, so eventually he took off his T-shirt and wiped it over his face, chest and neck, but the fabric felt thick and damp.

Still no one appeared along the path, so although watching the falling water was soothing, and the plashing sound almost mesmerising, Tony decided to make the effort and scramble further up the hill, thinking that he really would bathe in the next, more private pool; he hoisted his rucksack onto one shoulder, with his T-shirt knotted around its other strap, and set off, arriving at the higher pool rather breathless. He took off his sandals, and sat with his feet in the water, which, though cool enough to be refreshing, was not in any way cold; after a while, he slid down his shorts and eased off his tight trunks, and, working his way carefully a little further into the pool, sat waist-deep in the gently-flowing current.

It was very peaceful under the dome of leaves which sheltered the rocky dell; fewer blue-gold sun-shafts penetrated that part of the forest, and Tony sat, relaxed, in a cocoon of soft green light; the dull tinkle of the trickling fall which fed the limpid pool was soporific, and after a few moments, his eyes began to close. In his dozing daydream, it was a peacock which strutted down to the edge of the pool, and began to lap up the water with its hard little pebble-like grey tongue: turning to face the white man, it fanned out its beautiful tail, and in the misty, blue-green haze of the jungle, it seemed to Tony that he was being watched by many half-hidden eyes; but it was the shrill call of a much smaller bird, canary-coloured, which awakened him, as it flew out from the trees, dipped low over the water and, following the stream as it left the pool, swooped away down the wooded hillside.

The branch from which it had flown was still shaking; the movement rippled down the tree, reaching the lowest fork; from this, a small creature dropped, and scampered down across the rocks until it reached the pool, where it crouched, uncertainly, opposite Tony, and looked over at him, whimpering. Tony was, again, thrilled to see a monkey at such close quarters, especially as there were just the two of them, making it a particularly intimate encounter; and although of course he could not be sure, it looked like one of the more timid of the group which he had tried to feed the day before. For a few moments Tony again studied the wrinkled, leathery little face, watching the large, anxious brown eyes darting this way and that, the creature occasionally glancing up into the trees and then staring again at Tony, with a more animated outburst of nervous chatter.

Wanting to offer something, Tony remembered the cookies he had brought, and wondered if the monkey would take one from him: then, as he turned to reach over for his rucksack, a larger beast dropped down behind him in a shower of leaves, hitting the ground with a loud screech; it loped towards the bag, and started pulling at the flap.

"Hey!"

Tony raised himself from the water, and reached out to grab his bag by clutching at the T-shirt knotted to it, but the larger monkey had a tight hold, and, after uttering a string of piercing screams, started tearing wildly at the nylon with its teeth. Tony, hearing another screech from above, looked up, as the green canopy above him crashed into life, and monkeys began to drop to the rocks all around him, some from low branches, others slithering down the thick, hanging leaves and half surrounded him, their staccato calls building into a harsh, jabbering chorus.

But a group of young males jumped, bounced almost, over the rocks towards Tony's rucksack, the first to arrive biting deep into the shoulders of the monkey in possession, which, screaming in pain, released its grip on the bag for a moment, enabling Tony to drag it a little way towards him, but within seconds more of the tribe had reached it, and begun to pull it this way and that, all the while screeching, lashing out at each other with paws and teeth, and scrabbling desperately at the tough nylon fabric.

The rucksack disappeared under a struggling mass of fur: one monkey whipped round to Tony and hissed at him, viciously; Tony, by this time very much alarmed, had relinquished his hold on the T-shirt; he saw a flash of white as the Sheraton napkins were snatched from their shredded pouch, sending the chocolate cookies bursting upwards, to be leapt on in mid-air by the screaming creatures, each tit-bit savagely fought over by two or three males, with the females shrieking them on. Some of the females had started bickering and fighting amongst themselves: one grabbed a tiny baby from the teats of another, biting deep into its neck so that the head nearly left the body, then flinging the bleeding thing into the pool!; Tony watched as the deprived mother stared for a moment at the reddening water, then leapt at the throat other attacker, whose wild, chattering mouth was dripping with carmine foam.

Others still tore at the rucksack, and Tony could see the hotel towel being tossed aside as another, larger, monkey shot out from the undergrowth, uttering grating, rattling cries, and bounded towards the group fighting over his possessions, cannoning into them and knocking them aside; muttering, they crouched on the rocks, as the newcomer snatched the remaining contents from the wreck of the bag.

Tony stayed seated naked by the pool, too nervous to move and call attention to himself: he watched as the new monkey bit into his tube of suntan cream, sending up a thick white fountain, and ripped into the packet of Marlborough, showering out the crushed cigarettes all around him, in a frenzy of frustration. Thinking that he must try to go, Tony began slowly to reach out for his shorts, but the monkey saw him, threw down the torn guidebook it had been shredding and, letting out a string of cough-like gasps, chuah, chuah, chuah, followed by a hoarse, angry scream, leapt to the shorts and tugged at them, its teeth bared, a whining snarl vibrating from its throat. It seemed important to Tony to keep holding on; he thought of his wallet, his cards. Flecks of bubbling spittle flew from the creature's mouth as it jerked its head from side to side, and, as it scratched awkwardly at the ground with its back legs, Tony realised that he was face to face with the animal with the flattened back paw.

Other monkeys were screeching again now, and the piercing, tribal noise was sickening; Tony felt very much alone. Suddenly, the monkey in front of him dropped the shorts, lunged forward, and grabbed at Tony's bright metal wristwatch; Tony shouted "No!" and pulled his arm away; but the creature leapt forward again and bit him, savagely, on the forearm, and gibbered up at him, its mouth brimming with scarlet froth. Staring at the swelling, crimson beads, welling from the wound, Tony heard a movement behind him, and half-turned as one of the females hurled herself at him, biting into his fleshy right shoulder before clinging to his back with her arms at his neck, pressing her sharp bony fingers hard into his throat at either side. Oh God! – but it was difficult to shout; the crippled male lunged at him again, and although Tony couldn't feel it, he could see that the animal had bitten a lump from his thigh, as there was a deep pink hole in the ginger-haired white flesh, which was slowly filling up with blood. The other monkeys were closer now, and they all seemed to be screaming, so Tony couldn't concentrate, but he tried to stand up, which was difficult, because of the uneven rocks, and also because grabbing, stabbing things were pulling him down from behind, and there was a thick, rank, foxy smell.

At about that time, Doctor Loh and his wife, who ran the Happy Pet House, were standing by the roadside, and staring at the pile of rotting fruit which marked the monkeys' feeding-place. Mrs. Loh sniffed, and pulled a face. "What did the tourist people say?"

"They asked us to come and have a look, that's all, since that woman wrote to complain about the monkey biting her daughter's ankle."

"I suppose they're afraid of another outbreak, like last time. Maybe they should start some selective culling again."

"Oh, no, you can't blame the monkeys; and don't forget how close this place is to the Indian temples; at least one of their shrines is dedicated to the poor little beasts."

"I've never really understood all that."

"Me neither, but I think it's something to do with the spirit of place; the monkeys are of the hills, and they're here to watch over their patch, protect it, perhaps... they're very territorial. But when they overdo it, it certainly doesn't do the tourist trade any good; give the press five minutes, and they'll whip up a rabies scare."

"This place is disgusting; it can't be because they haven't enough fruit to eat."

"No, I don't think it's the fruit that's the problem." The doctor glanced over the rubbish lying on the scrubby grass, sifting through it with the toe of his shoe, then stooping to pick up a piece of torn cellophane. "'Yusuf Bakery.' I thought it might be this; they've started dumping all their stale stuff here again; I imagine it's cheaper than paying the refuse men." They walked over to the old man with the hand cart, who was just preparing to leave. "Uncle, a packet of those."

"But, today, monkeys don't have."

"It's okay." As the man trundled his cart away, the doctor took a bun from the packet, and broke it open to show his wife the bright yellow centre. "They love all this sugary stuff, and it seems they get plenty of it. No wonder they don't bother with the fruit any more."

"And the aggression?"

"Well, this stuff wasn't made for animals; tartrazine, amongst other junk. It just sends them, as one might say, apeshit."

"Darling."

"... to coin a phrase. I guess I'll have to get onto the health people, see if they can put a stop to all this dumping."

"There don't seem to be any of the monkeys around today."

"No, but they're not far away... can't you hear them?" They stood and listened for a while; from somewhere up on the hill, they could quite clearly hear a chorus of whoops and shrieks.

"Anyway, it looks as if we're in time to stop anything more serious. Let's go home."

Now You See It Now You Don't
Francis King

Now You See It Now You Don't
Francis King

In the late afternoon, the two middle-aged men strolled along the Corniche. Toby, stocky and bow-legged, wore a pair of crumpled shorts, a grubby tee-shirt and sandals, a broken thong of which he had that same morning maladroitly repaired with a length of string provided by the hotel bell captain. Noel, gangling and elegant, wore a white tropical suit and a wide-brimmed Panama hat. Toby, having inherited a fortune from his father, dawdled through life. Noel, a successful, and not always scrupulous, antiques dealer, sprinted through it.

A tall, muscular boy, sixteen or seventeen at a guess, with large hands, a large, misshapen nose and a tousled mop of hair, loomed up in their path. He was wearing a tattered, stained djellabah that all but covered his trainers. "Hello!" he greeted them. "Hello," Toby eagerly responded, flashing his charming smile.

"Oh, do let's get a move on!" Noel raised fingers to his nose. There was an acrid odour emanating from the body stubbornly planted in front of them.

"Where you from?"

"Where are we from? From England. From a town called Brighton. Have you ever visited England?"

Had he ever visited England? What a ludicrous question, Noel thought and almost said.

"No visit. Never." The boy pointed at his chest. "Poor. Want visit England. But – poor, poor. No money. How many days Luxor?"

"Well, we arrived – let's see – two days ago. We plan to stay for another five days. And then – then maybe we'll go on to Cairo or Aswan. Or even both. That's how we like to travel. No fixed plans. We go as the spirit takes us."

"You go West Bank?"

"Oh, for heaven's sake!" Noel slapped out at a fly that kept hovering around him. He might have been slapping out at the boy.

"Yes, we were there this morning. And we plan to go there again tomorrow."

"You want taxi?"

"Well, we usually get one outside the hotel..."

"I have cousin. Good taxi. Very cheap. Hotel taxi, much money. I arrange taxi tomorrow. I come with you. Guide. Yes? My name Abdul. Abdul. Everyone know Abdul."

"Well... Well, that's very kind of you. What do you think, Noel? That hotel taxi was far more expensive than it should have been."

"You know exactly what I think."

But Toby had suffered what he was later to call a *coup de foudre*. "I'd like to give his taxi cousin a try. I really would. Would you mind? Please. I'll pay." Although, from his appearance, anyone might suppose him to be far poorer than Noel, he was in fact far richer. He again flashed that smile, artless and winning, that people could never resist. "The truth is – I find him really rather C-U-T-E." He spelled it out, though there was little likelihood that the boy would have understood the word. "I think – I think I've fallen for him. Yes, I do, I really do."

"Oh, not again!" Noel did not fall for people, any more than he fell for a new pair of socks or a bottle of gin casually bought and then in due course no less casually replaced. "He's hideous! He's dirty."

"Well, where's this taxi?" Noel had been obliged to take two Immodium that morning, and the back pocket of his trousers was stuffed with lavatory paper. He had all but decided to spend the day at the hotel.

Abdul pointed up the steep, uneven path that led from the crowded West Bank quay into the village above it.

"But all the taxis are here."

"Cousin wait in cool place. Not far. Taxi cool."

Noel's stomach was again churning, and he had suddenly become aware that his new shoes were pinching feet swollen in the heat. Should he swallow one more of the Immodium tablets that he was carrying in the breast pocket of his jacket? "This is ridiculous. The taxi may be cool, but we're getting extremely hot trudging up this path."

Toby did not answer. He now had one hand on Abdul's shoulder. He was talking animatedly. Abdul shuffled along stiffly, head lowered. Noel guessed that he was embarrassed by this all too public demonstration of affection.

"There is taxi!" Abdul said. But what he was pointing at was a pristine minibus, with 'Cleopatra Tours' emblazoned on its side.

"That's not a taxi," Noel protested.

"Yes, yes, cousin's taxi."

The driver, a middle-aged man with a straggly moustache and a face pitted with either acne or smallpox, put aside the newspaper that he had been reading and descended stiffly from the driving-seat. Unlike Abdul's brown, stained djellabah, his was white and spotless. "Hello!" he greeted them. "Me Mohammed."

Noel did not respond. Toby went forward, extended a hand, and beamed. "Good morning. It's a beautiful day, Mohammed. My name is Toby and my friend here" – he pointed – "is called Noel." As so often Noel wanted to exclaim "Oh, cut the crap!" But at the same time he felt a reluctant admiration for Toby's unfailing bonhomie.

"Well, let's get moving!" Toby said.

"We'd better first fix a price."

"Oh, don't let's bother. I'm sure he's not going to cheat us. Not if he's Abdul's cousin."

Noel realised that, as always, he would have to conduct the bargaining.

When asked to name his price, Mohammed replied firmly: "One hundred fifty. Egyptian pound. Cheap. Special price. You friends Abdul. Abdul my cousin."

Noel became indignant. Ridiculous! The day before they had paid a mere fifty Egyptian pounds for a taxi for a whole day. The two men began to bargain. Finally, a sum of sixty was reached. Both then felt satisfied. Toby had taken no part in the argument. He would often tell people that he hated any disagreement, fuss or row. Such things made him feel ill, he would say.

"Well, that's settled." Having clambered into the mini-bus, Toby rested his hand on Abdul's knee with a sigh. "Now we can enjoy a lovely day." He was amazed and delighted when the boy took his hand in his and with the other hand began to stroke it. There was something exciting both in the spontaneity of the move and in the abrasive contact of that callused palm.

By now Noel, sunk scowling in his seat beside Mohammed, had decided that he had worked out for himself the truth about the 'taxi'. Cleopatra Travel must employ Mohammed as a driver, ferrying customers from and to the airport and around the town. This was his

day off. He had 'borrowed' the mini-bus to make some extra money.
Of that extra money, Abdul would no doubt get his cut.

The flank of a mountain embraced the whole site of the Hatshepsut
temple like the wings of some vast, hovering solar disc. The three
terraces, stacked one above the other, radiated an almost unbearable
heat and dazzle. Noel began to ascend ahead of Toby and Abdul, until,
looking back before starting laboriously to mount the ramp to the
second terrace, he saw, with a sense of angry abandonment, that they
had given up. Far below, perched side by side on a slab of masonry,
they were deep in conversation. They had forgotten him.

When he descended, they had vanished. At the same time, he felt
a slithering in his gut, as though some reptile were lazily moving there,
followed by a sharp tweak of pain. Christ! Unable to find any lavatory,
he wandered off into the blazing heat, across a bare landscape littered
with stones and fragments of masonry, and eventually squatted
behind an empty hut, its door ajar and its wooden floor rotten. If
anyone saw him, too bad! Just as he had lowered himself into position,
his immaculate trousers trailing in the dust round his ankles, he heard
a scrabbling sound. Oh, hell!

But instead of the expected tourist or labourer, it was a long-eared,
jackal-like dog, its coat a dusty grey. Having sloped round the hut, it
seated itself four or five yards in front of him. It stared at him. Then
it closed its slanting, mica-black eyes, raised its head and slowly
opened its mouth, revealing small, sharp teeth. Noel thought that it
was going to emit a howl, but instead it merely yawned. Once again
it fixed its eyes on him. He had seen a head exactly like that in the
Museum the previous afternoon. It belonged to a statue of the god
Anubis, who escorted the souls of the dead into the presence of the
judge of the infernal regions. He and the dog stared at each other for
several seconds. Then Noel felt passing through him the emotional
equivalent of the reptilian gliding through the gut that had brought
him to this spot. In panic he defecated in an explosive burst. Then,
half standing, half crouching, he scrabbled in the back pocket of his
trousers for some tissues.

As he returned to the temple, the dog pattered behind him. But, on
their approach to the crowds at its entrance, it suddenly shot off at an
angle, to make for Toby and Abdul, who were standing by a stall selling
souvenirs. Having reached them, the dog jumped up at Abdul, its

paws on his knees. Abdul reared away in terror. Then he kicked out at the dog viciously. The dog let out a shrill squeal, bared its teeth and, tail between legs, scampered off, zigzag, into the crowd. Noel felt a queasy horror.

Toby waved. It was as though he had been totally unaware of the incident. "So there you are! We wondered what had happened to you."

"I had another attack of the squitters."

"Oh, gosh! Poor you! Are you all right now? Frankly, you don't look all that good."

"Thanks. You know how I hate to be told I'm looking unwell."

"Oh, sorry, sorry! Abdul's just been telling me that this is where that massacre took place. D'you remember? Lots and lots of tourists machine-gunned. Mostly Japanese and Americans." Toby spoke with a strange, disconcerting elation.

Abdul was smiling beside him, head cocked on one side. His panic over the dog and subsequent brutality might never have occurred. He nodded. "Many, many killed. There – there!" he said in the same elated tone. He pointed. "Much blood." He gave a staccato laugh, which seemed to erupt from the back of his throat.

"Where's Mohammed?" Noel demanded shortly. He wanted to get away. "This place gives me the creeps."

"Oh, but it's so beautiful," Toby said.

"You've hardly looked at it," Noel pulled a face. "It stinks of death. Haunted by all those wretched murdered people."

Toby now wanted to spend every hour of every day with Abdul.

"Oh, do join us!" he pleaded with Noel over the vast breakfast buffet, from which many of the hotel guests would surreptitiously filch the wherewithal for their lunches. "He's really awfully sweet. I don't know what you've got against him."

"He's a bore. And it's embarrassing to be seen in the company of someone so scruffy and so young. No one could possibly mistake him for a guide or a friend of ours."

"I know you'd enjoy the trip to Banana Island. And, with this wind, it'll be the perfect day for it."

"And who owns the felucca? A friend? A cousin?" The night before Noel had reluctantly accompanied Toby and Abdul to a restaurant, said by Abdul to be owned by another cousin of his, above a spice shop in the souk. The food had been so disgusting that he had left most of what had been piled on his plate, and the bill had been so exorbitant that, much to Toby's and Mohammed's dismay, he had ended up shouting first at the waiter, who knew no English, and then at the proprietor, who had shuffled out from a curtained recess, puffing at a long, malodorous cheroot. Eventually, having realised that he had met his match, the proprietor had murmured "Okay, okay. For my friends I take away twenty," and had amended the bill. Noel's only response had been "What barefaced cheek!"

"Well, yes, the felucca does belong to one of the family. A brother-in-law, I think. But he's taking us for about half of what people usually have to pay."

"Oh, you're such a push-over!"

Toby bit into his croissant and swallowed. "You've got him wrong, you know. He's really awfully sweet. And a hundred per cent honest. Truly – you've got him wrong."

"I don't think so."

"Anyway, if one's so poor – one's father dead, a number of younger brothers and sisters dependent on one – it's understandable that, having met a foreigner... I mean, to them we must seem like millionaires. Do you realise that what we're charged each night for our rooms is more than the average monthly wage? Abdul told me that." He leaned across the table. "Oh, Noel, do come with us! Do! Why not?"

"Please, Toby. You have your fun. And let me have mine. I came here to see tombs and temples and to enjoy this wonderful climate. I didn't come here to trail around with a smelly little tart."

Toby's face was momentarily convulsed with shock. Then he said in a soft, sorrowful voice: "That's really not a nice way to talk about him. He's not a tart, not at all. He never asks me for money. Sometimes I give him something, of course, I do. But he often doesn't want to take it from me. I think in an odd way – he – he really cares for me." He swallowed. "Loves me. As a son loves his father," he added hastily. "His father died when he was four."

"Loves you! Loves your wallet, more likely."

Soon after that, Toby picked his room key off the table and got slowly to his feet. He felt both hurt and guilty. "Well, I'll see you later. I'd better be off now."

It was at that moment that Noel reached a decision. He would tell Toby that he was going to travel down to Aswan by boat the following morning. Toby could accompany him if he wished. Otherwise, he would return in four or five days, so that they could travel back together on the plane to Gatwick.

A small boy in an overlarge djellabah carried out most of the work of sailing the felucca, at the barked instructions of the stout, taciturn captain. Unlike most Egyptians, the captain made no attempt to ingratiate himself with the foreigner. He grunted as he put out a hand to help Toby aboard. He pointed to where Toby and Abdul should sit on some cushions. Then he turned away, to squat as far away from them as possible.

As the felucca lazily tacked back and forth from one side of the river to the other, Abdul and Toby, perched side by side, held each other's hands. They talked little but from time to time one or the other would turn his head and they would smile simultaneously.

Once in midstream, the captain began to roll himself a joint. Having puffed at it for a while, eyes half-closed, he slowly got up, waddled over to Abdul and handed it to him. Abdul drew on it three or four times, gave an abstracted smile, and then extended the pinched remains of it to Toby.

Toby drew back. "Oh, no. No, thank you. I don't smoke." From the smell, he knew what he was being offered.

"Good," Abdul said. He gave that joyous laugh of his that always had the effect of filling Toby with an answering joy. "Good," he said. "Make happy."

Toby wanted to say "But I'm happy – wonderfully happy – already." But to please Abdul he took the joint and cautiously drew on it. Then he held it out. "Thank you."

"More, more!" Abdul urged, laughing.

Toby shook his head.

Leaving the captain and the boy on the felucca, Toby and Abdul wandered through the banana plantation. Recklessly, even though they kept meeting other tourists, Toby would from time to time succumb to the perilous craving to embrace Abdul, his mouth glued to his. Abdul resisted at first, then showed an equal ardour. Toby could feel the boy's cock hard against him, through the thick, stained fabric of the djellabah. On one occasion three Japanese women came on them in one of these embraces. One put a hand up to her mouth and giggled behind it, one let out a brief squawk, and the third stared, round-eyed. Briefly they halted. Then, like startled deer, they swerved off on to another path. Eventually, Abdul caught Toby by the hand and attempted to drag him down an incline towards a rubbish tip. But Toby, remembering the recent case of a group of Cairo men savagely sentenced to four or five years in prison merely for having attended a gay party, pulled away and shook his head.

As they boarded the felucca, he thought what a coward he had been to reject that opportunity. But then, as first the sky and then the waters began to darken, and he sat beside Abdul, an arm round his shoulders and their bodies so close that the two of them seemed to have been melded into one, he had no regrets. I have never been so happy, he thought. Never. He removed his hand from Abdul's shoulder and ran the fingers of it through the boy's dry, dusty hair. Abdul laughed and ran his own callused hand over Toby's almost totally bald pate.

Soon after that, the felucca ran into trouble. Having hugged the west bank of the river for a considerable time, it all but tipped over at a capricious gust of a wind and grated to a standstill. The captain shouted angrily at his diminutive assistant, who, still in his djellabah, at once jumped into the opaque water and began to tug on a rope thrown down to him. The captain then struggled with a metal shaft protruding from the middle of the boat – to raise the rudder, Toby assumed. Abdul joined him. The two men tugged in turn. At last the boat began to move. Abdul laughed, then held up his hand. Somehow he had managed to nick his middle finger on the metal shaft. Blood trickled from it.

"Oh, look what you've done!" Toby cried out in dismay. He felt in the back pocket of his shorts and produced some tissues. "Here."

"Nothing, nothing."

"Don't be silly. Come here!"

Abdul went across. He held out his hand.

Toby surprised himself by what he did next. Instead of wrapping the finger in the tissues, he raised it to his mouth. He sucked on it.

The blood tasted strangely metallic and sweet. He had never tasted blood like that before. Greedily he sucked on it again. It filled him with a dizzying rapture.

Toby knew that the calèche driver was making a huge detour on the way from the restaurant owned by another of Abdul's 'cousins' back to the hotel. But so far from objecting, he was glad of it. Heavenly, heavenly, to sit like this, so close to Abdul, his hand on his cock and

Abdul's hand on his, with the immense sky, pricked by innumerable stars, above them, and the emaciated horse, from time to time galvanised into a stumbling trot by a lash of the whip, clip-clopping up one narrow, dark, deserted street after another.

There was a removable metal barrier across the entrance to the hotel drive. A soldier was seated on a stool beside it, a rifle across his knees. No calèche, the driver indicated, was allowed to proceed any further. Abdul jumped out and then held out a hand to help Toby down. The driver named a sum and, though he knew it to be exorbitant, Toby paid at once, not grudgingly but with a curious sense of euphoric liberation.

As the calèche creaked round in a half-circle, Toby suddenly thought of how Abdul would get home.

"Stop! Stop!" he called out. But the driver either did not hear or decided to ignore the summons for fear that Toby was going to demand back some of the overpayment.

"We must find a taxi for you."

"No, no! Not necessary! I walk to bus."

"But will there be a bus at this hour?"

"Maybe." Abdul did not seem at all worried.

"Oh, I wish I could take you into the hotel." Toby said it with an extraordinary intensity of longing. They had spoken about this before. But Abdul had said that it was out of the question, and Toby had known that he was right. Since the events of September 11, two armed policemen frisked anyone, even a tourist, who wished to enter the hotel. With Toby and Noel these two men had always been flirtatious. But they would not be flirtatious with Abdul, quite the reverse. There were also at least half-a-dozen men on guard in the grounds.

"Oh, I so much want to hold you in my arms in my bedroom – to show you how much I love you … Why, why, why do things have to be so difficult?"

"I find a way." Abdul nodded gravely, then repeated: "I find a way."

"But how? How?"

The soldier had turned his head and was staring at them. But, as in the banana plantation, Toby, usually so cautious and conventional, did not care. He took Abdul in his arms and kissed him on the mouth. "Goodnight, my darling." Once again he could feel that cock hard against him through the djellabah. Noel was wrong. The boy must, must, must have some feelings for him. It was not just a question of money. "We'll have to say goodbye here."

Again they embraced. Again Toby felt that cock hard against him.

As, alone now, Toby approached the hotel, he saw a greyish shadow imposed on the hunched shape of a bush to the left of the entrance. Oddly, the shadow seemed to flicker as though it were a paper cutout in a wind. He halted, peered. He had at first thought that it must be one of the feral cats that, voracious but wary, stalked the area round the poolside restaurant, waiting for someone to chuck over to them a scrap of gristle, a prawn-shell or a fish head. But now he realised that it was a dog. All at once he remembered that jackal-like dog with the long, pricked ears and slanting eyes, at which Abdul, in a panic, had kicked out. This dog exactly resembled that one. But it couldn't be the same dog. How could it have crossed the river? The breed must be a common Egyptian one. He was about to push at the swing-door into the hotel, then turned and looked round again. *Now you see it, now you don't.* He heard a faint click, as of a camera shutter. With that click, the dog had vanished...

Oh, no doubt, it had slunk back out of sight into the bush. But as the lift carried him the four floors up to his room, he felt a lingering unease. Yes, there had been a definite click and simultaneously an invisible hand had erased that tremulous, grey shadow. Weird.

Toby, who so often boasted that he fell asleep as soon as his head had touched the pillow, now could not sleep. He lay with his hands crossed behind his head on the vast double bed and stared up at the ceiling. He had forgotten the disquieting mystery of the dog. He still felt sexually aroused. He wondered whether to toss himself off. On his rare nights of insomnia, he had always found that that was the most effective sleeping pill of all. He began to imagine to himself Abdul's journey home – the waiting for a long deferred and overcrowded bus, the ill-lit, dilapidated ferry nudging its clumsy way across the river, the walk up the steep path to the mud-house, its windows unglazed apertures, that Abdul had pointed out to him...

He was aroused from his reverie by a tap-tapping sound. Was it coming from the next-door room, occupied by a young American couple with whom, from time to time, he exchanged a few words? He raised himself on an elbow, his senses alert. He was uncomfortably aware of the hastening beat of his heart. The tap-tapping was coming from the balcony.

He clambered out of bed, hesitated, then crossed over to the window. Cautiously, he pulled back the heavy curtain and peered out, a hand raised to his eyes.

It was Abdul. He was smiling, the tip of his tongue showing between teeth startlingly white in the moonlight. Toby hurried to unbolt the door and then to open the wire screen beyond it. Without saying a word, Abdul slipped into the room and closed the screen and door behind him. He was sweating from the exertion of having reached the balcony.

"How did you get up here?"

In his halting English, laughing excitedly between sentences and even phrases, Abdul explained. Workmen were renovating one wing of the hotel. There was scaffolding. Hadn't Toby noticed? He had crossed a field, that field overlooked by the balcony, scaled a low wall, and then climbed up the scaffolding. He had worked his way along the roof of the wing and jumped from that roof on to the one just above the fourth story. From there he had lowered himself down on to the balcony. It was lucky that the previous evening, as they had walked along the path between the river and the gardens of the hotel, Toby had pointed out his balcony, the last on the fourth floor on that side of the hotel.

"But you shouldn't have taken such a risk! Crazy, crazy!" But secretly Abdul's courage and enterprise thrilled Toby.

First Abdul had to inspect everything. He opened drawers, examined the various toiletries in the bathroom and even took off the stopper of a small flask of shampoo to sniff at it, flushed the lavatory, turned the air-conditioning up and down, switched the various lights off and on, and bounced on the bed. Then he pulled the dusty, tattered djellabah off over his head and, seated naked on a chair, removed his trainers. Toby went up behind him, stooped and put his arms around him. But first Abdul insisted on having a shower. For a time, Toby watched as the water cascaded over the muscular body. Then, on a sudden impulse, he hurriedly pulled off his pyjamas and himself stepped into the shower. He held Abdul close, his face against his shoulder. He gasped for breath as the water splashed on to the pair of them. They both began to laugh more and more loudly until Toby, mindful of the American couple, put a hand over Abdul's mouth. "Sh!"

Later, after they had made love, Toby scrambled off the bed and looked down at Abdul's still naked body. "Oh, if only I had a photograph of you! If only I had a camera! Noel's always the photographer on our expeditions."

"You want photograph?"

"Oh, yes, yes! So that when I'm back in England, I can look at you."

"I bring photograph. Tomorrow. French friend take photograph. I bring."

Toby felt a wasp sting of jealousy. "French friend? What friend? Do you mean lover?"

Abdul laughed. "Not what you think! Married. Travel on felucca, wife, children, two children."

Toby did not believe him. But he no longer cared.

When the dawn was about to break, Abdul said that he must go. Otherwise the police might see him. Hurriedly he dressed. Then, careful to make no sound, he opened first the door to the balcony and next the wire screen. Toby held out the handful of ten-dollar notes that he had fetched from his room safe while Abdul had been dressing.

"No, no!"

"Yes. Please! I want you to have this."

Without any further hesitation Abdul took the money and tucked it into a pocket inside the voluminous djellabah. "See you again."

"See you tomorrow. Same place. Eleven."

They kissed. Then kissed again and yet again.

"Don't forget the photograph."

"Photograph – yes, remember, remember!"

"Promise!"

"Promise. Abdul always keep promise."

Toby craned his head to watch as, with extraordinary agility, Abdul swung himself up from the balcony and on to the roof. For a moment the boy stood there, outlined against a sky now streaked with the pale yellow of the dawn just breaking. The air was chill. He waved, smiled, waved. Then he was gone.

Toby remained on the balcony in only his pyjama trousers. He clutched its rail, looked down. Suddenly, a grey streak seared his eyeballs, moving at extraordinary speed across the dim garden below. He thought: the dog!

Then he heard the shot. It was followed by three more.

Two days later Noel returned.

"I should have gone down."

"What would have been the point? He was dead. You would have been implicated. They might have arrested you. They'd have certainly questioned you. We might have missed the plane."

"I should have gone down. It was a kind of betrayal."

"Don't be silly. But what a crazy thing for him to do. Guards everywhere. Armed. Nervous. Trigger-happy. Crazy."

"It was my fault. My fault. I'll never forgive myself."

Until this conversation, they had been almost totally silent during dinner. Noel had repeatedly gone back to the buffet. Toby had eaten almost nothing.

After dinner, while Noel sat in the library rereading one of his guidebooks, Toby restlessly wandered the garden. He half hoped and half feared that he would once again see the jackal-like dog. But there was no sign of it. Three policemen sat round the pool, each with a gun across his knees. They were talking in low voices, punctuated by boisterous laughter. Perhaps it was one of them who had killed Abdul.

Toby decided to go up to his room. Without saying anything to Noel, he made for the lift. His two American neighbours staggered into it after him. This was not the first time when he had seen them drunk after dinner. They greeted him cheerfully and the man said: "Having fun?"

Toby merely shrugged.

As the three of them walked down the corridor, the American woman said: "You remember those shots the other night? Apparently it was someone trying to break into the hotel. That receptionist – the one with the squint – just told us. We're not supposed to know, of course. The authorities are trying to hush it up. Might put off tourists."

"It makes one nervous,' the man took up. "He could have been a terrorist. He could have blown us all to hell."

As he put his key in the door, Toby heard the sound of splashing. Had he left the shower on? Hurriedly he opened the bathroom door. The light was on, the floor was awash, as it had been on that night when he and Abdul had stood clutching each other under the battering of the water. But the shower was now off.

Puzzled and in growing apprehension, he left the bathroom and went into the bedroom. The window to the balcony and the wire screen were open. Then he realised that there was something on his pillow. He went over, stooped to pick it up. It was a snapshot of Abdul standing nude by open French windows, with the out-of-focus blur of a tree beyond him. Under the tree there was an amorphous grey shape. Was it – could it be – that jackal-like dog crouching there? Toby stared down at the photograph for a long time. He could not be sure.

Then he became aware of a stickiness on his forefinger and middle finger, and at the same time saw that something had been written across the bottom of the snapshot in Arabic.

He examined his fingers with a mixture of amazement and mounting terror. They were sticky with blood. He put the fingers to his mouth and sucked them. The blood tasted strangely bitter and caustic. He felt that he was about to retch. It might have been a poison.

Of course Noel had his explanations. He always did.

For some reason – probably the sort of blockage that constantly occurred with Egyptian plumbing – the water from the shower that Toby had taken before dinner had at first not flowed down the waste pipe. Or perhaps one of the floor staff had decided to take a shower while Toby was at dinner.

And the photograph? Well, it was not impossible that that same member of the floor staff had been a friend or even a relative of Abdul and so, having known of the affair, had decided to leave that image of the dead man on Toby's pillow. Why not? It was the sort of sentimental gesture one might expect from an Egyptian.

And the blood? Well, it could be that the person who had left the photograph had not, after all been a member of the staff. Perhaps, instead, it was the 'cousin' who had driven them in the mini-bus. In that case, he might have climbed into the room as Abdul had climbed into it and had then somehow cut his hand while doing so. Wasn't that a possibility?

But obstinately Toby kept shaking his head. "No, no," he said. Then loudly and decisively: "No!"

Back in Brighton, Toby showed the photograph to the Algerian lover of a friend of his. Could he translate the inscription?

The Algerian peered down, then looked up. "Oum Khaltoum," he said. He went on to explain that the words were from a song made popular by the most famous of Arab singers of her time.

"What do they say?"

The Algerian pursed his lips and frowned. Then he ventured:

"Death conquers life. But love conquers death."

Toby gave a little gasp and raised a hand to his eyes, as though to shield them from a sudden glare.

The Algerian again peered down at the photograph. "There's something else here. The writing is bad. An uneducated man must have written it. Yes." He himself was an educated man, a radiologist. He peered again. "'With my love. Forever'. And signed," he added. "Signed 'Abdul'." He looked up, laughed. "Who is this Abdul? A boy-friend?"

At first Toby kept the photograph on his bedside table, in a frame specially bought for it. Then, when he looked at it – which he did less and less – he noticed that it was beginning to fade. The sun must be causing that, he decided, and placed the photograph in a Florentine tooled-leather box in which he kept such things as studs, cuff links, collar-stiffeners and safety pins. On the rare occasions that he had recourse to the box he realised with a mingling of dismay and bewilderment that the fading was continuing.

Seven months later he and Noel had returned from what Toby described as an 'utterly blissful' holiday in Thailand. During that holiday, Noel had repeatedly told him that he was once again making a fool of himself – this time over a waiter in their Chiang Mai hotel. But Toby had not cared. The trouble with dear old Noel had always been that he had no idea at all of what it meant to fall in love.

That evening, even though neither of them was musical, they were about to make what they called their 'annual pilgrimage' to Glyndebourne. Toby opened the leather box to get out a pair of cuff links and studs for the old-fashioned dress shirt that he now so rarely wore. To his amazement he then found that the surface of snapshot had become little more than a blank, milky expanse. How could that have happened? As with the dog on that horrible night in Luxor: *Now you see it, now you don't.*

Oh, probably the man who had printed the snapshot had used some primitive process, he hastily told himself, that resulted in rapid fading.

But then – the thought suddenly came to him – why had both the bloodstain and Abdul's scrawl also vanished?

His lips trembled. The hands holding the snapshot began to shake uncontrollably. Nothing lasted. Nothing. That was the hellish thing about life. And death. And love.

With a single convulsive movement he tore the snapshot into two and then, in mounting frenzy, into innumerable tiny scraps.

My Brother's Shadow
Simon Lovat

My Brother's Shadow
Simon Lovat

The light here is hard and astringent, so unlike the soft light of my native country, England. The sun, which penetrates the high square window above the wooden desk at which I now sit to compose this narrative, illuminates everything, and leaves no lurking shadow in any corner. I find this revealing clarity both a burden and a painful pleasure. It is always hot on my little island, where I conduct my all but solitary existence, but despite the temperature outside – which experience has taught me is intolerable at this time of day – my room is mercifully cool. I have the builders of the house to thank for that. The walls are amazingly thick, and painted entirely white. No blemish or stain imposes upon them, as if no hand had ever leant against them for support, and no foot had ever scuffed the white wood skirt which runs all around, either by accident or in anger. Surely, in such an abode as this there is no place for dissimulation, and so I take heart. Difficult as my task is, I shall take this austere room as my model for the strange story that follows. Therefore, just as the sun pours undiluted past my elbow, apparently undisturbed by a single mote of dust, so let my narrative be clear and unaffected. And if my tale seems severe at times, dear reader, then blame the light; blame the Mediterranean heat; or if your conscience instructs you to do so, blame Sir John Foyle.

I will be three and twenty this coming April, in the year 18—, and remain, unfortunately, a bachelor. The reason for this unhappy circumstance no doubt lies in my weak constitution. I was a sickly child. From earliest memory, I have suffered from a fragile disposition, coupled with a disorder of the nerves, which left me confined to my bed, or to my room, for protracted periods. My mother consulted the illustrious Dr Thorne, of Leeds, in consequence of my condition, who recommended that I should be restrained from all but the most meditative of occupations, for the good of my health. He also suggested that I be excused from any agitating or difficult duties, and be shielded from unnecessary upheaval. Thus, his first edict ensured that I was forbidden to run, or to take part in any physical activity whatsoever, unlike my hearty brother and sister. My mother, erring on the side of caution, forbade me from walking at anything but the most funereal of paces, which rendered my melancholy existence, in those brief periods during which I was not confined to my room, still more so. Governed by the doctor's latter pronouncement, she further decided – whether at the suggestion of Dr Thorne, or on her own account, I cannot say – that any 'exciting' literature should also be excluded from my perusal, in order that I might not become unnecessarily agitated and make myself ill. Thus, the world of the mind, in which many invalids find solace, having been excluded from the real world, might also have been closed to me, were it not for my brother, Robert. My beloved twin.

Ah, Robert! Robert! With what pain and bitterness do I recall your memory? To have a brother is a marvel indeed, and one who loves you as much as Robert loved me, doubly so. But is there not pain attached to the recognition of one whose very existence demonstrates what you yourself might have been, in different circumstances? In looks, we bore a striking, almost uncanny resemblance to one another, but in all other respects we differed entirely. Robert was everything that I was not. Where I was shy and retiring, even amongst those I knew well and who loved me, Robert was gregarious; where I was pale and wasted, he was robust and hearty, his dark eye and handsome cheek able to captivate all who beheld it; where I was lethargic and enervated, Robert was entirely enthusiastic and energetic; where I watched life from my invalid window, Robert *lived* it.

"I brought this for you, from father's library," Robert said one day as he entered my room, producing from the folds of his clothing the first volume of an exciting, and therefore proscribed, novel. He smiled and sat beside me on the bed. "I had to steal father's key to get it."

"Robert!" I gasped – suffused with an admixture of censure and awe.

My brother waved away the remark with his hand. "Boundaries exist only to be broken, Charles," he told me. "The moral world, like the physical world, is not flat, as the law-makers would have us believe, and if you cross the border, you do not fall off the edge. You simply enter a new territory." He regarded my uncomprehending expression and laughed, somewhat bitterly, I thought. "My dear Charles, the truth is that you are fundamentally incapable of transgressing even the most stupid of rules, whereas *I*..." His sentence trailed off and he looked out of the window. A silence fell, punctuated by the shrill call of a solitary bird. Suddenly he jumped up and turned to me. "This afternoon, Rose and I will perform the tragedy of *King Lear* for you, in the usual place. Will you like that?"

"Very much, I hope. Is there any murder in it?"

"Oh yes. Murder, passion, and madness. It is a tragedy!"

"I am eager to see it, then."

"Good. Then I will go and consult Rose," he said, and marched out of the room without so much as bidding me farewell.

My relationship to my sister, Rose, was not so ambivalent. I loved her unreservedly. As I write these words, with what delight do I raise my eyes and rest upon a water-colour representing my dear sister, affixed to the wall above my desk? With what reverence do I behold her golden hair, gorgeous in the sunlight, falling so prettily in twisting cascades about her pale cheeks, framing that eye at once so full of womanly charm, wit, and intelligence. In Rose, the trope of much popular literature is confounded – where the fair maid is ever invested with beauty, but only in her dark sister is intelligence to be found – for in my sister, neither beauty nor intellect reigns supreme, but both coexist in gentle harmony. I speak not only as a proud brother of so worthy a sister. Her beauty and intelligence are a matter of objective fact. My sister's hand was sought by many eligible gentlemen, and my father, had he lived, would have had no difficulty in making a very fine marriage for her. She now resides in Italy with the Count Valcello, just outside Naples, and has two charming children, whom – alas! – I have never seen, as I am seldom fit enough to undertake to travel. (I made my journey to this remote island only in the direst need, and it has not been without its consequences.)

With what fondness do I recall those afternoons when Rose and Robert, my dear sweet brother and sister, would take positions on the gravel path that separated the house from the gardens, while I perched on the arm of a stuffed sofa, wrapped up against the air, and hung out of my narrow, mossy window to observe them as they sawed their limbs and declaimed the passionate imaginings of Shakespeare. I was forbidden to entertain both of them in my room at once, my mother fearing that it would prove overwhelming to my deranged nerves, so this occupation allowed us to be together as best we could during my periods of confinement. They would perform with the vast gardens stretching out behind them, as well as the well-groomed shrubbery –

laid out in symmetrical, geometric precision, just as my mathematical grandfather had designed it. My siblings were not greatly talented, but I was not a critical audience, and so the arrangement pleased us all equally. Robert derived particular pleasure from the exercise. He was aware that I was indulging in both proscribed company and prohibited literature at one and the same time, and even from my distant vantage point I could see his eye and cheek flush with a kind of triumphant exhilaration at our mutual transgression.

It was after one such theatrical rendition that I contracted the illness which subsequently proved so disastrous to my career. Perhaps I hung too long out of the window as my brother and sister performed *The Comedy of Errors* – a confusing piece when performed by two solitary amateurs of seventeen years. I cannot say. Perhaps their explanations that, although their names were the same, they were now portraying different characters, did indeed agitate my mind. Again I cannot say. The only fact, and I wish to adhere to the facts of this case, is that I became dreadfully ill. Once again, the magnificent Dr Thorne was summoned, and he at once diagnosed a pulmonary disorder of the severest kind. Strangely, I felt perfectly well, and communicated as much to the doctor.

"It is common in such cases for the patient to feel quite healthy," the doctor informed my mother, who stood by my bed with clasped white hands. Her eyes brimmed with copious pellucid tears, but nevertheless bore down on me in a manner I found disturbing. "However, I must impress upon you, that rest is the only certain cure," the doctor insisted.

Days passed, and still I felt as fit as I ever had. I fretted at my seclusion and forced inactivity.

"You must rest and stay quiet," my mother told me.

"Am I to have no visitors at all?"

"Rose will be in to see you."

"And Robert?"

My mother, who was occupied in pouring a pitcher of water into a bowl, halted and gave me an unreadable look. "Robert will... not be visiting you," she said, and abruptly left the room.

My interview with Rose came some days later.

"Oh Charles!" she sighed absently, and stared disconsolately across the room.

I picked up her hand, which lay gently beside me on the bed, and kissed it. "Do not worry," I told her. "I am not half so ill as everybody says I am. I feel quite well."

She smiled and I fell silent. I heard my mother's gentle tread in the passageway outside.

"Will you tell Robert that…"

"I can't tell Robert anything," she hissed at me in an urgent whisper, bending down towards me in a manner that I would have found alarming in a person less possessed of womanly gentleness than my sister. "I can't tell him anything, I say. He's…"

Rose was not permitted to finish her sentence. At that point the door suddenly burst open and my mother, usually so gentle, loomed in the doorway like a gaoler. "Rose," she commanded, "your interview is concluded. Go downstairs at once!" And my obedient sister left the room, throwing me a meaning look unobserved by my mother. Did I perceive this correctly, or was it the mere fancy of a mind more unsettled than it knew?

After this fracas, it was assumed that I had become over-excited, and the doctor was summoned once again. He prescribed small doses of laudanum, to aid my rest and sleep. Thus days, weeks, and months passed. How can I remain true to my purpose of objective fact in the disclosure of my narrative, when I cannot even be certain of how long I remained upstairs in my room? What I do know is that, like Rip Van Winkle, when I awoke from my dreams, I awoke to a world so radically changed, so utterly different from that which I had known, that it was rendered horrid to my ear and eye.

Who can say in what connection lie the brain and body? Not I. The philosophers of the age insist that such a connection exists. Will you not think it extraordinary, dear Reader, when I disclose that when I awoke finally, I awoke in such complete health that I was astonished? I felt reborn. I could detect no trace of my former malady, or indeed the maladies that had preceded it, in my body. And I hastily left my room and went downstairs in search of my brother and sister, to deliver this most marvellous of news. But alas, what hollow victory! The house was not as I remembered it. It was like a morgue.

At length, I found my mother in a small sitting room, and at once bade her give me news of recent events. "Mother!" I cried. "What has happened? Why is everything so quiet? Where are Rose and Robert?

Why do I not recognize any of the servants?" For it was the case that, as I had carefully negotiated the stairs and corridors in search of my mother, not a single face was known to me.

My mother rose, and invited me into the front drawing room. "Come in here, Charles," she instructed me with a brisk nod of her covered head. "I wish to speak to you."

I followed her into the cluttered drawing room, its dark narrow windows occluded by heavy velvet curtains. I sank into a chair, and my mother sat on an ottoman nearby.

"How long have I been ill?" I inquired after a moment of profound silence, during which a palpable dread settled upon me.

My mother looked at me solemnly, her mannish hands clasped upon her lap like weighty religious carvings. "It is now the end of August," she said.

A rapid calculation informed me that I had been ill for slightly less than three months. "And where is everybody?" I demanded.

"Your father is in Jamaica, dealing with his estates there. And Rose is travelling in Italy with your aunt and cousins."

I nodded. "And Robert?"

My mother abruptly rose from the ottoman and moved to the mantelpiece, where she began to rearrange, in a somewhat distracted manner, several small cherubs which stood there, and of which she was fond. "Robert is..." she began, her back turned. Then she swung round and faced me. "Your brother Robert is... dead!" She uttered the words in a strangely exultant accent, and her eye shone.

I was quite stunned by the revelation, and stared at my mother, who now gripped the mantelpiece for support. "How did it happen?" I stammered. "Surely, he cannot have been ill? Robert has never..."

My mother raised an admonishing finger towards me, and I fell silent at once. She composed herself by taking two deep, refreshing breaths, and seemed to grow taller and thinner as I watched her.

"It was an accident," she said. "In the stables. He was kicked. And now he is dead." And with that my mother glided out of the room like a galleon in full sail, still clutching one of the little cherubs.

I was disconsolate, unmanned. Alas! What news to absorb, and with no one close by to give me comfort! Poor Rose was in Italy, and of the servants I knew not one. I clasped my face in my hands and wept like a girl, and was satisfied. My dear brother, taken from me! And worse yet, by the laws of primogeniture I would now stand to inherit my father's estate upon his death, and become master of the house. It was a role I felt quite unfitted for, and which I regarded as abhorrent.

But thus does fate ever wear a crooked smile, for a few months later, my father's ship, returning from Kingston, was hit by a terrible hurricane that blew up from the coast of Florida, and I found myself master of one of the largest estates in Hampshire. My mother, afflicted by the triple blows of my illness, the death of her son, and of her husband, became a changed woman. She grew small and withdrawn, sitting for long periods in the drawing room, motionless as a statue, with the curtains closed. She spoke little, ate little, and smiled not at all. It seemed that she was becoming the invalid that I had been. Yes, there was something vampiric in our relationship! I drew life, vitality and strength from her as she drew sickness and lethargy from me. Long weeks passed in this depressing manner, and at length she took to her bed. Soon thereafter she died. It seemed that Death had stretched his hand particularly towards our family, claiming first one, then another, then another of us, whilst I had somehow struggled free. The realization left me with a heavy dread.

Now alone amongst strangers in the empty house, I at once wrote to my sister, informing her of our now dreadful, orphaned circumstances, and told her that I intended to quit the Meon Estate, so full of horrid memories was it for me. I had decided to continue my studies, so assiduously carried out during my long confinement to my room, up at Oxford, where I intended to pursue the natural sciences and philosophy. Rose replied that she understood, and that she would not herself return to Droxford. She also hinted that not all news of the heart was heavy, and that some joy might at last be had in our little family. She was, no doubt, referring to her beloved Count, whom she married the following year.

Little of my time at Oxford warrants inclusion in this narrative. I will simply declare that during my period of study I was exposed to many fascinating ideas and discourses, both philosophical and phenomenal, and made many transient friends. My health held. But I continued to ache for the company of Rose and Robert, and I am quite certain that for my fellows I made a disappointing and melancholy companion. I was withdrawn and shy, and gradually they left me to myself, where I reverted to the solitary existence to which I had grown so accustomed as a child.

However, the conclusion of my studies was coincident with my coming of age. At one and twenty I came fully into my fortune, no longer incumbent upon lawyers and trusts, and was at last a free man! But what was I to do, a man of almost no life experience? Those of my former fellows, numbering not a few, who were not to take up the noble academic professions, were making for London in order to establish themselves, and I decided that this was the course that I, too, would take. I wrote to Rose, who was then approaching her confinement for the birth of her first child, a sweet little girl, who – alas! – I have never seen, in order to inform her of my whereabouts and intentions. How could I know that Death was once again beckoning, in this seemingly innocent move? Thus it was that I soon found myself master of a small but comfortable establishment in St John's Wood. It will not surprise you to learn that my life in London was spent in very much the same manner as it had been at Oxford – reading, thinking, and entertaining. But everything changed the night I met Sir John Foyle, who came attached to a party that visited me one night on their way home from the theatre.

Sir John was a good-looking, well-made man about a dozen years older than myself, whom the years appeared to have touched but lightly. His manners and dress were impeccable, and he sat apart from his friends, saying nothing at all as the night wore on. He merely looked at me with his bottomless brown eyes, his head cocked to one side – as one listening intently, or as one engaged in deep thought – while my friends and I discussed recent events, or reminisced over our former days at Oxford. The persistence of his observation produced in me the most alarming sensation: I began to stammer and fall over my words, which caused me much embarrassment and inner recrimination, because I very much wanted to impress this silent man, whom I found unaccountably fascinating.

Two days later, Sir John sent me his card, and I sent him one in return, inviting him to call when he could. He came immediately. I soon discovered that he was possessed of the most brilliant mind. He was, he said, a confirmed auto-didact, like myself. He had read, and furthermore *understood*, Hume, Locke and Kant, and was able to recite vast tracts of all three. He was almost as conversant with the arts, and let it be known, as a matter of no consequence, that he spoke at least three languages. I at once responded to him as a kindred spirit. His real interest, he said, was as an amateur sociologist and psychologist, on the subject of which he advanced several theories. From all his talk I concluded that he had *lived*, and I found that particularly attractive. More accurately, he produced in me a profound ambivalence: both attraction *and* repulsion. Why this should be I could not say, although now I guess more.

Subsequent to our first successful interview, our meetings became almost daily, always at my residence, not his. Our conversations were always interesting, lively and surprising, lasting well into the night, and I enjoyed them immensely. One evening, as we sat with the fire gently crackling and twinkling at our feet, he looked at me with his ponderous orbs and said, "Tell me, Charles. Do you think that you could ever possibly commit a crime?"

I smiled, recalling Robert's assertion all those years ago that I was incapable of transgressing any law, through fear. "No, I don't think so," I replied.

Sir John looked at me seriously. "Then you would never kill another person – for any reason at all?" The atmosphere at once became thick and strange.

"No, not for any reason at all," I cried, and rose abruptly from my chair, strangely affected by his interrogation. "Why do you ask me such a bizarre question?"

Sir John raised his hands in an open gesture of apology. "I am advancing a certain hypothesis concerning twins," he told me. "Do not be alarmed."

I pretended some business at the far end of the room and retired there to gather my thoughts. "What hypothesis is that?" I said, my back turned to him.

"I am interested in the similitude, or indeed the difference, between twins," he told me. "When we know one twin, do we indeed know the other? When twins are separated at birth, do they maintain their similitude, or does the practice exacerbate their difference? What I am proposing, Charles – and I hope you do not think me heretical for saying so – is that not all character comes from God." He raised his hand, as if to stifle any objection I might have. In fact I had none. "On the other hand, I do not think it comes from parents, either. This is the opaque mystery that I am attempting to penetrate, Charles, and I believe that in the study of twins we will discover the answers."

"Then you misconceive your subject," I said, turning to face him once again. "I am indeed a twin, as those of our mutual acquaintance have no doubt informed you. But did they also tell you that my twin, my dear beloved Robert, died when I was yet a child? You see, Sir John, I am useless to you. You have no comparative study to make of me."

Sir John said nothing. He simply pressed his firm lips together, an exercise that ennobled his beneficent patrician appearance.

"When first you befriended me," I continued into the silence, "I marvelled that you would spend so much time with someone like myself, but now the reason is plain. And now, I suppose, we must say farewell. Your purpose is foiled."

"Not at all," Sir John countered, advancing upon me with smiling face. "You are a twin. Well, Charles – I, too, am a twin! Is that not the affinity which draws us toward one another, almost as if we were ourselves brothers?"

He rested an exquisite hand upon my arm. The 'affinity' – as he called it – that I felt towards him, which I did not understand, ran deeper than his mere person, which as I have said, was very agreeable. But it was not the affinity I had for Robert.

Disconcerted, I withdrew my arm from his touch, and removed myself to my chair once again. "I cannot say that I feel towards you as I did towards my brother," I told him.

Sir John's eyes glistened, and for a moment I imagined the astonishing sight of this robust, masculine creature weeping on my shoulder. But he only cocked his head to one side, just as he had that first night, and said, "Pray, do not misunderstand me. The affinity of which I speak is more abstract than you suppose. You see, I, too, have lost a brother."

I stared at him. "Your twin is also dead?"

"Not dead, no," Sir John answered slowly. "But we are not close. There is very little similitude between us, I am afraid." As he spoke his features were suddenly invested with an atavistic, animal hatred and disgust. "Indeed," he growled, "my brother is... he *innately differs...* from myself." And with that he turned and left.

That night I did not sleep. I turned over and over in my mind the conversation between us, almost to the point of monomania, always expecting that some clue would be revealed. Sir John was interested in living twins. I was a twin, but had no living brother, yet he maintained his interest in me. Why ? It made no sense. And what connection was there between twins and his first question, regarding murder? As dawn broke, I abandoned hope of rest and went about my daily life as best I could. At noon, exhausted, I retired to my bed, but fatigued as I was, sleep still would not come. Over and again I heard Sir John's words, '*my brother innately differs from myself,*' and once again experienced the tone of horror and disgust with which he had uttered them. I felt somehow complicit, condemned. As the day wore on and my brain became more fevered, I recognized the horrid sensations of agitation which had so often overtaken me as a child, and of which I had been so mercifully free in recent years. Then night fell, and with it came a dread of what was to come. Never before had I faced my illness alone. I avoided the clocks. Recognition of the slow march of seconds, minutes and hours, all without sleep, finally renders sleep impossible. Defeated at last, I roused myself and rummaged in my drawers for the small bottle of laudanum that I had been keeping for just such an emergency as this, and surrendered to Morpheus.

I received no visit, and no word from Sir John for several days. Coincident with this, I began to experience nervous palpitations, no doubt caused by the obsessive mental activity engendered by our last conversation. I ate little, and found myself unable to concentrate upon my books with any degree of satisfaction, so tossed them aside. Instead I gave myself up to brooding, to staring out of my windows, from one of which I could glimpse a small portion of Regent's Park. My mind was dull, my eye bright and feverish. It was during this period that an explanation for Sir John's words began to form themselves in my mind: Sir John was brilliant, cultured, calm and urbane. His brother, then, was the opposite. Uncouth, violent, stupid. The brother had probably committed some terrible act of violence. Yes! He had committed murder! And Sir John, aghast that someone so intimately connected to himself was capable of such base action, was concerned that beneath his civilized exterior, he too might be capable of it. Thus he had taken it upon himself to search out twins, in a desperate attempt to demonstrate the falsehood of his awful hypothesis! Dear Reader, although this explanation seems clearly preposterous to you, in my agitated mental condition I made no such judgement, and I fixed upon it as if it were holy law, and nothing could shake me from the conviction.

One afternoon, as I stared out of the window, a card arrived from Foyle. I glanced at it for but an instant and had him sent in. How can I convey my shock at the change wrought in the man? If I had declined, with all my listlessness and agitation, then Foyle had positively metamorphosed. It was Foyle, and yet it was not. His dimensions were the same, and yet he was smaller; he was as well-made, and yet not so pleasing. I find these changes difficult to express in words because they were so subtle. But how much less subtle was the change in his voice!

"Mr Grant," Foyle, cried, extending his hand in greeting. "So pleased to make your acquaintance." His voice was light and insubstantial, quite unlike his usual voice, and his touch was feathery as he lightly gripped my hand.

For a moment I stood before him, immobile. One of us had lost his mind, or both! Foyle had met me dozens of times. Why did he behave as if we had never met? I attempted an easy laugh, but achieved only a ghastly creaking in the back of my throat.

"I trust you are well?" I said.

Foyle nodded fussily. "Ah yes. Quite well. I thank you. And yourself, Mr Grant?"

I touched my forehead, which was damp with a cold sweat. "I... I have been a little unwell, I think."

Foyle stood before me and pursed his lips in concentration, his hands clasped in front of him in the attitude of a womanish parson. "I am sorry to hear that, Mr Grant. It is nothing serious, I hope?"

"Oh no. It is a mild recurrence of a childhood malady," I said. "I do not think it is serious." And I seated myself in a chair, indicating that Foyle should do likewise.

There fell an awkward, sterile silence, which was terminated at last by a question so unlooked for that I certainly feared for my sanity. For Foyle looked at me with a knowing smile and said:

"Did you enjoy the play, last evening, Mr Grant?"

"The play?" I repeated stupidly. "I saw no play last evening."

Foyle pursed his lips once more. "Why certainly, you did. I myself saw you there. A... gentlemen of my acquaintance, and I." He nodded in an uncharacteristic manner.

Thoughts whirled in my brain at terrific speed. What was Foyle attempting to do? Why was he deliberately frightening me, with his strange behaviour and stranger assertions? Was this another of his bizarre experiments? "I can assure you that I was at no such play last evening," I repeated. "As I have said, Sir John, I was unwell."

Upon my last utterance, Sir John's face drained of colour. He clasped his hands tightly together in his lap with a small, sharp intake of breath, and stared at me.

"Whatever is the matter?" I cried, my nerves now so deranged that the slightest occurrence was likely to terrify me. "Why do you stare at me so?"

Foyle cleared his throat. "I do beg your pardon, Mr Grant. It is simply that I had no idea that you had already made the acquaintance of my... brother."

"Your brother?" I cried in a fit of agitation. "Please, speak plainly, I beg you. I cannot think! You are driving me mad with your insinuations!"

"Then I am Sir John's brother, sir. I am *James* Foyle." He raised both hands, exactly like Sir John, but now the gesture appeared intensely effeminate, and affected. He emitted a high, quiet laugh. "I realize our mistake. You mistook me for my brother?"

Suddenly I relaxed. Everything made perfect sense now. The man before me *was* a stranger.

"Yes. I am afraid I did. I am a great friend of your brother's, and yet, I was mistaken."

James Foyle looked around him uneasily, his eyes sliding across every object in the room before returning to me. "My brother comes here often?"

"Quite often, yes. He is a brilliant man."

"Brilliant, yes," James repeated, nodding. Then, placing his hands on his knees, he looked at me, as if making a tremendous effort to speak. "And has he never mentioned my existence?"

"Indeed he has," I said.

"And what did he say?"

James cocked his head to one side, just like his brother, but the effect was so different that I thought I should go mad. Once again, Sir John's words came back to me: *my brother innately differs from myself*, and suddenly, with awful clarity, I knew what he meant, and shuddered. All thoughts of murderous intentions on James's part were banished, only to be replaced by more disconcerting ones.

"He said only that you were not alike," I offered carefully, "although he neglected to mention your physical similitude. You might make a remarkable sensation upon the stage."

James Foyle smiled knowingly. "The stage, yes indeed," he said with another nod, "And so could you!"

With that remark, the fragile sense of normality that had reasserted itself in the room shattered at once, and my heart was gripped by palpitations and a horrid dread. "I? How could I make a sensation?"

"Why, with your own double, whom I saw last night at the theatre!"

I clutched at my head, as if by this action I might slow my accelerating, deranged thoughts. "But I have no double," I cried. "My brother is dead! My brother is dead!"

James Foyle, now seriously alarmed, rang for the servant, who brought me some wine. He sat by me whilst I drank it and studied me hard as my ragged breath returned to normal.

"I am deeply sorry," I stammered. "By way of explanation, I can only repeat that I have been ill of late. Can you forgive me?"

"Of course, dear sir, think nothing of it," James said, patting my knee delicately as he did so. "It is all my doing, no doubt. I should never appear, where my brother has been before me." And so saying, he collected his gloves and walked daintily out of the room, before I had time to ask him what he meant.

If my thoughts had been in turmoil beforehand, how much more were they disturbed by this interview! I perceived, but dimly, a vast net enmeshing me, but of so crafty a design as to render it invisible. My poor nerves were wretched. Listless and agitated, I resorted to the laudanum once more, and fell into syrupy dreams in which I was visited by half-formed dreads and inconclusive proofs of villainy.

I cannot say how many days I languished in this manner, but some time afterwards, I received a visit from my friend Sir John, who was himself in a state of high agitation. I felt, perhaps, that I was heading towards some kind of resolution to the strange affair, and welcomed it, either for good or for ill.

"You have seen my brother!" Sir John exclaimed at once. "Oh! Our friendship is ruined!"

"No, indeed," I assured him. "You are not your brother. It is you who are my dear friend!" And I clasped him warmly.

Sir John held my arms and looked long into my face with a smile. "That is not what I meant. But I wonder if it is true, in any case." He broke away from me. "In point of fact you know me but little. Our minds meet, indeed they do, but..." Sir John pulled an elegant cigarette case from his pocket and began to smoke, something he had never done in my presence. For the phlegmatic Sir John, this demonstrated extreme discomfiture.

"I am afraid, Charles, that due to my brother's interferences," he said, contemptuously blowing smoke from his mouth as he did so, "I must raise an unpleasant subject. Unpleasant to both of us, perhaps. Please, sit down. Such news is best absorbed when reposed."

I sat, and my body thrilled with fear.

"I wish to talk to you on the subject of your brother. Robert."

"My *brother*?"

Sir John looked at me with his deep eyes. "Yes. He is in London."

"Are you mad? Are you wholly insane?" I cried, leaping from my chair as if scalded. "My brother is dead. He died five years ago. Why do you, and your contemptible brother, insist that he is alive? I tell you, my double – if double there be – is not my brother." I had lost control. I was screaming now, and took hold of Sir John and shook him with tremendous force. A strange, satisfied smile played on his lips, which infuriated me still further.

"I understand that you *believe* him dead," Sir John said, stepping away from me in a brisk, deft movement. "I am familiar with the story – garnered, as you rightly surmised – from your acquaintances at Oxford, some of whom are... friends of mine. But how much do you actually know? At that time you were ill. You have it on hearsay only, albeit from your mother's lips."

I laughed. "Do you seriously propose that my mother lied to me on so grave a matter as the death of my brother?" I cried in disbelief. "I had considered you a man of profound intelligence, but..."

"There are things worse than death, Charles, believe me," Sir John interposed. "Especially for a mother. Has it never occurred to you that she might have sent him away?"

I brushed his remark aside and shook my head wildly. "I hardly think it credible that so devoted a brother as dear Robert, were he living in London as you claim, would not come to see me!" I said.

"That would entirely depend, would it not, on the welcome he might expect to receive from you. Would he not be too ashamed – as he ought to be?"

"Why... should he feel ashamed?" I stammered.

Sir John smiled at me. "Your brother was banished for committing unspeakable acts, Charles! And you were protected from the truth for the sake of your nerves!"

I backed away from him, my sensations of anger now transmuting into feelings of horror and repugnance. "It is impossible!" I whispered, my eyes wide with alarm. "I don't know what you mean."

"Do you not?" said Sir John, advancing upon me with that same, strange smile. "Is it not true that to know one twin is to know the other? Does it not follow that the predilections of the one are replicated in the heart of the other? I have studied him long, Charles, and know his vile secrets. Tell me, do you not share them?"

My mind raced with the warring emotions of repugnance and attraction that I felt for the man who stood, now silent, only inches from my face.

"Your brother committed abominable acts, in the stables," Sir John repeated in a level voice, his eyes bright. "Will you deny it? Or will you kiss me?"

I hardly knew what I did next. I took his neck in my hands and squeezed and squeezed, my heart racing with cold fury. "It is a lie! A damned lie!" I cried. "My brother was a saint. I will not have you defame his memory. I will not!"

Sir John's flesh was warm, and I could see the blood pumping through a large vein in the side of his neck as I throttled him, my eyes afire. He made no attempt to escape, or move. He simply stood before me, as his breath rasped in and out, with that enigmatic smile upon his blue lips. I released my grip on him and he sagged forward into my arms. I stepped away and he slid noiselessly to the floor. I myself was breathing heavily, my hands trembling as I stared at the recumbent body at my feet.

At that moment I heard an altercation in the hall outside, and James Foyle rushed in, followed by a remonstrating servant.

"It's perfectly all right, Steven, let him in," I said, my voice belying the thumping of my heart. The servant hurried out.

"Mr Grant, Mr Grant, have you seen..." James Foyle stopped still as he beheld the horrid scene before him. He raised his hand to his temple and shut his eyes, then checked his brother's pulse for signs of life. "Then I am too late. Too late!" he wailed as he stood up. "What has happened here?"

"He besmirched the good name of my dead brother," I told him, "and I... I..." I broke down and collapsed on the sofa. By my own hand I had killed a man.

James Foyle sat next to me and made simpering gestures of condolence, touching me lightly on the knee and forehead.

"Do not touch me! What kind of man are you, who does not show rage at his own brother's murder?" I babbled, hardly knowing what I said, so full of contradiction and confusion was I. "I suppose it was you who corrupted my dear brother!"

"Dear sir! Take hold of yourself, I beg you," James Foyle cried. "Am I to find you in this wretched condition every time we meet?"

I attempted to steady my wild emotions, and concentrated my attention on Sir John's epicene brother as he continued to speak.

"John was quite brilliant, quite brilliant," he murmured, as if to himself, "but he was also deranged. I was his doctor. He had a monomanic interest in twins, and an unhealthy preoccupation with the possible configurations of... of the sexual act. It always enraged him that I was quite normal in that respect, whereas he..." James Foyle fiddled with his gloves, brushing imaginary lint from the fingers. "He has *known* your brother, Mr Grant."

I covered my ears, and my mind screamed for unconsciousness that stubbornly refused to come.

"He yearned for oblivion, Mr Grant. I was required to maintain an almost constant watch on him. But lately he had been very calm, due to your influence, I believe, and I grew complacent. Nobody could have known that he was intent on employing you to commit the act that he was not courageous enough to commit himself."

I stared at James Foyle with new eyes. Of course! His manners, although fussy, were not actually effeminate. Rather, they were an expression of Hippocratic fastidiousness. With the benefit of this revelation, I revolved in my mind Sir John's final words, and thought I saw new meaning in them. They were not a goad, but a *plea*. Yes! I had transposed the two brothers utterly.

"In every sense, he committed suicide," Foyle went on. "I suppose he did not struggle?"

I shook my head, remembering Sir John's compliant posture as I choked the life from his body, and the smile upon his lips.

"It is as I thought, then. But the police will not be so accommodating. You must flee, Mr Grant, and flee immediately. Go far away. At once."

My flight from England was simple enough, as Dr Foyle delayed for several hours before alerting the authorities, and I was fortunate enough to catch a boat to France late that night. From there I made my way to Kefalonia, a barren deserted Greek island that suits my solitary nature perfectly. And here you find me, dear Reader, with blood on my hands, as I bare my soul and commit the truth to paper. I have not yet written to Rose. I do not know what I can say to that sweet creature on this subject. That her dead brother lives, in infamy, and that her living brother is a murderer?

There are still unanswered questions, that come to me at night: which brother did I truly serve? Was it Sir John, who so hated himself that he wished to die? Or was it the illustrious James, whose deranged and inverted brother threatened to utterly damage his good standing – and by whose removal he might benefit? Did Sir John, on discovering how much he differed from his brother, attempt to discover two *like* twins, in order to undermine James's avowal of his normalcy? Or did he *rely* on that difference? Sometimes I fancy that he asked Robert – and how it pains me even to write his name! – to perform for him the act that I finally performed, and that he refused. And on being so refused by one twin, Sir John sought out his entirely differing brother, who may, perhaps, be goaded into murder. Does that not at last make sense of Sir John's strange question on our first meeting? And finally, but in no wise least in importance, what of myself? Which of Sir John's hypotheses do I prove, or disprove, if I admit to you here, that I do indeed share the vices of my brother?

The Name of the Wine

Anthony McDonald

The Name of the Wine
Anthony McDonald

I had hardly been in Cambridge two days before I was startled by the apparition of old Parry emerging suddenly from the doorway of a newsagent's. There was no mistaking him though I daresay I had not seen him in twenty years. Here were the same spectacles, seeming almost too thick to see through, the same thinning hair – quite white now – the same ill-fitting clothes that had once been expensive, the same aristocratic disregard for their shabbiness and failure to match and the same apparent absence of a face as a focus for the whole ensemble. Everything looked somewhat older than I remembered, but then of course it was.

Parry had been nearly, but not quite, head of the History department at Bristol when I had arrived there all those years ago as a very junior lecturer. I remember those spectacles peering out from an armchair over the issue of *Speculum* in which my first paper on the Forest Laws had just been published. I had been feeling very pleased with myself. "Nigel," the spectacles had said, "you are an unsystematic young man. Alarmingly unsystematic." A few years later our paths had diverged. I had an idea that he had gone on eventually to a fellowship at All Souls'. We had not met since.

To my surprise Parry recognised me as quickly as I had him. He showed no sign of surprise himself. Looking back, it occurs to me that he might have had some prior knowledge of my appointment through his contacts at the university – for he himself would have been retired for a good many years by this time. "Hello, Nigel," he said benignly, "What brings you to Cambridge?"

I told him about the Readership at Peterhouse. He treated this as news and I was duly congratulated. We stood and chatted for a few minutes. He now lived, he told me, a few miles outside Cambridge on the Royston road, at a place called Bearpark. By the time he had spelt this odd place-name, explained that it was a corruption of the French *Beau Repaire*, that it had originally been a sort of holiday home for some thirteenth-century Benedictine monks, and then indicated with the aid of both hands how one would find the place if arriving by car, he had little choice but to invite me to visit him. We fixed on Saturday lunchtime and I made a point of noting the date in my diary to show him how systematic I had become.

I drove out to Bearpark accordingly on what proved to be a fine, dewy October morning but when I reached the spot to which Parry's painstaking directions led me I was quite astonished. Instead of the country cottage I had been expecting, I found Parry's home to be the imposing gatehouse of an immense mansion which was partly visible further up the long drive. Both buildings were flamboyant eighteenth-century neo-gothic: all ogee arches and fancy crenellations. Parry was sitting outside his pointy-arched front door in a garden chair, sipping a whisky. He had clearly thought it worth braving the lukewarm sunshine in order to relish the astonished look that must have appeared on my face as I caught my first glimpse of his rural retreat.

Inside, the house was a good deal less than immaculate but even more exotic than the exterior. It was full of exquisite furnishings and ornaments of different periods and styles, each one of which must have been priceless but which, taken together, created an impression of spectacular unease and disharmony. The principal room was too large for comfort and an enormous mirror over the mantelpiece effectively doubled its size and halved its cosiness. Nevertheless, a cheerful log fire burned in the grate and when a large whisky was pressed into my hand the room took on a more friendly aspect altogether.

"And you live here all alone?" I said. Idiotically really, because Parry had been a lifelong bachelor when I'd first known him in his mid-fifties, and that was hardly likely to have changed now. Besides which, there was no sign of anybody's presence in the house except his own. He was looking his usual self. His sports coat might have come from Saville Row, though it looked as if he had been gardening in it. He frowned at my question as though I'd asked him something difficult. Then he said: "Yes, I live alone," pausing before adding, "My lover shot himself last April."

There was a dreadful silence. I had not the smallest idea what to say. I had been taken totally by surprise. Not so much surprised that Parry's proclivities lay in that direction (the lover had been *him*self not *her*self) but that Parry had proclivities at all. I had thought of him, when I thought of him at all, as sexless; I had seen nothing beyond the ill-assorted clothes and pebble-thick spectacles. Clearly I had been wrong. I now had to come to terms with the fact that the elderly scholar who sat opposite me, faceless behind spectacles, bow tie and lead-crystal whisky tumbler was, despite an acquaintance that spanned more than twenty years, an almost complete stranger.

"I'm sorry," I said. "I really don't know what to say." I paused again. "I don't quite know how you expect me to react, that's all."

"Don't react at all then," Parry said blandly. "And don't bother about how I react to anything *you* say. You strike me – always have done – as far too worried about what other people think of you. Yes, I know you. But as for me," – he took a sip of whisky, "I couldn't care a fig. At least, not now."

It was the *yes I know you* that I found disconcerting.

"I was surprised, if you really want to know, that you should want to talk about something like that with a... with someone you only know slightly. I was also surprised... I mean... I didn't know you were... 'so'."

"So!" Parry almost boomed. "What an extraordinary, old-fashioned turn of phrase. How clever of you to dig it up. A euphemism from the past. And much more descriptive to my mind than... gay. Hardly dignified. Especially as one approaches eighty. Thank you, Nigel, I'd forgotten that one. You've given it back to me. I shall remember it now. Now where was I?"

"Your lover," I said. I felt I had turned red. "I'll happily change the subject if you like. On the other hand..." (I thought this was quite perceptive of me) "... it may be that you'd like to talk about it, and in that case I'll just as happily listen."

I had never been aware of Parry's eyes before. Now, suddenly, I was. They were narrowed like a hunting cat's as they peered at me through their shatterproof windscreens. "You must be nearly fifty, Nigel," he said, "yet you're still making pretty little speeches like an eighteen-year-old boy. You haven't changed a bit." There was a hint of amusement in his voice that I disliked. I felt a small shiver run down my spine. "But thank you for your indulgence," he went on. "Yes, I would like to talk about Alan. But just for a few minutes. Not all through lunch, which would be tedious. Bring your drink. We'll take a turn round the garden while I tell you about him."

The sun was warmer and the dew had gone. We rambled round

lawns and shrubberies and the following – I have tried as far as possible to recall his actual words – is the story Parry told.

"I first met Alan more than forty years ago. Long before Bristol, long before I set eyes on you, Nigel. Do you know what Alan did for a living? He worked on a building site. Called himself a 'brickie'. We met in a... On second thoughts I don't think I'll go into that. You've probably got enough experience to work it out for yourself."

Which I had. It wasn't something I liked to think about though, and I was horrified at the idea that he had guessed it for himself.

"He was very, very handsome. And only nineteen. We had only known each other a short time before we fell in love. Fell, as if from a sea cliff into the waves below. Not something you'd ever plan to do – or be able to reverse after it had happened. There was no possible question, at that time, of our living together. I was a very junior lecturer at UCL. Setting up home with a nineteen-year-old bricklayer would have been professional suicide. I don't need to remind you that this was several years before homosexual acts were decriminalised. And it was just as impossible for Alan. His workmates would have... well, you can imagine. So for years, and I do mean years, our social lives never touched. I never met Alan's friends and he never met mine. The times we spent together were hard-won. Something as simple as a drink or a visit to a cinema had to be planned like a military operation.

"But then I went to Bristol and Alan came with me. And now he did move in with me. It seemed extraordinarily daring at the time. (I'm still talking about more than thirty-five years ago.) But we weren't really very brave, looking back on it. I still never met his workmates, nor was I mentioned in their company. We never met each other's families. If one of us entertained at home the other had strict instructions to stay out of the way."

I interrupted at this point. "I came to your house, I don't know if you remember, with Doctor Sanders. It never occurred to either of us that you didn't live alone."

"Quite so. And we never went anywhere together where we might be recognised. It made life together difficult, even dangerous but... also... exciting. You see, real romance sometimes thrives in the pragmatic squalor of deception. The need to keep a job down, the need to keep the dull old world turning. But there was a reward for all this, for all this inconvenience, for all these small deceptions. The reward? Call it magic. Call it what you will. It kept us bound together for a – for his – lifetime."

The garden was extensive. Most of it actually belonged to the big house though Parry evidently had the run of it. As well as rolling sweeps of lawn and planted borders there were wild areas and there was even a lake picturesquely surrounded by trees. He named plants as we strolled, but I was getting interested now in the story of himself and Alan. "What did he do in Bristol?" I asked. "More building jobs?"

"No," said Parry. "You can't go on swanning around on scaffolding for ever. He took a job in a warehouse for a while but found indoor work didn't suit him and so he went to work for the Parks and Gardens department of the City Council. He never became at all middle-class in his occupations or attitudes. Moving in with me was as far as he was prepared to go in that direction. Even then his accent became more aggressively cockney as the years passed. But he did develop one or two tastes that were rather endearingly out of character... No, not out of character, just at odds with his background. Wagner, lobster thermidor, Shakespeare's sonnets, Chateau Yquem with the rhubarb crumble. You know the sort of thing."

I supposed I did.

"Eventually we went to Oxford. I was never happier than when I was there. I knew I was never going to get a chair and somehow it was almost a relief. You can be quite second rate and still be happy in Oxford, as you'll find for yourself one of these days. Alan worked at a school for problem children. At first as a handyman-gardener. Then he took over some of the woodwork classes. And I think that's when he really found himself. He had a natural gift with the little toughs, and the school authorities let him take on more and more responsibility. The kids loved him. We were at Oxford for nearly twenty years and they went in a flash. But because all good things come to an end, Oxford ended. I retired."

"But why retire back up here when you were both so happy in Oxford?" I asked.

"Look around you," Parry answered. "It is all rather splendid, isn't it? The big house belongs to a cousin of mine, while my flamboyant gatehouse was left to me in an uncle's will, many years ago. Alan and I used to spend holidays up here, and as time passed he grew as fond of it as I was. If he hadn't taken to the place I'd never have asked him to pull up stumps in Oxford."

"But he gave up his job," I protested. "A job he loved. That must have been a terrible sacrifice."

Parry looked grave behind his glasses. "Unfortunately you are right. And equally unfortunately, neither of us realised it at the time. One of us would have to sacrifice something, and he, I'm sad to say, convinced himself that his sacrifice would be the smaller and more easily made, because he was captivated by the idea of living here," he gestured widely with both arms, "with these glorious gardens and in our small, higgledy-piggledy palace. As he said, Bearpark had the casting vote. Unfortunately, it cast it wrong."

"You mean he couldn't settle?" I asked.

"Oddly enough it wasn't that. He loved being here. You see, although it's a bit bleak and uncosy in winter, that didn't matter when there were two of you. Alan took an almost childish pleasure in all this... opulence. Never mind that it was a faded, unkempt, ill-assorted kind of opulence. All those chandeliers, Persian rugs, inlaid writing desks and monogrammed sheets, they were the stuff his childhood dreams were made of. And although I don't doubt that he missed the challenge of his old job (he became a gardener again) it wasn't that that made things go wrong. Nor was it the fact that we were under each other's feet rather more now that I was retired. We were pretty used to each other by this time. No, the real problem was something else."

We had turned the last corner of the garden and were heading back towards the house and – I hoped – some lunch. Our whisky glasses were empty.

"The thing was," Parry resumed, "that everybody up here seemed to know about our relationship and nobody could give a damn. And, ironically, tragically, this was the one thing that Alan was not prepared for. Here he was among all sorts of new people, gardeners on the estate, people in the village, old colleagues of mine at the university, and they all seemed perfectly ready to accept him for what he was – a pansy. He had always cherished the belief, I suppose, that if anyone ever found out they would refuse to believe it. He with his rugged, bearded face and broad shoulders and cockney accent, he couldn't be 'like that'. And I realised for the first time that something that the rest of the world was beginning to accept as quite natural was something that he could not accept at all. At the very moment in this country's history when you could at last arrive at a party and say quite simply, 'This is Alan', just at the time when we could begin to share our social lives, we found – what? That Alan, God rest his immortal soul, had never admitted to himself that he was a bloody poof. I tried to explain to him that the world was changing and old prejudices and stereotypes disappearing. Homosexuals like us – I mean of course, homosexuals like Alan and I – " (he said this with an exaggerated carefulness that I did not much care for) "were suddenly socially acceptable. But my arguments were to no avail. Alan sank slowly, oh so slowly that I didn't even see it at first, into a profound depression until, about eighteen months ago, I realised he had become unreachable. He was like someone living the other side of a glass wall. We could see each other but not, so to speak, hear, or talk, or touch. It was unbearable. Then last year, one spring day, he borrowed a shotgun from the head gardener and went decorously away to the edge of the lake..." he turned round and pointed towards it "... where, considerably far removed from the silk wall-paper, the brocades and the monogrammed sheets, he shot himself tastefully in the mouth."

We had arrived at the front door. Parry paused on the threshold. "I loved him as I have loved no one else. But now I think that is enough about Alan." He motioned me to go in ahead of him and when I did so I was astonished to be met by a demure, grey-faced woman who announced that lunch was ready in the dining room.

"Mrs Craig is my daily woman," Parry explained when she had withdrawn. "It's a courtesy title only, though. She comes in once a week – and cooks occasionally if I have company."

I had to admire Parry's composure. Within minutes of his finishing his tragic tale we were both spooning away at watercress soup and discussing, if I remember rightly, construction methods used in early pianoforte manufacture. Lunch was really excellent and, surprisingly, the conversation never morbid. We washed it down with a bottle of Gevry-Chambertin. But it was this, coupled with the tendency I share with most academics of wishing to show off in front of more senior colleagues, proved, as the meal drew towards its end, to be my undoing. "Now was it Belloc or was it Chesterton?" I said, and quoted: "'I forget the name of the place, I forget the name of the girl, but the wine was Chambertin.'"

"Belloc, almost certainly," said Parry. "Chesterton would have forgotten all three." Then he looked straight at me across the table and for the first time ever his eyes were so clearly visible, so wide-open and so blue that I scarcely saw the spectacles. And he said. "I forget the name of the place, I forget the name of the wine, but the boy was you."

"Oh my God," I thought, but I must have said it aloud; it must have slipped out, because Parry then said, in a flat voice, "I appear to have been unsubtle." And I was thinking: behind those spectacles he's been watching me all this time, watching and waiting, knowing just who and what I was, for all these years.

"Do you know something?" Parry said. "I never really saw your face until the other day. My glasses have got thicker as the years pass and human faces have come to seem more of a blur and less coherent. Any system behind the arrangement of the features seems to be lacking. Then, as I saw you outside the newsagent's, your face sprang into focus for the first time. There was a system behind the features. No criticism intended."

I said a chilly "thank you". He was not to be put off. "And now, Nigel, I am thinking I should like to make you a proposition. No, don't flinch. I don't mean that sort of a proposition. Where do you live?"

"In college," I said.

"And do you like it?"

"I have two rooms. My own bathroom."

"And are you comfortable?"

"Yes," I said. "It's splendid. Couldn't really be better. Nice view and a genuine medieval window to admire it through. Warm, cosy, and all meals provided."

"And you hate it," said Parry matter-of-factly. "I know. I wish I had someone to share this place with, Nigel. Not a lover, I think, at my age, but a companion. And since we met last week I have found myself thinking, perhaps unwisely, that it might be you." He peered at me again, leaning halfway across the table to do it. "You find the idea abhorrent? Impractical? Liable to misinterpretation... or what?"

"I don't want to appear rude," I began, but he cut me off.

"You see, Nigel, in some ways I think I know you better than you know yourself. And I am aware (as you are not, so that you will think me a monster of arrogance for saying this) that I could possibly be good for you."

"How dare you," I said, and stood up.

"Yes," Parry said calmly, "I did think that might be your reaction. There's blackberry pie on the sideboard. And cream. Do help yourself. Mrs Craig will have gone home."

"I really couldn't eat any more," I said – and heard the expression 'through clenched teeth' in my head.

"Nigel, do sit down. And if you like we can change the subject."

I stayed standing. "I don't want to change the subject, thank you very much. You've been talking to me as if you own me already. But nobody owns me and nobody's ever going to. You have in your mind some idea of me, some image of me, filtered through those God-awful spectacles, but that isn't me. It's you who you're seeing. It's you who has never loved or been loved in his life. I don't believe Alan ever existed. He was just a figment of your warped spectacles and..." I gestured around the opulent room, "... and your distorting mirrors. You invented Alan. Just as you're trying to invent me."

"And there you rest your case," said Parry quietly, sitting back in his chair. To my astonishment he took out a small cigar from a case in his pocket and lit it before he continued. "It would suit you down to the ground if Alan never existed. But he did. In the churchyard, where we can take a walk after lunch if you like, you will find a stone with his name on it. The verger will tell you how he remembers Alan. Mrs Craig, when you next see her, will happily tell you his favourite menus. Or I can give you her phone number if you wish to conduct your own researches. On Monday morning you can even ask your own head of department, Professor... Professor... hell..."

"Professor Williams."

"Thank you. Professor Williams met him. Alan cut down some trees for Professor Williams that were keeping the light off Professor Williams' garden and if you go there you will see the stumps! Three in a row. The ivy has hardly begun to grow over them." Parry got to his feet, slowly. "Oh yes, Alan was real. Very real. And so am I. You fail to discern me behind these spectacles of mine because you are incapable of perception, incapable of seeing, incapable of feeling anything much at all. How mistaken I've been. For a little while I'd been thinking that you had a face, Nigel, or were beginning to acquire one. But now I look at you more closely it seems to be fading away. Fading slowly away. These extraordinary glasses. I'm afraid, Nigel, you are once again... just a blur. Now, shall we adjourn to the living-room for some coffee?"

Needless to say, I didn't stay for coffee, but made my escape as quickly as I could, and I wish I could say that that was the end of the matter. But honesty compels me to admit that, over the next few days, I found myself thinking quite often, in my dreary college rooms, about Parry's unexpected proposition, and to my further surprise, considering it quite hard. The material considerations were a bit of an inducement after all, and Parry had stressed that he was looking for a companion, not a lover. But a little whisper of newly acquired self-knowledge warned me that I would find even that hard to cope with. I had not exactly risen to the occasion when Parry had bared his soul to me. And he, not I, had been right as to which of us was the faceless one. It was mine that proved to be wanting. Behind the learned articles, the Readerships and Fellowships it was I, not Parry, who lived in a world untouched by the rays of love or friendship. I was probably not even up the challenge implied by his possibly justified belief that he could be good for me.

I decided to give myself one more chance. I wrote him a conciliatory letter in which I thanked him for lunch and invited him to dinner at college High Table.

But he never replied.

The InBetween
Joseph Mills

The InBetween
Joseph Mills

"Dehydration."

"No kidding!"

"It wasn't even like it was a desert or anything: I got locked in an old coal bunker in a derelict house. Nobody even knew it existed until weeks later when they pulled the place down and found me. 'He would never have wandered off,' my dad kept telling them. He didn't tell them that I'd *run* off – or why. That's why they never really looked hard enough: they thought I'd been abducted or murdered."

"Well I *was*," said the surly fourteen-year-old sitting next to Billy. "And believe me, I'd rather have been in that bunker."

"Oh yeah? let me tell you this, Seymour – right next to the bunker was an old generator still chugging along, pumping heat into the house and the life out of me. They said I could have survived without food for that long if it hadn't have been for the heat."

"Don't talk to *me* about heat!" Seymour was indignant. "I was roasted alive by White Supremacists. Any idea what it's like to smell your own body burning?"

"OK, Joan of Arc," Mohammed lisped. "We get the picture. How about being raped by homophobes then buried alive because they said you wanted it – your own people!"

Rebecca had only let this go on because the three boys were still relatively new. And the young were always the most bitter about their deaths. True, everybody in the InBetween endlessly replayed their final moments – especially those who'd had life taken from them – but the young ones felt it more, watching their contemporaries grow up, always focusing on those that were doing the best, imagining that would have been them.

"Let's just concentrate on why we're here today," Rebecca said, trying not to glance down at the water beneath the Suspension Bridge. Where she had drowned. "*I* died of a broken heart and that beats you whining babies hands down."

Besides which this was her day. They would get to America soon enough.

"Right, the bastard's coming. Concentrate."

Brian Devlin stepped onto the bridge cautiously. He paused, held onto the railing. Young and old were striding past him casting curious glances. This was getting ridiculous. Every time he crossed the bridge it got worse. He was convinced it was Multiple Sclerosis. Or a brain tumour. Or epilepsy, diabetes, the mercury they put in his fillings. The truth was he hadn't a clue what it was. All he knew was that every time he crossed over this bridge his legs felt like jelly and the concrete like sponge.

Slowly he began to walk, got exactly halfway over, then suddenly felt as though he were walking on mud. His feet seemed to be sinking further into the concrete with every step. And when he passed the spot where Rebecca had jumped, marked out so thoughtfully with fresh flowers and cards, a new thing happened; what felt like a thousand volts shot through him from feet to fontanel. Then it was as though the bridge had disappeared and he was falling down into the river, down to the bottom of the Clyde. His legs buckled beneath him and he slid down to the concrete.

"Result," Rebecca shouted. "I knew I could bring that bastard to his knees."

Billy and Mohammed hi-fived with Seymour. Seymour, black, and Mohammed, gay and Muslim, had teamed up with Rebecca and Billy because The Majority – hetero dead white males – were generally more interested in helping their own kind with their haunting. Rebecca was especially grateful for their help because, as a suicide, most felt she was her own murderer.

"If you kill someone's will to live with adultery and cruelty then you're just as much a murderer as someone who does it with an axe," Rebecca argued, but only other minorities listened.

She watched Brian desperately trying to coax his hair back into place and almost felt pity. Her one remaining bitter-sweet memory was of their last date: Brian insecure, swaggering along the street with all the vanity and vulnerability that goes with a new haircut.

He was helped to his feet and struggled off the bridge past an STV presenter doing a piece to camera. Rebecca hoped Brian's humiliation would be broadcast to the nation that night, then wondered, as she and the others passed in front of the camera, whether some image of them would be recorded, as sometimes happened.

Billy and Mohammed were walking on, Seymour trailing. The first two had bonded more because they had implications of guilt in their own deaths in common. There were homophobes on the InBetween Council as there were in life; enough anyway to suggest Billy and Mohammed had 'led on' their abusers. Seymour had a rock-solid status but he knew that the backlog of murdered blacks was so extensive it would be a long wait before his case was dealt with.

"We've got brothers killed in the '60s riots still waiting," he was told. "And don't talk to me about South Africa!"

Seymour, like Billy, Mohammed and Rebecca was way down the Council waiting list. So, like many other frustrated spirits, they had formed their own breakaway group.

To their delight, Brian was so spooked he did not go to work that day. He turned left and walked along the edge of the Clyde, paused at Glasgow Bridge, then walked up to St Enoch's to get a tube back down south to the latest in a series of bedsits he'd rented then abandoned when strange and terrifying things happened there. The spirits had found that haunting wasn't half as easy as they made it look in the films. People deserted homes they'd spent half their lives in when scary things happened more than once. The *benevolent* spirits got away with a lot, though: nobody cared much about a half-remembered vision of a loved one at the bottom of the bed. They passed a bunch of benevolents chatting at a bus stop. Rebecca recognised old Mrs Malone who'd passed away in her sleep at ninety-two. She was playfully blowing her granddaughter's hair over her eyes.

Mrs Malone gave Rebecca and the others a disdainful look. The benevolents had carried their beliefs in Heaven and Hell beyond the grave. They were convinced that revenge was a sin, however justified, a sin that would confine you to the InBetween – or worse – for eternity.

Easy for them to say, Rebecca thought. Anyway, spirits just faded away willy nilly with no rhyme or reason. To God knows where. Some benevolents were there for years, some revengers faded with the death or despair of their murderers. Nobody had any more answers now than when they were alive. Only the questions were different.

Rebecca had not been there a long time: there was still a lot to learn about the afterlife. At the moment though she was more interested in strengthening her power over the living.

They did a bit of mirror stuff with Brian in his flat, distorting the face every time he looked, at it – 'make him look like a witch' – until he smashed the glass in the sink. But Rebecca sensed the boys were getting bored with her obsession for now.

"There's the funeral of a guy who was queer-bashed to death in the States," Mohammed said. "We could do that then come back to Brian."

"Yes," Rebecca smiled. "Let him think everything's gone back to normal."

Here you travelled through experience, mental development. Although, when you arrived at where you were going, when you were ready to be there, you had also seemingly journeyed in space and time.

At the funeral the young man who had been pistol-whipped and crucified by homophobes was listening to one of his murderer's girlfriends explain: "He only wanted to teach him a lesson."

There was quite a crowd of spirits there. Some well-fed, exuberant; old-timers, bursting out of their concentration-camp clothes (must remember to ask them how you get fat here, Rebecca thought, relishing the thought of joining the Jews in mockery of their Earthly bodies), were summoning up wind and rain to ruin the 'God Hates Fags' placards the religious right had brought to dignify the murder victim's burial with.

Mohammed was talking to the young victim. Dead for only a few days, his spirit face had not been cleaned up and sanitized as his corpse's had. It remained the way it was when he died: a mask of blood, save for the line of a tear from his right eye.

Mohammed was trying to cheer him up, pointing out happy spirits in the crowd; the young English mother who had been raped and murdered next to her son, a son she'd replaced for the time being with the toddler murdered by two boys, who was playing with the children whose mother had strapped them into a car then pushed it into the river.

"And there's Stephen," Seymour said, "with that guy they dragged along the road until his head came off."

They gathered round the murder victim.

"You've no idea how many ways you can spook someone with a severed head," Mohammed told him, laughing.

"The fun we're going to have with that crucifix!" Billy roared.

Rebecca wiped the blood and tears from the young man's face and he smiled, the first of many smiles.

Just Curious
Neil Powell

Just Curious

Neil Powell

You could tell there was something a bit off about Mangy Yates. He sat in the back row, of course, because his name began with Y. The class had been arranged in alphabetical order for the first few weeks, until the masters got to know everyone's name; but he stayed where he was put even after that, as if it were an inheritance he wouldn't surrender. I sat in the back row to watch Mangy Yates.

He was an unspectacular child, apart from his hair, which resembled some sort of infested fur, and apart from his peculiar inquisitiveness. The ancient desks in our form-room, designed to incorporate metal or perhaps even porcelain ink-wells, had holes a couple of inches across in their top right-hand corners. The ink-wells, like their attendant ink-monitors, were things of the quite recent past, but the holes which had contained them were phenomena of inexhaustible fascination for Yates.

Within minutes of a lesson beginning, his right hand would edge tentatively across the desk and his fingers would start to explore the inner circle upon which the countersunk rim of the ink-well was supposed to sit. Though this presumably held nothing more remarkable than encrusted ink overlaid with dust, Yates would dutifully withdraw, minutely examine and surreptitiously sniff his fingers before embarking on his second expedition, through the hole to the underside of the desk, where the only imaginable trophy might have been a fragment of congealed chewing-gum. What made this whole process all the more remarkable was the fact that he always sat at the same desk, which must surely have restricted its potential for revelation – although other classes used the room when we were elsewhere, and they might have left their own mementos.

Elsewhere, indeed, Yates's curiosity seldom lacked something to engage it. In the Geography Room, there were fiendishly-designed desks with metal frames and hinged benches, all in one piece, suitable only for little matchstick-men. Others would slam these benches up and down before the teacher arrived, with the intention of making as much noise as possible. Not Mangy Yates. Given the chance, you'd find him contemplating the hinge, evidently at pains to discover how and why it squeaked at that particular pitch in that particular place. Or he'd be examining a door-handle, turning and re-turning it until he was satisfied with every aspect of the mechanism's design and function. It was as if, unblessed with X-ray eyes, he felt compelled to analyse the insides and other sides of things until he'd created a mental model of them. And not only things: he was banned from the Biology Lab after attempting, in the middle of a lesson on the reproductive habits of the potato, to take a gerbil to bits.

The teachers naturally couldn't stand him. It wasn't that he was dim or uninterested – characteristics which would have seemed wearily familiar to them – it was that he was always interested in something else. Books and detentions and gym-shoes were flung at him almost daily, and once a brick. Mr Gilbert, who taught French, kept the brick in his desk as a last resort: it was made of foam rubber, but from a distance and especially at high velocity it looked extremely convincing. It bounced harmlessly off Mangy Yates, of course, though it may have had some lasting psychological impact. It certainly did on me. I can't to this day pass a building-site or see a stray brick in a gutter without feeling uneasy.

I don't know when I first articulated the idea to myself – perhaps it was the evening when I saw him trying to get his enquiring head inside a huge enamel tea-pot, like some juvenile relative of the Mad Hatter – but I remember thinking that it would be very hard to imagine Yates grown up. Whichever way you sliced the notion of adulthood, it was impossible to see how it might accommodate Mangy.

But he did in a sense grow up: at least, he disappeared, which may have amounted to much the same thing. One dull wet Thursday in November – it was the day of 'O' Level English Language for which, being supposedly literate, I'd been entered two terms early, though Mangy of course hadn't – we trooped back to our boarding-house to find his bed in the dormitory stripped, all trace of his ghastly self eradicated. There was no explanation: just an absence at meal-times, in assembly, in class; an empty space which was larger and more conspicuous than you'd have thought possible. Some people speculated on criminality and expulsion, but most settled for a family crisis involving bereavement or insolvency or both. And stories about his crazy antics blossomed to fill the gap he'd left until, months later, someone actually began a sentence, "Of course, in Mangy Yates's day..." and then we knew he'd become part of history.

By then, it turned out, he was in fact at a crammer's getting himself quite efficiently crammed, so perhaps his abrupt departure from school was due to nothing more sinister than parental dissatisfaction with an education which he had so devotedly confined to the interiors of ink-wells and tea-pots, and the squeaking of hinges. I suppose I should have guessed that he hadn't vanished for good.

All the same, I didn't expect to find him, an incongruously bright university scarf wrapped round his shabby neck, walking towards me across a new midland campus three years later. He was looking at his feet, but that hadn't prevented them from becoming thoroughly coated with the contents of several muddy puddles.

"Bloody hell," I said, "it's..." And stopped, because 'Yates' would have been an old-school-tie archaism and 'Mangy', though no less apt with the passage of time, seemed impossibly rude. His first name was Derek, but if I'd ever known that I'd forgotten long ago.

He stared at me incuriously. "What are you doing here?" he asked.

It hadn't occurred to me that he might consider my presence at all freakish. "I was about to ask you the same thing."

"Engsci," he said. Though it sounded like a Russian philosopher, I knew what he meant. Many of the courses had affectedly trendy names, and scientists were either Molecular or Engineering: Molsci or Engsci.

"Let's go for a drink," I suggested, "and you can tell me what you've been up to."

"Okay." He didn't seem keen.

When we reached the bar, however, he ordered with surprising confidence a Newcastle Brown, which at that time for a southerner indicated quite specialised beery knowledge, and eyed my pint of M&B Brew XI with the contempt it deserved.

"So," I said, "you're still getting inside things to see how they work."

He looked slightly pained. "All science, as Rutherford said, is divisible into physics and stamp-collecting."

"And an Engsci is a kind of physicist, of course."

"Maybe." He tried on his unconvincing replica of a smile. "I'm a stamp-collector, though. I'd have been a Molsci if I could."

That stuck in my mind, as well it might.

Mangy Yates, however, proved oddly elusive as a student. I imagined him toiling away day and night in the white-tiled slab-faced Engineering Science block, inventing wonderful and useless devices. I heard he'd moved into a flat near the by-pass and had an off-campus life in which Newcastle Brown figured largely.

He worked hard enough to get a decent degree and, after that, a respectable-sounding job – the sort of pseudo-academic research post in the electronics industry that gets expensively advertised under 'Graduate Opportunities' in up-market newspapers. Again I imagined him harmlessly beavering away and boring his colleagues in the staff canteen with the arcane results of his latest research. Secretly I even hoped that he might stumble upon something of demonstrable value to the human race: the everlasting lamp bulb, say, or the solar-powered electric shaver. He earned a salary that I could envy and after a while he bought himself a solid terraced house in Bow, about equidistant from Mile End tube station and Victoria Park. If I'd thought about it at the time – if I'd been in touch and had thought about him at all in those crowded years – I'd have sensed in that move something out of character, something too fanciful or imaginative for the Mangy I remembered. We exchanged Christmas cards, it's true, but that was about all; his were invariably of the chain-store variety pack sort that you wince to glance at, let alone attend to or display. He was clearly proud of his house, however anachronistic it may have seemed to me, and sent a surprisingly elegant change of address card to proclaim his arrival there, but he never invited me to visit him.

So much came out at the trial, and in the feature-length press coverage, that it's hard to be entirely innocent of hindsight in recalling Mangy's early career. (That house, for instance, was no more than an address to me: I know it was solid and terraced because the papers told me so, and I know where it was in relation to Mile End and Victoria Park because I've checked in the *A–Z*.) I suppose I should have some special knowledge or privileged insight, having to some extent grown up with him, but although I can reach towards answering the question "Why?" I'm still baffled by "How?"

How did he persuade the first boy, Kenneth or Kevin, for on this detail his scrupulous notebook is uncharacteristically vague, to come home with him that night? Money, obviously: he'd picked him up in the Golden Lion, and it can't have been charm which lured him all the way to Bow. All the same, that choice of where to live had been anything but whimsical: there was the conflux of tube lines at Mile End, the unsurprisably rough East End boys, the green spaces of East London, and Epping Forest only a short drive away. I'd been so wrong about that, about it being out of character: he'd probably selected the street with compass and set-square.

And there was Kenneth or Kevin from Newcastle, just like the beer: perhaps that was the opening gambit. He was skinny, as they all would be – subsequently, Mangy would get them on the bathroom scales and dutifully log their weights – and no taller than around 5' 8". Did Mangy Yates know what was going to happen that evening? Or was he simply a lonely research scientist in search of some vaguely envisaged sexual excitement? I think that's so, though it entails believing some of his creaky evidence and attributing to him a naivety consistent with that adolescent self I couldn't imagine ever growing up. I don't think he knew what he wanted.

When he discovered, he'd have reacted in two contrasting though compatible ways: he'd have been surprised, even shocked at himself; and he'd have at once contained and translated that surprise, automatically, just as he had always done, into scientific enquiry. He hadn't planned it in advance. They went back to Bow, drank some vodka and then, according to his own later testimony, he 'fucked K senseless', the ill-chosen cliché going some way to undermine the plausibility of the entire account. Anyway, the boy upped his price, switched into 'I'm only fifteen and I know a reporter on the *Sun*' mode (which with such a comically insignificant punter was as unapt as it was inept), and Mangy strangled him with a dressing-gown cord – an end which, judged by his subsequent criteria, was simply so *uninteresting*. He'd have begun to formulate ground rules as he lugged the body down to the cellar: they mustn't be too strong, in case of a struggle, nor too heavy nor too tall, given the state of the cellar stairs and his own health. And as soon as he'd thought that, he'd have started to envisage a pattern of skewed scientific research, probably in the form of an imaginary academic thesis: '*An Enquiry into London Boys: Some Comparative Data and Preliminary Conclusions*, by Derek Yates BSc.' Perhaps he even gave himself an imaginary doctorate to go with it.

That glimpse of a pattern would have been an invitation he couldn't refuse: my own guess is that the sex was almost incidental, that he may not even have thought of himself as gay, but that he was tempted to explore the possibility by that quirkily disinterested curiosity which ruled so many of his actions. He was, as he'd said that day in the student bar, by instinct a stamp-collector: in search of interesting specimens, rare examples. And so next Sunday afternoon he drove out to Wanstead – he'd enough sense to avoid the nearer green spaces – and wandered around the park, ending up at a recreation ground where a few lads were kicking a football about. One of them, taller than K but slim and sinewy-looking, kept glancing in his direction: so openly, indeed, that Mangy must have begun to worry that his new-found hobby was in some way dangerously conspicuous. After a while, the players began to drift away, and finally one of them went off with the football. Mangy followed his boy towards Eastern Avenue: it was dusk on a chilly late autumn afternoon, the streetlamps were just flickering into life, and the road was clogged with traffic returning from weekends elsewhere.

"Fancy a drink?" said Mangy.

The boy eyed him pityingly. He had curly black hair and would soon say that his name was Gary. "It's Sunday. Pubs round here don't open till seven."

"Well, my place then. Till the pubs open. It's not far."

His place. It was, of course, further than Gary supposed: but the car was warm, the bloke seemed nice enough apart from his funny hair, and there was the promise of a few drinks and some extra cash. Gary was fit: he could look after himself. He could handle any trouble. Easy.

Sensing this, Mangy wondered whether he'd miscalculated. He considered dropping the boy off with a fiver and an excuse, yet the added sense of danger brought with it a quite new edge of excitement.

"By the way, my name's Gary," said the boy. It wasn't. It was Raymond John White. And Mangy knew this: he'd heard the other boys shouting "Ray!" as they kicked the ball around. "What's yours?"

"Neil," said Mangy, borrowing from a friend he'd almost forgotten. "Much further?"

"Not much further."

"Good." He gave Mangy's leg a friendly squeeze. "I'm getting thirsty."

"Nearly there."

His place. He was the kind of man who'd pride himself on a lack of taste, suspecting that aesthetic sense – or, worse, expense – was morally frivolous. Most of his furniture had come from a junk shop off the Mile End Road, where it had looked more at home than it did now. There were copies of *New Scientist* strewn about, and dog-eared technical manuals. In the kitchen, in the shed, in the cellar, there were working gadgets, broken gadgets, and tools for making gadgets work again. Neighbours would ask him to mend things for them and often, annoyingly often, he managed to do so. They knew, though he never allowed them to see it, that there was an extensively equipped workshop in the cellar, where there was also, sealed in heavy-duty plastic sacks, K's neatly dismembered body.

Here Mangy's ingenuity failed him: he was good at collecting and dissecting things, hopeless at disposing of them. Those black sacks, so soon to be accompanied by others, had to go. He planned to dump the first batch later that evening, in a bankrupt builder's yard he'd discovered out towards Waltham Cross. It was full of festering rubbish: no one ever went there. Yet that seemed an inappropriately random conclusion to so orderly a crime.

Meanwhile there was Gary to get drunk, drugged, dealt with. The trouble was that as subjects for analytical study live human beings could prove deeply intractable and dead ones scarcely less so. Mangy must have felt something like simple gratitude when the boy pointed him towards an obvious solution.

"You're some sort of scientist then," said Gary, glancing round the room as he swigged his vodka and waited for the man to make his cumbersome move.

"Yes, that's right." And he suddenly saw how this truth, subtly improved and spiced with a touch of the Molsci he had never been, might assist him. "A kind of social biologist really. In fact I wondered if you'd mind helping me in my research."

"You what?"

"Oh, it's all right, there's nothing complicated about it. Just a bit of weighing and measuring, so I can incorporate your personal data in a few charts. Anonymously, of course."

"You serious?"

"Perfectly."

"It sounds a bit of a laugh to me." He sniggered. This one was a real screwball and no mistake, if that's all he was after. "Don't see why not. I've always wanted to be a statistic."

"Good," said Mangy. "You will be."

"Fuckin' hell, you are serious."

"Yes. Come on, I'll show you. Bring your drink."

Mangy led the way upstairs, clutching the vodka bottle. Later visitors would comment on the cork-tiled walls, but Gary may have been too amused by this innocent spectacle of a mad scientist to notice. He himself was under-skilled, under-qualified, an electrician's dogsbody trainee, and he viewed these supposedly brainy tossers with a degree of puzzled tolerance. Two open doors disclosed a bleak, deeply unerotic bedroom, a large functional-looking bathroom – the third door was tightly shut – and there was the clinging warmth of central heating turned up too high. In the bedroom, Mangy refilled Gary's glass. It had begun to look like the expected scenario after all.

But it mustn't. Mangy knew it mustn't. "Right," he said, attempting the brisk authority of doctor-dentist-schoolmaster, "just get undressed. This won't take long."

"Do I get paid?"

"Yes."

"How much?"

A swift calculation: too little might be more credible than too much if he was a penurious scientist rather than a wealthy punter. All the same... "Twenty. And I'll buy you a drink in the pub afterwards. Not bad for half an hour's work spent drinking my vodka."

"All right." Gary grinned. "You're on." He stripped off quickly, piling garments on the bed, hesitating for a winsome moment in his underpants.

"Don't be shy."

"Oh, I'm not shy." He stepped out of them with a stripper's flourish. "Da-da!"

"Good. Now let's get you weighed." Mangy, carrying a stiff quarto notebook, led the way into the bathroom.

The Book was an innovation. In it he had already laid out grids to encompass the most methodical information on his subjects, one of whom was to notice that it had a mottled, splashed design on its cover, like a stain of tears. He hoped Gary wouldn't wonder where the previously collected data had got to. K, of course, hadn't figured in The Book, though there would be some less formal retrospective notes about him by way of an appendix.

Gary stood on the ancient scales, while Mangy read off "Nine stone eleven" in the voice of a speak-your-weight machine.

"Here, sit on my face and I'll speak your weight," said Gary. He was, Mangy realised, not only rather drunk but also probably queer after all. The irony of this depressed him slightly. He noted the weight in The Book.

"Now let's do these measurements. The tape measure's in the bedroom. Come on."

"What's in there?" Gary pointed at the dosed door as they passed it.

"Skeletons."

"What?"

"Skeletons in the cupboard. You know, secrets. Actually, just a lot of old books and other junk."

"Oh, right."

They stood facing each other in the bedroom, and for an aberrational instant Mangy found the slender naked boy in front of him attractive. Gary smiled encouragingly at him. "Are you just a bit kinky, or are you a proper scientist?"

"Of course I'm a proper scientist."

"What, with a degree and everything?"

"Yes, look." Among the room's few hints of individually was his framed degree certificate. With the residual pride it still inspired, he unhooked it from the wall and held it in front of Gary, struck just too late by the mistake he was making.

"But it says here you're called Derek. You told me..."

He'd blown it in one stupid unthinking gesture. "That's right. It's because I use the research data anonymously that I prefer to work incognito myself."

To his astonishment. Gary grinned in benign, willing comprehension. "Me too," he said. "My real name's Ray. But I'd rather you kept on calling me Gary. I like that. Now where's the fucking tape-measure?"

It was in the bedside cabinet, with the other things he'd need. He fetched it, and with exemplary detachment set about his task. Neck, biceps, chest, waist, inside leg ("Knew you'd get there sooner or later," said Gary), feet, hands: he wanted to record anything that could be turned into a number.

"That's fine. And now there are just a couple of more intimate details. If you're sure you don't mind."

"Course I don't mind." He leered vaguely, but he no longer had a clue what the man was on about. "I could do with a piss first."

"Good, that's marvellous. You know where the bathroom is. You'll see some specimen jars next to the loo. Just fill one of those, will you, before you pee it all away."

"What?"

"It's important to have a sample of body fluid at the time the other measurements were taken."

"Fuckin' hell." He lurched unsteadily through the door; the vodka – 90% proof that Mangy had bought for the purpose – had done its trick. There was a good deal of splashing, and Gary's voice muttered "Oh fuck". Then he crashed back into the room. "I'm sorry. I must be a bit more pissed than I thought." He sat down on the bed, his head in his hands.

"No problem. One more thing and that's the lot. It's a measurement I'm sure you're proud of."

"Oh yeah?" Mangy's meaning dawned on him. "You must be joking. In my state? And I suppose you want to crank it up? Is that it?"

"No, you can do that. I've got to hold the tape-measure, remember."

"This is bloody stupid."

Mangy rummaged in the bedside cabinet and produced a whitish tablet.

"Take this. It'll help."

"What is it?"

"A mild stimulant. Wash it down with a drop of vodka."

"Good. Now, relax, lie back on the bed and have a good..."

"Yeah, yeah, I know, J Arthur."

With the drink and the sedative, he was knocked out and snoring in a minute or two. Mangy sat astride him and slapped his face gently, just to make sure, then took the roll of industrial adhesive tape from the cabinet and wound it carefully round and round his head, covering mouth, nose, eyes until he looked like a sort of high-tech mummy. It was a pity about that last measurement, Mangy thought: that would be interesting to have in future cases, and the ruses he'd have to employ would make it all the more worthwhile. He glanced at his watch: there were some delicate operations he wanted to perform on this specimen when he'd taken it down to the cellar, as well as the rubbish-dumping run to fit in. It looked like a busy Sunday evening.

*

I know, I know. I've been cheating again. There are details, attributed thoughts and invented conversations, which I couldn't possibly be sure about. Yet from what I must reluctantly describe as my privileged position, I feel more certain of them than I'd have dared to hope when I began this peculiar task. Just as a sophisticated computer can reconstruct lost or damaged parts of recordings or pictures, so the imagination's still more subtle technology can discover hidden elements in the life of Mangy Yates, using the disparate source-materials available to it: adding to whatever inside knowledge it may possess those exhaustive profiles in the Sunday papers and the data, exhaustive in such a different sense, from his own notebook.

What worries me, as I focus more closely on him. and as he becomes alarmingly more strange, is that I begin to feel almost at home with Mangy Yates. I begin, at last, after all these years, to know him. And that's a dangerous thing to do.

His notebook. 'The Book' as he proudly called it, is exactly that – a book of notation: like a musical score, it looks uncommunicative until it's interpreted. Once he'd invented it, The Book became both catalyst and justification. Because it seemed to restrict the range of data he could record, it urged and obliged him to obtain that data. By imposing limits The Book set him free. Every subject was identified by a single name, which of course may not have been his real one, and a four-digit code number (Gary's was 2310) representing day and month: it may be significant that Mangy didn't use six figures and include the year, perhaps sensing that this was a show which couldn't run for ever. Each page began with a passport-like summary of physical characteristics: height, weight, colour of eyes and hair, distinguishing features (Gary apparently had a mole just above his left thigh). Then there was a table for everything that could be measured, with several lines labelled 'Other' for inspired additions. There was a section for the method and time of death, with a space for 'Comments'. Most disturbingly – in view of the effect it was to have on Mangy as well as on his victims – there was a section marked 'Samples'. Listed on Gary's page, and tagged with the number 2310 in the cellar fridge, were a swatch of black hair, a sliver of flesh, two small containers of fluid. It was going to get worse.

Yet for a while at least the practical effect of The Book was delay: having organised himself on paper, it was time for Mangy to organise other aspects of the scheme before proceeding further. On a page at the back, next to his retrospective notes on K, he made a shopping-list. Then he went off to B&Q and bought plastic sheeting, heavy-duty cable, and some extra attachments for his Black & Decker. From a mail-order catalogue he chose handcuffs, ankle restraints, a rubber hood and gag. He hesitated over a harness and decided against for the time being. During November, as he waited for the mail-order firm to deliver, he made only one pick-up – a boy called Mick (1711), about whom his record is unusually reticent and who, coincidentally, is the only victim whose remains haven't been found. Perhaps he miscalculated with the Black & Decker and shamed himself into disposing of the body so thoroughly that even he couldn't relocate it.

It was a winter alternately bright with frost and blurred with fog, hazards Mangy may have underestimated when it came to offloading the black plastic sacks.

Yet this didn't seem to deter him. At work, his colleagues noticed a change in him without for an instant guessing at its cause: he seemed more sure of himself, more smartly turned out, they'd recall, apart from that dreadful stuff on top of his head; the word most often used to describe the impression he made during those months was 'motivated'. People also noticed, with no less astonishment, that he'd begun to develop something almost resembling a sense of humour.

In the first week of December he went, he drily noted, 'Christmas shopping': on the way home, he wandered through Soho, calling at Comptons (which he found oppressively noisy, festive and full) and the Golden Lion. He hoped something would happen, for among his purchases was an expensive shirt, meant for a body less paunchy than his own, which he proposed to offer, and re-offer, as a gift. But the right boy wasn't there, or wasn't sufficiently approachable. Disappointed, he went for a last drink before heading to a cellar bar near Leicester Square.

Though alcohol had blurred his judgement, it had boosted his confidence, and he had no doubt about the hungry, hollow-cheeked boy lounging in an alcove with a well-warmed half of lager. Without realising it, he had got to know the symptoms of paradox: recklessness allied to vulnerability, insouciance to need.

They ate at the Pizza Hut in Cambridge Circus. Money and a hint about the shirt were enough to persuade the boy home: he seemed so lost that he may have been grateful just for a roof over his head. He said his name was Jake, and probably it was. He spoke with the classless anonymity of the home counties – he'd grown up in Redhill – but he was new to London: he accepted the humiliating change to the Central Line at Holborn without question, and was sufficiently innocent to giggle at the robotic voice repeating 'Mind the gap' at St Paul's. For Mangy it had long ago blended into the rest of life's background noise.

Eventually they were home, and Mangy poured the usual huge vodkas – his drowned with tonic, Jake's practically neat. "How come you're adrift in London," he asked, "if home's so close?"

"My parents threw me out."

"Oh I see. Why was that?"

"They – there was something I had to tell them."

"Yes?"

Their eyes met. Mangy knew, and both of them knew he knew. 0612 became an almost empty page.

"Listen, I'm sorry. I'd have told you – you know – before anything happened. It's just a question of playing, well, safe."

"Yes. Look, I'm sorry too, but that's really not what I had in mind. I think it might be better if you went. You can have some money." He reached for his wallet.

"Couldn't I stay the night anyway? I've got nowhere else to go. You can forget the cash."

"No. No, I'm afraid that wouldn't be a good idea." There was no telling what he might stumble upon, and no way he could be let out alive after that. He took notes from his wallet. "Here's enough to keep you going for a day or two."

"You fucking miserable bastard." For a moment Mangy thought Jake was about to hit him, but instead he snatched the money and marched out of the house.

The following evening. Mangy was back m the West End. The sentimental part of him wanted to find Jake, to apologise and offer him the spare bedroom for as long as he needed it; the obsessive part, so maddeningly cheated, desperately needed a healthy fit boy to fill a page in The Book. Jake, of course, had pocketed the cash, gone straight to Victoria, caught a late train to Redhill and negotiated a reconciliation with his distraught parents; so to that extent Mangy needn't have worried. In any case, he discovered a boy calling himself Nick (0712! Thank God, thought Mangy) in the gents of the very first bar he visited and struck an expensive, easy deal: a less obstinately innocent man might have been troubled by Nick's unflappable air of professional readiness, but he simply felt grateful. Nick was short, blond, with nautically windswept skin, inquisitive blue eyes and a single earring; the visible bit of reassuringly skinny arm showed a hint of tattoo.

Back at home in Bow, did Mangy do his scientific research act to get Nick weighed and measured? There was probably no need.

"Tried advertising in the escort columns once," Nick said as he undressed.

"Really?" Mangy was surprised and interested: it was somewhere he should have been looking, though the expense would be against it.

"Yeah. Waste of time. Too many sweaty phone-calls and not enough action." He chuckled. "Sailor Boy. That's what I called myself. Or Nautical Nick. Nautical – naughty – get it?"

"And were you – a sailor?"

"Certainly I was." He laughed again. "Essex fisherman. That's sailing, i'n'it?"

"It certainly is. I suppose you got a few odd clients."

"You want to hear about them? You should be dialling one of them numbers. The weirdest one – he was a Tory MP and he wanted the same trick every time, it never failed – used to make me dress up in his school rugby shirt, red and white stripes, and blue shorts. They was a bit tight even on me. Then he'd chase and tackle me and he'd up hugging me in a scrum on the bed – we had to pretend there was a full pack of forwards round us – while he got the shorts down and his head under. After that we'd go into the bathroom and take a shower together, singing rugby songs and cheering for the school team. He was a bit weird."

"Yes, he was." Mangy felt he'd gone white with shock: he'd seldom heard of anything quite so unforgivably and pointlessly odd, but then he hadn't much liked school. At least after that, he could assume there'd be no problem with his own requirements. Baffled but unoffended, the boy submitted to the routine with bathroom-scales and tape-measure, gigglingly allowed Mangy to record his most prized dimensions ("Not exactly a scale model, am I?"), and pretended to be crestfallen when told to go and piss in a jar, in the interests of medical research.

"You know what?" said Nick, returning from the bathroom. "You're the weirdest yet."

"Why's that?"

"Because there's one thing wrong. I don't mind doing things. I don't mind being watched. But you're not enjoying it."

"I'm not?"

"Don't seem like it." He glanced at his watch. "Come on then, what's it going to be?"

"Right," said Mangy, sounding like a dentist, as he often did at dangerous moments. "This won't take long." He produced handcuffs and ankle restraints from the bedside cabinet.

"Hold on. No unprotected fucking and no whipping, unless we agree terms first." Mangy shook his head. "Right. And if you're going to play with them things, it'll cost you extra."

"How much?"

"Tenner per wrist, tenner per ankle. That's forty."

"All right."

"Right," Nick seemed mollified. "I suppose them cork tiles are there for a reason, but if I get upset I can make a lot more noise than they'll keep in."

At times it must have seemed like hard work, but eventually there was 0712 Nick cuffed and restrained and vaguely expecting that the next thing he'd feel might be Mangy's tongue between his legs. That was how it usually went. Instead, with a snap release of the energy and dexterity he'd primed up for the day before, Mangy slammed the gag on him, then the rubber hood. The boy was trying to splutter something – "You stupid bugger," it sounded like – as he wriggled.

"Don't struggle," said Mangy, lips close up to Nick's hooded head. "If you resist I'll have to suffocate you. Got it? Now listen. This won't take long, and it won't hurt." The boy was motionless in a tense, tentative way. "Good. Don't move, just relax a bit, and don't worry."

He'd pored over medical textbooks to get it right, but his hand shook slightly as he gripped the syringe. He'd wanted to do this since the day they threw him out of the biology lab at school. And it was what had been wrong with the others; strangling, suffocation seemed so unscientific, so out of keeping with all the logged data and the samples.

"Thank you for your co-operation," said Mangy, holding the hood with one hand while he checked the pulse of a cuffed wrist with the other. "It really won't be long now." He was contemplating the tattooed arm and wondering which of his workbench tools would enable him to add that artwork to his little museum.

*

He was making mistakes. Jake had been a fiasco, Nick had almost got out of control. These West End boys were going to be trouble, one way or the other, so he cruised East again, sizing up the pubs of Stratford and Leyton. That week, he picked up a hungry-looking Indian boy at Forest Gate who said his name was Manjeet. "Man-cheat, you mean," said Mangy recklessly. It was a bad start. When they reached Bow, it turned out that Manjeet had relatives in the next street and thought he might call on them. Mangy saw that he had to act quickly and strangled him with the emergency length of electric flex. The data on 1312 contains notable omissions.

He was getting careless: things were going wrong not from ignorance but from mere stupidity. One Sunday afternoon, pondering as so often on the perfect scientific death, he was struck by what seemed a good and obvious idea. He rushed upstairs to the spare bedroom, the one he'd jokingly told Gary was full of skeletons.

It was full of dust, books, scraps of furniture and a cheap metal-framed bed. He flung off the mattress: it was just as he'd supposed, a tight wire grid held in place by springs. If he could work out a way to wire it up... He felt the frustration of a child who's invented a new game and has no one to play with. He could at least check the feasibility of the thing. He fiddled delightedly with cable, plug, screwdriver, pliers, knowing in the sensible bit of his head that it was a crazy thing to do. Then there was an explosion in the fuse-box which shook the terrace; the next-door neighbours, woken from their habitual after-lunch television-watching sleep, came to voice their protest. It was his power-drill, he said, no damage done, terribly sorry. And that's another thing, they said, that drill in the cellar going at all hours of the day and night. It won't happen again, he said, really.

Worst of all, he thought he might be going slightly mad: he began to recognise characteristics in himself which struck him as a bit unpleasant. He blushed to recall some of the things he'd unexpectedly done. Even on the Sunday of the fuse-blowing, he returned later to the spare bedroom, his inventive instinct unsatisfied, and attached an old electric fire to the underside of the bed-frame so that the whole thing heated up like a grill. He was calmly wondering how long it would take to cook a boy when it dawned on him – in a moment of, I suspect, quite genuinely appalled surprise – that this was hardly scientific research. Christmas with his family in Hampshire intervened, and it might be supposed that this gave him a rest from his obsession. I don't believe it: I think that in the conversational longeurs over the turkey, in the desultory doze after the pudding, the images kept returning. He burnished them and refurbished them in his mind. He returned to London with a renewed sense of urgency and took one more chance on the West End. It was a good time to do so: there were plenty of boys on the streets, estranged from their families, who'd discovered that Christmas at MacDonald's wasn't quite the same and who'd be pitifully grateful for a square meal, no matter what went with it. Nevertheless, Rory (2912) was almost a problem.

For a start, he was conspicuously unattractive: one of the mysteries about Mangy's strange career is his apparent ability to pick up good-looking boys, but on this occasion he failed, or didn't bother, or simply lost his touch. Anyway, Rory, whose real name was Michael Braithwaite, was tall, mousy-haired, sallow-cheeked and far too clever. Worse still, he was as crazy as Mangy himself. He looked round Mangy's second-hand living-room with a sneer and declined the offer of a drink – "Afterwards, dear." Upstairs, he stared unbelievingly at the cork-tiled walls. "Well, bugger me, I suppose you're rewriting *A la Recherche du Temps Perdu*. Perdu's the word. I'd say." As he loosened his tie, and as Mangy wondered why he'd never before brought home anyone wearing one, he said: "Well then, what's it to be? Some stuff with plenty of equipment, I shouldn't wonder. Not much equipment on you, anyway."

Mangy, under pressure, reached for the only act he felt happy with, the one about the research scientist collecting data. "Jesus," said Rory, "don't make me laugh. Tell you what, we'll do a deal. Anything you can do I can do better: I'll record your data and you can record mine."

"I don't think..."

"I don't expect you to think. I just expect you to do as I say."

"All right," said Mangy, "you can have the money. Let's leave it at that."

For a moment Rory looked dangerous, then deflated. "Oh, all right, I'll play your ridiculous game."

Perhaps Mangy over-reacted to his close escape with Rory; but later, going through his clothes, he found a knife in the boy's pocket, so the danger had been even greater than he'd guessed at the time. Anyway, he decided there and then that prowling the West End wasn't for him, and he never went back. Of course, East London had its built-in drawbacks too: the boys were more likely to be local, living with families, known to friends, liable to be missed and ultimately traced. Yet that now seemed the lesser risk and the more interesting one: he'd be a mystery man with a name in newspaper stories, the 'Stratford Panther' or something (anything but Bow); he would read about his supposed exploits, hear himself discussed in pubs. He realised he'd always wanted fame.

Rodney Hollings was twenty-one but looked sixteen: people sometimes tried to speak kindly of his open expression when they described his vacant look, and the locals in the Prince of Wales called him the village idiot with a sort of proprietorial pride. He drank large quantities of a very weak draught lager, which he thought immensely strong: he believed it came from Australia, and had been known to pick fights with people who told it was made in Romford. Otherwise in the Prince of Wales Rodney was chiefly famous for having once publicly got his prick stuck in a milk-bottle; an ambulance had been called, but by the time it arrived they'd smashed the bottle and repaired the luckily minimal damage to Rodney with Elastoplast.

Mangy had been back three times now: Rodney had something of the windswept blond charm which had so beguiled him in Nick the Fisherman. There was groundwork to be done: through skilful eavesdropping, he had to discover roughly where Rodney lived, so that he could offer a lift as they coincidentally left together, find themselves going the same way, suggest a drink as a nightcap. He'd noticed that Rodney, though evidently valued as a comic accessory to pub conversation, always arrived and left alone. He listened and watched carefully, believing himself to be invisible, but more eyes than he could have guessed were watching him.

The absence of a problem was almost a problem in itself. When, outside the pub, he fell into step with Rodney and made his proposal, the boy agreed at once and then, turning with his celebrated open look, asked: "You a poof?"

"No," said Mangy automatically, "at least..."

"Don't matter. I like poofs. They like what I got. You want to see it?"

"Later."

"Right, later. You're a poof, then."

Most of it went, as Mangy recorded, like a dream. "Nice place you got," said Rodney, the first and last person ever to admire his home. "That's good stuff, too," of the vodka. He couldn't wait to strip off, loved the idea of being weighed and measured and used for research, flexed his muscles in a sequence of ludicrous beefcake poses. He was certainly the hunkiest of Mangy's boys, the one who could if he'd turned nasty have inflicted serious damage. But nastiness seemed not to be in his repertoire. Merrily drunk, he lay back on the bed, playing with himself.

"Hard to swallow, that's me. Rod by name and nature. Wanna try it?"

"Later."

"'S what you always say. Oh fuck." Reaching sideways for the freshly-replenished glass of vodka, he almost slipped off the bed.

"Just one more thing to do."

"One more. Jesus."

"I'm going to put this on you for a moment." He produced the rubber gag.

"I think I'm gonna puke."

"No you're not." He fixed the gag in place. He'd intended to get the boy unconscious and take it from there, but the possibility that Rodney might indeed vomit, and choke messily on it, alarmed some suppressed houseproud instinct in him. "Come on." He helped the boy clamber up from the bed and with his free hand took the handcuffs from the cabinet. Rodney must have thought he'd be guided towards the bathroom; instead, Mangy led him into the dark second bedroom and eased him gently downwards onto the bed. He recoiled as his back met neither bedclothes nor mattress but wire struts. Mangy reassured him, smiling down in the half-light: "Don't worry, this may hurt a bit. I know it won't bother you, though: it'll soon be over and you'll have your money. Now, just stretch your arms above your head." The handcuffs snapped on, round the frame. "That's fine." Mangy darted momentarily out of the room, returning with the hood and pressing it down over Rodney's face: he felt the boy choking, vomiting. "Messy little bugger."

When he'd flicked the switch, he stood back and quietly admired the warm amber glow steadily seeping out from the radiant bars beneath the body. Then he noticed the unmistakable acrid smell of singeing hair – not from the hooded head, which was beyond the area of the improvised grill, but from further down.

He'd come back in a few minutes, after he'd entered 0401's details in The Book, and perhaps see if he could turn the body over; to make sure – he glimpsed a joke – that the meat got properly cooked. He felt damp and loose with excitement. It was a truly beautiful invention: he wondered if there was any way he might get a fully conscious boy on it and monitor the responses without upsetting the neighbours. It was worth thinking about.

That was the night the police tailed him to Epping Forest, after he'd been seen loading black plastic sacks from the back yard into his Vauxhall Astra. Once there, they watched from a discreet distance as he disposed of his rubbish. There were others ready to surround his house.

They didn't break in: they waited until, at around 1.00am, Mangy got home. It must have been a poignant moment for so lonely a man, returning as he thought to his almost-empty house, to discover insistent males emerging from the shadows around him and demanding admittance. At that point, of course, the police picture still resembled random bits of incompatible jigsaws. They knew Mangy had picked up Rod outside the pub; they knew about several other missing East End boys, including Ray and Manjeet; and now they knew that Mangy had disposed of sacks containing human remains – though these at first glance wouldn't seem to belong to any of the missing persons they were seeking (they were Rory's, and had been in the freezer). Though clearly a murder investigation of some sort, it was for a frustrating hour or so one in which the victim and the corpse appeared to be different people.

Detective Sergeant Robert Mason, waiting in an alley for Mangy's Astra to pass along the street in front of him, was sure of only one thing: that whatever held these elements together, if anything did, was going to be a bit odd. He watched the car arrive; saw it carefully parked; and then, followed by three other officers, confronted Mangy on his doorstep. There was hardly scope for argument in the circumstances, and none took place: Mangy, slipping back into his accustomed role of a shy and deeply uninteresting research scientist, simply let them in. Of course, there must have been a perfectly straightforward sense in which he wanted to get caught – to break the whole obsessive, dangerous, unsustainable cycle. But he didn't want to get caught at exactly that moment.

D.S. Mason later said that the first thought to strike him, as he entered the house, was that this was a man who didn't clean his oven: there was a heavy stench of stale cookery, intensified by the excessive warmth of the central heating. His second thought was that this wasn't quite right. And his third, an instinct rather than a thought, told him that the premises had to be searched at once, luckily by men in mid-shift who hadn't lately eaten a volatile meal. For the nose is what must be followed: D.S. Mason's led him upstairs to the small bedroom, where he found the body of Rodney Hollings, gagged, hooded, and handcuffed to a metal bed-frame. The pathologist's report would confirm that he died from asphyxiation, having choked on his own vomit. Otherwise the bedrooms seemed relatively innocent of evidence for the sequence of murders which Mangy Yates, once taken into custody, was to describe with such matter-of-fact precision: there were one or two modest items of bondage gear, such as any sex-shop might have legitimately supplied, a rather ominous-looking syringe, and – also in the bedside cabinet of the main room – a book simply labelled 'The Book'.

This was more than enough, and yet somehow not enough. It was a young constable, whose recent deployment as a 'pretty policeman' might easily have led to an invitation from Mangy, who surmised that a house of that age must surely have a cellar and wondered what was in it. There was no obvious door, but beneath the kitchen table he noticed a rectangle of linoleum with what appeared to be a small recessed handle, like the ring-pull of a can. The staircase below was rickety, and the two bottom steps had rotted away completely, but there indeed was the cellar, methodically fitted-out with shelves, workbench, tools, a huge second-hand fridge and an even more elderly freezer (Mangy had found it on a skip outside a closed-down corner-shop, and given the bankrupt owner a tenner to help him get it home).

It was the method of it all which most upset D.S. Mason and his colleagues, who would have felt more comfortable trying to make sense of chaos. There were sealed sample jars of fluids and polythene envelopes containing hair, fingernails, skin – in one case exhibiting the fading pigments of a tattoo: all neatly labelled with four-digit codes, like a parody of scientific sanity. The whole cellar was like a distorted mirror-image of the police forensic lab.

They were waiting for the Chief Inspector to arrive. Detective Sergeant Mason felt no anger, and had scarcely any voice, when he asked the intolerable question. "Why?"

"I don't know," Mangy told him. He was calm, thoughtful, effortlessly reasonable. "I suppose I was just curious."

That was the attitude he sustained – or rather, the attitude which sustained him – throughout the trial. He was animated and engrossed, leaning forward to follow the exchanges between counsel and expert witnesses as if he were watching an extraordinarily interesting yet hypothetical debate; they were taking something to bits, to find out how it worked, and it didn't much matter that this time the something was himself. When he spoke of his own actions and motives, it was with the due scientific caution of a man ascribing thoughts to someone he didn't properly know... "I might have wondered..." or "I suppose I wanted to discover..." He proved to be an exemplary witness, eager to please and constantly at pains to recall details which might somehow be of use. But he couldn't explain.

Mangy Yates was a disappointment to the vast, expectant public he had at last acquired. The crimes had promised them a monster and instead delivered this earnest little chap with his tweedy jacket and his drab furry hair. When the judge spoke of 'an almost unimaginable catalogue of evil and depravity', you felt – as Mangy himself felt, by the look of him – as if you were witnessing a quite ludicrous case of mistaken identity. And it's true, I think, that he wasn't evil; for a knowledge of evil implies an understanding of good, and Mangy had neither. An innocent spirit of enquiry – which, differently shaped, might have made him a librarian or a surgeon or simply a train-spotter – compelled him, as it had always done, to investigate. It wasn't an excuse, it wasn't even any kind of mitigation: he was, as he'd himself said, just curious. The oddest thing of all about Mangy Yates is that I can almost believe it. Almost.

Touching Darkness
Patrick Roscoe

Touching Darkness
Patrick Roscoe

First things first:

You were not the prisoner; I was not the warden with the keys.

There was never a cage, never a cell. No bars of iron, no heavy chains.

Let's get that straight from the start.

Since appearances can be deceptive.

Once again, as originally, the room might at first glance look very neat rather than quite bare. Sparse furniture – a single bed, a night table, a wardrobe – is as unexceptional as its setting. A window, set fairly high in one wall, looks over our back yard; even when closed its venetian blind lets in light. The uncarpeted floor is laid with tiles, either much faded or never bold, of uninteresting design. The white walls are decorated with several generic prints of ships at sea. A large closet contains unmarked cardboard boxes whose obscure contents somehow do not intrigue: anything of value has surely been removed from them; nothing important enough to merit concealment probably remains in them.

Undisturbed dust dreams in silence.

Unbreathed air waits to be consumed by throats, caressed by lungs.

Certainly not a sinister or disturbing place. The room at the back of the house neither evokes nor deserves such description.

Perhaps only I, knowing it is there, am able to detect the slight stain on the tiles to the rear.

The subtle scent that lingers like a memory or dream of love.

For years we used it as a spare room, a guest room, a room to hold odds and ends which do not clearly belong in other rooms. Infrequently entered, except when something missing is searched for without particular hope within its walls, the room possesses an air of neglect born of indifference: neither of us feels sufficient interest to invest it with his attention, his energy, his taste. We do not really need the space; it is almost beside the point: we can bear no heirs. Often I forget the room entirely, as if nothing lies behind its door.

Kept closed, the door has no lock or key.

As your last wish, you will wordlessly beg for those interdependent mechanisms that deny entry.

Or prevent escape.

Yet finally this unremarkable space will be spoken of in the most lurid language.

Chamber of Horrors.

Dungeon of Death.

(Never mind that the room is situated on the ground floor and not in the basement. Upon the prosaic surface of the earth, not within its murky depths. Outrage often eschews accuracy.)

Prison of Pain, they will inevitably howl.

You would smile, I know.

If you could.

When you begin to sleep in the room at the back of the house, I am not unduly concerned. There have been a number of occasions during our long union when one or the other of us has felt the need to sleep separately for a time. A night, a week; at most, a month. Such nocturnal vacations from each other do not necessarily result from disharmony. There is no question of rejection, of withdrawal. Eventually the occurrence does not even require explanation, can pass without comment: for we are assured it will have a positive result. From our state of extreme intimacy, which to outside eyes may already appear suffocating, we move apart in order to come back even more closely together than before. We learn to miss and to want and to need each other fiercely again. To tremble anew at what was perhaps becoming an overly familiar touch. To receive fresh pleasure in the length of your body against mine, in the weight of my head upon your chest.

Simultaneous orgasms, syncopated sighs, osmotic dreams.

Our reconnection can possess the heightened excitement of the first encounter enriched by the wealth of erotic knowledge gained from ten thousand subsequent encounters.

But this time you do not return to our communal bed after a night, a week, a month.

I have no way of knowing that you will never share it with me again.

No understanding of what has ended, of what has begun.

At the time, as it happens, I am working and you are not. There is nothing unusual about this. Often we alternate holding employment; our life of love has always been more important than any amount of income. One leaves the other free to tackle long-postponed projects around the house, to assume the main burden of cooking and cleaning. Then more of our time together can be devoted purely to the act of love. (Though in more than just a sense every one of our shared activities – for example, putting up the storm windows in autumn – is a sexual exchange.)

It is a system that has worked well for us.

Until now.

Because I sleep poorly without you beside me, I come home from work tired after my first solitary night. I do not have energy to wonder why you have not prepared supper. (This is precisely when you would be apt to fix my favourite meal as reassurance, however unnecessary, of your unfaltering love.) Why you remain in the spare room instead of sharing the meal I end up making. Why you don't feel like going to the cineplex, the café, the gym. You have already eaten, I think. You wish to spend a quiet evening at home, alone. During these phases when we do not join together physically, we often remain apart in other ways too. I shrug at the silence that leaks from the spare room. You are reading, you are resting, you are writing a letter. Once or twice during the evening, I find myself listening for hints of your nearby presence. When I pass down the hallway, the spare room door proves closed. Moving the sprinkler in the back yard, I glance toward the appropriate window and see that the room you inhabit is already dark at ten o'clock.

Mentally, I shrug again.

We have always respected each other's secrets.

The closer we have grown, the more important and necessary those secrets become.

The unknown is erotic. Darkness is aphrodisiac.

The gap between what I don't know about your interior and all I know of your exterior can make me swoon.

Several days later I suspect you rarely leave the spare room while I am at work. The rest of the house lacks evidence of your presence. No crumbs litter the kitchen counter. No CD rests in the audio system. No damp towel drapes in the bathroom.

You continue to decline to share the meals I make, as you still do not wish to cook, to clean, to shop for groceries. While I am at home, you stay behind the closed door of the spare room, and are not overly responsive when I open it to say a few words at morning, after work, before bed.

Yes, you smile, when I ask if you're OK.

We have always told each other the truth.

Checking the odometer of your Jeep, I learn that the number does not change from one day to the next.

Of course you do not leave our house if you do not leave the spare room.

The other room, as I begin to think of it.

As it assumes greater importance, grows equal in significance to our room.

Or what was our room.

On the fifth day after we begin to sleep apart (or is it the sixth? I grow dreamy without the reality of your touch), I return from work to find the house filled with what feels like a new kind of silence. As if it has been empty for many hours during which all traces of human presence drained slowly from within its walls. Immediately my heart relaxes; just as suddenly I realize how tightly it has been clenched. I do not fear you have left me; the impossible is inconceivable. (Anyway, your Jeep rests in the driveway.) Instead, I hope that since morning you have been strolling beside the river or climbing the sweep of hill to where perfumed pines stir and moan in breeze. You have looked increasingly pale (I know it is difficult for you too to sleep alone) and the weather is especially fine this June. (That last June, I will later think, as though June has never come again, as though all months, even current ones, are only memories now.)

When I knock on the door of the other room, your voice does not answer. I open the door. You are sitting on the floor beside the bed; it is as neat as if it has not been slept in for more than just one night. Your face is turned toward me. I suspect your eyes have been watching for the appearance of mine since I left for work ten hours ago. All day you have done nothing but wait for me.

For my touch.

Our sexual life has always been intense. It is the reason we have remained together. (Only those few – in my experience, they are not many – who have fully explored the realm of all senses understand what a complete reason this can be.) Finely tuned bodies and sleek skin; swollen muscles and strong limbs; a pair of large penises: such is the medium of our communication, and to preserve this instrument of interchange we take considerable care regarding diet, spend several hours in the gym each day, forsake smoke and drink and other drugs. What I wish to tell you about who I am, how I feel, what you mean to me: all this is said through the language of touch. Now your and then my penis speaks slowly or quickly; the anus answers eagerly; lips elaborate the point. The few people to enter our daily life and observe us together invariably comment upon the extent of silence between us. Yet I doubt words could say more precisely or clearly what your hand conveys resting on the back of my neck as we drive into the mountains in search of the first or last snow of the ski season; what my multilingual lips say as they explore the various countries of your skin. In a unique, private sign language, your caressing fingers spell endearments upon my back. Intricate concepts, complex emotions: though silent, this idiom is not necessarily simple.

Before finding each other, we both experienced lovers who did not wholly understand the speech of sex, the tongue of touch.

That has allowed us to appreciate each other all the more.

Now my first touch in five or six days tells you I want you, I need you, I will never leave you.

More, you say soundlessly, unsmilingly.

(But that was long ago. Sometimes now, when the rooms around me are most silent, and the clock ticks its loudest, I can believe I inhabit this house alone. There is no sign of another presence, except for the scarcely distinguishable yet permeating scent of rot that travels from the room in the back. I can almost forget that in your ultimate, invisible form you are still there. Where you want to be. Need to be. Must be. Why? Love is the final puzzle of the world, the last secret of our galaxy, the true riddle of the Sphinx. I have had years to muse upon the question of what became of us. Like reaching out to grab darkness and ending up with empty hands, the answer still eludes me.)

The quality of your touch has changed since five or six days ago. It speaks with new force about hunger and need. After our initial, urgent dialogue is complete, you turn at once from me, curl into a ball on the hard floor where we have come together. You want me to leave when before our tactile conversation would continue long after the first explosion of semen.

Unlike myself, the single bed is undisturbed.

Leaving the room, I do not realize the full significance of the bed's unrumpled state. Or of your silence before, during and after our act of love.

The next day I come home to find you have fastened heavy black cloth over the window of the other room in such a way that no light enters, not even a crack at the edge. The following day I discover you have removed the bulb from the light socket in the ceiling. Two days after that you rid the room of its furniture, the walls of their prints, the closet of cardboard boxes. You begin to use a bucket for your wastes. You no longer dress. When I enter the room, your naked body shrinks into the farthest corner from the light that falls in from the hall. Your eyes close until the door has shut and complete darkness returned. You have transformed the space into a void around you. Besides the bucket, there is nothing in the room except yourself; nothing to dilute that essence. No clothes interfere with my touch. No furniture stands between us. No light offers our eyes distracting, unnecessary images. Now we see only each other. See through touch, see through smell. To a slight degree (quickened breath, contrapuntal moans), through sound.

But you have ceased speaking in words.

And my voiced speech makes you cringe, as if it were fists.

The darkness is pure, your fingers spell upon my back.

The darkness is holy, they insist.

Would I have acted differently if at the time I had known that I would never hear your voice again?

That you would never leave the dark room to appear before me in light again?

The heartbreak of hindsight.

Your touch soon informs me that it is not necessary to bring you carefully prepared and balanced meals twice a day. You will eat only a crust of bread, drink only a half cup of water. Nor is it important that I empty the bucket of waste regularly. All you want from me is my touch. As if this touch contains all light, all nourishment, all the comfort you desire.

What do I desire?

The same thing as always: your happiness.

I give you what you want, what I can, what I have.

More, your touch demands.

Harder, it urges.

Don't stop.

Driving home, I fear what latest development will await me there. I park next to your Jeep and from the outside contemplate the structure we share. It appears more or less the same as the other modest houses on this quiet street. Innocent, innocuous. The old woman next door, whose sidewalk we shovel in winter and lawn we mow in summer, waves until I lift my arm in response. (We have taken pains to ingratiate ourselves with our neighbors in order to forestall any unease they might otherwise feel from your presence, as in a foreign country one is careful to soothe potentially hostile natives.) A small boy pedals his tricycle furiously down the sidewalk, repeatedly rings its tinny bell. A sprinkler pirouettes with perfect grace upon green grass. Blue smoke from barbecues slants through the golden air of six o'clock. The scent of burning charcoal and cooking meat mixes with that of freshly cut lawns to produce the bouquet of suburbia.

The small boy's name is Billy. Often when you are working out in the yard, he will tag at your heels, tug at your sleeve, ask question after question. Changing the oil in your Jeep, you patiently explain each step, allow him to hand you tools. He stands beside you, scarcely reaching half way up your long legs. His face tilts to find your eyes above. Your hand rests lightly upon his tawny head.

From what I understand, Billy has no father. My source of information, the old woman next door, shakes her head when speaking of him: plainly, she could say more.

I have seen the way you look at the son you will never have.

It makes the strings of my heart knot, tangle, twist.

From the driveway's perspective and distance, it is easy to summon such terms as 'breakdown' and 'psychosis' and 'illness' to describe what is occurring in our house.

It seems obvious that intervention and assistance are required for you, of me. In the end, they will ask why I didn't save you. Call that failure a crime, give it another name, turn it into something that demands punishment.

I will not try to explain.

That to drag you from the other room and to call an ambulance would have been failure to our eyes.

We have never lived for the world's eyes.

We have always lived for love alone.

Perhaps all lovers must believe they embark upon a unique adventure, undertake a brave new experiment, engage in unprecedented experience. You are daring me to follow you deep into the darkness. To search for the source of love, elusive as that of the Nile, which lies far beyond practical procreation and sanctified desire and convenient passion; only there at its origin, before becoming contaminated by time and space, is love pure.

Long ago, I suspect, you planned this journey we are taking now, waited patiently until able to bring it about, always kept the larger picture in mind. An unremarkable house on a quiet street in a drowsy suburb far from the sleek centre of the city: this particular setting is important to the success of your meticulously conceived design—as the room at the back of the house, the old woman next door and the small boy half way down the block form further crucial pieces of the puzzle you hold whole in your head. And you selected me specifically because you believed I would not fail the challenges of your experiment, however difficult they might be. Half a dozen images of you closely considering me montage through my mind. You are wondering:

Am I strong enough, brave enough, man enough to love you?

The tricycle bell fades in the distance. I continue to feel you waiting within the house for me. For several days, I realize, I have come home hoping to find you gone. For one moment I am tempted to turn the ignition key and restart the still-warm engine, to drive away and not return.

This is my last chance to leave you.
From here there is no going back.
Slowly I approach then enter our house.
Honey, I hysterically think of calling, I'm home.

Gradually I stop thinking of the space you occupy as 'the other room'.
It is simply 'the room'.
The original room, the only room.
As if no other exists.

Sometimes your silence taunts me.
Sometimes it shrilly screams.
Seduces, begs, insinuates, cajoles.
Increasingly, what is left to me is interpretation.
Or rather: understanding that in love, always, interpretation is only what we have.
The adoring expression in his eyes, the tender tone of his voice: our own emotion, fatally subjective, elects the adjectives it requires to survive.

The air enclosed within the room becomes thick and heavy with the odour of your unbathed body, with the stench from the bucket of waste. It grows difficult for me to respond to your silent summons. I must remind myself that this aroma is produced by, and is part of the being I love; therefore, I must love it also.
In love there can be no selective throwing out of chaff to keep the grain.
Take me as I am.
All or nothing.
In sickness and in health, till death do us part.
Threadbare clichés echo tinnily inside my head.

The darkness around you assumes the properties of solid matter. I stroke its skin, I squeeze its entrails. Rub it between my fingers, feel its texture. Touch it, learn it, know it.
Love it.

It requires increasing effort for me to touch you with the force you desire. I grow nostalgic for the days when the lightest pressure of my fingertips could make you quiver, cry out, come. In the darkness I read in braille a historical romance that features your clean hair's scent, the gaze of two green eyes, the precise pitch of a laugh. More and more, I feel I am making love with the past.

Or committing adultery with your ghost.

I wonder if our emphasis upon touch as profound communication was misguided all along. As your silence lasts, I am perversely compelled to speak to you in words, must fight to stifle that urge. When your birthday arrives, and then our anniversary, I feel helpless to convey the significance of these days. Especially since, exactly when its subtlety is most needed, my touch becomes reduced to blunt blows.

Still harder, you mutely beg.

Of course it is painful to realize that your body is losing weight, your muscles their firm tone. In the second that the door is open, as I enter or leave the room, a glimpse reveals how pale you have become. Gaudy sores and cuts and bruises decorate your skin like the haphazard work of some tattoo artist suffering a deficiency of sustained attention. With the nails of your toes and fingers, you matted hair grows long. But in the darkness your eyes shine more brightly than ever. Your touch tells me over and over that this is how you wish to live. Your previous experience was compromise.

Now you are completely satisfied.

Perfectly happy.

Summer passes slowly. I go to work each weekday. I visit you each evening. I mow the lawn and wave to neighbors and watch Billy pedal his blue tricycle back and forth in front of our house. He is hoping the sound of his bell will draw you to him. That you will play catch with him. Tell him about when you were a boy his age. Promise that one day he will grow to be as tall and strong as you. As loved as you.

When I return the emptied waste bucket to the room, you tend to shift it one or two feet from where I have placed it. After a moment, the metal's glint shows you have moved it half way back to where it was. In my mind gleams a dozen occasions from the time before the room when you seemed to meditate upon the position of some unimportant object, consult a blueprint in your head, adjust the arrangement of the landscape to match it. The blueprint is of the past; what to me seems unprecedented is in fact repetition: this has happened before. I slowly understand how crucial it is that the room is at the back, not the front of the house. That the woman next door is old rather than young. That, for purposes of replication, Billy's hair is tawny instead of dark.

In my dream I sponge your body until it sings with cleanliness. I cut your hair and clip your nails and dress your sores. I feed you, cradle you, croon to you. In our dreams we do what is denied when awake.

Our telephone and doorbell have never rung often; we have always been enough – everything – for each other. Now when an acquaintance calls for you, I say you are at the gym, at the store, in the shower. When the old woman next door wonders once or twice why she hasn't seen you lately, I explain that you have gone away for the summer. By autumn I will say you have left me, I don't know where you have gone. I leave the keys in your unlocked Jeep until it is stolen. I scrawl 'moved' on your mail, send it back. Calls for you cease; with one exception, questions about you stop.

You have gone.

You are not here.

Like any dream erased by dawn.

In what was our room, on what was our bed, I study photographs of you. Once I would have said, with complete conviction, that I would never have to do this. No matter how far you went away, no matter how long you stayed away. Light seeps from your snapshot skin, spills from your emerald eyes, escapes your Kodak smile. Women and other men turned in the street to catch that light; they did not realize it was only a faint approximation of the dazzle to flood me when we were alone. During our twelfth year we have wanted each other more than during the first. In the supermarket your broad shoulder brushes mine and I am nearly knocked off balance by the force of electric charge. Spotting you in the gym, my fingertips graze your wrists and blood rushes to the lush surface of your skin. Always the taste of your saliva blooms in my mouth. Always from us wafts the spice of our mingled semen.

I do not possess a vial containing the precious essence of your original scent.

No recording of the voice that throbbed my blood.

Before or after the last leaf falls from the maple behind our house?

I do not realize precisely when I begin to think of you in the past as well as the present tense. When the being in the room, though still 'you', assumes an identity separate from the one I originally loved. You have divided into two – pre-darkness and post-light – like some organism capable, with only the assistance of time, of self-reproduction.

Which half received the indivisible heart?

Only Billy doesn't believe you have gone. He persists in knocking on the front door and asking for you. As I explain your absence again, he peers behind me for sight of you. Dragging his heels, glancing over his shoulder, he leaves reluctantly. His unconvinced face is pinched more sharply than ever with hunger.

At my least sound, you shake with such force I fear you will convulse. Now we do not even moan or grunt when we come together. There is only the dull thud of my fist against your face, the slap of my hand upon your skin. My kick, my push, my shove: all these gestures of love produce their particular sound, speak their specific language. It is unfamiliar to me; I can't understand it. Only you are fluent in this idiom.

I wonder where and when you learned it.

With whom.

We have always worn each other's clothes. We are the same size.

Seeing you in my green shirt could make me feel we are interchangeable, identical, one. I would experience the same pleasurable confusion as of waking to wonder if the arm flung over my chest belongs to you or to me. Now I wear your clothes exclusively. At morning I look in our closet and imagine what you would wish to wear today. The faded yellow sweatshirt with a small hole in the left shoulder, an old favourite? I like to believe my dressing in your clothes allows you to share my experience within them.

To live in light as well as in darkness.

In our former room I make loud, guilty love with your photographed self. Sense you stiffen with outraged jealousy in the darkness across the wall. On my next visit, you retreat to the back of the closet and won't come out. Though I have long ceased receiving pleasure from our physical contact (except in the sense that your pleasure is always mine), on this evening I leave the room overwhelmed by unsatisfied desire.

Though the autumn proves surprisingly mild, I never feel warm in bed, wonder if your naked body suffers equal cold upon its bare tiles. Beneath heavy blankets I curl around my shivering self. The first time I waken to the sound of crying, I believes it comes through the wall. Then I understand this sound is produced by myself. Soon I am accustomed to being roused by weeping; it is no more extraordinary a nocturnal phenomenon than, say, darkness.

As you continue to deteriorate within the room, I grasp more tightly to life outside it. I do not miss a day of work. Attend the gym religiously, read the newspaper thoroughly, clean the house carefully. Leaves fallen from the back-yard maple are raked, air freshener to combat the odour that leaks beneath the room's door is bought. My car is tuned, my teeth are examined. Respectful of the calendar, I have candy on hand for Hallowe'en. (This year Billy is a cowboy; last year he was an Indian.) At Thanksgiving I cook a turkey with all the trimmings, eat enough for both of us. When the first snow falls, I am acutely aware that you do not know the world has become white. As perhaps you are uncertain whether today is Tuesday or Friday, whether night has replaced day. (Or in your dark zone have you developed strategies, based on sounds from outside, to keep track of time as in the cemetery corpses methodically count off the weeks until their resurrection? Only the blunting of senses necessary for me to bear the room prevents me, surely, from hearing within it the song of birds and calls of children beyond.) At Christmas I am at a loss as to what gift I can give you. Then, on that silent, holy night, for the first time my hands draw your blood. At once I comprehend how much this excites and pleases you. You greedily lick the liquid that spills from your nose. I listen to the slurp, suck, slurp and recall the time I entered the room to see, in that second of illumination, you tilt the bucket of waste to your opened mouth. Then swallow, then lick lips, then burp.

Sometimes I wonder if my memory is confused. If it were I who unscrewed the bulb from the socket in the ceiling, removed the furniture, placed heavy black cloth over the window, took away your clothes. Sometimes it seems my body possesses physical memory of performing those actions. Then I shake my head: no. It has always been difficult to know where one of us begins and the other leaves off. Only that has caused my confusion.

At other times I ask myself if I could remain with you in the darkness. Share it with you as we have always shared everything important. Yet I know this is not possible.

I must remain in light so you can enjoy darkness.

I am the light, you are the darkness.

Complete love is the union of these opposite elements.

I repeat the formulae by rote, puzzle upon where I learned them, speculate that while I sleep someone stands beside the bed and whispers concepts and instructions that through the darkness sink into my subconscious to emerge as apparently my own thoughts upon waking.

There are moments, during daytime, when I can almost recall the sound of that voice.

Its familiar tone, its known timbre.

Anyway, if we did love lastingly in the darkness, our electricity would soon illuminate and destroy that element. Even now – still – sparks seem to shoot from our touch, swirl in haloes around our heads.

Repeatedly it strikes me how comfortable you are in the dark, bare room – as if you have lived this way before.

You have realized in three dimensions the blueprint of the past that for years hovered only flatly in your head. (Sometimes, entering the room, I feel I am stepping into the dark chamber of your mind.) Or (to take the longer view) as if, over centuries of evolution, your species has adapted to these conditions until they have become a natural environment you can enjoy as well as endure.

Yet I can't permit myself to contemplate how you pass the hours while waiting for my next touch. What you remember of the past, what you experience in the present, what you hope for the future. I can't allow myself to calculate the number of dark hours you have survived so far. The thought causes a twinge of pain to shoot through my head.

Spring comes, spring goes. Suddenly it is a year since you entered the room. I mark the date by remembering:

The last words you spoke to me.

The last squint of your sun-drenched eyes at me.

The last cup of coffee you made for me.

If nostalgia is a second-rate emotion, surely sentimentality occupies a still lower plane.

In the back yard I catch Billy looking up at the window covered with heavy black cloth. He quickly runs away. The boy has always avoided me as much as, inversely, he has been drawn to you. He is aware that I know the truth about him. That I recognize the hunger in him. That I understand what he is prepared to do to save himself from starvation.

Need corrupts.

When you were not looking, his innocent grey eyes have leered at me.

His tongue has licked his pink, petalled lips enticingly.

If the woman he lives with – a relative of some kind, say my next door neighbour – is in fact an alcoholic recluse, a mean and twisted spirit, that is really no excuse.

It could be much worse.

As I should know.

And you, I will learn, even more.

I abandon my habit of wearing your clothes. I do not want even to imagine your sharing the experiences and emotions I now have within them.

Certain stresses I must suffer and tensions I must bear because of the stupidity of the world.

Let's just say it has not been easy to sustain myself outside the room.

Arguably, you enjoy an easier existence within it.

Yet I do not resent the alignment of our roles.

Selfishly, unsuccessfully, I try to subvert your unspoken wishes, your undeniable happiness. At high volume I play certain music you have especially loved with the idea that it might draw you from the room. With similar hope I prepare the one dish whose tantalizing aroma you have never been able to resist. For one week I refrain from bringing you bread and water. Going away for a weekend, I deprive you of several visits.

None of these stratagems works.

I can almost sense you smirk at the naivety of my ploys.

Clearly you are the one in control here. The one to dictate the course of events.

I am merely your pawn, your prisoner.

Factor X in your investigation into the truth about love.

One evening during the second year you do not shrink away when I enter the room. For once the moment of light from the hallway does not seem to disturb you. Curious, I leave the door open and move silently toward your favourite spot to the rear of the room. When I wave my hands before your eyes, they do not blink. A clap near your ear fails to make you recoil.

You are blind, you are deaf.

Correspondingly, your touch becomes more urgent, more forceful, more demanding.

More, more, more. Each time leaving you, I am exhausted from trying to fulfil your need, surprised by the sustained vigour of your response. I doubt I will possess the stamina to love you the way you need to be loved much longer.

Who is growing stronger?

Who weaker?

Yet I continue to close the door behind me upon entering or leaving the room. I cannot bear to witness with my eyes (it is difficult enough to accept what touch tells me) pus oozing from open sores, bones jutting sharply beneath skin coated with a second skin of dirt and blood, feces and urine. After each visit, I scrub myself mercilessly with powerful soap, but wonder if a trace of your decay clings to me still.

Unvanquished microbes.

Unbudged bacteria.

You have seeped into my skin, sunken deep inside my marrow, dripped into my DNA.

You are not deteriorating, I tell myself.

You are evolving.

I have failed still to rediscover how to sleep soundly alone. Perhaps this is a skill that once unlearned can never be acquired again? Where you occupied our bed yawns a bottomless pit beside which I huddle fearfully until dawn. (On the other side of the wall are you awake too?) And the voice that speaks to me in my sleep is waiting to pounce if I finally do drift off. Now it barks, growls, snarls obscene instructions. The morning mirror reveals a drawn, anxious face. My head throbs steadily. I fumble through the days as if half-blind, half-deaf. At work I continually make simple mistakes. My colleagues express concern. Those who have known about your presence in my life believe they witness evidence of suffering caused by your desertion.

It is not just a question of sleeping alone. I do not know if I am able to live alone. Millions do, I remind myself. Yes, but they have not known you. Often in the evening, battered by the pain in my head and the voice of my sleep, I sit on the hall floor, rest my back against your closed door, from your presence beyond seek to draw sufficient strength to carry on for one more day.

Billy's blue tricycle becomes a green bicycle. One Saturday I see him bent over its prone frame. One of the pedals is broken. No, he replies when I ask if I can help. He looks at me with a mixture of suspicion and dislike and fear. He believes I have taken you from him. Made you disappear.

Perhaps I am disappointed in the boy.

Perhaps I thought that, deprived of you, he would turn to me.

As if it were recently left there, or had been patiently awaiting discovery all along, a file concerning yourself, dated twenty-one years ago, appears at the bottom of the bag where you kept your hockey equipment. (I have been sorting through your things; it is time, snaps the voice of my sleep.) I glance quickly at the papers in the file. Medical reports, psychiatric records, police dossiers. Without assimilating their information, I stuff the papers back into the bag. If you had wanted me to know the contents of this file, you would have shared them with me. For reasons I can't articulate, it seems essential that I refrain from digging into your secrets now. The prospect makes the dull pain in my head sharpen.

We did not bring our pasts to our union. We were born anew with our first kiss. Yet I have vaguely gathered that no parents or siblings or close friends peopled your existence before myself; this kind of uncrowded history was one more attribute we shared. No one will look for you. Make inquiries. File a missing persons report. Even given the circumstances, it is astonishing that a human being might vanish without a murmur from the face of the earth. As if he were never here at all.

Melt away like snow that leaves no trace of itself behind.

Displaying what was there underneath all along.

After a certain point in the third year, there is no way to describe what passes between us in the room as sexual activity, however broad the scope encompassed by that term. Suddenly, swiftly, your touch grows weaker; you can no longer hold me, clutch me, grasp me. Eventually you do not have the strength to expel your wastes into the bucket, to swallow bread, to sip water. Your teeth have abandoned your gums. Your hair has deserted your head. Huge in your gaunt face, open wide, your blind eyes are covered with a film of white. Your limbs, apparently broken some time ago in the course of our meetings and never properly healed, dangle at odd angles from your torso of bereft bone. You become an inert mass upon the tiles. Now I am required simply to enter the room and kick the shape of darkness. I must kick as hard as I can for you to feel the touch. That kick is all that keeps you alive.

It would be an act of violation, an explicit rape, to cradle you in my arms, rock you gently, whisper into your unhearing ears all the words of love that for three years have been building up inside me, festering like the pus that drips from your open sores.

Something snaps. With your last strength you sever the unbreakable thread that has joined our physical selves for so long.

You perform this superhuman act for the sake of my survival – or, more exactly, since you are me, for our survival. I no longer need to crouch outside the room at evening: what remains within its walls is dross; what is essential, our love, lives on within my walls of flesh. Though free from the contents of the room, from force of habit I can't help continuing to visit it, to consider it, to think of it as you.

Very carefully I sweep the house of all your belongings, wipe your fingerprints from the walls, destroy every piece of evidence that you were here. As a back yard fire consumes photographs of your face and identification from your wallet, as smoke from the liberating flames annoyingly tears my eyes, I remind myself that I require no sentimental souvenirs, no nostalgic knick-knacks. Long ago, I repeat, you were imprinted upon my cells, written into their code. Every expression of love between us was an act of genetic engineering.

I frown with irritation. The file of documents I left in your hockey bag lies open upon my bed. Yet I distinctly recall taking the canvas bag, in a load of your possessions, to the dump at the edge of town. I press my thumbs into the corners of my eyes; neither aspirin nor more potent medication relieves the pain of the headaches which have become a constant factor in my life. In addition, the dreaminess that I have suffered since your entry into the room has steadily grown stronger; my job performance has been affected to the point that last week my supervisor called me into his office for an interview that was highly unpleasant in its implications. (Once the golden glow that surrounded me – the radiance created by the light of our love – caused this man to blush whenever I looked at him, stammer whenever he spoke to me.) As a side effect of the headaches or of the dreaminess, or under their combined influence, I sometimes find myself now at a location without the least idea of how I got there.

It is a somewhat disorienting experience.

Almost disturbing.

The other night I woke up (perhaps, more correctly, came to consciousness) outside the house half way up the block where Billy lives. I could not recall the series of steps which led to my crouching there upon the dirt, beside the chinaberry bush, beneath his window. My most recent memory was of opening and then quickly closing the door of the room. For the first time failing to transform my disgust of the stench and filth within into love for the substance that is its source. For the first time failing to enter the darkness and to satisfy the remains of its occupant. Beneath Billy's window, the spring dirt smelled amazingly rich: I would describe the scent as a clean darkness. Through the pores of its skin, the earth beneath me breathed in, breathed out. Pulsing at the edge of the yard, crickets kept time like a clock in the May night, reminded ascendant stars that they still had hours to glitter the dew. The touch of a breeze against my face reeled my head; the gleam of grass dilated my eyes; above, the hallucinogenic heavens swam, swirled, spun.

From the way this world overwhelmed my senses, I might have just emerged from three years within a dark, bare, fetid room.

From the nearest streetlamp, a path of light carried my vision inside Billy's window, exposed his perfect, unmarked face upon the pillow. Though slightly flushed with sleep, his face appeared pale under this illumination. I could see his chest rise and fall a pyjamas top patterned with what looked like super heroes; below, the covers tangled around his waist, left his concealed lower limbs to interpretation. The same breeze that touched my cheek lifted and let go the curtain of Billy's open window, with a delicate gesture offering then taking away my view, tantalizing, teasing.

Suddenly I felt quite angry.

How careless to leave the window open like that.

How irresponsible.

Inviting anyone to enter.

Even a sleepy suburb like this is not safe.

(Especially a sleepy suburb like this, I sometimes think.)

All at once the pain in my head became much more severe. I blacked out; that must be what happened. I next found myself standing in the shower, with powerful soap scrubbing and scouring my skin of its stink.

Your stink.

Apparently, at some point after leaving Billy I overcame my revulsion and visited you after all.

Perhaps my vision of Billy compelled the visit?

My vision, my experience.

I intuit an image is missing from my memory: its absence nags.

As the sound of Billy's bicycle bell reminds me of something I can't quite recall.

Something in the darkness I can't quite touch.

Something significant, I suspect.

Something known to the possessor of the voice that addresses me during sleep.

Trying to piece together what has happened during the blank spaces caused by the headaches in turn causes the headaches to grow worse.

I feel caught within a closed circuit.

The synapses in the circuit are produced by a struggle to escape it?

I reluctantly pick up the file on the bed. Quietly, as if across the wall you can hear, I examine its contents:

A physician's report concerning the physical condition of a boy who, it is estimated (see concurring psychiatric and police reports), spent seven years enclosed within a dark, bare room. Malnutrition: severe. Muscular coordination: poor. Sensory responses: poor. Inability to withstand light: temporary. Muteness: see psychiatric report. Recovery: excellent (underlined). Prognosis: no lasting physical damage.

A psychiatric diagnosis. Trauma: severe. Loss of speech: temporary. Loss of memory: severe; limited recovery anticipated. Loss of affect: severe; limited recovery probable. Perception of reality: poor. Sexual fixations: several. Prognosis: permanent psychological damage; eventual functioning at minimal levels. (For detailed analysis of case, see *International Journal of Psychiatry*, Vol. XXIV, No. 3, pp. 217–249.)

Social services report. Placement of subject into foster care. Follow up visits: social (home and school) difficulties: noted. Sexual disturbances: see psychiatric records; acted out. Discipline difficulties: noted. Concern of foster parents: noted. Status: ongoing monitoring required.

Police file. Efforts to establish identity of Case No. _____: unsuccessful. Investigation into circumstances of criminal confinement: unsuccessful. Possible suspects in confinement: none. Possible motives: unknown. Final status of case: unsolved; closed.

Court document. John Doe No. _____ will henceforth bear the legal name _____.

At the bottom of these documents lie petitions, dated eleven years later, for their release to their subject.

I close the file.

In one sense, it has been closed for twenty-one years; in another, it is still open.

Those twenty-one years form a blank space for you?

A synapse in your closed system?

A period of limbo between one bare, dark room and the next?

Between one dream and another?

Across the wall, once more in darkness, you struggle to close the file.

Forever, for good.

If I did not know you better, this information might seriously disturb rather than briefly disappoint me. Initially, I must confess, I am somewhat surprised by your failure to destroy, long ago, documents which are essentially without meaning, which obviously bear no real relation to our love. I wonder at your decision to allow them to survive for my discovery. To risk our very special, very intimate experience being polluted this way by the uncomprehending world outside. Were my love for you less strong, it might now be soiled by the rough, clumsy touch of those systems which must always seek to control and to explain our existence.

Quickly correcting my mistaken sense of disappointment, I reject the documents as wholly as I reject the systems that produced them.

They mean nothing. They explain nothing.

They illuminate only the incomprehension of the unevolved world around us.

The stupidity.

Clearly, you left this information for me to destroy.

Call it a final invitation to partake in your experience.

A lover's last gift.

Once again, I am happy to comply with your wishes.

Another match scratches. More fire is fed.

Passing our house these days, Billy quickens his step, stares straight ahead. No longer looks lingeringly, hungrily toward where you once lived.

The smell of rot within the room is so intense I must hold my breath for the few moments I manage to withstand it. Though I continue to replace the bread and water that go untouched from one evening to the next, my visits are now perfunctory at best. More would be unnecessary. The entity upon the tiled floor bears as little relation to our love as did the documents I have destroyed. Frankly, I grow impatient with this mass of blood and skin and bone that you have left behind. I am almost resentful at your delegating me to deal with it. There is a danger that if your remains linger too long they will cloud the meaning of our love as much as the contents of the file threatened to do. The most important act of love I could perform at this moment might very well be to free us entirely of this mute, motionless mess.

This matter, this muck.

The periods of darkness – or blank spaces; or synapses – occur more frequently and last longer, as far as I can tell. Obviously, I am disinclined to seek relief from the medical profession for them or for the worsening, accompanying headaches. The quacks and charlatans have done enough damage as it is. Instead, I take the self-prescribed medication which, due to the stupidity of our legal system, I can obtain only with some difficulty. Unfortunately, it renders me unable to pursue certain activities which have long played a central, stabilizing role in my life; for example, I am unable to attend the gym. Also prevented from working, I take advantage of the considerable vacation time that has accumulated during these past three years.

The telephone rings unanswered.

Unopened mail accumulates.

Between the blank spaces I visit the cash machine, the supermarket, the supplier of my medication. At a building supply store I purchase a sack of lime, as the voice of my sleep has instructed. These excursions are necessarily as brief as possible: I must take care that the blank spaces occur within the house; to fall into them outside would be to expose myself to risk in several ways. Yet there is continuing evidence that I still wander during the dark episodes; that I do not come to consciousness in places I am without memory of travelling to is hardly a relief. It only means I do not know where I go or what I do during those times of blackness.

Guess, chuckles the voice of my sleep.

The unknown is dangerous, beats the pain in my head.

Interestingly, of late I have often 'woken up' to find myself naked in the room. I am not equipped to describe the appalling loneliness of that experience. How the darkness tells me only that I would do anything, even leave life, to escape it. (I have never liked the dark.) More than once, I have discovered my hands to be stained red, as if with bright blood; a strange, bitter taste would haunt my mouth. For several days after my first encounter with these phenomena I was puzzled by the elusive nature of their source.

Abruptly, unexpectedly, the explanation slid to the front of my mind from its dark rear.

The house half way down the block.

The chinaberry bush.

Billy.

*

The obscure substance upon the tiles seems to produce a very weak, scarcely audible sound.

Mama.

Help.

Or so I think I hear.

The sound resembles the voice of a small boy who is frightened of the dark.

It is produced by my imagination, of course.

(The medication has more than several inconvenient side effects.)

The (imagined) voice does not speak again – at least, not while I am in the dark room.

I must have accidentally cut myself during a recent fall from consciousness.

There is a deep gash in the flesh of my inner arm. The sharp sting appears to cause the pain inside my head to recede, if only temporarily. Perhaps one hurt erases the other. I work my tongue into the wound as my penis stiffens.

In the back yard I touch a match to a piece of cloth. As well as torn, it is soiled with what looks like the red juice of chinaberries. The pattern upon the cloth is made of men of comically exaggerated strength; they are patently capable of rescuing any situation no matter how desperate, of saving any being no matter how imperilled. Flames drop upon the site by the back fence where ash indicates other flames have fallen. A sound in the near distance lifts my head. The old woman next door is watching from her back steps. Realizing I notice her, she fades back into her house.

I wonder why I have not seen Billy lately. Since school is out for the summer, he should be playing on the block during these sunny days. Perhaps he has gone away to a camp situated among green, scented pines, beside a blue lake of crystalline water. With other boys like him, he swims and hikes and canoes; after dark, they gather around a fire to sing sweetly. Their voices lift high into the clear night, reach to touch glittering stars.

I can't help notice that lately I see better in the dark, as if my eyes have adapted to a prolonged lack of light. In the room I believe I notice the matter at its rear stir slightly. Bending closer, I realize this movement is in fact that of worms wriggling in and out of soft liquefying flesh. Matter is changing form, transmutating. I smile. This reminds me that our love has never been static; it has always evolved.

Progress keeps it vibrantly alive.

I waken to hear Billy's voice cry through the darkness for help, mama, help. Something has happened to him at the summer camp beside the blue lake, amid the green pines. An accident. He has drowned in crystalline water or has plummeted from the cliff of a mountain trail. Long after its actual end, his voice continues to echo through the night. Though it travels from far away, the voice is distinct and clear as a voice within this house.

The proliferation of wounds I find on my skin suggests that when most heavily under the influence of medication I must be quite clumsy. I must allow myself to exist in too near proximity to sharp instruments. In the kitchen silver knives wink knowingly. The axe leers from the back porch; seductively, a razor shimmers in bathroom light. Where opened to the air, my stinging flesh sings so sweetly. My tongue tingles in anticipation.

Once such summer weather would have drawn me outdoors at every free moment; but each week I leave the house even less frequently than the one before. It is not that I fear falling into dangerous darkness beyond these safe walls; apparently, the synapses have ceased for the time being. There is no indication either that I persist in undertaking journeys and performing acts without conscious knowledge: it seems that phase has ended too. What needed to be done in darkness has been successfully accomplished, I assume.

(I can only speculate, at this point, upon those developments occurring within and around me; each new day I peek cautiously at whatever unexpected event unfolds. For you still control the execution of your secret master plan; and only the owner of the voice that speaks to me in sleep seems to share in advance that privileged information. Kept in the dark. This worn figure of speech now acquires fresh potency as its figurative and its literal meanings rub against each other, set off a vibration I feel in my teeth. In both senses of the phrase, as they pertain one to you and one to me, it is you who does the keeping in the dark.)

Still my head pounds, still that voice snarls during my sleep, still the curtains remain closed. Medicated, I stumble through shadowed, scented rooms. The one or two times I venture outside, I don't bother to greet my neighbors with a friendly wave, to interpret and to match their false expressions. The minor role played in my life by these unknowing people has been concluded; they don't matter any more. (However, someone perhaps should warn the old crone next door about the direction in which she watches from her window, from her steps. Too late, she might come to regret the unwise habit.) Oddly, the street seems empty not only of Billy but of all children. It is the kind of absence that insists upon itself, like the silence that screams.

I am not surprised when you begin to speak from inside me. It is no secret that your essence entered mine some time ago; I have not mourned you because you did not leave. It is startling, however, to recognize that this is the same voice that has delivered instructions to my sleeping mind. Quickly I understand that the seeming harshness of its tone was due simply to the extra vocal force that is necessary to penetrate unconsciousness. For reasons not yet clear to me, your voice must now communicate during daylight as well as in darkness.

Of course it is overwhelming to hear again, after all that has happened during such a long time, the push of my lover's vowels, the catch of his consonants. At first I am so enchanted by your voice I disregard the words it forms. In some way, beyond the requirements of current circumstances, you sound different. I wonder if your voice itself has altered, if my memory of it is incorrect, or if my interpretation of its qualities has changed. Beneath the erotic throb that lifts the hair on my arms bites a cold, hard edge. Perhaps it was there all along. Carefully disguised, unperceived.

Hurry, it says.

The sack of lime, it insists.

Before it's too late, it commands.

The voice requires obedience. If its instructions are not carried out, I sense, the speaker will swiftly become enraged.

Summer heat has hastened the decomposition occurring within the room at the back of the house. The odour produced by this process is perceptible from the end of the driveway, from the farthest reaches of the back yard; slightly sweet, almost cloying, it mixes with the perfume of flowers grown by the old woman next door. Entering the room for the first time in several weeks, at your order, I notice at once that my approach raises numerous flies or gnats from the remains. They tremble above their source like visible ions of darkness. Then I see that the bones are nearly bare of flesh.

They look quite small.

I bend nearer.

This is the skeleton of a child, not of a man.

Someone has secretly substituted a boy's bones for yours?

What are you waiting for? hisses your voice.

I sprinkle lime over the bones.

It sifts through the darkness like a child's midnight dream of snow. In the morning we will toboggan down the big hill behind St. Cecilia's. You ride in front; behind, I wrap my arms around your waist, hold on tight, close my eyes as we speed faster and faster like the nuns' beads in the night. If we spill upon the snow, our arms will make angels until Sister Mary calls us in to feast on bread and water, all that is needed by orphans who have the rich, sweet nourishment of Jesus to enjoy.

Pay attention, snaps your voice. What are you doing?

I shiver as an angel's wing brushes my shoulder in the dark.

Start as a heavy lid slams in my mind, seals St. Cecilia's tight inside the coffin of the past.

Blink at my powdered fingers. Lick lime, taste chalk.

Rather than interfering with nature, I am aiding to quicken its process.

I remember how we would never ingest steroids to stimulate our muscular growth by artificial means.

For some reason the memory now strikes me as touching, tender.

It becomes necessary to turn more and more to my medication in order to silence the voice that otherwise speaks incessantly, steadily, scarcely pausing for breath. Yet you were never voluble; quite the opposite, in fact. Perhaps this stream of language is composed of all the words you did not speak to me during the twelve years before entering the room.

Late at night, exhausted, I am prevented from sleeping by the constant chatter.

It is malicious, cynical, inimical.

It delights in enlightening me on the subject of countless infidelities committed by yourself from the very beginning of our union. It gleefully paints in pornographic detail every illicit fuck and suck you experienced, and how your excitement in each encounter was heightened by my ignorance of its occurrence. Droolingly, it describes what really gave you pleasure, how your true desires were never satisfied in our bed, the way you only went through the motions with me, why you considered yourself a skilled actor for stifling yawns of boredom both beneath and above me.

Of course this voice is not yours.

The possessor of this voice has only imitated you in order to deceive me.

You would never do the things this voice describes.

Sickening acts. Disgusting deeds.

The motive here is laughably obvious. It was clear, right from the start, that the extraordinary combination we made would provoke inordinate jealousy and inspire all kinds of attempts to sever us. In each other's arms, we used to joke about the pathetic efforts made by those who panted to come between us. Their begging to join us upon the sheets. Their offering of large amounts of money to watch us. Instead of driving us apart, such machinations inspired us to dive more deeply inside each other.

The envious owner of this voice does not seem aware that now, more than ever, efforts to divide us are doomed to failure.

But I can reason this out only with difficulty: for the venomous voice is screaming inside me.

It shrieks out, over and over, one obscene scenario which above all others you enjoyed.

You don't believe me? shrills the impostor.

Ask the kid yourself. And why not give him a whirl while you're at it.

Afraid you might like it?

I am not offended by such an implication. I know what I have and have not done. Only that matters. It is interesting that, despite its purported omniscience, this voice isn't quite so all knowing after all: Billy's accident, that unfortunate fatality, seemed to have eluded its notice. As to the real identity of the speaker, that is of negligible significance. Clearly, this voice is composed of all the frustrated longing, all the thwarted need, all the unsatisfied desire of all the cowards who populate the world around us. For the time being, for my own purposes, I am perfectly content to allow the voice to believe it maintains the upper hand.

Naturally my feelings were hurt by not being invited to Billy's funeral. It appears I will not even be informed belatedly of his death; the sad event will be kept secret from me, like the weddings and anniversaries and baptisms that constantly take place beyond the edge of my vision. Despite this slight, and the resulting tardiness, I consider bringing a tasteful wreath to the woman halfway down the block who was charged with Billy's care. My impulse is quickly killed by anger that such a being would be given a child to raise. I have seen this sorry excuse for a human from a distance; I can guess, quite accurately, almost as if they happened to myself, what sort of experiences Billy suffered at her hands. The kind of experiences that refuse to be buried despite the passing of twenty-one or more long years. Maybe the boy is lucky to be out of it, after all. I glare accusingly at the street from behind my window. The nondescript block lined with modest houses appears hushed, holding its breath, in suspense or in fear or in horror.

When I next enter the room (I am not certain how much time has gone by; the medication interferes with my ability to calculate clearly the passing of days), the remains on the tiles to its rear resemble perhaps finely crushed bone meal, perhaps the end product of the crematorium's furnace.

(Now my vision has grown poor, as if my eyes have strained for too long to see in darkness.)

I sniff what seems to be an unfamiliar odour – something acrid, acidic, chemical. Something besides the sweet smell of decay, the smothering smell of lime. A further substance that has been added, by an anonymous assistant or by myself, to encourage the disintegration of bone?

I allow the puzzle to pass. There are more important matters to worry about.

I dig the mixture, whatever the full nature of its components, into the flower beds that edge our back lawn.

The lawn is brown from lack of watering, I notice dully.

The flower beds are choked with weeds.

The simple task is almost beyond my strength. My movements are clumsy, my coordination poor.

Weakling, sneers the voice.

Patsy, it snipes.

I have no idea if this concoction of bone and lime and other ingredients will act as fertilizer or as poison.

Finish what you started, orders the voice.

I dispose of the waste bucket at the dump.

Remove the heavy black cloth from the window. Reinstall the single bed, the night table, the boxes.

Hang the prints of ships upon the walls. Screw a bulb into the ceiling socket.

Scrub the floor with disinfectant.

Open the window to allow fresh air to enter.

Once again the room might appear very neat rather than quite bare.

Only a slight stain, perhaps invisible to unknowing eyes, remains on the tiles to the rear.

Despite the opened window, a subtle scent lingers like the memory of love.

For the first time in three years I am permitted to rest. Relieved of the painful pressure inside my head, apparently by the simple act of returning the room to its original state, I wander this shadowy house as if to reacquaint myself with it after an extended absence. I have been far away from here.

During my long journey, the mirror informs, I have grown old. My face is pale and drawn and deeply lined. My hair is mostly grey; my eyes dull. My body is cadaverous as an anachronistic victim of the concentration camps. Beyond these physical effects, no souvenirs exist to speak of where my journey has taken me and what has happened to me there. There is no sign of what may have transpired within this house while I was away. What the world will call a crime. For which it will insist on finding a convenient scapegoat and on exacting harsh punishment.

I notice the outside of the house needs painting.

Inside, the clock ticks more loudly than I remember.

I move down the hall, past the door that, though without lock or key, remains closed.

Behind it undisturbed dust dreams in silence.

Unbreathed air waits to be consumed by throats, caressed by lungs.

The voice that once spoke within these walls is silent. It has received what it wanted.

Surely satisfied, it is able to return to sleep behind the closed door. At least until the next time it is woken by desire.

Forgot something, teases the voice, with an approximation of a giggle, just when I am convinced of its dormancy.

I look around again. I am certain no evidence remains of the experience of love to have occurred during my absence.

The latest experience.

Of course I know, as I have always known, there have been other experiences in the past and there will be more in the future.

There are always more.

And I won't tell you what, chortles the voice.

A clue has been left behind by the owner of the voice. A piece of evidence has been deliberately dropped to tie me to its actions.

I am its victim, after all.

I will pay the price for its desire's fulfilment.

The pain in my head returns with vicious vengeance.

I reach for the medication, the instruments of injection.

Pale blood swirls the syringe.

The sting of the stab silences the voice.

I wait for the heavy fists to pound on the front door, the curious mob to gape from the sidewalk beyond, the television cameras to capture the easy images, the surface truth.

Darkness, pure and holy, creeps up behind me. Softly, quietly. Shadows gently stroke, obscurity caresses. I wait for the absolving hands of darkness, its tender touch of love.

Mama.

Help.

Understand.

Forgive.

A Perfect Time to be in Paris
Jeffrey Round

A Perfect Time to be in Paris
Jeffrey Round

It was supposed to be the perfect time to be in Paris. Indeed, the weather could not have been better – sunny, sultry afternoons and long, cool evenings – but it was barely a month after the death of Princess Diana, and the pall cast by her tragic end, as well as the layer of scarcely breathable smog hanging overhead, dimmed and dulled the otherwise magical appearance of the City of Light.

I'd arrived hoping to escape an unsavoury feeling that had been hanging over my own head in much the same way, a feeling exacerbated by the recent departure of my lover due to an emotional restlessness, otherwise known as a change of heart, which Albert seemed to have undergone recently for no reason he could put his finger on other than that he needed 'time away', and the consequent knowledge that I was the object from which he was in need of temporal distance. Only to myself, and scarcely then, could I admit that it was the arrival into our enclosure of loyal friends of a certain Nick – a young Greek possessed of stupendous legs and torso, and closer in age than I to Albert – that had precipitated the beginning of the end for us, and that 'time away' from me meant 'time with' Nick on Albert's part.

Whether Albert was aware of my knowledge of his emotional defection, I don't know, but I do know that I'd come to Paris in hopes of relieving myself of the burden of constant reminders of him, the way a car of a particular colour and make recalls the handsome neighbour who once lived on your street and drove such a car, and who returns now with all the vividness of an actual physical encounter merely by virtue of the chance appearance of just such a car: or, similarly, how the refrain from a hot dance-hit of summers past is enough to evoke memories of that summer's romance, as its melody revives intangible reminders of the former loved one until you realize the feelings you held for him were never dead at all, but merely buried beneath a Herculean effort of self-willed forgetting. It was all this I'd hoped to escape when I fled to Paris that particular September. I had not, of course, failed to remind myself it was a trip both Albert and I had looked forward to taking for the last year, as I lovingly described to him each place we would visit – the Arc de Triomphe, Montmartre, the Champs Élysées, the Eiffel Tower, and, of course, the grave site of my beloved Marcel Proust – all things we were to have experienced in our treks together around what was arguably the world's most beautiful, and perfect, city.

For me, that trip should have been comprised of mornings spent in street cafés sampling their delicate pastries and harsh beverages, afternoons contemplating the exquisitely erected buildings lining the grand avenues as well as the alabaster skin and striking faces of the men and women who strode along them, and the gloaming twilight – Proust's 'blue hour' – experienced like a silk scarf brushed lightly over the skin, a nightly fanning of casual strollers with the softness of a lover's caress. Albert and I were to have known all these things, savoured every nuance of our trip together, then returned home cherishing the memories like photographs carefully preserved as time hurtled their more real, more solid, counterparts ever onwards to oblivion. Instead, what I had encountered in my week there, apart from a few sordid bars where I had no interest in the other tourists hanging about in darkened corners, nor they in me, had been the underpass where Diana met her untimely death, with the remnants of a British flag flying sadly overhead. These, and the cimetière du Père-Lachaise with its other famous dead, including the graves of both Proust and Oscar Wilde, fellow queers and lovers of young men, as well as a consort of rough-looking male prostitutes, spectral guardians haunting the tree-lined pathways between the rows of stone chapels and graves, were all I had seen.

It was no use to run, for everything served to remind me of Albert – the turn of one young man's thigh or another's hair, a softly quavering laugh that recalled his own, the smell of his favourite *frites* hanging in the air outside some local diner – colouring all I saw with grief at his invisible presence, just as Proust's protagonists are always wallowing in jealousy over their lovers' betrayals, or drowning in the reflection of love's lost glories, reliving again and again the shadows of what they had once experienced, tucked away in the heart's memory as the burnished blush of sun on the skin of a grape is safely stored inside the bottle of a vintner's best stock, to be uncorked and enjoyed at some supper ages hence when the warmth of the sun's glow on that far away day is gone past recalling by all but the most loyal of Time's memoirists.

Nothing offered me respite from my feelings, no place to hide from the pain that had taken up what seemed to be permanent lodging inside me. Even sex had not proved a panacea, for my sole attempt in that direction ended in dismal failure, though a failure in no part due to the pains taken by the young man with whom I spent the better part of one of those frail afternoons with the sun highlighting the sills of the hotel windows as I caressed the ribbed flanges of his youthful body.

I met him in the Tuileries outside the Musée de l'Orangerie, one of a host of young skateboarders who'd shed his outer layers of clothing in order to take advantage of the fine weather and the appreciative eyes of the tourists, and even the occasional Parisian, who bestowed upon their young bodies the rapt gaze of a more inveterate age of Lust, and its urbane cousin, Desire.

The boy insisted on calling himself Renoir, while we sipped coffee later in a sidewalk café. At first I suspected the name was born as a result of having fashioned himself after the desires of the easily-fooled tourist who no doubt would be generous of his flowing coffers in exchange for the likewise flowing kisses from the honeyed lips of this Gallic Adonis. I half-expected to hear him declare himself an artist who plied his bodily trade only to support his artistic ambitions, but indeed, when I asked his price, Renoir red-facedly insisted he was but a student and interested only in partaking of a mutually shared experience of love-making. These suspicions at the time stemmed, at least in part, from my fearing the impossibility of being truly desired by anyone ever again, and so when we returned to the hotel I was not surprised to find myself unable to fulfil his wishes, lying inert beside him while he roused himself to a furious passion. There was no denying the veracity of desire on his part – it was I who could not reciprocate his physical affections and ended up satisfying his needs orally, performing such ministrations as I could on his ample member until he was fully satiated. Afterwards he clung to me happily, whispering reassurances that it had not been a problem, that he was pleased with my performance and did not require more from me. Oddly, it was only then, as Renoir playfully hugged me and kissed my cheek with such vehemence I was forced to push him away, that I clearly understood what I desired.

"No more kisses, *bébé*," I insisted, rejecting the efforts of this flawless cherub to prove his amorous intentions toward me, unwanted as they were at that moment, though at another time they might have been all I could desire. I made him dress quickly and we left the hotel exchanging hasty vows to 'get together' later in the week. Thus freed, I rushed to the nearest metro and once again followed the circuitous route back to the gates of Père-Lachaise where the sun was already falling. I made my way past the grave of Jim Morrison, where fresh-cut flowers adorned the site along with the melted stumps of burned candles from some obsessive midnight ritual, farther along to the burial place of Edith Piaf, where a grey-haired man stood in solemn mourning. He looked up briefly and nodded. "*Oui – elle est là*," he intoned, as though reassuring us both that she had indeed existed in bodily form after all, and only now could no longer resist his ardent devotions.

I hurried past toward that winged, emasculated gryphon proclaiming the gigantic tomb of Wilde, also betrayed at the hands of a beautiful young man many years earlier than myself. It was there I caught sight of my prey hulking off to one side of the path, and quickly caught up with him so there could be no mistaking my intention. He smiled and nodded as I approached, as though he had been waiting for me. I noted that his face was heavily tanned and dirty. As well, his nose had been broken and a ragged scar snaked along the space between it and his upper lip. What's more, he was older than he appeared from a distance. All of this pleased me now, whereas normally I would have experienced a pang of regret over the breaking of such an illusion.

"How much are you?" I asked, as if he were some sort of animal flesh I desired to purchase by the pound.

"It depends what you wish, monsieur," he replied simply.

"I'll pay whatever you cost, if you do what I ask," I assured him.

He paused, waiting for me to take the lead.

"Do you have a hotel? With a bed, perhaps?" he asked.

"No. I wish to do it right here," I answered.

"Here?" Despite the inquiry, he did not seem surprised.

"Yes – here. Come with me."

He shrugged and followed me down the footpath to Proust's modest black grave, cut off from view by a somewhat larger stone edifice.

"Here," I said, dropping my pants and turning my back to him.

He came up gently behind me, taking my waist in both hands. The smell of something sweet, yet at the same time earthy and nauseating filled my nostrils as he paired his stomach against my back. The skin of his fingers was rough as he caressed my sides in what I took to be a gesture of tenderness. I was not interested in the foreplay and simply bent over, spreading my cheeks with my hands. His cockhead probed delicately the entrance to my asshole, inserting itself partially once or twice and then withdrew without entering me fully.

"Fuck me," I commanded.

"But, monsieur, we must use a condom."

"I don't care about that. Just fuck me!"

He demurred and pulled back. Luckily, I remembered the condom stuffed in my pocket during the abortive escapade with Renoir that afternoon. I pulled it out and handed it to him without bothering to unwrap it. He peeled back the plastic wrapper and began to work its contents around himself. I bent over the marble tablet again, spreading my legs in anticipation. I heard him spit, and steeled myself as once again he put his member against my asshole.

"I am called François. What is your name, monsieur?" he asked softly, like a doctor attempting to divert his patient's attention from painful manoeuvre.

I pretended not to understand. For some reason, I did not wish to him my name spoken aloud in the graveyard. He did not persist.

"How do you like it, monsieur?"

"Hurt me," I answered without thinking. "I want you to make me feel bad," I declared, wondering if I'd gotten the nuances right in the French language.

I gasped as his cock pushed angrily inside me and filled my entire asshole with pain.

"Is it too big, monsieur?" he asked.

"No – do it," I urged. "Just fuck me. Hard!" I braced myself against the stone and awaited François's assault on my insides.

He fucked me just as I'd asked, banging away until I thought I would have to tell him to stop, but my own cock was rigid and unflagging muscular twinge and ache. I knew I would be sore the next day and possibly the day after that, but there was no way I would not hold out for as long as he continued to inflict sensation on my body, taking away some of the ache, the longing I felt for

Albert that had until then not ceased for a moment to cause me anguish.

"Nick," I blurted out. "I want you – to call me – Nick!"

"Yes, Nick – I am fucking your beautiful ass!"

When François finally stopped, I realized he had been asking me something for several moments. It took me a second to decipher his French – he had already come and wondered if I wanted him to continue his assault on my sphincter.

"No," I said. "That was fine, François. Thank you."

I allowed him to pull out of me and retrieved my pants from around my ankles.

"You are a very nice man, Nick," he gushed, letting the used condom fall to the ground with a soft 'plop'. After I paid him he made signs of hanging around, perhaps hoping I would ask to see him again, or possibly just feeling happy with how well he had performed. In any case, I wanted to be alone. "Leave me now," I said. "Go away."

He crept off into the evening shadows as I collapsed across the marble slab, rolling onto my back and looking skywards like a sacrifice stretched across an altar, beseeching an invisible god for a much-desired absolution. The pain in my posterior was already slackening, but I had felt it and knew it to be real – at least as real as anything I'd felt in the months since Albert's departure. It was enough for my body to know it could begin again, enough to forget, however slowly, and allow something to take the place of the pain that had been my sole companion of late. And as I lay there, I felt I understood what was at the heart of Proust's long-winded imaginings beneath all those perfect Parisian skies at the beginning of a century only now just ending, felt I knew what had driven him to recreate his life in five thousand pages of remembered experience over the course of more than twenty years, which is that we all are driven with the unceasing desire to be loved by one person of our choice, or, if that is not possible, then at the very least to believe we have been loved by that one person, however briefly, at some time in the perfect, unchanging past.

Falling
Lawrence Schimel

Falling
Lawrence Schimel

When I first saw him, he was having sex with another man.

I have never really been superstitious about anything, like that it means seven year's bad luck to break a mirror or walk under a ladder, and have openly scoffed at the more saccharine notions like falling in love at first sight. But at the same time I've always imagined that if the latter were to happen to me it would occur as it did in the movies: gazes locked across a crowded room and then slowly, inexorably, we make our way toward each other.

But that's not how it happened. We were in the Parque del Oeste, near the Templo de Debod. This 4th-century BC Egpytian temple is a bit incongruous in the center of Madrid, where it was reconstructed stone by stone. It was given to Spain in 1968 in recognition of the help of Spanish engineers in constructing the Aswan High Dam, which inundated the temple's original site. But despite its easy accessibility, it is seldom visited by Madrileños – with the exception of homosexuals, who've used the surrounding area as a twilight cruising grounds for decades.

The man my gaze was locked with was tall and lean, with deep-set eyes that were dark pools of shadow. He had unruly black hair that fell across his face, casting further shadow across his features. He stood with his legs spread apart and his pants unbuttoned; a man knelt before him, sucking his dick. I wanted to be that man on his knees. I wondered how they'd react if I joined them; if I could perhaps displace the man on his knees with my superior worship of this sullen dark idol. I felt a pang of envy as I watched the back of a head bobbing before his crotch, then a cold shiver of anger at having arrived too late, the injustice of timing.

And all the while the man watched me, quite steadily, his dark eyes finding mine again and again, and I began to realize that I might be feeling something more than just lust, although I couldn't quite identify the feeling. It was something I wasn't quite comfortable with. It wasn't fear, but I distinctly remember feeling afraid, though I couldn't identify its source.

And then there was a scream, and he and I both turned and saw a body falling from one of the buildings on Calle Ferraz that faced the park.

We stood frozen a moment, he and I. The man on his knees kept sucking, oblivious to the world beyond the dick in his mouth.

And then we were both running toward the place where the body must have landed. He managed to keep pace with me, even as he buttoned up his jeans again. I think it was at that moment that I realized I was falling in love with him, or perhaps that I had already done so. So many men wouldn't have bothered to try and help. They wouldn't have gotten involved. Or they'd have waited to come beforehand. Like that man who'd been sucking his dick, who'd stayed in the park, and perhaps was already sucking the cock of some other man, lost in his own private world of sexual need.

We plunged from the crepuscular world of the park with its trees and shadows onto the wide lamp-lit street of man-made structures. There was little traffic and we dashed across the street, falling into pace with each other so smoothly that it was uncanny. I couldn't say if he led and I followed, or the reverse, we simply both went.

And then we both stopped, quite suddenly, faced with the surprise of the sidewalk. There was no body.

Later I realized it was curiosity I'd seen written on his face, as if he were surprised by something. Surprised that I'd run to help. Surprised that I'd seen anything at all.

But at the time I mistook the look on his face for sexual interest. I'd already been looking for sex, of course, and had been hoping for sex with this man when that scream distracted us. I think the desire for sex is a natural response in the face of death – or the fear of it. A primal, physical affirmation of life and pleasure.

So when I looked up from the sidewalk where the body wasn't and saw him looking at me with that expression on his face, I smiled at him and tried to think of something to say: the usual cruising overtures seemed inappropriate. Could one just ignore what had just happened, or at least, what we'd both just seen happen? There was no doubt for either of us as we stood there in silence. Neither one of us needed to stammer inanities to reassure our sanity; we'd both seen the body falling.

His dark liquid eyes were locked with mine as I debated with myself, and I'm not sure why but I began to blush. I don't normally get this flustered when trying to pick someone up. But all the rules suddenly seemed different. What had just happened, the connection we had without ever having spoken or touched, the unusual (for me) desire that this be the start of something more – everything seemed to indicate that our having met was of some import.

I broke the eye contact, looking down at the sidewalk where a dead body should've been. I couldn't help glancing at his still-swollen crotch, thinking about his dick, that stranger's saliva still on his cock, what it would taste like to suck his dick right now with another man's spittle still on him. My own dick was rock-hard in my jeans, and I stared down at the empty space between our feet, thinking about the strange missing body to try and take my mind off my dick for a moment and figure out what was going on.

Because something had happened, of that there was no doubt.

When I looked up, he had turned and was walking away.

"Hey! Wait…" I felt again that surge of anger at arriving too late, of missed opportunity. And I was confused. Because I thought I'd been offered a second chance. And I didn't want to let that opportunity just fade away, not without a fight – or at least an explanation.

He looked back over his shoulder.

I didn't understand anything. I read desire in his look, the equal to if not greater than my own. But there was also that curious look, of surprise, or fear, or both.

He turned again and kept walking. I watched him walk away, unable to either move or think, mind and body both frozen by the tumultuous events of the past few minutes.

As he disappeared around the corner, I suddenly came to life again. I deserved more than this.

"Wait," I cried out again, following after him. But when I turned the corner, the street was as empty as the sidewalk where I'd just stood, where a dead body should've been.

I went back the next afternoon when I got out of work. First to the sidewalk, where he and I had come so close to… something. Intimacy? Not just sex but something more than that. It went beyond the physical. I couldn't get him out of my head.

I'd gone home after he disappeared, since anything was bound to be a let-down after the intensity of what had happened. Even if it felt like everything had just stopped halfway to the climax, and I'm not just talking about the physical release of orgasm. It was all a mystery, an enigma: the body falling but not landing, the scream that he and I both heard but which attracted the attention of no one else, this mysterious stranger in general and the connection I'd felt with him, from the moment our eyes first locked...

It's not surprising that I went back.

But the sidewalk offered no more answer the day after than it had when he and I had stood where the body should've fallen in those moments just after we saw it plummeting.

I turned and headed toward the Temple and the trees and bushes surrounding it. It was early still, and there were few men about. By day, the Parque del Oeste, where the Temple now stood, had its share of mothers and nannies who took their kids to this patch of greenery, mostly to let them loose on the jungle gym built a few blocks from the temple while they would sit on the benches and gossip with one another. As night fell, the makeup of the park's inhabitants changed dramatically.

I strolled around the area where I'd first seen the stranger the day before, but even as I went looking for him I knew he wouldn't be there. I came to cruise by the Temple on occasion, but I don't think I'd ever come two days in a row. Of course, last night I hadn't managed to get off, at least not out here – I'd jerked off at home, thinking about the stranger, his eyes locked on mine as if he were watching me from my own fantasy, seeing how my hand flexed as it stroked along my cock...

But I came looking for him anyway, on the off chance that he, too, felt this sense of incompletion, this urgency to figure out what had happened, what was happening (this strange feeling I still felt, nagging at the back of my consciousness like an itch or a headache that didn't quite happen), what was going to happen.

I repeatedly ignored the overtures of men who tried to initiate something with me: mere sexual urgency paled in comparison to the impulse that sent me looking for my stranger, evening after evening. I had never before felt myself so obsessed with anyone, and on such scant basis. After all, we hadn't had sex. We'd not even touched. Except perhaps, and I know this sounds freakishly New Age, soul to soul, when our glances locked. Or when that man screamed, that body fell, and no one but we saw it.

I didn't lose interest, but after nearly a week of fruitless searching, of desire unfulfilled, of mysteries that would remain unsolved, I began to wear down, like an old battery whose charge is failing. I wandered up to the Templo de Debod and stood between the two long pools of water that extended from its front door, staring down to watch the sky reflected above me. I looked at my own shadow cast upon the water, tried to imagine the shadow of that stranger appearing behind me... but it was no use. If force of will alone could have summoned him, I would've resolved this aching emptiness a week ago.

Bitter and angry, I turned away from the temple and headed for the bushes, resolved to forget that stranger in the embrace of some other man or men, to exorcise a phantom with pure physical release.

I didn't have to wait long before someone approached, and looked at me with want. The intensity of his gaze was a pale imitation of my mysterious stranger, but this man was present, and I followed him deeper into the greenery, and tried not to think but just feel as he knelt before me and unzipped my pants.

I was still being sucked off when another man appeared, and watched us. Watched me, really, since he hardly glanced at my crotch, the glimpse of cock sliding in and out of moist lips, at the 'action' that a mere voyeur would've focused on. His gaze sought my own, and I had an eerie sensation of dislocation, of roles being reversed, a sort of _déjà vu_ of that moment when I had seen my mysterious stranger. This new man who watched me did not resemble either myself or that sullen dark idol I'd been obsessed with these past days. But that feeling of semi-familiarity remained, a suspicion that I had seen him somewhere before, or had been in this situation before. The man who was sucking me paid no attention to the interloper, and for a moment I wondered if it might be the same guy who had been sucking off.

And then I heard a familiar scream.

I wasn't sure, at first, if I was remembering having heard it or if I were actually hearing it now. But the man who was watching me turned his head, and my gaze followed his, and once again I watched a body falling from a building on Calle Ferraz.

Before I knew it, I was running toward the sidewalk, the cocksucker forgotten, even the new watcher forgotten. My attention was focused on that man with sunken eyes who I felt certain would be waiting at the sidewalk where the body should be but wasn't.

But the sidewalk was once again empty. No body. No mysterious stranger.

Only, a few seconds after my own arrival, the new man who'd been watching as I was being sucked off.

I felt almost dizzy with uncertainty. What did the falling body mean? Whose was it? And where did it disappear to? Or appear from? I had no idea what was happening – all emanating from that encounter. Was he harbinger or catalyst? How and why had I become involved with all of this?

And now this new stranger...

I felt almost as if I were expected to now walk around the corner without saying a word to this new man who had been watching me, who had become the 'me' from the last time this scenario played out.

But before I could decide anything, the man spoke.

"Shit, that was freaky. I could've sworn for a moment that I heard a scream and saw a body falling."

The world was suddenly back to normal. I felt calm, like the sudden hush that happens in the eye of a storm.

"Yeah," I replied. "Bizarre."

We stayed a moment longer in silence, gazes locked. I didn't think about anything, just looked.

He broke the silence again, "You didn't finish back there."

I realized that somehow I had my pants on properly again, zipped up without having any memory of the action. Which must have happened while I was running.

"Maybe you'd like to finish off with me?" I didn't respond, but I looked him in the eye, and my lack of an immediate denial was enough for him to proceed. "We can go back to my place. I live here. In this building. That's why it was so freaky to think of a body falling. For a moment, it had looked like it was falling from my balcony." He laughed, a nervous chuckle to try to reassure himself, to lighten the mood, and moved toward the doorway, pulling a set of keys from his pocket.

I still hadn't moved, trapped in that calm of final realization.

I remembered that curious look on the face of my sullen, dark obsession as we stood in this same spot. The look I'd confused with desire, or fear, and which I realized now was curiosity mixed with surprise. That I'd heard something, seen something. Something I shouldn't have seen. Something which hadn't happened.

Something I was somehow involved in.

"Sure," I said, and followed him into the dark portal of the door he held open, toward an inexorable destiny.

T@ngled

Stuart Thorogood

T@ngled
Stuart Thorogood

"Are you sure you'll be all right on your own?"

"Yes, mum," sighed Luke. "I'm eighteen."

Luke's mother just shrugged. She smiled. "I won't be back late, anyway."

"Stay as late you want," said Luke, hoping she would. She kissed him on the cheek and pulled her coat on.

"I'll see you later then."

"Bye, mum."

"You sure you'll be..."

"Mum!" he laughed. "Will you just go?"

She laughed and left the room. "See you later!" she called out, as Luke heard the front door open.

"Bye. Don't do anything I wouldn't do!" Luke smiled to himself, alone in the house at last. He stood up and went upstairs, feeling his dick getting hard already.

Thank God for the internet, he thought, as he sat himself down in front of the PC.

Luke wasn't out. Not really. Not properly. He was out to himself, yes, but no one else knew. None of his (very) few friends, nor his mother, and they were the people that mattered most in Luke's life. Luke didn't know why he wasn't out. Surely now was a time when gays were more accepted by society than ever before. But, for some reason, Luke just didn't feel that now was the right time.

It didn't matter. It was quite nice really. Quite nice to have secrets. And what a big secret that was.

This was the reason Luke so liked – *loved* – the internet. Full of all those chat rooms, where you could be anyone and anything you wanted to be. Luke loved it. He loved having all these different aliases, chatting to all these guys, turning them on, letting them turn him on. Wanking away happily while they typed out what they'd love to do to him...

Mmmmm...

Luke switched the PC on and typed in his password. He clicked on the Explorer icon and waited for the AOL homepage to appear. Quickly, he typed in the required URL.

www.freeserve.co.uk

Luke knew of other chat rooms that offered a wider range of possibilities, such as gay.com, but these all seemed a bit too confusing, him being new to the web and all.

Luke waited a few moments while the system authorised his password. The screen was a dull grey and Luke waited in anticipation, wondering how many 'members' would be resident in the room that night. He knew a few of the regulars. Well... he recognised some 'handles'. No one really knew each other in a chat room. But that was the beauty of it.

Finally, after what seemed like forever, the screen finished loading.

Sixteen members. Not bad. Not as populated as some of the other rooms around but then this was an unmoderated room, so you could 'say' whatever you wanted.

Oh, and people did.

Luke smiled to himself as he saw his nickname register itself.

queerlad9000

Several of the regulars were in there too. 'sweetgayanalsex', 'twohotgayguys', 'sexy_mark2002' and 't_dot' were just a few of the names he recognised.

Luke was pleased his mother was out with the girls from her office. He hardly ever had a chance to enjoy himself in the chat room while she was home. As soon as he got going he'd hear her calling up the stairs, "Luke! Get off that thing! I need to use the phone!"

He typed his first message of the evening. Instantly, it clicked into the general room, viewable to all sixteen members.

queerlad9000>hey room

There was no response. Everyone was probably off in his or her own private conversations. Luke decided to up the ante. He wanted more action. He started to type a line.

queerlad9000>ne1 wanna talk dirty to a horny 18-year-old gay lad??????? P2P ME NOW!!!!!!!

Within seconds a grey box appeared in the left-hand corner of the screen with the words, *HotGuy is requesting a Person To Person chat with you...* **hi queerlad, a s l plz?**

ASL meant that HotGuy was requesting Luke's age, sex and location.

Eagerly, Luke clicked on the 'CHAT' button in the grey box. In the space that appeared, he typed his message.

queerlad9000>hi hotguy. 18, m, bucks

The response was almost immediate.

HotGuy>cool. What u in2?

Luke knew he was onto something here and wasted no time getting into the swing of the chat.

    Queerlad9000>what u got?
    HotGuy>everything.
    Queerlad9000>cool.
    HotGuy>describe yourself for me.
    Queerlad9000>blonde floppy hair, green eyes, 8″ cock uncut, toned tanned athletic body four tattoos

Luke hit RETURN with a mischievous smile, knowing that the description wasn't quite accurate. He didn't have four tattoos and wasn't *sure* how big his cock was.

But, after all, this was an internet chat room; certainly no place for facts. His smile widened as he saw the reply pop up.

    HotGuy>WOW! Sounds a right turn on :)

Oh, how Luke loved this! He felt his dick get hard. There was something so utterly sensual about being absolutely anonymous, able to sexually arouse guys whom you'd never met or were ever likely to meet. But that was another thing about the net. For how were you to know that these lines of type didn't come from someone Luke *did* know? Who was to say that this HotGuy wasn't Luke's next door neighbour, his best friend, the manager of his local off-licence?

But it didn't matter. Not to Luke. Who cares? he would think. Who cares who it is?

The important thing was that they didn't know who Luke was. He turned his attention back to the screen.

HotGuy>u want fone fuck, m8?

"Shit," muttered Luke. He hated when this happened. Why couldn't blokes just be satisfied with a bit of dirty typing? Wanking off in front of their computer screens like Luke did. Why phone each other up? Didn't that defeat the whole purpose of the internet?

He'd tried it once, phone sex; had given out his mobile number to some bloke on the net.

Big mistake.

They warned you not to do that. But Luke had been feeling randy and, as usual, had thrown caution to the wind. The guy had sounded very old and after a few grunts and groans had shot his load and then hung up. Luke, of course, thought that that would be the last he'd hear from this anonymous guy. Wrong. The bloke had phoned him for weeks, wanting more of the same, wanting to meet up with him etc. It had been a nightmare. Finally, the calls stopped, but that was enough for Luke never to indulge in that particular activity ever again.

He typed his reply.

Queerlad9000>sorry don't do fone
HotGuy>y?
Queerlad9000>2 personal
HotGuy>ok u got cam then m8?

For fuck's sake, thought Luke. If I think talking dirty to someone on the phone is too personal then I'm hardly likely to let someone watch me wanking on a webcam, am I?

Queerlad9000>no sorry no cam
HotGuy>ok bye

Great, thought Luke, feeling his erection completely disappear.

He sat there for about five minutes, waiting for someone else to 'person-to-person' him. No one did and five minutes slowly became

ten minutes until Luke decided to take matters into his own hands.
He double-clicked on one of the names.

essexguy12345

A new box flashed up and Luke typed his opening P2P message.

queerlad9000>hi m8 u up 4 dirty chat with horny 18 yr old?

Luke waited. And waited. And waited. Until eventually...

essexguy12345>hi u in2 fone?

Luke sighed.

queerlad9000>sorry m8 no
essexguy12345>ok where r u??????
queerlad9000>bucks
essexguy12345>too far for sex m8 sorry bye

Luke was getting pissed off. The number of people visiting the chat
room had gone down now: only seven remaining. He decided to send
out another general message to the main room, not wanting to make
the first move on anyone again. He was pretty sure all they'd want was
either phone sex, cam sex, or to meet him in some park to shag him.

queerlad9000>NE1 OUT THERE WANT TO MAKE ME CUM????

He hoped his use of capital letters would emphasise the urgency of his
request.

Five minutes passed and when no responses appeared Luke padded
downstairs in his socks to get a beer. He took a Kronenburg out of the
fridge, popped it open and took a long swig.

"Mmmmm," he said to himself, under his breath. The house was
eerily silent.

Suddenly, for no apparent reason, he actually felt afraid.

Stupid twat, he thought, shaking his head. He laughed, but in the
silence of the house, it sounded strained. The laugh seemed to fall to
the floor and smash, like glass.

Luke went back upstairs with his can of lager.

On the screen, a P2P box had appeared in the top left hand corner.

SHADOW WEAVER is requesting a Person 2 Person chat with you
I do.

I do? thought Luke. And then he remembered the message he'd sent out to the general room before getting his drink.

NE1 OUT THERE WANT TO MAKE ME CUM????

Well, it looked like someone did.

> **queerlad9000>**hi m8
> **SHADOW_WEAVER>**u wanna be my sex slave boy?

Luke swallowed hard and felt his cock begin to swell again. He loved being 'dominated' on chat rooms. Made him feel vulnerable. Sexy. Aroused.
He typed his reply.

> **queerlad9000>**love 2 be m8
> **SHADOW_WEAVER>**gooooooooooooooood boy

Cool, thought Luke, rubbing his hard cock. He undid his trousers.
Mmmmmmmmmmmm.
Luke watched as more words from SHADOW_WEAVER popped up onto the screen.

> **SHADOW_WEAVER>**what u wearing stud
> **Queerlad9000>**white t shirt black socks white boxers and black trousers
> **SHADOW_WEAVER>**u gonna do what i say boy?
> **Queerlad9000>**yesssss... what shall i call u?
> **SHADOW_WEAVER>**u call me MASTER boy
> **Queerlad9000>**yes master
> **Queerlad9000>**i'll do what u say master
> **SHADOW_WEAVER>**good boy
> **SHADOW_WEAVER>**u want humiliation? u want verbal abuse? u want 2 b tortured, boy?

Luke felt his dick get very *very* hard. Straining against his cotton boxer shorts. His best mate Rick would say, "You got a tent pole down there, mate!"

Luke loved this kind of talk. Loved the idea of an older man wanting to do things to him... dirty things... filthy things. Oh, what it would be like to have an older man using him, holding him down, stripping him naked... sticking his cock right up him and not caring if it hurt Luke.

Luke would often ejaculate to these thoughts and afterwards would feel dirty and disgusting; a pervert. What kind of bloke am I? he'd think. Getting off on strangers telling me dirty things?

It was always like that. Even when Luke masturbated – away from the internet – when he'd lie there naked in his bed, thinking of making love with some hot guy.

After he'd shot his load it would always be, *Luke, mate, what the hell are you doing?*

But at this point, all of that didn't matter. It turned him on, made him tingle, brought him to *that* point.

Mmmmmmmmm.

Luke typed into the screen.

Queerlad9000>yes
SHADOW_WEAVER>yes WHAT boy?
Queerlad9000>MASTER yes MASTER

Luke tingled with the excitement of being anonymous and he considered that word 'torture'.

Torture implied violence. Suffering. Pain. Agony.

Yet here, now, in the darkness of the room, alone, with nothing but the throbbing, softly glowing screen of the computer it meant so much more to Luke. It meant pleasure, indulgence... *sensuality.*

SHADOW_WEAVER>ready for me to tell u what to do boy?
Queerlad9000>yes master
SHADOW_WEAVER>take your top off and your socks

Luke felt that tingle of excitement again, stronger now, more desperate. It pulsed beneath his skull.

Queerlad9000>yes master, just a sec
SHADOW_WEAVER>hurry up boy

Quickly, Luke pulled his top off and his socks. He loved this – *loved* it! He ran a hand across his chest, which was toned with muscles from his swimming and gym workouts. He wished he did have a webcam, so SHADOW_WEAVER could actually see him. Oh, how Luke would've loved that!

Queerlad9000>ok master, top and socks off. What next?
SHADOW_WEAVER>stroke your chest
Queerlad9000>yes master stroking chest
SHADOW_WEAVER>what's it feel like?
Queerlad9000>toned and tanned, firm, master

There was no immediate response. Several minutes passed and Luke quickly grew impatient. He knew that it was probably because SHADOW_WEAVER was also chatting to other guys concurrently. Luke nearly always did this, too. But this time, with this guy, he felt like he didn't want to talk to anyone else. Lest he... miss something.

Odd... after waiting a few more minutes, he typed a new message.

Queerlad9000>master? U there?

The response was literally immediate, the words exploding onto the screen.

SHADOW_WEAVER>impatient little cunt! U wait for me to contact u boy!
Queerlad9000>sorry master

Luke felt his excitement return. This is what he wanted; this is what he liked. To be used and abused... and yet all of it fake and safe and anonymous. All at a distance, barely even real. How perfect it was!

SHADOW_WEAVER>now. imagine I'm standing behind you, boy
Queerlad9000>yes master
SHADOW_WEAVER>feel my hot breath on your dirty little neck
Queerlad9000>yes master

And as soon as Luke had typed the two words, he actually felt – sensed – a breath of hot air on the back of his neck. He froze, hands suspended in mid-air above the keyboard. He was sure he'd felt that. Positive of it. He shook his head in one, brisk motion. Idiot, he told himself. Fucking idiot.

He looked around him, feeling like a small child, then back at the screen. No new words had yet appeared. Luke picked up his can of Kronenburg and took a nervous swig. Then he laughed quietly to himself, a dusty little chuckle.

SHADOW_WEAVER>u like that don't u boy?
Queerlad9000>yes master
SHADOW_WEAVER>you're a dirty little boy aren't u slut?
Queerlad9000>yes master
SHADOW_WEAVER>you like being punished
Queerlad9000>yes master
SHADOW_WEAVER>tortured?
Queerlad9000>yes master
SHADOW_WEAVER>abused?
Queerlad9000>yessssss massssssssterrrrr
SHADOW_WEAVER>good boy

There were no new messages for the next few minutes and Luke took another swig of his beer.

SHADOW_WEAVER>take off your jeans now boy
Queerlad9000>yes master

Luke quickly unbuckled his belt and slipped out of his jeans. He felt so horny sitting there in just his underpants, his cock bulging through them.

Queerlad9000>ok master jeans off
SHADOW_WEAVER>imagine me standing behind you still as you stroke yourself.

Queerlad9000>yes master stroking my cock for you master.

Luke swallowed thickly and irritably and he became very aware of his

Adam's apple in his throat as it bobbed up and down, almost painfully.

Even though he felt turned on like hell, the thought of some guy standing behind him made him feel strangely uneasy. He'd done this kind of thing before, of course he had, but this time it all felt kind of... well, eerie. As if this guy could actually see him, as if he really did have some kind of control over him, as if he knew who Luke actually was.

A new line of type had appeared.

SHADOW_WEAVER>you look real nice boy. Gonna enjoy torturing you boy.
Queerlad9000>yes master
SHADOW_WEAVER>beg me slut
Queerlad9000>please... please master
SHADOW_WEAVER>more
Queerlad9000>PLEASE! PLEASE MASTER! TORTURE ME MASTER!

Luke waited for a couple more minutes.

SHADOW_WEAVER>ok that will do for now. get completely naked for me slut

Luke wasted no time in complying and quickly pulled off his boxer-briefs, almost ripping them in the process. His penis sprang out and he started to pump it.

SHADOW_WEAVER>don't start wanking yet

Luke froze as he read the latest line. He pulled his hand away from himself and read and re-read it. Then he smiled, thinking of what an idiot he was. As if he was being watched or something! Don't be pathetic, Luke, that's just how these things go.

Queerlad9000>no master. What happens next?????
SHADOW_WEAVER>I'm still standing behind you. I place my hands on your shoulders. Hard.

Luke grinned and started typing.

But as he did, he suddenly felt a sharp jolt in both of his shoulders;

kind of like a muscular spasm. Like something was pushing down onto him. Something grabbing hold of him that felt like...

... two hands.

Two male hands.

And then it was gone. Just as suddenly as it had come, it was gone. Luke whirled his head, as if expecting to see someone behind him. But of course, the room was empty save for him.

He wanted to laugh out loud, wanted to tell himself that this was simply his imagination running away with him. But he didn't. Somehow, he couldn't. He looked back at the screen, read his half-finished line of type.

Queerlad9000>yes master. Your hands feel

Feel what? Real? They feel as if they're really there? Really on me? Muscular fingers curling around my bare shoulders?

Because that's what it *had* felt like. As if a man – a strong man – had been clamping his hands down hard on Luke's shoulders.

He swallowed thickly, finished the line and hit ENTER.

Queerlad9000>yes master. Your hands feel strong

I'm being stupid, thought Luke, and this, he decided, had to be the understatement of the year. No, the decade. No... the century. He rubbed his shoulders, a half-smile forming on his face.

And then the next line of type, the next message from SHADOW_WEAVER clicked onto the screen.

SHADOW_WEAVER>they are... they're very strong Luke

Luke felt his breath turn to glass in his throat. He'd never revealed his name! Not to SHADOW_WEAVER, not to anyone on these chatrooms. Ever! It was the first rule... the cardinal rule. You never, ever, *ever* revealed *anything* about your true identity on these things. Never!

Luke sat very still. Very still. He stared hard at the screen and his eyes zoomed in onto one word in particular.

Luke.

In a blood red font it was, seeming to stare out at him. Blood red. *Blood.*

SHADOW_WEAVER>you still stroking yourself boy

Luke's eyes were transfixed on the screen. Slowly, he read the new message. He couldn't respond. Felt like he couldn't even move. He was a prisoner. Paralysed.

And his eyes wandered back up to that four-letter word again. His own name. His own name that he had not given out. That he had *never* given out.

Irrational, foolish explanations began to pirouette inside his head.

Someone I know is doing this, he thought. Someone is getting a kick out of this. Knowing what I'm doing; knowing what I'm feeling. They...

But they didn't. They didn't!

Luke got up. He felt so vulnerable, standing there naked, the only sound in the room the soft hum of the computer.

Luke walked in a slow circle around the room. He touched the walls.

It was just a house; just a room.

Plaster.

Glass.

Wood.

Nothing more.

"Twat," said Luke aloud to himself. He sat back down in front of the computer screen and read the words once more. He read them again. Twice, thrice, four times...

He had thoughts, but they were distant. His thoughts seemed to have travelled a long, long way away. Out of his body. His thoughts floated around him, without meaning anything to him.

This is stupid, he told himself. Ridiculous!

So how does he know my name?

Luke read his name again on the screen. He typed a new line.

Queerlad9000>is this someone I know?????

No immediate answer. Luke considered the possibilities. Who would know he was in a chat room? A *gay* chat room, at that.

Rick? Yvonne? Gavin?

No. None of them would know. So who was this person? How did he know Luke's name?

A new line appeared on the computer screen.

SHADOW_WEAVER>no one you know

Luke shivered. This was too weird. Am I imagining it? he thought.

SHADOW_WEAVER>you'll suck my cock now boy

Despite everything, Luke felt himself get hard again. Hard as a rock. He stroked the shaft of his dick, fondled his balls. They felt very heavy and he slapped them against his thighs a couple of times.

SHADOW_WEAVER>open wide boy

Luke grinned and started to pump himself with his right hand. With his other hand, he leaned over the keyboard to type his response.

Queerlad9000>yes master

He was shocked at the come-back.

SHADOW_WEAVER>lying cunt. I said OPEN WIDE BOY

Luke's eyes bulged as he read the line. What the fuck was going on?

SHADOW_WEAVER>I am your master and you are my sex slave you dirty little fucking slut-cunt boy. You do what I say when I say it and you do not fucking lie to me.

Oooohhhh-kayyyyy, thought Luke. He was annoyed. This was no longer enjoyable. Who the fuck did this SHADOW_WEAVER character think he was? It was one thing taking on fantasy role-plays over the net, but this was just getting a *little* too intense for Luke's liking.

You can piss right off, mate, he thought.

Luke, his hard-on rapidly deflating, leaned over to get the mouse and dragged the little arrow into the top right-hand corner of the screen, over to the tiny 'x' which would shut down the Internet chat room.

He didn't make it.

His shoulders, quite involuntarily, leapt backwards against the chair, pinning him to it, as if by their own accord.

What the...? he thought, utterly stunned. His eyes became very large, massive with fear. He jerked his head from side to side and struggled, but to no avail. This invisible force was just too strong. He felt something squeeze his arms. It felt like two hands. Two strong, male hands. He looked down at his upper arms and saw the skin twist, and grow red, as if the invisible man was pinching it hard.

Luke's mouth opened as he cried out in pain.

He looked at the screen, watched with his fear-widened eyes as a new line appeared.

SHADOW_WEAVER>you didn't do what I asked, cunt. You need to be punished. Now. Suck. My. Cock.

He felt the tip of it slide in. Big and fat, slippery with pre-cum. A huge, fleshy cylinder. A man's large cock. A man's large *invisible* cock. Luke gagged as the dick pushed to the back of his throat, filling his mouth, making it difficult for him to breathe.

In and out, *in and out, IN AND OUT...*

Violently pushing against Luke's tonsils. Harder and harder. Faster and faster.

The pain subsided from his arms as the invisible hands released him. But the respite was all too short-lived.

Luke felt the hands on the back of his head next, gripping tightly, pulling his face forward, the cock pushing deeper and deeper into his mouth.

Thrust thrust thrust thrust...

He thought he was going to suffocate, right then, right there, at the hands of this... this *thing*, whatever it was...

And then it stopped.

There was nothing.

Nothing at all.

Luke whirled his head from side to side again, feeling absolutely terrified. What had just happened? *What had just happened?*

His mouth felt bruised; raw. He had had a dick in his mouth. He knew it. He *knew* it.

But... how? What...?

Terrified, Luke knew that enough was enough. Whatever was going on here, Luke wanted out right now. He leaned forward, grabbed the mouse and dragged the arrow up to the 'x' in the right hand corner.

He clicked the mouse button.

Nothing happened. The chat room remained on the screen.

What the fuck?

He clicked again. And again. Three times. Four.

Nothing.

The thing refused to shut down.

Confusion spun in Luke's head. This is not right, he thought. This is so far away from right it isn't even true.

New words appeared on the screen.

SHADOW_WEAVER>gonna fuck u now, boy. Gonna fuck you hard. U ain't getting out of this yet, bitch.

The whole thing was ridiculous – utterly ridiculous. But still, Luke felt scared. After what had happened with the phantom blowjob, he was sure this SHADOW_WEAVER character meant what he said.

Luke leaned forward and typed.

Queerlad9000>leave me alone. I'm not interested.

Luke waited. His breath came in hot spurts. He was scared, all right. Scared to death.

A new message appeared.

SHADOW_WEAVER>I don't think so.

Luke stared at the message in sheer disbelief. He shivered, naked and alone. He wished for his mother to come through the door and rescue him.

But rescue him from what? This was stupid! There was no one there. It was just the internet. No one could see him; no one could touch him. What was he so afraid of?

Once again, he reached for the mouse, dragged the tiny arrow towards the 'x', trying to shut the bloody thing down.

He clicked once; twice, three times.

Nothing happened. It just wouldn't just shut down.

Fuck this, thought Luke, and he stood up. He went to leave the room, but something stopped him. Boy, did it *stop* him.

As if by a pair of huge, invisible pliers, he was thrown to the ground.

"Get the fuck off me!" he screamed.

A huge blow to the side of his head met his request, as if a large fist had just ploughed into his left temple.

He gasped, and froze, right there, on all fours, naked as the day he was born.

Something was holding him there.

Something big.

Something *strong*.

This is crazy, thought Luke. He was alone, utterly alone, yet he was being mauled. Raped, he told himself. The invisible man is raping me.

He felt something push against the nape of his neck. Something forcing him over. Forcing him into this pushing.

The words from the screen, the words from SHADOW_WEAVER, filled his head. *Gonna fuck u now, boy. Gonna fuck you hard. U ain't getting out of this yet, bitch.* And Luke knew it was going to happen. He was going to be fucked. Fucked by the invisible man.

He felt his arsehole widen, pain shooting through his body. It felt like fingers, big, large, manly fingers spreading his tight virgin hole. He screamed out in pain and was rewarded with another hefty cuff around the head.

"Unghh!" he spluttered, through clenched teeth.

The pain was unbearable. He felt more pressure on the back of his neck as he was forced down. "Ungh! Ungh! Please! Stop! Please!" he managed to get out.

Then he felt the tip of the phantom cock again, pushing slowly into his arse. He felt his un-lubricated hole spread around it. More went in. Luke felt his skin split. Felt his own warm blood trickle down his legs as the invisible cock made its way inside him. The pain. Oh, the pain! It was utterly unbearable. And still the cock shoved deeper. The sheer size of it! As it penetrated Luke, he screamed in agony, struggling against the strong grip of his invisible assailant. In and out, it went, opening him up wider, splitting his flesh, and causing the blood to flow, hot and fast.

"Uggggghhhhhhhh! Please stop!" he shrieked.

But his screams only brought more torture.

In and out, in and out, faster and faster.

Blackness swam before Luke's eyes. He felt himself grow dizzy as the spectral penis continued its relentless onslaught.

In and out, in and out, faster and faster...

No, thought Luke, as consciousness gradually began to fade. This isn't real, this isn't real, this isn't real.

The pain was unbearable. Luke felt his eyelids begin to drift down, blocking out the agony as he was fucked harder and harder and harder.

Darkness flooded his vision like a thick, evil blanket.

Dark.

Darker.

Darkest.

Patrice felt more than a little tipsy as she came through the front door. She wondered what time it was.

She pulled out her mobile phone and checked. Just gone midnight. So she wasn't too late in.

She wondered if Luke was still up.

Probably on that bloody internet, she thought. She'd started to worry about her son of late. He always seemed to be on the internet. Patrice didn't know what it was he was looking at. As far as she was concerned, computers were none of her business.

It had been a good night out with the girls though. She'd been a bit concerned about going, her being much older than the others and everything. But it had turned out to be a great laugh. It was about time she got her social life sorted out after the divorce anyway. No point sitting around moping all day, just because David had got himself a younger model.

Wanker, thought Patrice, heading into the kitchen to make herself a coffee.

"Luke!" she called out, flicking the switch on the kettle. "You still up?"

When no answer came, Patrice simply shrugged. She felt a little dizzy. Shouldn't have had all those cocktails, she thought, thinking back over the evening. Screaming Orgasms they were called. The girls had been raving about them. The trouble with cocktails, though, was that you could get completely steamboated on them and not even realise.

Oh well, she thought. When was the last time I had a good night out?

Patrice finished making her coffee. Mmm. Nice and hot.

She decided to go up and see Luke. Give him a kiss goodnight. He'd be embarrassed, she thought, but that's what mothers were for.

Carrying her coffee carefully, she mounted the stairs. She felt almost naughty and giggled to herself. She really had over-done it with the cocktails that night!

"Luuuuuuuuuuuukkkkkkkkkke!" she sing-songed.

She knocked on his bedroom door.

And went on in.

It looked as though he'd been torn in half. The room was so full of blood. Patrice had never seen so much blood. Had never imagined she ever would.

She went to scream but nothing came out. She could only stare. Could only stare at the two, large pieces of flesh that had once been her son. That had once been her Luke.

What the fuck had happened to him? What the fuck had happened to her baby?

His clothes lay on the floor, crumpled in a heap beside his mangled carcass. She could see his insides oozing out onto the carpet.

She felt the bile rise up in her throat and swallowed it back down. She looked around the room. Saw the computer. Saw that it was still on. There were words on the screen.

Patrice began to read.

SHADOW_WEAVER>sleep well boy. U were a good fuck for your master. Pity it had to be ur last, eh?????? :)

Patrice felt a heaviness engulf her. She swayed slightly, throwing back her head, opening her mouth to scream.

But the only sound to hit the air was the heavy thud of her body collapsing to the ground.

Alfredo and the Leather Mouse
Michael Wilcox

Alfredo and the Leather Mouse
Michael Wilcox

It wasn't quite the review that Henry Lesser was expecting. He knew from past experience that *The National Graphic*'s music critic delighted in singling him out for special derision, but surely his heroic, yet lyrical assumption of Alfredo in last night's new production of *Die Fledermaus*, which had so delighted the packed Edinburgh audience, deserved better? How dare that myopic and vicious bitch, Julian Bunker, describe him as 'a camp leather queen'? It wasn't his idea to dress the cast in sweaty, imitation leather. And Bunker's headline, 'Handbagging for *Die Fledermaus*' might have raised a titter in Morningside, but the chorus wags had beaten him to it weeks ago with leather jokes. Most of them habitually wore leather posing pouches under their costumes, anyway. Thank God, Henry Lesser was on the train to Newcastle for a one-night stand, singing the tenor solos in Hexham Abbey's *Messiah*. Besides, Hexham's first gay sauna, which had opened the previous week and made the national news, should be worth a visit.

What had caught the nation's attention was the way the Hexham Constituency Conservative Party offices in Beaumont Street had been sold as part of a fund-raising exercise. But when news of what their sacred building was to be used for leaked out, all hell broke loose. Local opposition to 'Hadrian's Hot House' had been intense, but the case for equal opportunities and social inclusion had finally won the day at ministerial level. To make matters worse in some eyes and more delightful in others, advertisements in the *Hexham Courant* for young Antinouses to work as bathhouse attendants had received an overwhelming response from local lads. The irritation Henry Lesser felt at being ridiculed by the hateful Julian Bunker was more than compensated for by the prospect of rural mischief.

Henry dumped his bags in his room at The Beaumont Hotel, took a quick shower and walked down the road to Hexham Abbey for the afternoon's rehearsal, and past the offending sauna opposite. He'd sung *Messiah* a hundred times, but every conductor had his own ideas about editions and what was or wasn't authentic practice. Henry preferred to decorate the vocal line with some restraint, especially after the heavy night he'd had in Edinburgh, but the conductor wasn't having any of it. He demanded the full works. The four old pros, under the expectant scrutiny of choir and orchestra, exchanged glances and proceeded to try to outdo each other with vacuous runs and ludicrous, if exciting, interpolated high notes. "Mad scenes from *Messiah*, anybody?", whispered the wicked soprano during the tea break. With relief, Henry left the Abbey with three hours to kill and headed straight for 'Hadrian's Hot House' across the road.

What he discovered inside exceeded all expectations. He was welcomed by a fallen cherub in a clean and flimsy Roman tunic, who directed him to the changing-room. The décor wouldn't have disgraced a fifties Hollywood sword and sandals epic. The towels had period patterned borders and, wrapping one around his waist with the *élan* of a tired centurion, Henry set off to explore. For a start, he needed a shower. The attendant gave him an account, in a charmingly indecipherable dialect, of what was where, with Henry noting the words 'oracle' and 'catacombs'. In the 'Ablutions Block', Henry was showering himself when he was joined by a bearded man with a dick like a cucumber, which Henry thought would not have been out of place on a centaur. Refreshed and fired up, Henry set off to explore what else was on offer.

He passed the central plunge pool, around which lolled a couple of senatorial senior citizens, and headed for a door marked 'Galley Slaves'. Here he found a themed room with wooden benches and oars disappearing into the walls, complemented by an array of whips and shackles for those with a penchant for punishment. When the centaur from the 'Ablutions Block' slipped into the room behind him and leered at him menacingly, Henry retreated rapidly and followed the signs for 'The Oracle'.

Down a long, dark corridor, a golden mask was lit by candle light. There was the smell of incense in the air, and the sounds of distant cicadas. He approached the mask and stood there for a moment, expecting it to speak. Nothing. Silence. Then there was the sound of a slight movement behind it, out of sight. Henry instinctively let his towel fall and, with a sense of wicked excitement, thrust his growing penis into the oracle's mouth. At once, he found himself on the receiving end of an invisible blow job. Henry almost pulled out with surprise and then indulged himself for a short while, but not for so long that a one-shot specialist like himself would come before the rest of the complex had been explored. Besides, the oracle could always be revisited.

Henry withdrew and crept away. As he did so, he was aware of a figure shuffling away from behind the mask, as though in pursuit. Henry hastened for 'The Catacombs'.

The door to 'The Catacombs' swung open and Henry was met by a hot wall of steam. He entered the darkness like Orpheus searching for the ghost of Euridice, and groped his way past dimly lit alcoves in which wraith-like figures could be glimpsed at play. This time, there was a maze of corridors and ante-rooms, each lit differently. The intense steam made it difficult to see anything clearly, but he was aware of his body being stroked and explored by invisible hands as he travelled deeper into this dramatic underworld. Soon Henry had lost all sense of direction and was groping, hands outstretched, wondering which turn to take. A tongue started to explore his buttocks, while another teased his balls. For a moment he was transfixed like a rabbit in the fast lane of a motorway, wondering which way to shoot. Then a hand clutched his and started to draw him away. Wondering what further extraordinary sensations awaited him, Henry followed meekly. It was not until he had been guided out of the hot mists of Hades that he was able to see his guide with any clarity. To his intense alarm, Henry realised that the man still clutching his sweaty hand was the myopic Julian Bunker, chief music critic of *The National Graphic*, and Henry's sworn enemy.

Bunker's distinctive glasses were safely locked away with his clothes, and he showed no sign of recognising the distinguished tenor, Henry Lesser, as he dragged him through the door marked 'Galley Slaves'. Henry, for his part, had no intention of giving the game away. In a trice, he had shackled the squealing Bunker across an oily oar and seized, to Bunker's evident delight, one of the whips that lay, so conveniently, around the tacky floor.

"Row, you bastard!" muttered the threatening Henry.

"I'm doing my best, sir," grinned the reptilian Bunker, playfully.

Henry lashed him across the back. "Try harder!" To himself, Henry was thinking, "So... my Lohengrin 'lacked poetry'." Whack! "My Samson was 'blind to the beauties of the score'." Whack! And I was 'miscast as Siegmund'." Whack!

Only the arrival of the bearded centaur, evidently still unsatisfied, saved Bunker, who by now was in an erotic ecstasy, from being beaten to a pulp. "He's all yours. Don't take no for an answer," whispered Henry, still unrecognised, to the centaur before leaving the galley slave to his fate. When he reached the cold plunge, Henry dived in with a shout of triumph, splashing the angry old senators, and delighting the fallen cherub in the trim tunic.

Later that evening, in Hexham Abbey, one of the more remarkable performances of *Messiah* took place. Henry had regaled his fellow soloists in the Green Room with his adventures of the afternoon, and the totally unexpected arrival of the despised Bunker. They, in turn, recognised the critic's glinting glasses halfway down the nave as they took to the platform at the start of the performance, but none had seen his beatific smile before. With rebellion in the air, Henry ignored the excesses of the conductor and sang his opening recitative and aria with scrupulous musicianship and a dramatic intensity that set the standard for the rest of the evening. The chorus and orchestra were inspired to ignore the apoplectic antics of the man with the stick, and sang and played their hearts out, taking their cues from each other in a defiant act of inspirational music making. The roars of approval and standing ovation that greeted the final 'Amen' moved many present to tears.

After the performance, the conductor, white as a sheet and with teeth clenched, hid himself in the toilet and was sick as a dog. In an unprecedented gesture, Julian Bunker, more relaxed than any had seen him, came to the Green Room to congratulate the artists on the finest *Messiah* of his lifetime. Henry, still unrecognised from the afternoon's adventure, quietly understood the relationship between the more sordid excesses of everyday life and supreme artistic achievement.

Legend of Albion
Graeme Woolaston

Legend of Albion
Graeme Woolaston

I always know when he is summoning me. I become restless in both body and mind: I cannot sit still, I cannot concentrate, I cannot read, music cannot distract me, television bores me, the computer screen is merely a dancing of colours. If I am to find peace I must get up and go out, whatever the weather, and take the road that leads west from the village; I turn up a farm track and strike off through the trees, down to a clearing where a stream runs into the lake.

If there is no moon – the summons always comes at night – I have a lantern which I place on the ground. Then I take off my glasses and wait. Because of my short-sightedness the world becomes no more to me then than a meaningless pattern of grey and dark; the moon herself, if she is in the sky, is an amorphous blob of light pulsing as my eyes pulse, and her reflection on the lake a shimmering streak.

I never hear his approach, and only know he is with me when he first addresses me. I turn towards his voice and put on my glasses again; the world snaps back into substance, and out of the shadows he is formed, standing in front of me. I bow to him, shallowly and stiffly, because it is so alien a custom for us moderns, "My lord Arthur…"

He is a man of my own height, below average for our time but tall for his. His appearance is always in accordance with the phase of the moon. When the moon is new he is beardless and young, startlingly young for what he already was by that age, a leader in battles. At the first quarter he is still young, but bearded and thicker-set; this is how he was on his wedding-day. At the full moon his kingliness is at its height; he is the overlord. By the third quarter he is greying and his face has become careworn, for the shadow has fallen on his reign. And in the last days of the moon he has the air of an old man, ill and stooping, though in bodily years he was younger than I am now; this is how he looked on the eve of the battle in which he fell.

He is always dressed plainly, either in tunic and breeches or with a cloak fastened at the shoulder by a simple brooch; he wears no gems appropriate to his rank. As a young man he is very beautiful, with dark curly hair and grey eyes which glint in the light from my lantern; they are often laughing. He knows his appeal to me in that form and is untroubled by it, since he lived before lies darkened the world. But when I see him as a mature man his handsomeness is an expression of the greatness he had achieved by those years; then I understand why the best men of his age were drawn by the hundred to his court.

Occasionally field-mice and the like appear at the limit of my lantern's glow to investigate who disturbs the night, and sometimes waterfowl shimmy across the lake towards us with low cries. But no animal shows any fear of him, and I feel none.

Our talk is of the things we have in common across fifteen centuries. We are both men of a time when a religion is dying, in his case to give way to a new faith, in mine to a world of none or many. Both of us have an enemy in the Church, which vilified him though he made war on the English whom it had yet to conquer. Nonetheless the Church perhaps judged correctly; when he was a child he learned too much from his people's wise ones to trust a creed which teaches that the eternal has only one face and voice and name.

He sometimes speaks of the most famous of them: "Merlin said that the new god would reign unchallenged for a thousand years, but that the day would come when the old altars would be honoured again – even the temple on the great plain."

"You know that for centuries people believed it was he who built Stonehenge?"

He laughed: "There are many things believed about us..."

"He was right about the thousand years – from your time to the Renaissance. That's exactly correct."

"And then?"

"And then the challenges began. Gently at first, very gently, but gathering strength and gathering strength, till now..."

"Till now?"

"Till now the Church's god is just one among many."

"Was he not always?"

"In Britain, I mean."

I saw wrinkles of laughter at his eyes: "But not dead?"

"Can any god die?"

"Ah! The question of questions!" He turned towards the lake and looked up at the moon, which that night was full. His lips began to move without sound, but from their shape I could tell that he was addressing the goddess in his own tongue.

When he had finished I asked, as politely as I could: "What does she answer?"

"She answers as she always answers."

"I don't understand..."

"She answers: 'Look on my beauty and give thanks'."

I thought for a while.

"That isn't an answer," I protested.

"Is it not?"

"No. Beauty isn't godliness."

"What is beauty, then?"

I risked impudence: "Beauty is what you possess as a young man."

To my relief he laughed: "Oh, we are all such fools! I thought the same once – that beauty is shapeliness of form. I sought it many times, and found it." His tone changed: "But consider where that idea of beauty led me... my wife, my best friend..."

I was startled; he had never before referred to the disaster which began the destruction of his monarchy.

"They were beautiful, both of them," he went on, more as if he were remembering aloud than addressing a listener.

"They were beautiful, and I saw it, and that was why..." His attention returned to me: "That was why I could do nothing. That was the failure of my kingship. I saw beauty, and I could not act."

I was regretting my flippancy: "Of course, there are many kinds of beauty," I said to correct my earlier remark.

"And none of them are godly?"

I wished I hadn't started this discussion: "I suppose, intellectual beauty... Yes, intellectual beauty. It isn't of the world of the senses, it can't become corrupt, it exists as a thing-in-itself – it would exist even if no one perceived it, even if there were no one who could perceive it."

He looked up at the moon: "So does her beauty. So did her beauty, when the world below her was without life." He turned back to me: "And what of love?"

"Love?"

"Another quality men have called god." He looked towards the moon again: "She has never asked for love. But the new god wanted love – the new god demanded love. 'Love me or perish'." His eyes went to the shadows around our feet. "I did not love him," he said quietly, "and I perished."

"But once again – there are many kinds of love," I ventured.

He raised his eyes: "We have still to say what is godliness."

I mused: "Not beauty, not love..."

"'Truth' answers nothing."

"What then?" I challenged him. "What?"

"The gods bring unity," he said.

"Unity?" I exclaimed.

"Why does that surprise you?"

I saw a need for tact: "Because in my experience gods don't bring unity. Rather the opposite – conflict, slaughter, civil wars, and even wars between nations."

"You are thinking of the god the Church worships. But other gods, of other peoples, do not resemble him." He looked again at the moon, which by then was westering across the lake: "She shines on every living thing, without favour."

I remembered the New Testament: "The god of the Church is alleged to have said something very similar."

"And also taught: 'By their fruits shall ye know them'. Is there a wiser saying of the Church?"

"And it condemns them out of their own mouths."

He simply nodded.

I went back to an earlier remark: "I still don't understand – what do you mean when you say 'the gods bring unity'?"

"I mean that where there is hatred between men they are not living as the gods wish – the true gods. The true gods bring harmony even to former enemies." Again he indicated the moon: "She has never inspired discord or war. Look on her beauty now – look!" He can still command like a king; I obeyed. "Look, and give thanks that such beauty can calm the warring hearts of men."

For some time we stood in silence together. Then I risked: "These are strange words from a warrior king."

"I fought only from necessity, because we had to fight to save our country from..." – he laughed. "From your ancestors."

"From my ancestors," I admitted.

"But once we had secured what was ours, then I sought to create one realm of all who were under my rule – a kingdom centred on my court, on my throne..."

"On the fellowship at your table."

"Indeed! A kingdom at peace. And I achieved it. I achieved it."

I saw that his thoughts were full of the glory of his famous capital, before the shadow fell on it.

"*Ynys y Cewri*," I said, in the language descended from his own.

"The island of the mighty," he said in mine. "Yes, that was our hope – an island of one people, strong in unity." He became sombre: "But after I departed... the hope was lost."

I said quietly: "After you departed there was no man equal to the task of ruling such a realm."

He smiled at the flattery – as well as the strengths of a king, he has the failings.

"But perhaps, after all, it is needful," he said, looking once again to the moon.

I was baffled: "What is?"

"That there should be a cycle of life for men as there is for her. Kingdoms must wax and wane, nothing can be permanent. Perhaps that is needful, to permit growth."

I remembered a line of poetry I learned at school, long ago. It was perfect for the moment, but, in his presence, I hesitated before I found the courage to speak the words Tennyson put into his mouth: "'The old order changeth, yielding place to new...'"

For obvious reasons he laughed. But he took up the quotation: "'Lest one good custom should corrupt the world...'"

"By preventing growth?"

"Perhaps that is what..." He laughed again: "What the speaker means."

"Nonetheless," I said. "It seems to me it is a tragedy that when unity has been achieved, it should be thrown away."

"It is. But men will always quarrel, just as men will always lust."

"How to deal with human discord?"

"That is the question we all ask our gods."

I saw that the moon was now well to the west and low in the sky, so his next words did not surprise me: "But the time of my departure is close."

We part with little ceremony; once again I bow, and he acknowledges me with a nod. Then I take off my glasses. Immediately he dissolves into a blur, together with everything around us. I turn away and wait for perhaps a minute; when I turn back and put my glasses on again he is gone.

I pick up my lantern and make my way through the woods, to the road which leads to my home.

Steven's Photograph
Richard Zimler

Steven's Photograph
Richard Zimler

The face of a Caravaggio + a lean powerful body = at least three months of great sex and maybe even love.

That's the calculation I make when I first see Steven. He is spooning quinoa out of a bin at the Fillmore Natural Grocery in my San Francisco neighbourhood. To tell you the truth, I hate quinoa, no matter whether the ancient Mayans lived to a hundred and twenty on it or not. But Steven has long chestnut hair and intelligent eyes. And a sleek way of walking that I find very sexy. So I sneak up behind him and say, "Hey, you like quinoa, too!" as if it's our secret little discovery.

Steven stares at me, seemingly scared by something.

"I'm sorry if I startled you," I say.

Some words catch in his throat. He brushes hair off his forehead with a gesture of impatience. "What... what was the first thing you said?"

"Just that I never saw anyone except me buying quinoa before."

He forces a smile, then turns away and heads off. His coldness leaves me stunned. I trail him through the store from a discreet distance, reading labels whenever I think he might be watching me. After he pays, I see him dart a look of interest back at me.

Our paths cross again about a month later. It's in the frozen food section this time. He spots me but makes believe he hasn't, wears a stern face of forced constraint. I finally speak to him more out of sympathy than anything else. At that moment, he's trying to choose a flavour of frozen rice cream.

"About to torture yourself?" I ask.

He feigns surprise. "Oh, it's you... Torture ...what's that supposed to mean?"

"Only that that substitute ice cream is really bad. My mom coats it on her roses so the Japanese beetles don't eat the petals."

Steven rolls his eyes as if pronouncing the verdict that I'm an idiot. He turns his back on me and walks away. I catch up but remain silent;

I'm searching for something to say that won't scare him off. I begin with the healing properties of carrot juice and, when I see that that isn't about to get me any response, move on to the exorbitant price of shampoo. In desperation, I finally admit that I hate quinoa. He doesn't so much as smile or frown. When we reach the check-out line, I apologize for being so dogged. I fight back more sensible options and ask if I can call him sometime.

"I don't think so," he replies in a bored tone.

I can't speak or look at him after that. My embarrassment makes me shiver and I move to the other check-out line.

When I reach my car, Steven suddenly walks up to me and pushes a business card into my hand. He rushes away behind the turned-up collar of his jacket as if he's afraid of being stalked.

His name is Steven Mason and he has his own graphic design studio on Polk Street.

It's Monday afternoon when I get this card from him. I waffle between throwing it out and calling him until Friday morning. "My name is David," I say when he answers the phone. "You met me at the Fillmore Natural Grocery, remember? I said some silly things. And you gave me your card."

"Yes," he answers dryly.

"Would you like to go out tonight? Get some dinner maybe?"

"Where?"

"Well, what kind of food do you like?"

Silence.

"Steven...? You there...?"

"Yes, what?"

"I was asking what kind of food you might like? Do you like Mexican, Thai, Italian...?"

More silence. As I'm wondering what I should say, he whispers, "Whatever you want."

"You're sure?" I ask, because he sounds so doubtful.

"I'm sure," he answers, as if he really isn't.

Our meal together is clearly the worst ever. Steven refuses to eat more than a few bites of his lemon veal and says nothing when I ask him why. He picks around it hopelessly while I finish my pasta. All evening, he refuses to answer any of my questions in anything but monosyllables.

He keeps his eyes down most of the time. When he does look up at me, it is with the glum face of a puppy who's just been whacked for chewing the veneer off a table leg. In consequence, I try to be encouragingly amusing, and, when that fails, move on to poetic gentility. I'm sure I'm coming across as manic. But I only give up when he whispers, "Is it okay if we don't talk?"

After that, I wolf down the rest of my tortoni and pay. In the car, he presses his forehead up against his window like some forlorn alien trapped on a distant planet.

"Sorry," I say when I let him out in front of his flat.

He accepts my apology with a stoic nod.

I don't phone him again. But it's then that the story takes its strange turn; he calls me.

"I'm sorry about the other night – I'd like to see you again," he says.

"How'd you get my number?" I ask.

"You mentioned where you worked."

It is my turn to be weird, and I let a long silence fall between us. Then I say, "But why do you want to go out? It's only too obvious that you had a terrible time?"

More silence. I don't know why, but a sudden feeling of solidarity grips me, so I say, "I'd like to see you, but I don't enjoy having such a bad effect on people. You really are sure you want to?"

With careful sincerity, he replies, "Yes... yes I do."

I suggest a movie. He agrees. I don't dare to touch him, but in the middle of *Babette's Feast* at the Castro Theater, Steven slithers his fingers up my thigh. I think he might want my hand and offer it gently, but he pushes it away. He starts kneading my cock through my pants.

Perhaps it is my growing feeling that Steven is way beyond me in his thoughts, but I can't even get the initial twinge of an erection. "Sorry," I whisper.

On the way out of the movie theater, I figure I'm going to have to apologize a lot if I pursue this relationship, and I all but wish Steven a nice life. But he says, "Never mind all that, would you like to come to my place for some tea? Or maybe some wine?"

He is staring at me with wild, hopeful eyes. And it is only then, under the pressure of my sexual fear, that my interest is aroused. I wonder about his desires, about my own. I agree to come over.

As soon as we reach his flat, Steven disappears into the kitchen. I drop down into a plush white couch and page through a corporate magazine that he's designed. I'm impressed. "This looks great," I say when he returns.

"Thanks."

He pours tea. We sit next to each other like two adolescents afraid to touch. Steven clears his throat, gets a pack of cigarettes from his jacket and offers me one. I refuse amiably.

After he lights his, he tries the offer again, this time saying, "Would you, for me?"

"I don't think so – I try not to get lung cancer for other people," I answer.

I smile when I say that and hope to elicit a reciprocal gesture, but he looks at me instead as if about to burst into tears. He jumps up suddenly and walks to the window, turns back with anger in his eyes. "You don't... you don't understand," he stammers.

"Maybe I should just go," I say.

"Yeah, I think so," he concludes with a self-assuring nod, looking away from me as if I'm betraying him.

I walk to the door. "Bye," I say. "Thanks for the tea."

"No wait." Steven stubs out his cigarette and runs to me. He tugs a hand through my hair as if trying to change its style and looks into my eyes until I get the feeling he's searching inside me for something he's desperate to own. He feels for my cock again and kisses me on the lips. I sense I'm about to enter a world I'll never understand. I hug him tight in order to try to reach some warm, familiar ground.

In bed, he winces when I penetrate him. I pull back and say, "I must be hurting you."

"Just shove it all the way in!" he whispers.

He grimaces when I'm fully inside him and closes his eyes. He pulls me to him with all his strength. With each thrust, he grunts. When tears well in his lashes, I stop. I began to pull out.

"No!' he says. "Keep going. Give it to me hard – as hard as you can!"

He cries till I come. Afterward, I feel ill, as if I've killed something. But he's very calm and just asks me to light him a cigarette. When I do, he smiles genuinely at me for the first time. Then he starts to cry again, inconsolably, like an abandoned little boy melting into despair. I fight against my instinct to flee and try to hold him, but he pushes me away.

When I finish dressing, I ask, "Why did you want me to make love to you like that?"

Steven's tears are gone by then. He laughs in a single exhale, looks away and shakes his head as if commenting sadly on a distant memory. He is silent for a long while, then leans across his bed and takes out a photograph from his night-table drawer. It's a black-and-white of a young man who looks as if he could be my brother. He is holding a prized fishing catch, a giant flounder or fluke, is smoking and grinning the way models did in cigarette ads from the 1950s.

I look questioningly at Steven. He nods up at me and whispers inside an exhale of smoke:

"Because that's the way my daddy used to do it."

Acknowledgements

'The Notorious Dr August' by Christopher Bram is taken from the novel of the same name, published by William Morrow, an imprint of HarperCollins Publishers, New York, 2000; an earlier version of 'The Weeds' by Perry Brass appeared in *Out There: Private Desires, Horror and the Afterlife*, published by Belhue Press, New York, in 1994; an earlier version of 'In the Interests of Science' by Peter Burton appeared under the title 'A Marriage of Convenience' in *On the Line: New Gay Fiction*, The Crossing Press, Trumansburg, New York, in 1981; 'Touching Darkness' by Patrick Roscoe originally appeared in the magazine *Exile* and constitutes a chapter from his novel in progress *The Truth About Love*; 'A Perfect Time to be in Paris' by Jeffrey Round first appeared in the *Harrington Gay Men's Fiction Quarterly*.

I would like to thank the contributors to this volume for their excellent stories and I would like to make an especial note of thanks to Simon Lovat (who wielded the word processor) and to Tim d'Arch Smith (exemplary bookdealer, for turning up – over more than three decades – so many relevant texts).

Peter Burton

Further reading

This is not a bibliography of the sinister, it is a basic checklist, the aim of which is to point the interested reader in the direction of some of the writers and some of the books in the popular genre. Editions cited are those on my bookshelves, not necessarily firsts:

Barker, Clive: *Books of Blood, Volumes One – Three* (London, Weidenfeld & Nicolson, 1984)
   Books of Blood, Volumes Four – Six (London, Sphere Books, 1985)
Winter, Douglas E: *Clive Barker: The Dark Fantastic* (London, HarperCollins, 2001)

Beckford, William: *Vathek* (London, The Folio Society, 1958)
Mowl, Timothy: *William Beckford: Composing for Mozart* (London, John Murray, 1998)

Benson, E F: *The Collected Ghost Stories* (New York, Caroll & Graf, 1992)
   Raven's Brood (Brighton, Millivres Books, 1992)
   The Inheritor (Brighton, Millivres Books, 1993)
   Colin (Brighton, Millivres Books, 1994)
   Colin II (Brighton, Millivres Books, 1994)
Masters, Brian: *The Life of E F Benson* (London, Chatto & Windus, 1991)
Palmer, Geoffrey, & Lloyd, Noel: *E F Benson As He Was* (Luton, Beds., Lennard Publishing, 1988)

Blackwood, Algernon: *John Silence: Physician Extraordinary* (Thirsk, N. Yorks., House of Stratus, 2002)
   Best Ghost Stories of Algernon Blackwood (Thirsk, N.Yorks., House of Stratus, 2002)
   The Dance of Death and Other Stories (Thirsk, N. Yorks., House of Stratus, 2002)
Ashley, Mike: *Starlight Man: The Extraordinary Life of Algernon Blackwood* (London, Constable, 2002)

Burton, Peter (Ed.), *The Mammoth Book of Gay Short Stories* (London, Robinson, 1997)

Chopping, Richard: *The Ring* (London, Secker & Warburg, 1967)

Davies, Rhys: *Nobody Answered the Bell* (London, Heinemann, 1971)

Fleetwood, Hugh: *Foreign Affairs* (London, Quartet Books, 1976)
Brothers (London, Serpent's Tail, 1999)

Forster, E M: *Collected Short Stories* (Middlesex, Penguin, 1967)
The Life to Come and Other Stories (Middlesex, Penguin, 1975)

Hartley, L P: *The Collected Macabre Stories* (Leyburn, N. Yorks, Tartarus Press, 2001)
Wright, Adrian: *Foreign Country: The Life of L P Hartley* (London, André Deutsch, 1996)

Heard, Gerald: *Dromenon: The Best Weird Tales of Gerald Heard* (Leyburn, N. Yorks.,Tartarus Press, 2002)

James, Henry: *Collected Stories: Volume Two* for *The Turn of the Screw* (London, Everyman, 1999)

James, M R: *The Penguin Complete Ghost Stories of M R James* (Harmondsworth, Middlesex, Penguin, 1984)

King, Francis: *Voices in an Empty Room* (London, Hutchinson, 1984)
Punishments (London, Hamish Hamilton, 1989)
The One and Only (London, Constable, 1994)

Linton, Gordon: *The Sacrifice* (London, GMP, 2002)

Lorraine, Jean: *Monsieur de Phocas* (Cambridge, Dedalus, 1994)
Nightmare of an Ether-Drinker (Leyburn, N. Yorks., Tartarus Press, 2002)

Maugham, Robin: *The Black Tent and Other Stories* (London, W H Allen, 1973)

The Boy From Beirut and Other Stories (San Francisco, Gay Sunshine, 1981)

Raven, Simon: *Doctors Wear Scarlet* (London, Anthony Blond, 1960)
  The Roses of Picardie (London, Blond & Briggs, 1980)
  September Castle (London, Blond & Briggs, 1980)
  The Islands of Sorrow, (London, The Winged Lion, 1994)
  Remember Your Grammar and Other Haunted Stories (Broze, France, The Winged Lion, 1997)
Barber, Michael: *The Captain: The Life and Times of Simon Raven* (London, Duckworth, 1996)

Rice, Christopher: *A Density of Souls* (London, Pan Books, 2002)

'Saki' (H H Munro): *The Bodley Head Saki* (London, The Bodley Head, 1963)
Langguth, A J: *Saki: A Life of Hector Hugh Munro* (London, Hamish Hamilton, 1981)

Stenbock, Stanistaus Eric: *The Child of the Soul and Other Stories* (London, Durtro, 1999)
  Studio of Death (London, Durtro, 1996)
Adlard, John: *Stenbock, Yeats and the Nineties* (London, Cecil & Amelia Woolf, 1969)

Walpole, Horace: *The Castle of Otranto* (Oxford, Oxford University Press, 1998)
Mowl, Timothy: *Horace Walpole: The Great Outsider* (London, John Murray, 1996)

Walpole, Hugh: *The Old Ladies* (London, Macmillan, 1924)

Waugh, Evelyn: *The Complete Short Stories* (London, Everyman, 1998)

Wilde, Oscar: *Complete Works* – including *The Picture of Dorian Gray* and *Lord Arthur Saville's Crime* (London, HarperCollins, 1994)
Bartlett, Neil: *Who Was That Man? A Present for Mr Oscar Wilde* (London, Serpent's Tail, 1988)
Sinfield, Alan: *The Wilde Century: Effeminacy, Oscar Wilde and the Queer*

Moment (London, Cassell, 1994)

Schmidgall, Gary: *The Stranger Wilde: Interpreting Oscar* (New York, Dutton, 1994)

Wilson, Angus: *The Wrong Set and Other Stories* (Harmondsworth, Middlesex, Penguin, 1959)

Such Darling Dodos and Other Stories (Harmondsworth, Middlesex, Penguin, 1960)

About the authors

Neil Bartlett is the Artistic Director of the Lyric Theatre, Hammersmith in London where his acclaimed productions have included Wilde's *The Picture of Dorian Gray*, W Somerset Maugham's *The Letter*, Terence Rattigan's *Cause Célèbre* and Robin Maugham's *The Servant*. He is a dramatist and translator and his books include the novels *Ready to Catch Him Should He Fall* and *Mr Clive & Mr Page*. He lives in Brighton, England.

Sebastian Beaumont is the author of *On The Edge, Heroes are Hard to Find, Two, The Cruelty of Silence* and *The Linguist*. He regularly reviews for *Gay Times* and lives in Brighton, England.

David Patrick Beavers is the author of *Jackal in the Dark, The Jackal Awakens, Thresholds, The Color of Green* and *Pathways*. He lives in Los Angeles, USA.

Kevin Booth has worked in various performance-based media, and has had five plays performed, including *100 Metres*, which toured Buenos Aires and the Canary islands. Born in New Zealand, he now lives in Barcelona, Spain.

Christopher Bram is the author of *Surprising Myself, Hold Tight, In Memory of Angel Clare, Father of Frankenstein* (filmed as *Gods and Monsters*), *Gossip* and *The Notorious Dr August*. He lives in New York, USA.

Perry Brass is the author of *Warlock: A novel of possession, Mirage, Out There: Stories of private desires, The Harvest, How to Survive Your Own Gay Life* and *Angel Lust: An erotic novel of time travel*. He has been nominated several times for Lambda Literary Awards (in the categories Poetry, Science Fiction & Fantasy and Religion). He lives in New York, USA.

Scott Brown balances writing with a career in hospitality management, but would like to be able to write full-time. He is working on a novel but in the meantime 'Justice Armstrong-Jones' is his first published fiction. He lives in a quiet corner of Essex, England.

Peter Burton is the author of *Rod Stewart: A life on the town, Parallel Lives, Talking to...* and *Amongst the Aliens.* He edited *The Black Tent and Other Stories, The Boy from Beirut and Other Stories* and *The Mammoth Book of Gay Short Stories.* He is Literary Editor of *Gay Times,* Commissioning Editor of GMP and lives in Brighton, England.

Richard Cawley had a successful career as a designer for a fashion house before becoming a food writer (nine cookbooks) and television chef on programmes such as *Ready Steady Cook* and *Can't Cook Won't Cook.* He is the author of one novel, *The Butterfly Boy,* and 'The Pink Tower' is his first published short story. He has homes in France and London, England.

Jack Dickson is the author of *Oddfellows, Crossing Jordan, Freeform, Banged Up, Some Kind of Love* (the latter three featuring private investigator Jas Anderson) and *Out of This World.* He lives in Glasgow, Scotland.

Neal Drinnan is the author of *Glove Puppet, Pussy's Bow* and *Quill.* He edited *Best Gay Erotica 2002.* He lives in Sydney, Australia.

Stephen Gray is a lecturer and poet and is author of *John Ross: The true story, Time of Our Darkness* and *Born of Man.* He lives in South Africa.

John Haylock has taught English at universities in Baghdad and Tokyo. His novels include, *See You Again, It's All Your Fault, One Hot Summer in Kyoto, A Touch of the Orient, Uneasy Relations, Doubtful Partners, Body of Contention* and the forthcoming *Loose Connections.* He divides his time between the Far East and Brighton, England.

Steve Hope is currently working on a collection of short stories – of which 'Mirror Man' is the first to be published. He lives in Oxfordshire, England.

Alan James is a graduate from the Royal College of Art and he has exhibited three one-man shows. 'Monkey Business' is his first short story to be published. He currently divides his time between the Isle of Wight and Bangladesh.

Francis King published his first three novels while he was an undergraduate at Oxford and since then has written another forty books. His novels include *A Domestic Animal, Act of Darkness, Voices in an Empty Room, Punishments, The Ant Colony, The One and Only, Dead Letters, Prodigies* and the forthcoming *The Nick of Time*. He frequently reviews books for *Gay Times*. He lives in London, England.

Simon Lovat is the author of *Disorder and Chaos* and *Attrition*. He regularly reviews for *Gay Times* and lives in Brighton, England.

Anthony McDonald is the author of *Orange Bitter, Orange Sweet*, and the forthcoming *Adam*. He lives in London, England.

Joseph Mills is the author of *Towards the End* and *Obsessions*. He edited *Borderline: The Mainstream book of Scottish gay writing*. He lives in Glasgow, Scotland.

Neil Powell has been a teacher and a bookseller. He is a poet, critic and biographer of Roy Fuller. He is author of one novel, *Unreal City* and edited *Gay Love Poetry*. He reviewed (mainly) poetry for *Gay Times* for several years. He lives in Suffolk, England.

Patrick Roscoe was born on the Spanish island of Formentera and spent his childhood in East Africa. He was educated in England and Canada and later California and Mexico. He is author of seven internationally acclaimed books of fiction. He currently divides his time between Sidi Ifni, Morocco, and Sevilla, Spain.

Jeffrey Round is a much-published poet, short-story writer and editor. His first novel, *A Cage of Bones*, was published in 1997. He lives in Ontario, Canada.

Lawrence Schimel is the author or editor of over fifty books including *His Tongue, The drag Queen of Elfland, The Mammoth Book of Gay Erotica*,

Two Hearts Desire: Gay Couples on their love (with Michael Lassell), *Boy Meets Boy, Things Invisible To See: Lesbian and Gay Tales of Magic Realism, Kosher Meat*, and *Found Tribe: Jewish Coming Out Stories*. He has won a Lambda Literary Award and has also been a finalist six times. Born in New York City, he now lives in Madrid, Spain.

Stuart Thorogood is the author of *Outcast* and *Outside In*, inter-novels, the third of which *Over and Out*, is scheduled for publication in 2003. 'T@ngled' is his first published short story. He lives in Buckinghamshire, England.

Michael Wilcox is a dramatist and his plays include *Rent, Lent, Green Fingers* and *Mrs Steinberg and the Byker Boy*. He is the author of *Outlaw in the Hills* and *Benjamin Britten*. He edited *Gay Plays* (Volumes 1–5) and regularly reviews books for *Gay Times*. He lives in Northumberland, England.

Graeme Woolaston is the author of *Stranger Than Love, The Learning of Paul O'Neill* and *The Biker Below the Downs*. He is a regular contributor to *Gay Times*, and lives in Glasgow, Scotland.

Richard Zimler is the author of the international bestseller *The Last Kabbalist of Lisbon, Unholy Ghosts* and *The Angelic Darkness*. He has translated a great deal of Portuguese poetry and prose into English. American born, he lives in Lisbon, Portugal.